PRAISE FOR SANDIE JONES

'One of the most twisted and entertaining plots'
Reese Witherspoon

'An absolute corker – wickedly relatable story, wonderful
characters and a great twist. Should definitely be on
your reading list for this summer'
T. M. Logan, bestselling author of *Lies*

'A nice twist. I enjoyed the increasingly barbed exchanges
between the mother and the prospective daughter-in-law
– I think a lot of readers will probably identify with
events in the book!'
Jojo Moyes

'A twisty, deliciously fun read'
Sarah Pekkanen,
bestselling author of *The Wife Between Us*

'What an incredible read. Pammie was such a compelling
and unique villain . . . It's a definite must–read this
summer!'
Hollie Overton, author of *Baby Doll*

'Knocked my socks off! Psychological suspense at its
most addictive, with a shocker of an ending. I couldn't
put it down!'
Michele Campbell,
author of *It's Always the Husband*

THE FIRST MISTAKE

SANDIE JONES is a freelance journalist and has contributed to the *Sunday Times*, *Daily Mail*, *Woman's Weekly* and *Hello!* magazine, amongst others. If she wasn't a writer, she'd be an interior designer as she has an unhealthy obsession with wallpaper and cushions. She lives in London with her husband and three children.

Also by Sandie Jones

The Other Woman

SANDIE JONES

THE FIRST MISTAKE

PAN BOOKS

First published 2019 by Pan Books
an imprint of Pan Macmillan
20 New Wharf Road, London N1 9RR
Associated companies throughout the world
www.panmacmillan.com

ISBN 978-1-5098-8522-0

3 5 7 9 8 6 4 2

A CIP catalogue record for this book is available from the British Library.

Typeset by Palimpsest Book Production Limited, Falkirk, Stirlingshire
Printed and bound by CPI Group (UK) Ltd, Croydon, CR0 4YY

For Rob

Who taught me to believe that anything is possible

PROLOGUE

She looked at me with real warmth in her eyes, as if she trusted me with her life, and for a moment I thought I couldn't go through with it.

But then I remembered what she'd done and I suddenly felt calm again. What goes around, comes around, and she deserves everything that's coming her way.

Trust is a funny thing; it takes such a long time to build, yet it's broken in a second.

She shouldn't trust me – it will be her undoing.

1

'Sophia, let's go,' I call out from the hall. 'Livvy, where's your homework?'

She huffs and rushes off to the kitchen. 'I thought you'd put it in my bag.'

'I'm your mother, not your slave. And besides, you're eight now, you should be taking more responsibility.' I'm exasperated, though in truth, I'd happily pack her school bag for another ten years if it meant I could hang on to my baby who, it seems, has disappeared within a blink of an eye. How had I lost that time?

'Here,' she exclaims. 'Have you got my swimming cap?'

'Olivia! Oh, for God's sake, is it swimming today?'

She sticks one hip out to the side and rests her hand on the other, with all the sassiness of her fifteen-year-old sister. 'Er, yeah, it's Wednesday.'

'Run upstairs quickly, look in your top drawer. I'll count to five and you need to be back down here. Sophia, we're going.' I'm shouting by the end of the sentence.

What my elder daughter does up there I don't know. Every day it seems to take her five minutes longer to straighten her hair, scribe the black kohl under her eyes, inflate her lips with self-plumping lip-gloss or whatever

5

else it is she uses. She looks undeniably gorgeous when she does eventually appear, but is it all really necessary, for school?

'I can't find it,' Olivia calls out.

'We're late,' I shout, before huffing up the stairs. I feel a heaviness in my chest, a spring tightly coiled, as I rifle desperately through her socks and knickers. 'If I find it in here . . .' I say, never finishing the sentence, because I'm not quite sure what I'm threatening. 'Did you wear it last week?'

'Yes,' she says quietly, aware of my mood.

'Well, do you remember bringing it home?'

'Yes, definitely,' she says confidently, knowing that any other response will have me blowing a gasket.

The grip on my chest releases as I spot the matt rubber cap in the back corner of the drawer. 'Great,' I say under my breath, before adding as I run down the stairs, 'Livvy, you really do need to wake up. Sophia, we're getting in the car.'

'I'm coming,' she shouts back indignantly, as if she's said it three times already. With her music playing that loudly, how would anyone ever know?

She skulks into the passenger seat of the car and instantly pulls down the sun visor to inspect herself in the mirror as we drive.

'Haven't you just spent the past hour doing that?' I ask.

She tuts and flicks it back up with as much attitude as it will allow.

'What time will you be home tonight?' I ask, ten minutes later, as I lean across and offer my cheek. She kisses it reluctantly, which she's only just started doing again, since we struck a deal to park slightly further away from school.

'There's a maths revision class, so I'll probably go to that,' she says. 'What's for tea?'

We've just had breakfast, are at least four hours away from lunch, and she wants to know what's for tea? I do a mental scan of the fridge. It doesn't look too healthy. I might be able to rustle up a pasta dish, at best.

'What would you like?' I smile.

She shrugs her shoulders. 'Don't mind. Something nice?'

I pull her towards me and kiss the top of her head. 'Go on, go. I'll pop into Marks and Spencer if I get time.'

She smiles and gets out of the car. 'See you, divvy Livvy.'

'Bye poo face,' giggles her little sister from the back seat.

I put the window down as we drive past her and call out, but she's already locked into her phone, unseeing and unhearing of everything else around her. 'Look up,' I say to her silently. 'You'll never know what you might miss.'

Olivia and I do a light jog into school, which isn't easy in these heels. 'I love you,' I say, as she rushes off to join a playground game of netball without looking back.

'Mrs Davies, can I have a word?' calls out Miss Watts from across the playground. I purposely avoid eye contact. I don't have time for this. I look at my watch to let her know I'm under pressure.

'Sorry, it won't take a minute,' she says. 'Would you like to come into the classroom?'

I look at my watch again. 'I'm running late, can we do it here?'

'Of course. It's just that . . .' she looks around surreptitiously, but it's early enough not to have too many other parents within earshot. 'It's just that we had a little incident yesterday, in the playground.'

My heart lurches and I can feel my brow furrowing. 'What kind of incident?' I ask, forcing myself to stay calm.

The teacher rests a reassuring hand on my arm, though it feels anything but. 'Oh, it's nothing serious,' she says. 'Just a falling out between a few of the girls.' She rolls her eyes. 'You know how girls can be.'

'Was Olivia involved?' I ask.

'Apparently so. There were just a few nasty words bandied about, and Phoebe Kendall says that Olivia threatened not to play with her anymore. I'm sure it was nothing more than playground antics, but Phoebe was a little upset by it.'

I imagine she was. 'Olivia didn't mention anything last night. Did you speak to her?'

'I had a quiet word yesterday,' she says, looking

around again before continuing in a hushed tone. 'It's just that it isn't the first time that Olivia has been involved in an altercation of this type.'

I look at her, trying to read what's going on behind her eyes. 'Oh,' is all I can manage.

Miss Watts leans in closer. 'She's normally such a bright and bubbly child, eager to be friends with everyone, but these past few weeks . . .'

I rack my brain, wondering what's changed things. 'I'll talk to her – see what's going on.'

'Perhaps it would be useful to come in for a chat,' she says, tilting her head to one side. Her condescending smile reminds me of a therapist I once had. The one who asked me to close my eyes and imagine I was lying on a deserted beach, with the sun warming my skin and the gentle waves lapping at my feet.

I hadn't gone back. Treating me like a five-year-old didn't work then, and it certainly isn't going to work now.

'I'd be happy to see you and Mr Davies after school today if you're available?' Miss Watts goes on.

'I'm afraid Nathan . . . Mr Davies is away on business. He's flying back this afternoon.'

'Ah, okay then, perhaps another time,' she says. 'I'm sure it's nothing to worry about, just something we need to keep our eye on.'

'Of course,' I say, before turning on my heels and instantly bumping into a group of girls playing hopscotch. 'I'll talk to her tonight.'

I make my apologies to the disgruntled children as I tiptoe over brightly painted numbers on the tarmac.

'Wow, you look a bit done-up for this time in the morning,' calls out Beth, as she streaks past me in trainers and go-faster Lycra with her daughter Millie trailing behind.

'Hey gorgeous girl,' I say to the petulant-looking eight-year-old. 'What's up?'

'*She* got up late,' Millie replies, as she rolls her eyes theatrically towards her mother. 'And now we're *all* paying for it.'

Beth turns around and pokes her tongue out at the both of us. 'Let me drop this little madam off and I'll walk out with you.'

I tap my watch. 'I'm running late,' I say after her. 'I'll catch you later.' But she's already gone and is depositing Millie in the playground. I start walking out, knowing that within seconds she'll be at my side.

'So where are you off to all dressed up?' she asks, half-accusingly, as she catches up with me. I look down at my black skirt; granted, it is a little tight. And my red top; perhaps a little low. But my jacket goes some way to covering me up. Suddenly conscious of what Miss Watts might have thought, I pull it closed.

'Do I have to be going somewhere to make an effort?' I laugh lightly, though Olivia is still nagging at my brain.

'Anything other than pyjamas or gym gear is abnormal

at this time of day,' Beth says. 'So yes, you looking like that, when us mere mortals haven't even had time to brush our teeth, is really not fair, and most definitely shouldn't be allowed.'

'It's just my normal work attire,' I say. 'Nothing out of the ordinary.'

My face flushes and she raises her eyebrows. Who am I trying to kid?

'*I* believe you, even if a thousand others wouldn't,' she says, giving me a wink.

I smile, though I feel the heat rise in my cheeks. 'Did you hear anything about the girls falling out yesterday?'

She looks at me nonplussed and shakes her head. 'No, why, what happened?'

'Miss Watts just told me that a few of them had a bit of a ding-dong. It seems Phoebe and Livvy were involved. I just wondered if Millie had said anything to you about it.'

'No, but I can ask her if you like.'

'Probably best not to make a big thing of it for the moment,' I say. 'I'll wait and see if Livvy mentions it.'

'Okay. You still on for tomorrow night?'

'Definitely! Nathan's back today and already knows he's on babysitting duties.'

'That's what I like to hear,' she says, laughing. 'A man who knows his place.'

'Where do you fancy going?' I ask. 'Uptown or do you want to stay local? There's a new place that's just opened in Soho. Nathan went there with a client and raved about it.'

'I don't mind, could give it a try. Though saying that, I don't get paid for another three days, so if it's expensive, I might have to save it until after payday.'

'No worries, it'll be my treat,' I say, and see her eyes momentarily narrow. I bite my tongue and immediately wish I could suck the words back in. I'd hate for her to think I'm being patronizing, but I'd genuinely like to help. It takes a little longer for my brain to catch up with my mouth and realize that she might appreciate a handout for something more worthwhile than an overpriced meal in a fancy restaurant.

'Don't be silly,' she says finally, and I let out a sigh of relief. 'Why don't we do a pizza night tomorrow and go uptown *next* week?'

'Sounds like a plan,' I say.

2

'So, are we going for the burgundy and gold for the drawing room at Belmont House?' I ask the team around me, as they contemplate the mood boards in front of them.

'I've tried working up a royal blue, with white accents,' says Lottie, our junior designer, as she absently chews on the end of a pencil. 'But it doesn't look nearly as decadent as the burgundy.'

'Great,' I say, gathering up the loose papers that I'd strewn over the table during the meeting. 'So, let's present them with that and see what they think. Is there anything else?'

'I've just got a few accounting queries,' pipes up Matt, 'but they can wait until Nathan's back from Japan.'

I look at my watch and my breath quickens. 'He's due to land in the next hour or so, all being well. If he makes good time, he might pop in. Are you sure it can wait until tomorrow if he doesn't?'

'Yeah, course,' says Matt. 'It's nothing urgent.'

'Okay, so if that's all?' I ask, looking around at the nodding heads.

'Can I have a quick word?' says Lottie, hanging back as the rest of the team file out.

'Sure,' I smile. 'What's up?'

'I just wondered if I'd be able to come to the meeting at Belmont House with you tomorrow?'

I consider it for a moment.

'It's just that I've got loads of ideas, and I really feel I could bring something to the table.' She looks at me, her mouth agape at the faux pas she thinks she's made. 'Not that there's anything wrong with what's already on the table,' she rushes on. 'It's *all* on there, *and then* some, and then you've wrapped it up in a big gold bow and put the Alice Davies signature on it . . .' She's rambling, and I wait with raised eyebrows.

'I can't see why not,' I say, when she stops to take a breath. 'In fact, you can lead it, if you like.'

An involuntary squeal escapes from her mouth that I pretend not to hear, even though it makes me smile.

I can't help but marvel at how far she's come in the short time she's worked here. She was as quiet as a mouse when she first joined AT Designs, barely able to look anyone in the eye. I remember asking at her interview where she saw herself in ten years' time, and she'd meekly whispered, 'Sitting in your chair.' The juxtaposition of her manner and her words had almost made me spit my coffee out. She had got the job on that alone.

She'd been almost mute for a week, just nodding and shaking her head at pertinent times, but I knew she was in there somewhere. I'd seen it, though Nathan refused to believe me.

'I'm telling you, you picked the wrong candidate,' he'd said over dinner after her second day. 'We need someone with something about them – she's not even going to be able to interact with clients.'

I'd smiled and shaken my head. 'She's young and shy, but she's quietly ambitious and has a real flair for interior design. She reminds me of someone I used to know.'

He'd smiled ruefully. 'I give her two weeks.'

Six months later and she's truly come out of her shell. She's not only able to interact with clients, but is working on one or two small projects by herself.

'I won't say, "I told you so",' I'd whispered to Nathan under my breath when she presented her ideas on a new restaurant concept we were pitching for last week.

'Smartarse.' He'd smiled, his blue eyes not leaving Lottie.

There was no denying that I felt a tiny sense of satisfaction at getting one over on Nathan. Our friendly competitiveness was part of who we were, whether it be in work, a game of tennis, or playing charades with the girls. But the overriding emotion was one of relief; that in Lottie I might have found a protégé who could take the pressure off me. Nathan was, *is*, brilliant at keeping the business side of the company ticking over. It's in better shape now than it's ever been. But, until Lottie joined, I was the only creative, and to have someone to fall back on, to take the heat off, has meant that I've slept a little easier at night.

Although he's not one to admit defeat, Nathan obviously concedes that having Lottie around is making a difference, as just before he left for Japan he'd championed her for a pay rise.

'She's worth her weight in gold,' he'd said, as he stood in the hall with his holdall in his hand. 'You should have seen her in the meeting with Langley Kitchens. She had them eating out the palm of her hand.'

'Er, you don't have to tell me,' I had said, laughing. 'I'm the one who told *you*, remember.'

'If I'd thought of it sooner, I'd have asked her to accompany me to Japan.'

'*Really?*' I was taken aback, even though I couldn't quite work out why. It had been my choice not to go.

'It's not too late if you want to come with me,' he'd said gently, taking me in his arms.

'Don't be ridiculous.' I had pulled away, my heart hammering through my chest. 'Of course I can't, I've got the children to think about.'

'Your mum would have them at the drop of a hat, you know she would.'

My mind had frantically run through what I'd have to go through to get on that plane with him. My breath caught in my throat as panic crept through every nerve fibre, tingling the tips of my fingers.

'We've discussed this,' I'd snapped.

'I'm just saying that there's still time,' he'd said as he pulled away from me. 'That's all.'

'I'll see you on Wednesday,' I replied. 'Enjoy yourself.'

'How can I if you're not with me?' he'd said forlornly.

'It's Japan, how can you not?'

'Be good,' he'd said with a wink as he walked towards his car on the drive.

'Call me as soon as you land, won't you?'

When I didn't hear from him, I frantically rang his mobile every few minutes as the horror stories played out in my mind. The plane had crashed, Japan had had an earthquake, there was a tsunami. By the time I'd eventually reached him, I'd convinced myself that there wasn't even a remote possibility that he was still alive.

'Oh my God,' I'd cried, when he eventually picked up. 'Are you okay?'

'I'm so sorry darling,' he'd said in a gruff voice, as if I'd just woken him from a deep slumber. 'I took a call as soon as I got off the plane and when I got to the hotel I crashed out for a few hours.'

'I thought something had happened to you,' I said, still with a slight hysterical lilt to my voice, though my chest had stopped hurting.

'I didn't mean to worry you,' he said patiently. 'I'm absolutely fine.'

I could hear ice cubes clinking in a glass.

'Are you all set for the big meeting tomorrow?' I'd asked. 'Got everything you need?'

'Yep, Lottie's sent it across and I've got all your mock-ups here. I'll chat through the scheme with them and make sure we're all singing from the same hymn sheet.'

'Even if we're not, I'm prepared to compromise,' I said, laughing nervously. 'I really want this, Nathan. This deal will put us up there with the big boys.'

'Where you deserve to be.'

'Where *we* deserve to be.'

'AT Designs is *your* baby,' he'd said. 'It was your and Tom's vision that started this whole thing.'

'That may be so, but having you beside me these past few years has made it the success it is today. I just know we can go even further.'

'It's a massive ask, Alice. Are you absolutely sure you can take it on?'

I'd known what he was implying, and allowed the enormity of the task to wash over me. I sat with that feeling for a little while, like I had a hundred times before, waiting to see how it would present itself.

'It's twenty-eight apartments,' he'd continued, as if reading my thoughts. 'Our biggest job by a long way. Do you honestly think you can handle it?'

'Absolutely,' I'd said, my commanding voice belying the panic in the pit of my stomach. 'I've never been more ready for anything in my life.'

And I'd meant it then, when I'd had a glass or two of wine inside me. But now, three days on, I don't feel quite so confident in my abilities or my emotions. Nothing's changed in that time, at least not in a tangible sense. But today it just feels different, as if the roller coaster I'm forever riding has shot straight past the station platform, where it's calm and orderly, and stopped at the top of the loop-the-loop, with me, hanging there upside down, waiting to be rescued.

'Have you got everything you need for your meeting with Temple Homes?' asks Lottie now, interrupting my thoughts.

'I think so,' I say, walking across to my desk. 'Is it definitely David Phillips that I'm seeing?'

'Yes, he specifically asked for you. He said he was a big fan of your work.'

My stomach turns over as I gather up a file and lined pad, avoiding Lottie's gaze.

'In fact, he referred to you as Al,' she goes on, as I concentrate on not blushing. Though the harder I try, the redder I go. 'I had to bring him down a peg or two and tell him that your name was Alice. I can't stand it when people pretend to know you better than they do.'

I roll my eyes and smile tightly, whilst silently saying, *He knows me better than most.*

3

When my satnav tells me I'm under a mile away from Temple Homes' headquarters, I pull over and check my reflection in the rear-view mirror. I wonder if he's changed – I wonder if *I've* changed. I brush my hair through and feather my fringe with my fingers. I could do with a little more mascara, so deftly paint my eyelashes jet black, taking extra care to lengthen them as much as possible with the wand. A brush of blusher, a dab of red lipstick and I'm as good as I can be without the benefit of plastic surgery or being able to turn the clock back some twenty years. It still doesn't stop me from trying though, as I pull my skin tight across my cheekbones, wondering where all that time's gone. I've never thought of it before, but I suddenly regret not having something done, so that I don't look too far off of when David last saw me. Ridiculous, I know, but doesn't every girl want to look their best when they meet their first love again? Not because you still want him, but there's a tiny part – okay a big part – that wants *him* to still want *you*.

'Alice, wow, look at you,' he says as he comes towards me in reception. He looks me up and down appreciatively and I'm pleased that I made a special effort. I kidded myself when I was getting dressed this morning that my 'look' was just a subtle extension of what I normally wear, yet it had been the first thing Beth noticed when she saw me, and Lottie had also commented on how the red complemented my skin tone. Maybe it wasn't so subtle after all.

'David, goodness, you haven't changed a bit,' I say, except he has, and I struggle to hide my shock. I've spent all these years imagining him as he was, as if he'd been somehow frozen in time, whilst I grew older. But he's grown older with me. His dark wedge has been replaced by a bald head, so shiny that the glare of the spotlights above him is reflecting off it, and his perfect physique, the six-pack that all the girls swooned over, has been recast with what looks like an extra six stone.

'So, how have you been?' he says as he kisses me on the cheek.

'Good, really good.'

'I heard what happened to Tom.' He leads me into the boardroom. 'I'm so sorry.'

People often say words to that effect when their back is turned. They're somehow under the misapprehension that it's easier that way. It might be, for them. But ask anyone who's been through it and they'll tell you that they'd rather people be up front than try to brush it under the carpet, or, even worse, avoid the awkward subject altogether.

'So, how are you doing?' he asks solemnly.

'I'm well, thanks. The business is going great, so it's all good.'

'And you married again?' It's more of a statement than a question and I'm taken aback, like I always am when people I haven't seen for years seemingly know more about me than they should. I wonder what else he knows.

'Yes,' I say. 'In some respects, I've been very lucky.'

'I'm pleased you were able to make a new life for yourself after what happened.'

I offer a closed smile. 'And you?' I ask. It seems rude not to at least pretend to be interested in what's been happening in his life since I last saw him. 'You've obviously made a great success of Temple Homes.'

He smiles, and his eyes disappear into the folds of skin around them. I can't even begin to compute that this is the same person, man or boy, who had taken my virginity one summer night, after the end-of-exams ball.

'The company's doing really well,' he says. 'But my marriage, unfortunately, was a casualty of its success.'

I drop my eyes, uncomfortable with the personal slant the conversation has taken. 'I'm sorry to hear that.'

'It happens,' he says. 'Perhaps you can't have it all.'

'But you must be very proud of what you've achieved here,' I say, looking around the boardroom and noting the various building certificates on the wall.

'Yes,' he says, puffing out his chest and sitting up straighter in his chair. 'But I think we can go further, hence bringing you in. I hope you didn't mind me contacting AT Designs, but I've seen your work around and I'm very impressed with what you do.'

'Not at all,' I say, smiling. 'That's good to hear.'

A phone trills around the room and for a moment I ignore it, as I'm sure I turned mine to silent. But when it continues, and I notice David's sitting on the table between us, showing no sign of life, I rummage in my bag.

'Sorry, excuse me,' I say, before seeing that it's Nathan and pressing decline.

'So, the Bradbury Avenue project is—' David begins, before the ringing of my phone interrupts us again.

'I'm so sorry, let me turn it off.' I hit decline again and turn the volume off, but panic is already beginning to set in and I can't concentrate on anything David is saying to me. I note everything down as the silent calls continue to light up my mobile, my writing becoming more frantic.

'Okay, so leave this with me,' I say, standing up, in an attempt to wrap up the meeting prematurely. 'And I'll give you a call once I've got some ideas to present to you.'

'Why don't we do that over dinner?' he says, holding on to the hand I've offered for a little longer than necessary.

'It's probably best to keep this professional,' I say, half laughing.

Without warning, his hands are on my buttocks, pulling me in to him.

'No one ever need know,' he breathes into my ear. The pungent smell of coffee permeates my nostrils and I turn my head. He makes a grab for one of my breasts, squeezing it hard. 'We were good together, you and me. I bet we still are.'

'Don't you *ever* do that again,' I hiss, pushing him away from me with two hands on his chest. He looks hurt, as if he can't understand what he's done wrong.

'But I thought—'

'You thought what? That just because we've been together before gives you the right to go for it again.'

'Well, y-yes,' he stutters, and it takes all my resolve not to slap his face.

I quickly gather up my things from the table and turn to walk out. 'This has clearly been a waste of my time.'

'But the project . . .' he calls out after me. 'What about the project?' I don't answer, leaving him to fill in the blanks.

I'm shaking when I get to the car and fumble with the handle, slamming the door behind me in indignation. How dare he presume that this would be anything other than a business meeting?

I look down at my blouse, undone by one button too many, and I slam the steering wheel in frustration. 'Shit!' I call out loud. What was I thinking? Aren't I as guilty as he is? What message had I relayed in my pathetic attempt to recapture a time long since passed? But then I pull myself up. No. *However* I choose to dress does not give him the right to invade my personal space.

In my incandescent rage I'd forgotten that Nathan had been trying to call me and as I look at my phone, I notice I've missed twelve calls from him and one from the girls' school.

'Shit! Shit!' I say as my mouth goes dry. My heart feels like it's beating at double speed.

'Nathan, it's me,' I blurt out when he picks up. 'What's happened?'

'Where are you?' he asks.

'I'm just out of a meeting,' I say, my voice frantic. 'What is it? Are the girls okay?'

'It's Livvy,' he says.

I feel like I can't breathe.

'Wh-what is it?' I stutter, already working out the quickest way to get to her. I'm turning the key in the ignition but it's not starting. Panic is building within me as I try it again and again. In a split second of clarity I remember that I need to put my foot on the brake first.

'What's happened? Where is she? Is she okay?' The questions are all coming at once.

'She's fine,' he says. 'But she's had a little accident at school.'

'What kind of accident?' I ask, leaving rubber on the road as I screech out of the Temple Homes car park and head in the direction of the school.

'It sounds like she's hit her head.'

It physically hurts as I inhale. 'Oh God.'

'Okay, now listen to me,' he says, his voice suddenly authoritative. 'I want you to take some deep breaths and calm down.'

I try to do what he says, but my lungs don't feel like they're working. They're not letting in the air that I need. My breaths are coming in short, sharp pants as I will the learner driver in front of me to put their foot down.

'Alice, listen to me,' says Nathan again. 'I need you to slow everything down and just concentrate on inhaling and exhaling, long and slow.'

If I could close my eyes it would be easier, but cars seem to be coming at me from every angle. Cutting across my path, pulling out in front of me. Horns are blaring but I can't tell where they're coming from or who they're directed at.

'You okay?' asks Nathan. I nod through pursed lips. 'Alice?'

'Yes,' I say.

'Do you want me to stay on the line until you get there, or shall I let them know you're on your way?'

'Can you call them?' I ask.

'Where are you? How long will it take?'

'I've . . . j-just left Temple Homes headquarters.'

I stutter because I genuinely can't remember where I am, not because I'm trying to hide anything.

'Where are *you*?' I ask.

'I've just left the airport and I was going to go straight to the office if that's all right with you.'

'Yes, I'll see you at home then.'

'Call me once you're with Livvy,' he says. 'I'm sure it's nothing to worry about.'

It only occurs to me then that he doesn't know about the conversation I had with Miss Watts this morning. I wonder if the problem is bigger than either of us thought.

'They don't sound that concerned,' he goes on. 'They're probably just worried about concussion and need to cover their backs.'

I end the call and turn up the radio in an attempt to drown out the noise in my brain.

When I reach the school, I park in the space reserved for the headmaster and half walk, half run into reception, trying hard not to look how I feel.

'Ah, hello Mrs Davies,' says Carole, the school secretary, careful to keep her tone upbeat. I'm quite sure they have a file on me with the words 'Handle with care – unexpectedly widowed' written in big red marker pen. 'Nothing to worry about, it's just that Olivia had a little fall.'

'Is she okay?' I ask, following her through the double doors.

The unmistakable stench of boiled cabbage wafts under my nose as my heels click-clack on the polished wooden floor of the dining hall. It's the same smell as my school dinner thirty years ago, even though we didn't have boiled cabbage then, and Olivia doesn't have it now. I know, because she memorizes the menu every week and tells me what she's having day by day. I almost feel sorry for her that chocolate sponge and chocolate custard, the monthly treat that was part of the staple diet of inner London schools back in the day, is no longer offered. But even on those special days, the school still smelt like rancid vegetables, and I find myself wondering why that is. Anything to keep my mind off what I'm about to be faced with.

'Your mummy's here,' says the school nurse, smiling at me. I half expect to peer around the curtain and be confronted by Olivia lying unconscious on the bed, with blood pouring from her head.

Relief floods through me as she looks up, a little forlornly. There's no blood, no bandage, not even a bruise. 'Hello, baby girl,' I say, my voice shaky, as I bend down to her level. 'You okay?'

She nods, and I give her knee a squeeze, fighting the urge to wrap her in my arms and breathe her in, if only for the nurse and Carole, who, no doubt, will add 'neurotic mother' to my file.

'It was only a little knock,' says the nurse. 'But just keep an eye on it. If she complains of a headache or experiences any dizziness, you ought to get her checked out at hospital.'

I smile and nod.

'What happened?' I ask when we're back in the car.

'Phoebe pushed me,' she says tearfully.

I picture Phoebe's normally angelic little face twisting into something ugly as she bullies my daughter. I can't bear the thought.

'She was being mean to me,' whispers Olivia, as if someone might overhear. 'So I did what you told me to do.'

I wait with baited breath, unable to remember what I said. I'm hoping I told her to give as good as she gets.

'I ignored her and walked away,' she says.

I can't help but be disappointed with my own advice.

'But she pushed me, and I fell onto the floor.'

'Well, that's not very nice, is it?' I'm careful to keep my voice light, all the time wondering how quickly I can get an appointment to see the head. 'I thought Phoebe was your friend. Is she always mean to you?'

She shakes her head, before immediately nodding. I'm not sure that she knows herself.

'Only sometimes,' she admits. 'She says bad stuff to try and make me cry.'

I gently push her flyaway hair back from her elfin face. 'What kind of stuff?' I ask.

She shrugs, as if trying to lift the weight of the world from her shoulders.

'Come on, you can tell me,' I press.

'She says that my first dad is dead.'

I'm momentarily speechless.

'But . . . but you know that Tom was Sophia's daddy,' I say, as she nods. 'He wasn't *your* daddy.'

'I know, but Phoebe says that he was my first daddy.'

I pull her to me, as much as is physically possible across the console of the car. 'Listen—' I start.

'And . . . and . . . she says that my second daddy is going to die like my first daddy.' Her eyes fill with tears and a big globule falls over her bottom lashes.

'Now, you listen to me,' I say assertively, keen not to pass on my own paranoid tendencies. 'What happened to Sophia's daddy was a one-in-a-million. Nothing like that will happen to your daddy.' I discreetly cross my fingers.

She looks at me, her big blue eyes glazed with tears. 'I promise,' I say resolutely. 'Now, how about an ice cream?'

'Yay,' she squeals, oblivious to her worries and sadness transposing from her to me.

4

'Daddy's here!' shrieks Olivia as she bounds down the stairs in her pyjamas, with Ned the Ted in her hand.

'Er, excuse me madam, aren't you supposed to be in bed?' I say, looking up from the mood boards that I've laid out over the dining table.

Her bottom lip sticks out. 'But I haven't seen him for like, ever,' she whines. 'Can I see him? Please. If I promise to go straight to sleep afterwards?'

'You were supposed to be asleep a long time ago,' I say, knowing full well that would never have happened. She gets so excited when she knows Nathan is coming home, and if he doesn't appear in daylight hours, I know to resign myself to her sleeping with one eye open, waiting for him.

'Please,' she begs. We can already hear his footsteps across the gravel drive.

'Go on then,' I smile.

'Thank you,' she says, squeezing me around my waist. 'I promise I'll be asleep in seconds.'

She runs down the hall and I hear excited shrills – no doubt Nathan has picked her up and is twirling her around. 'How's my gorgeous girl?' I hear him say. 'I've missed you. Was it a long one this time?'

I pick up my glass of wine and peer around the door frame. 'It's been four days, eight hours and twenty-three minutes,' Olivia laughs gleefully. 'But I think my chart must be wrong because it feels like a lot longer.'

He grips her tightly and ruffles her hair. I watch, smiling, waiting my turn. She's still in his arms as he comes towards me. He looks tired, but he's trying his best not to show it. His eyes twinkle and his mouth curls upwards as he looks at me.

'Has it felt longer to you as well?' he asks softly, before kissing me on the lips.

'Much,' I say.

'Have you missed me?'

'I always miss you.'

'I wish you didn't have to go away, Daddy,' says Olivia. 'Can you stay home now? For a long time?'

She curls her arms around his neck and drops her face onto his shoulder. 'You've got me for a while,' he says, tickling her under the arm. 'Come on, let's get you to bed.' He starts to climb the stairs.

'Do you want a drink?' I ask after him.

'A large gin would be good,' he says before he disappears around the corner on the landing.

I'd predicted as much and have already prepared three thinly sliced rounds of cucumber. I count four ice cubes into his favourite glass and fill the tumbler halfway with

Hendrick's. He likes to add his own tonic, so I open a small bottle – the bigger ones lose their fizz, he says – and stand it to the side.

He's changed into jeans and a T-shirt by the time he comes back downstairs.

'Is she okay?' I ask. 'I knew she wouldn't settle without seeing you.'

'I wouldn't have it any other way,' he says, smiling. 'How did it go at school? Is she okay? I didn't want to make a big thing of it.'

I nod. 'I think so. I'll keep an eye on her for the next twenty-four hours or so, but I might pop in, have a chat with the head, just to make sure everything's okay. Livvy says that Phoebe pushed her.'

He raises his eyebrows as he takes a sip of his drink. 'You know what kids are like.'

'Yes, but her teacher had a word with me this morning about a falling-out they had yesterday. I just want to make sure there's not something more going on.'

'Good idea,' he says as he pops an olive in his mouth and pulls me towards him. I immediately stiffen as I picture David doing the same thing. 'And how are *you*?'

'I'm okay.'

'You can't go getting yourself in the state you were in earlier, it's not good for you.' He doesn't know the half of it. 'The children are going to hurt themselves, they're going to have arguments with their friends, they'll fall out and make up again. That's all part of growing up.'

I smile tightly. 'I know, but it's just . . .'

'I understand, but you've got to learn to relax. Nothing's going to happen to them.'

'You can't promise me that,' I say, looking at him intently.

'Nobody can, but that's life. I just want you to enjoy yours.'

I pull away and take a long slug of my wine. I can feel his eyes boring into me.

'So, what were you doing at Temple Homes today?' he says.

I busy myself with looking for a colander to strain the rice I've cooked. 'A new client,' I say, far too abruptly. 'They need some interior solutions.'

'Isn't that David Phillips's company?' he asks casually.

'Mmm,' I say, bending down to find a chopping board that I don't need.

'Wasn't he your first boyfriend?' It sounds like he's talking through a smile, but I'm too nervous to look.

'Er, yeah,' I say, not sure whether I feel guilty about meeting him, dressing for the occasion, or the memory of his hands on my body, even though they weren't invited.

'Was it *him* you met?'

I nod.

'That must have been a bit weird,' he says, half laughing. 'How did that go?'

I wonder whether I should tell him what happened,

knowing that if I do, he is more than likely to go straight round there. I think better of it and let David off the hook, at least for the time being.

'It was fine,' I say. 'It was a long time ago.'

'So, no funny feelings in your tummy,' he asks, teasingly.

'Not on my part,' I say honestly. 'He's old, bald and divorced, not an attractive proposition.'

'I bet he took one look at you and rued the day he let you go.'

I throw him a withering look.

'I mean it! I bet he's thinking of you right now. He's probably lying in his single bed, remembering all the things you used to do, pretending he's doing them to you all over again.'

I shiver involuntarily. That's too close to the truth to be funny.

'Do you think we'll get his business?' he asks. 'It might be a nice little earner on the side. Something that can run alongside the Japan project.'

'I don't know if it's something we should do,' I say. 'We'll have our hands pretty full with Japan, if we get it.' I put the chopping board back. 'So, come on, tell me, how did it go?'

'Well,' he starts, unable to keep the smile from his face, 'I think it's all looking pretty good.'

'So, they liked what you showed them?'

He nods. 'They loved it, but what's not to love? It

doesn't take a rocket scientist to see how good you are at what you do.'

'What about the kitchen and bathrooms?' I ask, excitedly. 'Did they like the furniture choices?'

'Yep, they thought they were inspired.'

I feel my chest rise, my pride instantly buoyed. 'When do you think we'll hear for definite? Did they give you any idea on timescales?'

I absently top up my red wine, almost filling an already oversized balloon glass to the brim.

He eyes me carefully. 'All being well, they're exchanging contracts next Monday and completing the week after. But they want to have a designer on board as soon as they exchange.'

Butterflies dance in my stomach at all the possibilities, whilst my brain tries its damnedest to keep myself from racing ahead.

'How long will it take to build?' I ask.

'They're looking to do it in two hits,' he says. 'The first phase will be completed in twelve months and the second will be around six months later. It's a lot of work, Alice, and it'll all come at you pretty quickly.'

'It's what I've been waiting for,' I say. 'This is it. This is the big one.'

He trails my jawline with his finger. 'I only want to do this if you're sure you can handle it. I can't risk you having a relapse, so if you have any reservations, any at all, then you need to say.'

I remember a time, not so long ago, when the very thought of it would have had me running for the hills. A time when I was scared of my *own* shadow, let alone the one created by the black dog that seemed destined to be by my side forever more. Back then, I was so far down that hole that I even began to seek the darkness out, believing that it was my only true friend.

I could barely get out of bed, only doing so to deposit Sophia in the playground, before sloping back to hide under the duvet, where my thoughts would poison even the brightest of days. At three o'clock, I'd get up again and convince myself that no one would notice my stained joggers as I waited at the school gates, head down, trying to hide from anyone who was brave enough to look. Ironically, it might have only taken one person to show an interest for my faith in humanity to have been restored. But on the rare occasion I was looking, all I could see was embarrassment and avoidance. I knew I was being ridiculed and reviled, spoken about and ostracized, but I didn't care. I didn't care about anything other than being a mother, and even then, I was barely functioning. Just thinking about it makes my breath come in short, sharp pants.

'Are you sure you're ready for this?' asks Nathan again.

I nod my head, aggrieved at his lack of confidence in me, though I have to dig deep to find it myself. 'I'm absolutely ready for this, Nathan. I'm not going back to where I was.'

'Well, I'll be here to help and give you all the support you need, but ultimately it's *your* face that fronts the company, it's *your* talent that delivers results and it's *you* who people want to work with.'

I smile and hold his hands. 'But it's *you* who runs things behind the scenes and I couldn't do what I do if it weren't for you. We're in this together.'

He lifts my hands to his lips. 'And Sophia, how's she getting on with her exams?'

'She's got her final one on Friday,' I grimace. 'Maths, of all things. I mean, you wouldn't wish it on your worst enemy, would you?'

'That's because you haven't got a head for figures,' he says, laughing. 'Remind me what you got in your maths final exams.'

'Er, a U,' I mumble.

'What was that?' he says, leaning in with a hand cupped to his ear. 'Can you repeat that? Louder.'

I swipe him on the arm with a tea towel. 'A U,' I almost shout.

'And what does U stand for?' he says, holding himself up against the kitchen worktop for fear of falling to the ground laughing.

'Unclassified,' I say.

'So, you did *so* badly that they couldn't possibly grade it?' he manages.

'That's why I had to marry you,' I say triumphantly, as I kiss him. 'So you could do my numbers for me.'

'So, is she going to be okay?' he asks.

I look at him perplexed, momentarily forgetting what we were talking about.

'Sophia,' he says, reading my confused expression. 'Does she think she's done enough revision?'

'Well, she's a walking mass of hormones at the moment, so your guess is as good as mine.'

'We were all teenagers once,' he says, as he appreciatively takes a sip of his drink.

'I can't remember that far back,' I say, kissing him. 'Thank God.' I can taste the gin on his lips, the tang of the juniper berries reminding me of Christmases gone by.

'Urgh, can the pair of you get a room?' says Sophia in mock horror, appearing in the doorway. Or perhaps her revulsion is real – it's hard to tell these days.

'Hey sweetheart,' says Nathan. 'How's it going?' He opens out his arm for her to walk into and pulls her towards him, kissing the top of her head as it falls heavily on his shoulder. 'What's going on with you?'

'I hate my life,' she says, her arms dangling loosely by her sides. 'I can't wait for these exams to be over.'

'School is the easy part,' I say. 'Just wait until you're a grown-up.'

'Oh, here we go. Your school days are the best days of your life . . .' she mimics in a sing-song voice. 'Blah, blah, blah . . .'

I have to stop myself from laughing. Do I really say

SANDIE JONES

that? I wasn't aware I'd turned into my mother. I pull a face behind her back and Nathan gives me the stern eye.

'They are,' I insist. 'Believe you me, if I could have my time over again—'

'Except you wouldn't,' she says. 'You couldn't wait to get out of school. Grandma said you barely stayed long enough to sit your exams.'

She does have a point, but I'd prefer to give her my version of events than have my mother tell her how it really was. I cringe inwardly as I recall my high school days, remembering the misery I felt on a daily basis. I'd spent the first two years being bullied, and wishing, more than anything, that I was part of the 'in crowd'. I'd then spent the next three years in it, and desperate to get out.

Being hunted, for me, was somehow easier than being the hunter. I was never comfortable being part of the whispering huddle that the new girl at school had to walk past, desperate to be included, yet so quickly and thoughtlessly rejected by us without a second's thought. She didn't need to say or do anything to incur our wrath; Tracy, our ringleader, would already have decided she didn't like her, and seeing as we seemingly didn't have minds of our own, we'd just gormlessly follow her lead.

I'd ashamedly surfed Facebook over the years, trying to put right the wrongs I felt I'd been a part of. Unsurprisingly, Maxine Elliott, who I'd been forced to empty a glass of milk over, and Natalie Morgan, who

40

I'd been coerced into telling was ugly, didn't respond to my friend requests. Funny; after all this time I still use words like 'forced'. I hadn't been 'forced' to do anything. I wasn't held under water or nailed to a cross; I'd had a choice, and that's what still pains me today. In my fantasies, I imagine myself standing up to the draconian ringleader, instead of staying quiet and taking the coward's way out.

I think about Olivia and feel a tug in my chest. Is it possible that a child so young can be caught up in the same horror? A shiver runs through me.

'I just want you to enjoy it,' I say to Sophia. 'Because it'll get a whole lot harder before you know it.'

She shrugs and moves away from Nathan's embrace to get herself an orange juice from the fridge.

'We only want what's best for you, sweetheart,' says Nathan. 'Your mother's right, it might not feel like it, but this is the easy part. This is the only time in your life when you don't have any real responsibilities. You don't have to hold down a job, you don't have to pay bills, you don't have any little ankle-biters, draining your emotions and your bank account.'

She gives him a withering look, but the corners of her mouth are ever so slightly turned up as she battles with a smile.

'Honestly, it's tough out here in the big wide world. Don't be fooled by me making it look so easy.'

We each pick up a tea towel and throw them at him,

laughing as he ducks the missiles. But he's right – he does make it look easy, and I don't know that I always give him the credit he deserves.

It could have been so different – I could still be thrashing around in that black hole, if Nathan hadn't rescued me. Us.

I was going through the motions, but not really feeling anything, when I met him. I like to think I would have got myself back around the right way eventually – I would've *had* to, for Sophia. But as much as I'd drawn my strength from my daughter, in my efforts to protect, comfort and love her, I had been a shadow of my former self.

Even on the rare good days, I wasn't expecting to get a second chance. I thought I'd had the best that life was going to offer with Tom, and with him gone I'd been sure I'd never find love or happiness ever again.

But Nathan showed me that there was still a world out there and slowly, over time, I began to think there might be a place in it for me. He took on the challenge with such sincerity that I often found myself thinking it was all too good to be true. He'd take me and Sophia out for the day to the zoo and quite literally monkey around until her sides hurt with laughter, and he'd surprised us both on her ninth birthday with a weekend away on a boat. When she fell over, he was first in line with a plaster, and when she cried, he was there to offer a cuddle.

'We love you, and are always here for you,' he says to her now.

I look at him and smile, my heart feeling as if it might burst.

'Help yourself to some chilli,' I say. 'I'll just go and check Livvy's gone to sleep.'

As I pass the open door of our bedroom, I see Nathan's overnight holdall lying at the foot of our bed. I imagine what's inside; four pristine white shirts, each laundered by the hotel, ironed and folded perfectly in crunchy cellophane, as if he'd bought them new that day. Probably eight pairs of Calvin Klein underpants, all white, clean and folded in identically sized squares. His socks will be paired and rolled over just once at the top. My hand is lingering over his bag when he comes into the room.

'Do you want me to unpack for you?' I ask.

'No, I'll do it,' he says, coming towards me. 'There doesn't seem to be much point in unpacking really,' he says, carefully taking out four white shirts in cellophane and eight pairs of freshly washed underpants.

'Oh, why's that?' I ask. 'Are you going away again?'

'I'm probably going to need to go back to Japan if we get the contract. It'd be great if you could come too . . .' I feel my insides tighten as he looks at me, before he continues, 'It's okay, I understand . . .'

Except he doesn't – not really. He tries to, but how can he when I can't even work it out myself. 'I thought you said I didn't need to go,' I say, my mouth suddenly dry. 'You said I could work from plans if we got the job.'

He comes towards me again and pulls me into him. 'But wouldn't it be good to go to the site, to see it and feel it?'

I nod as he strokes my hair. 'And when the time comes, wouldn't you like to add the finishing touches yourself, instead of someone else rolling out the rug *you* hand-picked or hanging the curtains *you* specifically chose?'

I hear everything he's saying and when he puts it like that, it sounds perfectly plausible, but I can't leave the girls and fly halfway around the world. I simply can't.

'I'd love to, but . . .' I start.

'I was hoping this deal might change things,' he says gently. 'That it might give you the confidence to go, as you'll be so busy concentrating on the project that you won't have time to miss the girls.'

I feel my hackles rising and pull away from him. 'I don't *not* go away because I'll miss the girls, Nathan. Jesus, I thought you understood.'

'I do, but it's been almost ten years now, Al. If you're not careful, you'll go through your entire life without stepping outside of the home counties.'

'Don't make it sound like I'm some kind of hermit,' I say, my voice rising. 'We've been to France and Ireland.'

'Yes, with the girls,' he says bluntly.

'And you and I went to Scotland . . .'

'That was our honeymoon,' he says. 'We could go

anywhere in the world – we've got the money, and, with a little planning, we've got the time. I really thought Japan would be a new start.'

'Is that why you pitched for it?' I snap. 'To put me under pressure? Why would you do that to me?'

'You're being ridiculous,' he says. 'I know what AT Designs means to you and I did it because I thought you'd want to do it. Period. This isn't about me, Alice. This is about you, living the life you should be living.'

'Well, I'm perfectly happy as I am,' I shout as I go into our bathroom and slam the door.

5

'You're not going to let him get away with that, are you?' asks Beth, aghast, as we have dinner the following night.

I twirl spaghetti absently on my fork and feel surprisingly emotional. I suppose it's because up until now I'd convinced myself that what David did was no big deal, but Beth's reaction proves to me that it was.

'Have you told Nathan?'

I shake my head. 'I didn't know whether to or not. I might have done if we hadn't had a row.'

She grimaces, and I already regret saying anything. But she's one of the few friends I have who has nothing to do with AT Designs and no connection to Nathan. In fact, she still hasn't met him, and part of me wonders if I've kept them apart, albeit subliminally, so that I can say how I feel without being judged, or running the risk of it getting back to him.

'What did you row about?' she asks.

I instinctively look around the tables closest to us, checking for anyone I know. Not that they'd be able to hear us over the din of the birthday party that is thankfully beginning to peter out. There is only so much of

'Zac' and his excitable friends that one can be expected to endure, especially on the rare occasion that you're child-free yourself.

'Just the same old stuff,' I say dismissively.

She leans forward. 'Like what?'

'About me going away,' I say. 'It's the only thing we ever row about, and every time I try to explain myself, I think he understands, only for it to rear its ugly head again a few months later.'

She screws her face up in confusion. 'Where are you going?'

'I'm not, that's the whole point.' I no longer want to have this conversation, as I'm sure that once she hears my side, she'll think I'm just as mad as Nathan does.

'I'm not with you,' she says, half laughing. 'It's you *not* going away that's causing the problem?'

I nod. 'He wants me to go to Japan, if we get this big job that we're pitching for, but I've not been away without the girls since . . .'

My voice breaks, and she leans across to put her hand on mine.

'It's a weird and complicated thing, but I just can't bring myself to do it. Every time I think about it, I'm paralysed by fear.'

'That's understandable,' she says soothingly. 'Losing Tom like that was such a huge shock – I don't imagine anything will ever be quite the same in your world again. What is it that panics you the most? The idea of something happening to *them* while you're away? Or the possibility of something happening to *you*?'

'Them. Me. Both.' I shake my head. 'I don't know.' I feel tears welling up in my eyes and bat them away. 'Sorry, it's just . . .'

'You don't need to apologize, Alice,' she says.

'I just don't feel comfortable leaving them,' I say. 'Tom walked out the door one day and he never came back. I wasn't with him when he died and I'll never forgive myself for not being able to save him. If we'd been together, he'd still be here, and that's what constantly goes around in my head whenever I'm away from the girls. How can I save them if I'm not with them? It takes all my strength to drop them off at school each day. But Nathan doesn't get it. He thinks I should be embracing the opportunity to go away, and now there's a chance of us getting this job, it just feels as if I'll be under even more pressure.'

'Do you *want* the job?' she asks.

'Most days I want it more than anything,' I say honestly. 'It's been in the pipeline for months and it'll be such a huge coup for us. But on the days in between, I panic; about the stress it'll put me under and that I might be forced to leave the girls.'

'I get that, but the longer you worry about what *might* happen to them, the less time you've got to enjoy yourself and live the best possible life you can live.'

She sounds like Nathan.

'You, more than most, know how short life is.'

I nod. 'Yet ironically that makes me fear it all the more.'

'Look around you,' she says. 'You've got it all. A husband who clearly adores you, two beautiful children, a gorgeous house, money in the bank.'

I sniff and muster a smile.

'And not only that, but you're a talented interior designer who is, touch wood, in good health.'

I put a hand on top of my head. 'God willing.'

She does the same as she brings her glass to her lips.

'I'm sorry, I don't mean to be morose,' I say, holding back from adding 'or sound ungrateful', knowing that must surely be what she thinks of me. I look at her and chastise myself for bemoaning the amazing life that I lead when hers is a daily struggle.

'I'm sorry to ramble on,' I say. 'How's things with you?'

'Not bad,' she says sadly. 'I had an interesting chat with Millie yesterday.'

'Oh?'

'Yeah, she asked me about her dad.'

I look at her over the top of my glass, trying to read her expression. Her facial muscles contract and there's a pulse below her eye. Talking about her ex is always a thorny issue and I know her well enough now to gauge whether she's in the mood to talk about him or not.

* * *

Like all of us, Beth had been convinced she'd know if her other half was playing away. On one of our many nights out, my bravery enhanced by three glasses of rosé, I'd asked, 'Was there no part of you that heard alarm bells or saw the signs?'

'Nope,' she'd said. 'I was so in denial, or insanely trusting, whichever way you want to look at it, that I hadn't a clue.'

'So when did he last see Millie?'

'He hasn't,' she said, her words a little slurry, or maybe my ears just had a blush-infused mesh over them. 'He left when I was pregnant and we never saw him again.'

'He's not seen Millie since?' I'd asked incredulously, my brain unable to compute how a father could do that. How can life be so unfair? How can it give men children they don't want, and yet take away the fathers other children so desperately need?

She shook her head, her bottom lip trembling. 'How could he do it to me, Alice?' she remonstrated. 'I gave him everything.'

I fell back into my chair, feeling suddenly and inexplicably drawn to my friend. Here was someone who could begin to understand what it felt like to have the person you love, the man you've shared so much with, disappear from your life. She knew how it felt to have the rug pulled out from underneath your feet, tossing you up in the air and making you wonder if you'll ever come back down again.

I could have argued that at least her partner is alive, whilst mine is dead, but when I tried to put myself in her position, I was almost grateful that I was in mine. I couldn't bear the thought that Tom had *chosen* to leave my life, and that of our child. He wasn't given the choice – none of us were.

'How . . . how did you find out he was seeing someone else?' I'd faltered, unable to get my head around what she was telling me.

'Purely by chance. I'd gone away and had come back earlier than expected and there they were.'

A hand flew up to my mouth. 'Oh my God.'

'Yeah, so . . .' She'd looked out across the restaurant as her eyes filled with tears.

I'd reached across the table and placed my hand on top of hers. 'I can't even begin to imagine . . . Is he still with the woman . . . ?' I had almost added, 'he left you for', but it would have been too hurtful.

Sensing my predicament, she'd finished the sentence for me.

'I have absolutely no idea,' she'd said scathingly. 'I imagine they're playing happy families somewhere. Well, she got what she wanted, didn't she?'

I'd pulled back, looking at her quizzically. 'You sound like you're blaming *her*. But it's likely that she didn't even know you existed.'

'Of course she did,' Beth had spat. 'You know when the man you're with is supposed to be with someone else.'

I'd wanted to argue the case, but I could tell by her hardened features that it wasn't one I was going to win.

As a tear fell onto her cheek I'd moved to her side of the table, holding her close and gently pushing her auburn hair away from her wet face. 'How could he do it, Alice? How could I not have known what was going on?'

'How would any of us know?' I'd offered reassuringly, though I *would* reverberated loudly around my head.

'Don't you ever worry about Nathan straying?' she'd asked, as if reading my mind.

I had shaken my head. 'That's not on my radar. I've had worse happen to me, so when he's late home, I worry more about his safety than who he might be sleeping with.'

'I wouldn't worry about it,' she'd slurred. 'There's no way Nathan would ever cheat. I mean, just look at you for God's sake. He'd be out of his mind.'

I'd looked down at my slim legs, encased in tight dark denim jeans, and brushed imaginary crumbs from my cleavage, as it descended into the plunging neckline of a white T-shirt. I try my best to stay in shape, but my willpower isn't always what it should be. God *must* be a man, as no woman would be so cruel as to make chocolate, biscuits and crisps taste so darn good.

'So, I've made a decision,' says Beth, bringing me back to the here and now.

'Oh,' I murmur.

'I'm going to find him,' she says, abruptly.

'Why?' I ask. 'You've done fine without him up until now, what's changed?'

'Because now it's about Millie,' she says. 'I always knew this day would come – I was just hoping that it wouldn't be any time soon. But I promised myself that as soon as she started asking about him, started realizing that she was different to other kids, I'd tell her about him.'

'But she's still young. Won't it all be a bit much for her to take in and understand at the moment? There's plenty of time for her to find him if she wants to.'

'It wasn't the right time before,' she says, 'but I feel it is now.'

I look at her, square in the eyes. 'For you or for Millie?'

She bristles. 'For Millie of course.'

'You need to think very carefully about the impact of this on her. Once you open the can, the worms are going to keep coming out. You need to be ready and prepared for that.'

'I am,' she says confidently.

'So, what are you going to say to her when she asks why her daddy left? When she discovers that he didn't even stay long enough to meet her.'

Beth's face is clouding over, her fury and frustration close to the surface.

'I'm sorry if I sound harsh,' I say, my hand on hers, 'but I'm just playing devil's advocate. I want to make sure you know what you might be letting yourself in for.'

She smiles ruefully. 'I grew up without a father, and there isn't a day that goes by when I don't miss him and wonder what could have been. No child should have to endure that.'

I only have to picture Sophia's face, on the days when she's missing Tom even more than usual, to get a sense of the sadness that she carries with her everywhere she goes. My eyes fall to the table, for fear that I might sob at the injustice that they've both suffered. If I could take away Beth's pain I would. But as I can't, the next best thing I can do is support her in her mission.

'Why don't we see if we can find him first?' I say.

'We?' she repeats, her eyes wide.

'I'll do all that I can to help you,' I promise. 'But there's nothing to be gained from talking to Millie at this point. If you tell her you're looking, and he doesn't want to be found, it'll only lead to more heartache.'

She mulls it over. 'Mmm, you're probably right. I'll have a tentative look around, see if I can find any trails that might lead in his direction.'

'And if I can do anything to help, just let me know.'

'I might hold you to that.' She laughs.

As usual, we bicker over the bill, but as much as I genuinely want to pay for her, I'm aware that there's a very fine line between being generous and being patronizing. I only agree to go halves if she promises to let me pay next time.

'So, when will you know about the Japanese project?' she says as we reach her car.

'Monday, hopefully,' I say, crossing my fingers. 'Just as soon as they exchange contracts.'

'I'll be keeping everything crossed for you,' she says.

'Thanks for listening,' I say, leaning in to give her a kiss on the cheek. 'I'm sure everything will work out for the best.'

She hugs me tightly and I feel like I might cry. 'Good luck,' she says. 'Keep me posted.'

'Good luck to you too,' I say, and we both know what I mean.

6

'So, how's it going to work?' Lottie asks forthrightly, as we sit in our team meeting the following morning. 'When we're so far away from the site.'

'Okay,' says Nathan, looking to me for the go-ahead to reveal what we'd discussed. I give a small nod. 'Well, once we're properly up and running, we're thinking Alice will stay here, overseeing the project from the UK. And I'll be over there, making sure everything is received and in good order.'

'So, you're not going over there at *all*?' Lottie says incredulously, looking at me.

I stay focused on the random sketches on my pad. They say a lot can be determined about a person from their doodles and I wonder what conclusion would be drawn from the cubes and stars that are scattered across the paper in front of me.

'No, Alice will be based here,' says Nathan. 'But that does mean I'm going to need some help on the ground in Japan. Lottie, maybe that would be something you'd consider doing.'

It had been *my* suggestion, a way of getting myself off the hook, but Nathan had readily agreed. If he felt I'd manipulated the situation, he didn't say.

'Seriously?' chokes Lottie, her voice high. 'Oh my God, seriously?'

He smiles. 'Yes, seriously. What do you say?'

I choose to bat away the uncomfortable sensation that is swirling in my stomach; pretending that it's just nerves about the job. But as much as I try to disguise it, the green-eyed monster won't be silenced. *I wanted to be the one to pull it all together, be the first to see the end result.*

You could, the voice in my head says. *If you were brave enough.*

'It would be a really wonderful opportunity for you Lottie,' I say, with a smile fixed on my face. 'And we're confident you'll do it with aplomb.'

'I can't believe it,' she says. 'Of course, yes, yes, yes.' She instinctively jumps out of her chair and throws her arms around Nathan. 'Thank you, I won't let you down.'

Lottie's blonde hair swishes from side to side as she makes her way towards me, and I get up out of my chair, ready to receive her gratitude. 'I don't know what else to say apart from thank you,' she says, putting her arms around me.

'Well, we haven't got the job yet,' I say, seemingly conscious that we shouldn't be getting ahead of ourselves. But I half-wonder if I just say it to rain on her parade.

* * *

'How come you've got Daddy's car?' squeals Olivia as she jumps into the front passenger seat of Nathan's BMW later on, when I pick her up after school. 'Is he at home?'

'Because mine's in for a service and no, he's not,' I say.

'Aww, when's he going to be back? Will I see him before I go to bed?'

'I don't think so, sweetie, he's playing golf and then going out for dinner.'

'But he's always out,' she moans.

I wonder why she feels that way. It certainly doesn't feel like that to me, but maybe the perception of time veers wildly between the two of us. What's my hour must feel like her day, and my week, her month. That's how I remember feeling about my dad, as a kid. He very rarely went out, but on the odd occasion he'd go to the pub, straight from the building site on a Friday, with his bulging wage packet in his pocket, it felt like forever until I saw him again on Saturday morning.

'You'll see him tomorrow,' I promise. 'It's the weekend.'

'Yay,' she says, fidgeting with her seatbelt, not wanting to let go of the jam jar housing the painted lady caterpillar the school has helpfully asked us to look after whilst it morphs into a chrysalis.

'Forget it, little lady, you're not staying there. In the back.'

'But Daddy lets me,' she whines as she clumsily gets

out, dropping the hungry caterpillar into the abyss of the footwell.

'Livvy,' I shriek. 'Be careful.'

'Ooops!' She laughs.

'Well, he shouldn't,' I say. 'You're not allowed to.'

The lid has popped off the jar and the hairy slug-like insect is tantalizingly close to poking its head out. I reach down and under the seat, frantically feeling around for the lid.

'But why not?' she goes on.

I blindly touch upon a sharp object and instinctively pull my hand away, still no closer to locating the lid. I go in again, as if I'm doing a bush tucker trial, not knowing what's under there or where the sharp object is. I'm reminded of my Aunty Val, who'd have a panic attack every time she had to pop a letter in the postbox. She couldn't bear to have her hand there, just in case something came out and dragged her in. It got so bad that she'd pay me twenty pence to post her letters for her. In my infinite innocence I'd boldly stride up to the red pillar box, stand on tiptoes and peer into the slot, asking if anyone was in there. What happens to us between then and now, I wonder, as I gingerly poke my hand under the seat again. I come at the object from a different angle and am able to pinch it and pull it up to the light. I can't make it out at first and hold it aloft to the windscreen. I blink a couple of times, as if to clear my vision, but there's no mistaking the crystal pear drop earring that's dangling there.

'Mummy,' shrieks Olivia, 'it's crawling out.'

'Oh my God. Livvy, find the lid.'

'Why can't I sit in the front?'

'Because you're not allowed.'

'But Daddy lets me.'

'Livvy, find the lid.'

'What will happen if it crawls out?'

'Get in the back seat.'

'Will Daddy get into trouble?'

I look at the earring again. *Oh yes*, I think to myself.

'For letting me sit in the front.'

'The caterpillar's getting out.'

'Find the lid, Mummy.'

'Yes, because it's against the law for someone so little to sit in the front.'

'I can see it. The lid's back here.'

I want to go on like this. I want to continue our diatribe forever because the longer it goes on, the longer the earring has to change itself into one of mine. I so want it to be mine.

7

Sophia is already home when we get back, and once I've set Olivia up with her homework, I climb the stairs to my elder daughter's room. I sit on her bed and watch as she brushes her long dark hair through. God, she looks like Tom. Every now and then, I catch her at a certain angle, or see her pulling the very same expression as him. She doesn't know she's doing it of course, and if I asked her to do it again she wouldn't be able to, but just in those fleeting moments, I can see him so clearly. And I don't want to lose him. I squeeze my eyes tightly shut to try and hold on to him.

It's what I used to do in the months after Tom had gone; shamefully willing Sophia to metamorphize into him. My mind had been tricked into thinking that if I could just get Tom back, I'd happily sacrifice everyone and everything else. It was an insane thought, but that's what happens when you are momentarily struck with insanity. How else could you explain that I honestly believed that losing my daughter would somehow be easier to deal with than losing my husband? Maybe God heard me and decided to put my deluded theory to the test, because a little while later I *did* lose her.

Somewhere between a seemingly normal Wednesday afternoon and a dreary Thursday morning, the world that I'd kept tentatively spinning on one finger came crashing down. Looking back, the warning signs were all there; I'd not been able to sleep, preferring to immerse myself in the never-ending hell of being awake. I was unable to do even the most mundane task – I once confused a banana for a cucumber when I made tuna sandwiches for Sophia's packed lunch. My mother has never forgiven herself for not seeing what was hiding in plain sight, but how could she, when I couldn't even see it myself?

The switch that short-circuited my system came in the form of a badly made cappuccino in a coffee shop. Not that there was anything necessarily wrong with it, it just had chocolate sprinkles on, which I thought I'd expressly said I didn't want. An easy enough mistake to make you might think, but for me it was the straw that broke the camel's back.

As the unfortunate barista handed it to me, I felt something inside me go horribly wrong, as if the blood was rushing out of my body. All I wanted was a cappuccino with no chocolate sprinkles, but even that seemed an insurmountable task. Was I not worthy of even a coffee? Did the powers-that-be hate me so much that I couldn't even get the drink I wanted?

I felt as if I was drowning, unable to keep my head above the water, whilst everyone around me was pretending not to see the overwhelming panic that had paralysed me. The walls caved in, and the floor rose to meet the ceiling, leaving me trapped in a windowless room with just my poisonous thoughts to taunt me. *Why don't you just die?* I said to myself. *What's the point of living? Nobody would miss you. You're not even capable of ordering a coffee . . .*

After whatever was happening happened, I found myself sat under the counter, drenched in coffee, tightly hugging my knees to my chest to stop my body from shaking. I vaguely remember flashing blue lights, though whether it was the police or ambulance service I can't recall. I clearly needed both.

Seeing Mum at the hospital, her face etched with pain, still didn't convince me that I had a life worth living. 'Don't worry about Sophia,' she said as she held my hand, bringing it to her lips and kissing it. 'She's home with me.' I hadn't even given her a second's thought; my brain was empty, barren of emotions.

I stayed in the psychiatric unit for eight weeks and it was only on day twenty-one that I asked if Sophia could be brought in to see me. 'Let's see how you are tomorrow,' said the doctor, smiling gently, which I translated into, *Not until we're absolutely sure you won't scare her.*

Three days later my good behaviour was rewarded with a visit. My nervous-looking mum held Sophia's hand as she walked towards me, her face a complicated mixture of fear and adoration.

As soon as *I* smiled, *she* smiled, and she ran to me with her arms open wide. A flood of love rushed through me as I hugged her, my ravaged thoughts wondering how I could have risked losing her. Yet at the same time, I asked myself how I could possibly look after her ever again. I didn't feel responsible enough to keep *myself* out of harm's way, let alone *her*.

But each day I grew stronger, and when I eventually returned home, I started to think about how much Sophia needed me, rather than how much better off she'd be without me. I certainly knew I needed *her*, but I wasn't brave enough to do it on my own, so Mum moved in with us – a constant yet necessary presence.

Under her watchful eye, I learnt how to be a mother all over again, which was exhilarating and terrifying in equal measure. Every step felt like a leap into the unknown, but slowly we made it through to the other side.

Looking at Sophia now, all these years later, I shudder to think how I almost lost her. 'How did your final exam go?' I ask tearfully.

She gives me the briefest of looks – just to double-check I'm okay – before shrugging her shoulders. She's used to seeing me cry. 'Okay I guess.'

'Can you offer anything more?' I ask. 'Do you think you did all right? What questions came up?'

Her eyes are sad as she looks at me and I move closer to her, resting my hand on her knee.

'What's up?' I ask. 'You're free now. No more exams for another year.' I look at her excitedly. 'That must feel great, eh? You've got your freedom back.'

She shifts and rolls off the other side of the bed. 'I guess.'

'Sophia, what's going on with you?' I ask gently. 'You've not been yourself recently.'

'I'm surprised you'd notice,' she says.

My natural instinct is to recoil, but I know she doesn't mean to sound as scathing as she sometimes does. God knows, there's been many a time when her words have hurt me more; her sense of abandonment knowing no bounds, as first her father and then her mother left her. It's no wonder that she keeps checking I'm still here, both literally and figuratively.

'Hey, what's going on?' I stand up, walk around to her and pull her to me. She does little to resist. 'I *always* notice,' I say, breathing her hair in. 'Have these exams been getting you down?'

She nods mutely.

'But they're over now, no more pressure.'

'But what if I don't pass them?' she says, her voice cracking. 'What will happen then?'

'You're a clever girl. You'll be fine.'

'But what if I'm not?' A sob catches in her throat.

Her weight falls into me as if she's carrying the world on her shoulders. 'Stop worrying,' I say. 'Worst case scenario, you fail them all.'

'But then I won't get into sixth form,' she cries.

'If that happens, we'll work something out,' I say reassuringly. 'Now stop worrying. School's out for the summer, so go and enjoy yourself.'

She shrugs me off and falls onto her bed, picking her phone up.

'I've got some good news,' I say, as I ferret in my jeans pocket. 'Ta-dah. Bet you thought you'd lost this.' I hold up the earring.

She peers over the lifeline in her hands. 'That's not mine,' she says, and the hope that I'd been holding onto, willing myself to believe, is smashed into a thousand tiny pieces.

'It's not? Are you sure?'

'Definitely. Why? Where did you find it?'

I don't know whether I should tell her. Is her brain still as innocent as Olivia's? Or has it been violated by the evil on the internet and the trolls on social media? I'd hate for her to put two and two together and come up with five.

I chance it. 'It must be yours, it was in Nathan's car.'

I laugh lightly, conscious not to convey my suspicions to her. Even in the midst of her tempestuous teens, Nathan is still her hero and it would break her heart, just after it broke mine, if he was fooling around with someone else.

She stops tapping on her phone and looks up at me with a furrowed brow. 'In Nathan's car?'

I can see her brain whirring. Her expression tells me that she's come up with the wrong answer to the equation and I immediately regret telling her.

'Well, it must be yours then,' she says.

'Maybe it's one of your friends'?' I ask. 'Could it be Hannah's?'

A look of recognition crosses her features. 'Ah, yes, that must be it.' I don't know if she's trying to convince herself or me.

'Might Nathan have taken her home? Given her a lift?'

She nods. 'I think he dropped her back after Megan's party.' It feels as if she's clutching at the same straws that I am. 'And didn't he take Lizzy home from here the other night?' she adds.

'No worries,' I say, far too casually. 'Ask them when you next see them.'

What I really want to say is, *Can you ring them both, right now, so we can put an end to this and I can sleep soundly tonight?*

As expected, I lie awake, waiting for Nathan to come home from his weekly game of golf, which is invariably followed by an even longer drink in the bar. I've gone through every possibility in my mind and a headache is banging at the sides of my skull. The way I see it, there are only two feasible options. Well, only two options I'd be happy with. Either the earring belongs to one of

Sophia's friends, or it was dropped by a member of staff at the valet parking when Nathan left his car at the airport. It's a tad far-fetched, but it's possible.

I watch the clock on my bedside table change to 22.46 and tut in frustration before turning over, hoping that not being able to see the ticking of time will aid sleep. I force myself to think of something else and focus on the team meeting earlier in the day. It had gone well, from what I could tell. They all seemed fully committed to Japan, should we get the job, and were genuinely excited about the opportunities it might bring.

My mind goes to Lottie, and how she had reacted to the news that she'd be going to Japan. Nathan had embraced her awkwardly, as if she were a friend's teenage daughter. A man on guard, worried about what is deemed appropriate and what's not. Up until now, that's how I've viewed Lottie; a young friend of the family, an eager-to-please apprentice whom I've enjoyed mentoring. But now, as I lie here, picturing her body pressed up against Nathan's, I'm reminded that she is a twenty-two-year-old woman with the type of frame I've always envied; petite and narrow across the shoulders, her blouse seams sitting perfectly on her lean torso, with no real distinction between her waist and hips. A neat little package that makes me feel like a cumbersome giant.

Stop, I remonstrate with myself. I think the world of

Lottie, and anyway, that's just not my style. But then I remember the look she gave Nathan, the look he gave her – as if they shared a secret.

I scream into my pillow in exasperation. How has my brain turned something I know to be totally innocent into a guilt-riddled love pact, just because I've found an earring in my husband's car? This is ridiculous – what's the point in lying here in the dark, with every scenario tearing around my brain, growing more and more exaggerated with every passing minute?

I turn on the bedside lamp and feel for the earring in my drawer, bringing it up to the light to examine it even more closely than I already have. Who would wear something like this? It isn't real, I'm sure of that, so it must have been worn as dress jewellery. A little glimpse of bling to brighten up a dull outfit, perhaps? Or the pièce de résistance with a simple evening gown, elegant and understated? I picture two very different women, from either end of the social spectrum. This isn't helping. I swing my legs over the side of the bed and go to pick up my dressing gown from the chair beside me. Perhaps a cup of tea is what's needed.

I find myself wondering, as I wait for the kettle to boil, if there is a tablet that can temporarily rid the brain of its thoughts. Not the cherished memories or excited optimism for the future, but the toxic type, the ones that poison our minds and turn us into temperamental, untrusting versions of ourselves. But then I remember

I'm already taking that very medicine – the two tiny pills that I pop every night, just before bed, are designed to take the sharp edges off my thoughts and feelings, protect me from the darkness. So why aren't they working now?

I used to rely on them to get me through the day, so that I could wake up every morning without that weight on my chest, pinning me down on the bed. Over the years, what felt like a boulder had gradually been replaced by a rock, and the rock eventually felt more like a stone. It had been a great cause for celebration when I declared myself free of medical intervention eighteen months ago.

It had been liberating to be free of the blurry haze I'd been living in, after years of feeling lethargic with a brain full of cotton wool. Because that's what it was like on antidepressants; I may not have felt the lows, but my nerve endings were so dulled that I didn't experience the highs either – I'd just existed in the middle of a long road, with no colour either side, just grey all around.

'I remember a time when you couldn't have done this,' Nathan had whispered to me at a party a few weeks back. 'I can't tell you how proud I am of you – of how far you've come.'

Which is probably why I haven't yet had the heart to tell him that I'm back on the tablets. I don't think I could bear the look of disappointment in his eyes. I'm only on a minute dosage – they may as well be placebos. But I need that little lift, a crutch to lean on. It's coming up to ten years that Tom's been gone and what with Japan and Sophia's exams, everything feels like it's getting on top of me again.

I sit in bed with a cup of tea, made too milky, in the hope that it will kickstart my snooze button. My laptop is perched on my lap, forever ready to hijack my thoughts and make me superficially alert. The contradiction is not lost on me. But still, I can't stop myself. I stare at the blank screen. I don't even know where to start, and wonder if there's an online manual on how to find out if your husband is cheating. I laugh hollowly to myself – I bet there is. My fingers linger over the keys. *How do I know if my husband is having an affair?* I feel stupid even typing it in and I shield my eyes from the screen, as if doing so will mean that I'm not really interested in the answer.

This is what *other* wives do. Suspicious wives, who have every reason not to trust their husbands. I don't want to be like them. I *know* Nathan and I know that our marriage is strong, immune from the problems that blight couples weaker than us.

I open one eye to see a quiz with the same heading as my search, run by a national newspaper. I shamefully read the first question, if only for a laugh, I tell myself.

Does your husband go to the gym:
a) Every day
b) Every other day
c) Once a week
d) Never

C, I say to myself. If I answer in my head, I'm not really doing it.

Does your husband want to have sex:
a) Every day
b) Four times a week
c) Once a week
d) Hardly ever

I feel like my teenage self, who truly believed that my love life could be accurately predicted by one of these preposterous quizzes, which was no doubt devised by an office assistant not much older than myself. I can't quite believe that adults are still relying on them. Despite myself, I casually cast an eye over the *Mostly Cs* category and feel mildly satisfied to be told that my marriage is healthy, and my husband is definitely not having an affair.

I'm about to close my laptop when I see another page, a forum for women who believe they're being wronged.

I can't blame him. I was always too tired for sex, one says.

I'd let myself go and now he's with a woman who looks

like I did ten years ago. I should have made more of an effort, says another.

I'm incredulous that of the hundreds of posts from women who think their husbands are having affairs, barely any are blaming him. I read a message from a woman named Sylvia who, like me, has found an errant piece of jewellery that isn't hers. I feel a sense of camaraderie with her as she attempts to justify how a silver chain with half a love heart hanging from it could have found its way into her husband's suit pocket:

> Sylvia: I thought it might be our daughter's, but I can't ever remember buying her anything like that. It may be the babysitter's, as Paul often gives her a lift home . . .

> Anne: Is it definitely not yours?

> Sylvia: No, it's definitely not mine. Though I do recall having something similar when I was a teenager. I wonder if it could be that?

I absently turn the ring on my right hand, its significance slowly burning into my brain. I stare at it, as if shocked by its presence. Am I not as culpable as the man I'm accusing? This ring, that I've not been without for almost ten years, immediately consumes me with guilt. How can I have the audacity to be so self-righteous? To denounce my husband for an imagined wrongdoing, when all this time I've been wearing another man's ring. And I'll not take it off, come hell or high water.

It was from Tom, wrapped and ready to give to me when he got back from his skiing trip. But he'd never made it home – instead I found it four months later when I eventually mustered the strength to go through his things. It had been in the inside pocket of a suit jacket, wrapped in gold and tied with a perfect red bow. I'd left it untouched for days, putting it on his pillow, silently willing him to come back so that he could give it to me as he'd intended.

When I finally built up the courage to open it on our tenth wedding anniversary, I asked my mum to have Sophia for the night. I cooked beef stroganoff, Tom's favourite, laid the table for two, lit a candle and played Elvis's 'Can't Help Falling in Love', our first dance at our wedding. If I tried really hard, I could see him, sitting there opposite me, smiling.

'How was your day?' I had said aloud as I sipped on a chilled glass of white wine. I left time for him to answer.

'Do you want to see your present?' I asked. I imagined him nodding his head as I got up and walked towards the fireplace. With a flourish, I pretended to pull a sheet off the painting that hung proudly above it. 'Ta-dah.'

I could see his wonderment, feel his elation as he looked up at the Venice scene in awe. He would marvel at how the delicate brushstrokes brought the magical city on water alive, depicting perfectly the memories of our honeymoon there. We would reminisce about the gondola ride we took through the waterways, the exorbitantly priced pasta arrabbiata we had in St Mark's Square, and his morbid fascination with the Bridge of Sighs. But mostly, he would praise my ingenuity, for always knowing him so well.

'So, what's in the box,' I'd said, lifting it from his side of the table to mine. My fingers wrapped themselves around it, knowing that he was the last person before me to touch the shiny paper and tie the tiny bow. If I put it to my ear, I could almost hear his heart beating from inside.

I carefully unwrapped it, knowing that even the Sellotape that he used would be going in my ever-increasing keepsake box. The anticipation of what was inside was almost palpable. I didn't want to lift the lid, so I could savour the moment forever.

'Oh Tom, it's beautiful,' I gasped, as the diamonds on the platinum band sparkled in the candlelight. I had slid it on my finger, vowing never to take it off. 'It's the most perfect thing I've ever seen.'

And it still is, despite another, even shinier engagement ring and wedding band on my left hand. The admission fills me with remorse.

I'm still sitting up in bed when I hear the front door shut and Nathan's shoes as he crosses the hall, dropping his keys into the bowl on the console table. I hurriedly close my laptop, turn off the lamp and lie down in the darkness, my heart thumping. I don't know what I'm scared of. I guess it's the thought of being presented with the truth.

Four ice cubes fall noisily into a glass from the fridge's inbuilt ice maker and I picture him going through the post that I left propped up against the vase on the kitchen island. He's at least ten minutes away from coming upstairs; he'll need to check through his emails, lock all the internal doors, perhaps call his mistress to say good-night?

I banish the last thought from my mind; Nathan *can't* be having an affair. When would he have the time? If he's not in the office, he's with me and the girls, and if he's not with us, he's away on business. The poor man barely has a minute to himself. *Yet he manages four hours on a golf course and dinner afterwards*, I think, my brain contradicting itself. *And are all his work meetings really work meetings?*

Stop! my brain screams, just as Nathan comes into the bedroom.

I squeeze my eyes shut as he places the glass on his bedside and goes into the bathroom, careful to put only the low-amp wall lights on. I can't help but marvel at how considerate he is. Would he bother if he loved someone else?

He slides into bed and straight up to me, spooning me. I hear his breathing in my ear, smell the alcohol on his breath. His hand reaches out, stroking me. Despite myself I feel a pull in my groin, but I'm not going to respond.

He plants light kisses on my neck and I will myself to stay unmoving. His hand travels up and down my leg, around the curve of my bottom and I arch my back. He knows I'm alert to him, my body disappointingly letting my mind down. I murmur, and he gently turns my face towards him. I turn back but his lips are on my neck, his mouth working its way up to mine.

'I'm tired,' I say sleepily, pretending he's woken me up.

'Okay, so just close your eyes . . .' he starts, as his head moves down to my breast.

'Not tonight,' I say, rolling away from him.

'Seriously?' he asks, surprised by the refusal.

Him and me both. I can't remember a time when I've rejected him. But if he thinks he's going to go out, do what he wants, and have me as a subservient wife to come home to, he's got another think coming.

8

With other things occupying my thoughts, I completely forgot that my car still hadn't come back from its service, and it's not until the morning that I realize I can't drop Olivia over to Beth's house like I normally do on a Saturday.

'Is there any chance you can pick Olivia up from here?' I ask when I call her.

'Mmm, it's going to be a bit tricky,' she says. 'Is Nathan there?'

'Er, yes,' I say absently, wondering when, and if, I'm going to be brave enough to ask him about the earring.

'So, can you not borrow his car to drop Olivia over?' says Beth.

'I guess so,' I reply, wondering why she can't pick up from here, just this once. 'Actually, I might see if Nathan can drop her over. I think he's got a few things to do out and about this morning.'

There's a muffled silence at the end of the line. 'No, don't worry,' she says, suddenly. 'I'll come and get her, but can you have her ready to come out? I'll text when I'm outside.'

'Yep, sure. Is everything okay?'

'Yeah, I'm just running really late and I've got a million and one things to do.'

'Okay, well if you're sure you don't mind. I'll pick them up after dance class and drop Millie back.'

'Thanks,' she says. 'That would be great.'

I'm in the hallway, helping Olivia with her shoes, when the doorbell goes.

'Oh God, that'll be Beth,' I say as I struggle with the buckle. 'Quick, get your ballet shoes. They're in the bag in the utility room.'

I swing open the door to find a beaming woman standing on the other side, peering through the foliage of a huge bouquet of flowers.

'Are you the lucky lady?' she asks.

I shrug my shoulders nonchalantly, though my brain is working overtime as it tries to recall today's date and its possible significance. Have I forgotten our wedding anniversary, or the day we met? Both of which we normally celebrate.

'I guess so,' I say, holding out my hands.

'Mind, they're heavy,' she says. 'There's been a fair few quid spent on these.'

I don't need her to tell me how generous the sender has been. That much is obvious. 'Thanks,' I say, as I take the weight in my arms.

She's already in her van and pulling away by the time I've opened the card.

To my darling Rachel
Sorry, please forgive me.
I love you.
x

I re-read the card a couple of times in confusion, but the message is too short for me to have misread.

'Blimey, what have you done to deserve those?' asks Sophia sleepily as she comes down the stairs, rubbing her eyes. I quickly shove the card into my jeans pocket.

I smile tightly at her, my lips pressed firmly together. 'I have no idea.'

My phone is pinging with messages from Beth to say she is outside.

'Go, go, go,' I say to Olivia as she rushes past me in the hall, only to get to the front door and turn around to come back and give me a kiss.

'See you later,' she says. 'Love you.'

'Oh, you really didn't have to,' jests Nathan as I walk into the kitchen, the flowers weighing heavily in my arms. I watch him closely as he looks at them, waiting for some kind of recognition. 'I don't even think we've got a vase big enough. What's the occasion anyway? Who are they from?'

I look to him, to Sophia and back again. She must see the expression I'm trying so hard to disguise as she grabs a banana from the bunch going brown in the fruit bowl and scoots out of the room.

I resist the temptation to fix myself a stiff drink, even though I could kill for the shot of confidence that alcohol usually gives me. I reluctantly fill the kettle instead.

'Oh, by the way,' I say flippantly, though inside I'm anything but. 'Thanks for letting me use your car yesterday.'

Nathan looks up from his iPad and waits for me to continue.

The earring is burning a hole in my pocket. 'I'm not sure what it is, but I found this in it.' I fish around in my jeans and hold it up in front of him.

He looks at it quizzically. 'I'd suggest it's an earring.'

'Well, yes, I appreciate that, but whose is it?'

He looks to me then back at the earring. 'I don't know.'

'Well, who's been in your car? Perhaps we can narrow it down that way and get it back to them.' I'm aware of an edge creeping into my voice and try harder to keep my tone neutral.

He shakes his head. 'Sorry, I'm not sure what you're implying here.'

'I'm not implying anything,' I say. 'I'd just like to get the earring back to its rightful owner.'

'Perhaps it's Sophia's,' he says.

'No, I've checked with her.'

'Well, it's probably one of her friends' then.'

I watch as his brain goes into overdrive, much like mine has been doing for the past eighteen hours, the only difference being, he must know the answer.

'Have any of them been in your car?' I ask.

He shrugs his shoulders.

'You know what it'll be,' he says suddenly. 'I bet it's the valet parking company at the airport.'

Funny how our minds think alike.

'You hear all sorts of crazy things going on with them; some cars get taken home by the staff for the weekend, or even worse, get written off by some nineteen-year-old employee who thinks he can handle a three-litre engine.'

I nod, unconvinced.

'So, who are *they* from?' he asks, tilting his head in the direction of the flowers.

'You, I guess,' I say, bluntly.

He smiles. 'If I'd known what kind of mood you were going to be in this morning, I can assure you I would have sent them to put a smile on your face, but alas, I'm not a psychic. Maybe they're from lover boy.'

I look at him, momentarily bewildered.

'David Phillips.' He smiles. 'Crikey, how many possibilities are there?'

I pull the florist's card from my pocket and throw it across the worktop towards him.

'Who's Rachel?' I ask tersely.

He shrugs his shoulders. 'I haven't the faintest idea. Where did this come from?'

'You must think I'm stupid,' I hiss.

'What on earth . . .' he starts, as I snatch the card from his grasp.

'*Please forgive me*,' I mimic snidely. '*I love you.*'

He looks at me as if I'm mad.

'What have you done wrong, Nathan? Why do you need to apologize to Rachel?'

'This is ridiculous. What the hell has got into you?'

'Don't make this *my* problem,' I say, unable to stop my voice rising. 'Just tell me what's going on.'

He makes a good show of looking baffled and I can almost hear his brain whirring. 'I have no idea who Rachel is or what you're going on about.'

'So, these flowers –' I pick them up and throw them back down angrily – 'have absolutely nothing to do with you? That's really bad luck on your part if they've inadvertently been sent to your wife instead of your mistress.' I laugh sarcastically. 'You couldn't make it up, could you?'

'Are you honestly being serious?' He attempts to laugh. 'Where is all this coming from?'

I snigger derisively and shake my head. 'So you've no idea who they're for or who they're from?'

'No,' he says eventually. 'But if it makes you feel better, I'll give the florist a call – see what's going on.'

'You do that,' I snap.

Sophia gingerly puts her head around the kitchen door and I immediately hate myself for giving into my insecurities, knowing that they will only manifest themselves in her as well. I pack my anxieties away and resolve to only reveal them when she's not around.

'I'm going into town with Megan,' she says quietly.

'Do you want me to drop you at the station?' asks Nathan. 'I've got to get the car cleaned anyway.'

And check it for any other jewellery? I say to myself.

'Can we get Megan on the way?'

'Sure,' he says, and Sophia offers a smile before heading up the stairs.

I busy myself with wiping down the worktops. 'If I haven't got my car back in time, I'll need you to pick the girls up from ballet and drop Millie back to her house.'

He groans. 'Do I have to? That means I'll get stuck talking to another nutty mum from school.'

'It's Beth,' I say. 'She's as far removed from a nutty mum as you can get.' Though if he knew her life story he might beg to differ. 'She's the one I go out with.'

'You see her a lot, don't you?'

I nod. 'We get on really well. She's the only mum at that school who is remotely on my wavelength.'

'Yet I still haven't met her?' He poses it as a question, and when I look at him, he raises his eyebrows as if he expects an answer. 'For all I know, she could be a completely fictitious figure that you've invented as a cover story.'

'What?' I say, incredulously. 'Do you want to come on one of our girlie nights out?'

'Well, how do I know that's where you're really going? You could be doing anything. You certainly claim to see

"Beth" a lot.' He puts her name into speech marks with his fingers.

I can't help but laugh.

'It sounds preposterous, right?' he says.

'Absolutely.'

'So imagine how *I* feel when you bandy ridiculous accusations around. It wouldn't ever occur to me that you're doing anything other than what you tell me. I trust you with all my heart and I thought you did me.'

I bow my head, almost embarrassed for the way I've behaved. I'm not a vulnerable teenager in a tempestuous relationship. I'm a grown woman who has never questioned Nathan's loyalty in the nine years we've been together. So, why am I so quick to now?

'I'm sorry,' I say, going towards him and cupping his face in my hands. 'I don't know what I was thinking. The earring and then the flowers . . .'

He kisses my forehead. 'Why don't you take some time out this morning?' he says, with a look of genuine concern on his face. 'Have a breather – sit down and put your feet up?'

Maybe that's exactly what I need. How could I have believed, for just a second, that Nathan would be unfaithful to me? I chastise myself for allowing my drug- and, if I'm honest, alcohol-addled brain to think the worst. I have enough neuroses to deal with – I can't afford to let paranoia, created by the very poisons that

I take to dull my nerve endings, overwhelm me. How pathetically ironic.

'Okay, let's go, Sophia!' Nathan says, as he stands up and reaches for his car keys on the worktop.

'See you later, Mum,' Sophia calls out, just before the front door slams.

Overcome with relief, I sit at the kitchen island and contemplate the jobs I need to do with a renewed sense of purpose. There's the washing, the food shop and all the other wonderfully banal chores that Saturday mornings bring. But first, I should let Beth know that Nathan is dropping Millie back home.

I text:

Thanks for coming to get Liv this morning. Hope you've caught up with everything you needed to do. Just to let you know that Nathan will be dropping Millie back after ballet x

Even as I type it, I feel a little uneasy, after the conversation I've just had with Nathan. Of all the days for him to finally meet Beth, he goes and implies that she might not even exist!

I receive a message back from Beth almost immediately.

No, don't worry – I'll grab the girls x

Me: It's honestly not a problem x

Beth: I'll drop Olivia home, but can't stop x

Me: Okay, if you're sure x

Beth: Yep x

I leave a message on Nathan's voicemail and then call the florist to let them know of their mistake. I'd hate for poor Rachel to be none the wiser about the olive branch that was being offered by whoever had upset her. I couldn't have that on my conscience.

'Hello, Roses Florist, how can I help you?' I can hear Elton John's 'Tiny Dancer' playing in the background.

'Oh, hi,' I start. 'I've had some flowers delivered today, but they've come to me by mistake.'

'Oh goodness,' the woman on the other end of the line says. 'I'm so sorry about that.'

'It's no problem, I just want to make sure they get to the right person.'

'That's very kind of you. Most people wouldn't bother and would keep them for themselves.'

Really?

I give her my name and address and listen as she hums along to the song. I imagine her running a finger down a list.

'Ah yes, here it is,' she says. '24 Orchard Drive. That's the address I've got.'

'That's *my* address,' I say. 'But there's no Rachel here.'

She hums a little more. 'Well, I don't know what's happened there then, but they've definitely gone to the correct address.'

'Well, do you have the sender's name? Perhaps you could give them a call to make sure they've given you the right address?'

'The sender is a Mr Davies, but I don't seem to have a phone number for him. Oh, that's annoying.'

'Wait,' I say, as a buzzing sound rings in my ears. 'Nathan Davies sent them?'

'Yes, do you know him?' Her voice is hopeful, eager to solve the mystery.

'He's my husband,' I say, ignoring the band of pressure that is tightening around my head.

'Well, there you go then,' she says happily. 'They *have* gone to the right place.'

She has no idea what she's just done.

Tears fill my eyes as I end the call and stare at the phone in disbelief. Nathan must have ordered them to go to another address, but they've sent them to his billing address by mistake. I imagine how furious he must have been at their faux pas, and how well he kept his emotions in check whilst he was professing his undying love for me.

I take the stairs, two at a time, to our bedroom, feeling like a drug addict desperate for a fix. I want to numb the pain, but I know that once I find what I'm looking for, it will only multiply it tenfold. It doesn't stop me though – I *have* to know.

Nathan's wardrobe looks like a display in an exclusive men's boutique. A row of identical white shirts hang above a shelf of neatly stacked handkerchiefs, a separate pile for each colour.

I realize I don't actually know exactly what I'm

looking for as I carefully lift the lid of his watch box. I pull out the miniature drawers and finger his cufflinks; I recognize them all. His underwear drawer reveals nothing new and I even find myself looking at the bottom of his shoes, though for what, I'm not quite sure. Do I really believe my sleuthing skills are so advanced that I would be able to determine the ground type from the tiny pitted indents on his soles? And from that, establish that he visited a particular hotel, with a certain type of woman? I laugh hollowly at how insane this all is.

I bend to pick up the laundry I'd left by the door, and just out of the corner of my eye I catch a glimpse of Nathan's overnight holdall. It will be empty by now; he's been home for three days and it's not in his nature to leave things in there. He wouldn't be able to bear the thought of them getting creased. I drop the washing again and wander slowly towards the bag lying beside his shoe rack. I'm filled with a sense of foreboding, as if I already know that something incriminating is lurking in there. I almost wait for it to jump out as I approach, willing it to, so that I know my suspicions are warranted. Why would any wife wish that on herself?

I unzip the various compartments, saving the inner pocket, the section most likely to harbour a secret, until last. I pull out a small bundle of Japanese yen, folded around a piece of paper. If I knew my world was about to implode, I wonder if I would've just slipped it back in, zipped it up and walked away.

The headed paper is concise enough; *The Conrad Hotel*. I smile as I read *Room Service Breakfast*, imagining him sat at a table in front of a floor to ceiling window, eating his eggs Benedict, overlooking the vast metropolis of Tokyo below.

I think I'd already seen the $x2$, printed beside the à la carte breakfast, before I'd even pictured him. I guess it's the brain's automatic attempt to derail us; to un-see what's already been seen.

I gaily carry on tracing down the bill with my finger, in staunch denial of what I know to be there. I smile as I see he'd had five of his favourite G&Ts during his stay, but choose to ignore the four cosmopolitan cocktails. I marvel that he'd had time to get a full body massage in the spa, yet pretend not to see the word 'couples' written in front of it.

I make sure to fold it neatly, just the way it was, and fight against the overwhelming heat that is rising up from my toes. I try to stand, but feel giddy and collapse back down. I'm sure it doesn't say what I think it said. I must be mistaken. Perhaps I'll take another look later on, just to make sure I didn't see what I know I saw.

I'm not going to cry, but a ball of fear is pushing itself upwards through my stomach and into my chest. Once there, I know I won't be able to stop the tears and crushing feeling it will bring.

I look numbly at the washing on the floor. Nathan's socks are entwined with his handkerchiefs, and my autopilot kicks in. The laundry still needs to be done, regardless of whether its owner is being unfaithful or not. I pick it up and force myself to sing a song as I carry it down the stairs.

It's only after I load up the machine, set it to an express cycle and press start, that I allow the desolation to engulf me. I slide down the wall of the utility room, put my head in my hands, and sob.

9

I take a hot shower in a futile attempt to wash my poisoned mind clean, but the tears keep coming. As I close my eyes, my mind instantly races ahead, questioning, accusing, though of what I don't know. I will my brain to shut down, just for a minute, so I can have a moment of peace and quiet. But no matter how hard I try, I can't control the rattling in my head. It feels as if a dark secret is thrashing around in a cage, banging at the bars, desperate to get out. So much for the mindfulness techniques I've learnt during yoga these past few months.

Beth and I had suppressed our laughter as Monica, our spiritual guru, passed around the class and placed her fingertips to our temples, chanting in a meditative state.

'What good is that ever going to do?' laughed Beth as we had coffee afterwards.

She was more into the blood, sweat and tears of the gym, preferring a fifty-minute boot camp session to anything remotely holistic. I had to agree that I saw little benefit in lying in a dark room, humming and having my eyelids rubbed. Yet as the weeks went on, I found myself looking forward to the end of the sessions, relishing the prospect of Monica breathing in and out with me, her soothing voice helping me transcend into another universe, just for a moment, or at least until Beth's stifled cackle penetrated the quiet, mystical mood.

I don't know whether to be thankful or not when I receive a text from Nathan telling me that he's going to pop into the office for a couple of hours. It certainly gives me more time to get my head together, for although I may look just the same as when he left, so much has changed. Yet it also allows my mind to wander and meander, dwelling on where he's *really* going, and acknowledging how this thought will now be my immediate go-to whenever he leaves the house. For the first time, my anxiety isn't caused by the fear of something happening to him. This new feeling is more oppressive, more claustrophobic.

I desperately claw at the possibility that he's going to her; to tell her that I'm getting suspicious; that what they have needs to stop before anyone gets hurt. But what if my aroused suspicions push him the other way? Make him see that it's now or never. Give him the strength to tell me that he's met someone else and he's leaving. Will he feel relieved when it's all out in the open? Free to lead the life he clearly wants to lead. Or will I beg him to stay? Believing that an unfaithful husband and father is better than not having one at all.

* * *

My mind flashes back to the 'Girls Night In' that Beth and I had enjoyed at the Berkeley hotel in town a couple of months ago. We'd laid on the bed in our face masks, helping ourselves to the mountain of chocolate freely supplied, as we watched a chick flick: *The Other Woman*.

'What would you do if Nathan was cheating on you?' she'd asked, as room service knocked on the door with what looked like a lifetime's supply of Ben & Jerry's.

I'd rolled a Malteser around in my mouth. 'Can we define cheating?' I'd mumbled.

'What's *your* definition?' she asked as she brazenly answered the door, mud pack and all.

The man didn't bat an eyelid.

'Well, everything,' I said. 'From a kiss to the full shebang.'

'Okay, so if he kissed someone, what would you do?'

'Once?' I asked, for clarification.

'Does it matter?'

'Well, if it was a drunken slip-up, I'd be more likely to be able to see past it,' I said, matter-of-factly. 'But if it was more than once, or God forbid, more than once with the same person, then we'd have a bit of an issue on our hands.'

'So, if he had sex with a prostitute once, and kissed the same girl three times, what would you be less likely to forgive?' she asked, playing devil's advocate.

'Definitely the kisses,' I said, feeling slightly nauseous at the sight of her spooning Cookie Dough ice cream into her mouth. 'Are you honestly going to eat *all* of that?'

She'd looked around our luxuriously decorated room. 'Well, in the absence of a freezer, I might *have* to,' she laughed.

'I think there would be a lot to talk about if he had a one-night-stand with *anyone*, but if it happened more than once, then that would imply that there's a whole other level to it. I wouldn't be able to get past him having a relationship. If he had an emotional connection with someone, then he'd be out on his ear.'

'No questions?' she asked.

'Absolutely not. It would haunt me – wondering if he was thinking about her every time we were together. Every row we had, I wouldn't be able to stop myself from bringing it up, and every time he walked out the door, I'd think he was going to her. It would destroy us.'

'Are *you* about to destroy us?' I ask, out loud, as I look at Nathan's text message again.

Have you got time to pop in? I text Beth, all too aware that she may not give me a get-out clause from the adamant resolution I made when I thought it was just a hypothetical conversation.

I can't, sorry, she texts back.

Me: I could really do with speaking to you, just for a minute. It's about Nathan

I wait for what seems an eternity for her to reply. Is he home? she texts.

Me: No

Beth: Okay, I can't stop for long

Half an hour later she's at the door with a worried, furtive look on her face.

'Hey,' she says. 'You okay?'

It's a simple turn of phrase and one that she's probably expecting nothing more than a yes to. But the tears come as soon as I see her.

'No,' I blurt out. 'No, I'm not.'

She ushers the girls in and sets them up in front of the TV.

'Oh Alice, what on earth's wrong?' she says as she comes towards me, taking me in her arms. I'm oddly comforted by the warm, familiar smell of my dear friend. 'What's happened?'

'I just . . .' I start. 'I . . . it's just that Nathan . . .'

There's a sharp intake of breath, but I'm not sure if it's from me or her. 'Oh my God, is he okay?' she asks, as she no doubt wonders if history has repeated itself.

'Yes . . . yes, it's just . . .'

'Where is he?' she asks.

'He's gone into the office, but I . . . I think he's having an affair.'

She holds me at arm's length. 'You've got to be kidding me.'

I shake my head as she pulls me into her again.

I tell her about the earring, bouquet and hotel bill, hoping that saying it out loud will somehow make my suspicions implausible, though it only serves to confirm them.

'Jesus,' says Beth, as she falls back into the dining chair she's sitting on.

'It's not looking good, is it?'

She grimaces. 'Look, I know I've not met Nathan, but I'm trying to give him the benefit of the doubt. There may be a perfectly good explanation for all this. Only you know him well enough to say, hand on your heart, that something might be going on. They say a woman instinctively knows when her other half is up to no good, but hey, look at me – I didn't have a bloody clue.' She smiles to try and lighten the mood. 'What's your gut feeling? Has he got it in him?'

'Hasn't every man?' The words are no sooner on my lips than they're being furiously brushed aside by the thought of Tom. Not *every* man. Not Tom. 'I didn't think so,' I add. 'This time last week, I'd be happy to bet my life on it, but now . . .'

'Has nothing like this ever presented itself before?' she asks.

I shake my head vehemently.

'Was he with someone else when you first met?'

I think back to that day; our coming together, like most things in life, being entirely dependent on a 'sliding doors' moment. If the sun hadn't been shining. If I hadn't been sat on a bench in the hospital grounds. If I hadn't been frustrated about being held against my will in a place that looked after people unlike me. Then perhaps I wouldn't have been open to the idea of talking to a stranger.

But that day, for whatever reason, I turned at the sound of crunching gravel on the drive and watched as a man, dressed in a well-tailored suit, got out of a sleek Mercedes. He laid his jacket on the back seat and reached in for his briefcase. In that simple action, I was reminded that there was still a world going on out there. Without me in it.

I imagined him having just come from meeting important clients. Perhaps he'd won their business and was still flush from the thrill of it. My stomach lurched at the memory of how that felt; the adrenaline that rushed through my veins whenever AT Designs won a pitch. I closed my eyes and pictured the scene, wishing, more than anything, that *I* was in *his* day, rather than *him* being in *mine*.

It was a turning point for me. For the first time since losing Tom three months earlier, I wanted to be out there, living the life I still had to live. The sudden realization shocked me.

I didn't think the man would ever know the part he played in breathing air into my deflated lungs. Not until he came through the day room and out onto the terrace, shielding his eyes as the low sun sliced across his vision.

'If you take a seat here, I'll just go and see if Mr Miller is up to seeing you,' said Eileen, the only staff member who bent the visiting hour rules.

By the time she came back out to say Mr Miller was sleeping, the man in the suit and I were exchanging pleasantries.

'Thanks, I'll wait,' he said to Eileen. 'I'm Nathan, by the way,' he said to me, extending his hand.

And that was it. We'd talked until the sun had gone down that day; about his life outside the hospital and mine on the inside. I can't remember whether that was when he told me that he was going through a messy split, or whether that came later. It had felt like we talked about anything and everything. Poor Mr Miller didn't ever get to see his visitor.

'I think it was over by the time we met,' I say, in answer to Beth's question.

'You *think*?' she asks. 'Wouldn't you *know* whether your new boyfriend was still with someone?'

'Well, our early days weren't very clear cut. I wasn't my normal self and wanted to take things slowly. He was working away a lot, which suited me at the time, but now, come to think of it, perhaps he was still tying up loose ends with *her*.'

'So, he cheated on *her* with *you*?'

I'm taken aback at her accusatory tone. 'No, it wasn't like that. They'd split up – I'm sure they had.'

She raises her eyebrows. 'It doesn't make you seem like a great advocate for the sisterhood, does it?'

Didn't it? I'd never thought of it in that way. Had I blatantly ignored the silent code of conduct in my desperation to feel wanted and needed?

'No,' I say, shaking my head, denying the implication. 'He's not that kind of man, at least . . . I didn't think he was.'

'Once a cheater, *always* a cheater, is all I'm saying. A leopard never changes its spots, it just creates a smokescreen for them.'

'So, you think everything is pointing to him having an affair?' I ask, though I already know the answer.

She grimaces. 'There may be a perfectly understandable explanation, but . . .'

'So, what should I do?' I ask.

'Just keep looking for clues,' she says. 'Check his phone, his emails, anything that might incriminate him.'

'Isn't that crossing a line?'

She looks at me aghast. 'So, let me get this right. He gets to sleep with anyone he wants, yet you're not even allowed to look at his *phone*? There's something of a double standard going on here.'

I feel too foolish to even respond.

'Just carry on with what you're doing,' she continues. 'Check social media for any accounts that he might have set up. Keep an eye on the credit card bill. Find out whatever you can and when you're sure of the facts, front him up with it.'

I nod.

'What are you going to do if your worst fears are confirmed?' she says.

My face crumples, but I refuse to cry. 'My head says leave, but my heart . . .'

She puts her hand on mine. 'You've got to think of the girls,' she says.

'That's exactly the problem. They would be the only reason I'd stay.'

She looks at me, her brow furrowed.

'I can't let them down again,' I say in answer. 'Sophia has already lost one father, the fallout of which she'll always blame me for in some way. I can't be the reason for it happening again.'

'*You're* not the reason,' she says, '*he* is.' Her voice is loud and clipped and I put a finger to my lips to remind her of Olivia and Millie's close proximity.

'I will not be responsible for taking them away from their father,' I say, my tone suddenly authoritative. 'I will do everything in my power to make my marriage work before I allow him to walk away.'

'Jeez,' she says, puffing out her cheeks. 'You're a more forgiving woman than I'd ever be.'

'Do you want a drink?' I ask.

'I'll have a coffee if you're making one.'

'I was thinking of something stronger.'

'It's only three thirty,' she says, looking at her watch. 'What time is Nathan likely to be back?'

'Probably any time now.'

'I'd better get going then,' she says. 'It's not going to take a rocket scientist to work out what's going on if he walks into this.'

'Thanks for coming over,' I say, hugging her at the door.

'I'm here if you need me,' she says, before dragging a reluctant Millie down the path.

They bump into Sophia on the pavement and say a cheery hello and goodbye. 'You look like crap,' she says when she reaches me. 'What's up?'

If that's her way of showing she cares, I'll take it right now.

'I just haven't got any make-up on,' I say, as she alternates between looking at me and the phone in her hand. 'And I'd really prefer it if you didn't use that kind of language. You're at home now – you're not with your mates.'

'Soz,' she says, and I roll my eyes in exasperation at her inability to use complete words.

Her phone rings and she looks at me half apologetically as she answers it.

'Hiya,' she says with a smile. 'It's Nathan,' she mouths. I can't stop my features from hardening.

'He's asking if we want to meet him at the Cuckoo Club, near the office, for something to eat.'

I know exactly where it is. Does he think I'm stupid? Does he think that him asking us to meet him there verifies his whereabouts for the previous three hours? Is he using Sophia to test what mood I'm in?

I look at my watch. 'It's getting late,' I say. 'I'd rather do dinner here.' The thought of forced joviality, pretending to anyone looking on that all is well, is just not in my remit right now.

'Okay,' she nods. 'Yep, I'll tell her.' She turns to me. 'He's on his way home, says we can have a barbecue if you fancy.'

No, is what I think. 'Okay then,' is what I say.

Just a few days ago, I'd have proudly told anyone who asked that my stomach still did butterflies every time I heard Nathan's key in the front door. Now, I wait here, dreading it. How the hell did this happen?

I can't carry this burden with me into another day. It's eating away at my insides.

10

I wait until Nathan's put Olivia to bed before pouring us both a large glass of red wine and settling down on one of the oversized cream sofas, making sure I sit perfectly in the middle, so that he'll feel more inclined to sit in the identical one opposite me. I want to be able to watch every twitch on his face, every spasm of expression.

There's a churning in the pit of my stomach as I wait for him to join me, an unmistakable swirl of nervousness that will only dissipate when I have the answers that I need. I pull my legs up underneath me as he walks in, conscious of relaying a more relaxed mood. As expected, he sits down heavily on the sofa opposite and takes a slug of wine.

'How did it go in the office today?' I ask. 'Get much done?'

I tilt my head to the side, in another subconscious effort to put him at ease. Though why, I don't know. I guess it just feels that I'm more likely to catch him out if he's off guard.

'Yes, it's much easier when the phone isn't constantly ringing.' He clears his throat. 'So, are you going to tell me what was going on with you this morning, and last night . . . ?'

I wonder if he knows he's walking into a minefield, the severity of the explosion entirely dependent on the words he chooses to utter in the next few minutes. I take as large a mouthful of my wine as I can, in the hope that it might numb the pain. I'm almost a bottle in and still waiting.

'Steady on,' he says, and I defiantly knock back another gulp, my eyes never leaving his. 'What the hell is going on with you?'

I shake my head and shrug my shoulders. 'Nothing.'

'You've not been yourself since I got back from Japan,' he says, trying a different tack. 'Are you worried about the work involved if we get the job? Because you know I only want to do this if you're entirely happy. I don't want to put you under any unnecessary stress.'

'I'm not a five-year-old,' I say petulantly.

He sighs. 'You know what I mean.'

'No, actually, I don't think I do. What are you trying to say?'

I drain my wine and put the stained glass on the coffee table, both of us momentarily watching it wobble.

'I just don't want to risk you having a setback, that's all,' he says. 'You've come such a long way and I'm so proud of how well you've done.'

Tears jump to my eyes. I don't know if it's because I *want* to make him proud, or that I know he'd be

105

devastated if he knew I was back on medication. I guess they're one and the same thing.

'I'm still doing fine,' I say, hoping he can't sense my guilt.

He sits forward and looks at me earnestly. 'You *can* do this, Alice.'

'Which bit?'

'All of it,' he says, smiling. 'Japan is a big ask, I know that. But I wouldn't have pitched for it if I didn't think you were capable of doing it.'

I nod. I *am* capable, but that's not what the problem is here.

'You only have to say the word if it's not what you want, but it would be such a huge waste of your hard work. You've put your heart and soul into this . . . I thought it was what you wanted.'

It was, until I discovered that my husband is having an affair. Now, everything feels uncertain, as if I'm suspended in some weird, parallel universe. Hanging there in limbo, waiting for my strings to be cut.

'I've got a confession to make,' I start, half smiling. I can't go in too accusatory. 'I'm afraid I washed your white shorts.'

His eyebrows knit together as he watches me walk through to the kitchen and reach behind the last cook-book on the shelf. I pull out the hotel bill.

'Sorry, I didn't see it until it was too late, but this was in the pocket. I hope it isn't anything important.' I hand him the bombshell, which I've wet along the creases, just enough to give it the appearance of having seen better days, but without any of the incriminating evidence being destroyed.

I watch as he opens it carefully with his forefinger and thumb, a slight irritation to him now. He peels one side painstakingly slowly away from the other, so as not to damage the damp paper. How ironic that in just a few seconds he's going to wish he'd done the exact opposite.

He stares at the Conrad logo blankly before looking at me. I'm careful to keep my expression neutral, to make him think there's still a chance I haven't yet looked at it.

'What's this?' he asks.

I stay silent, waiting for the penny to drop.

'Oh, it's just my hotel bill,' he says dismissively, before folding it carefully again. 'No doubt I'll need that for accounts.'

'Are *all* entertaining expenses tax deductible then?' I ask casually, picking at imaginary fluff from a cushion.

A funny noise emits from his throat. I'm not sure if it's because he realizes I've seen it or if it's a derisory snort at my comment. If I look at him I'll be able to tell which it is from the expression on his face, but I don't want to know.

'It's not entertaining, Al,' he says. 'I was there on business.'

'Well, that all depends on how the taxman views it,' I say. 'I'm not sure he'd see a couple's massage as business, do you?'

He doesn't miss a beat. 'A couple's massage? Where on earth did you get that idea from? I was there on business. For AT Designs. For you.'

'Don't you dare make out that you're doing me a favour.'

'Jesus,' he says, standing up. 'First it's an earring, now it's a hotel bill.'

'Don't forget the bouquet to Rachel,' I sneer. 'What were you apologizing to her for? Have you had a lovers' tiff? I bet you tore a strip off the florist for delivering it to the card holder's address instead of your darling Rachel's. Is that where you've been this afternoon? Buying another bouquet and delivering it personally?'

He comes towards me. 'Listen to yourself,' he snaps. 'What the hell is going on with you?'

It takes all my willpower not to swing at him. How dare he insinuate it's all in my head? 'Do you honestly think I'm stupid?'

His jawline clenches involuntarily. 'I haven't got a clue what—'

'Look!' I shout, snatching the bill out of his hands. I'm not nearly as careful as he was opening it. 'There.'

His brow creases as he leans in to look at it more closely.

'I honestly have no idea what that even is.'

I roll my eyes, exasperated.

'Honestly, I don't know where that's come from. That's not my bill.'

'Are you kidding me?' I snap. 'Are you really expecting me to believe that?'

He takes it from me and stares at it, shaking his head. 'This isn't my bill.'

I fold my arms. 'So, you didn't pay $792.60?'

'Nowhere near. I only had a few extras, because the room was paid for in advance. They must have given me this printout by mistake afterwards.'

'You must think I was born yesterday.'

'Alice, I promise,' he says gently.

I want to believe him, and as I allow the possibility that it could all, somehow, be a comedy of errors, I suddenly feel spent. I fall back onto the sofa as all the nervous energy of the past couple of days consumes me.

'So, you're telling me I don't need to worry?'

He looks me squarely in the eyes. 'About Japan? Yes, we do need to worry because there's no guarantee we're going to get it and if we do, you need to be ready. But I swear on the girls' lives that I'm not having an affair.'

I flinch as he uses Sophia and Olivia to bet on.

11

Lottie sees me struggling with my mood boards from the window of the office and runs out to help.

'Is this all for Japan?' she says, tilting them this way and that to get a look at them. 'Wow, they're amazing.' Her enthusiasm is infectious.

'I changed some things up over the weekend. I just wanted to see how they sat against the walnut floors.' I don't tell her that I'd done it through the fog of a hangover after drinking myself into a stupor after Nathan had gone to bed on Saturday night. I'm still not feeling quite myself a day later – it seems to take me so much longer to recover than it used to. Though I can't imagine it helps when I'm mixing gin and wine with antidepressants.

'I think Nathan's on the phone now,' she says through a wide grin, as I hold the door open for her. 'Might it be the decision?'

My stomach does a somersault as I look at my watch. 'Oh God, it wasn't supposed to be happening until 11.30.' I let out an involuntary squeak, though I don't know whether it's from nerves or excitement.

I try to gauge Nathan's expression as I peer through

the striped glass panels of his office wall, but although he must see me, he shows no flicker of recognition.

'Do you want a coffee?' asks Lottie.

'Yes please,' I say. 'A strong one.'

The atmosphere is charged as Nathan moves, seemingly in slow motion, through the open-plan area and into my office. Six heads turn and watch his back as if it's going to give them the answer we all so desperately want to hear.

I feel a rush of heat to my ears as he closes the door behind him and stands in front of me. I can see his lips moving but the first few words he utters sound as if he's talking underwater.

'*I'm sorry,*' is the first thing I hear clearly.

My head falls into my hands, my elbows firmly on my desk.

'The developers aren't buying the land after all. They're not going ahead with the deal.'

It's in that moment that I realize just how much I'd wanted it. 'But why?' I ask, my voice high-pitched and sounding like a spoilt child.

'I don't know,' says Nathan. 'But what we need to take away from this is that if the deal had gone ahead, we would have definitely won the business. They said as much.'

I can't think straight. I just feel deflated.

'Did they even hint at what's happened to change their mind?' I say, finding my voice.

Nathan scratches at his head, his bemusement obviously as great as my own.

'I mean why would they just suddenly pull out at this late stage? AT Designs aside, I thought this was a massive deal for *them* as well.'

'It is. It was,' he says, rubbing at the five o'clock shadow that peppers his chin. 'It just doesn't make sense. I thought they were a hundred per cent committed.'

'All that work,' I say, 'a wasted trip to Japan.'

'It's the nature of the beast,' he says. 'I'm so sorry.'

He walks to me and pulls me up out of the chair. 'I'm sure we'll have other opportunities,' he says, hugging me and kissing the top of my head. I'm vaguely aware that the team are eyeing us through the glass – it doesn't take much to guess which way it's gone.

'I know,' I say. 'I'm just so disappointed. I really thought this was the big one.'

'We're already doing really well,' he says, holding me away from him, his eyes boring into mine. 'This year's figures are amazing. Don't beat yourself up about it.'

'It's not about the money,' I say. 'It's about putting ourselves on the map, building a reputation. This would have done that.'

He looks away for a moment, and I watch as he goes into thinking mode. 'Give me a sec,' he says, before turning and going out the door. Lottie's eyes follow him forlornly as he crosses the space between my office and his. She looks how I feel.

I'm surrounded by wood samples, fabric swatches and paint colours, all destined for twenty-eight apartments in Tokyo that no longer exist. I want to throw the whole lot out of the window in frustration.

Lottie pokes her head around the door. 'You okay?' she asks quietly.

I daren't look at her, as I'm sure I'll cry, and thankfully she takes the hint and backs out. *For God's sake Alice, pull yourself together*, I say to myself. *It's not as if somebody's died.*

But they have, and I suddenly picture Tom's face, his mouth breaking into a wide grin at being told we'd won the contract. I can feel his immense pride as he lifts me up in his arms and twirls me around, before we collapse into a giggling heap, unable to believe what we'd achieved.

This one's for you, is what I was planning on saying to him. But now I can't, and I don't know if I'm more disappointed that I've let him down, or overcome with guilt that it's *his* face I imagined sharing that moment with and not Nathan's.

'Can I just run something by you?' says Nathan, coming back in and interrupting my thoughts. He's almost bobbing from one foot to other, agitated.

'Go on,' I say, sitting back down on my chair.

He comes around to my side of the desk and sits on its leather top beside me.

'What if I told you that the land and the project is

still up for sale?' he says, staring straight ahead, out of the window behind me.

'What do you mean?' I turn and look up at him, confused.

'The sellers still want to sell – it's just the buyers that have pulled out.'

'O-kay,' I say hesitantly. 'How does any of that help us?'

'What if *we* buy it?' he says, his jawline tensing with every word he utters.

'What?' I almost screech. 'Don't be insane!'

'Listen to me,' he says, looking at me for the first time and taking hold of my hands. 'We could do this project ourselves. We could buy the land, build the apartments, design the interiors and sell them on ourselves.'

'Are you out of your mind?' I ask, laughing.

'We could do this, Al,' he says, his voice getting louder. 'Me and you. AT Designs. We could do this whole damn thing ourselves.'

I'm looking at him, shaking my head. 'This is far too big for us to take on. We don't have the experience, we don't have the money . . .'

'A million buys it,' he says. 'We could get a loan, keep the repayments super-low.'

'Okay, you're scaring me now,' I say, but the adrenaline is coursing its way around my body. Is this even a remote possibility?

'I've just spoken with the vendors,' he says, as if reading my mind. 'They're desperate. They were selling for £1.5 million, but they'll drop if they can get a buyer now.' He falls to his knees in front of me. 'We can do this Alice. I know we can.'

'We . . . we can't, I mean we can't just . . .'

'You wanted to hit the big time,' he says earnestly. 'Well, now's your chance.'

'We need to talk about it . . .'

'We can't wait around, Al – this offer's not going to be there for long. They'll have other developers biting their hand off – it's right on the 2020 Olympics site. It's a no-brainer.'

'I need to think,' I say. 'I can't think straight.'

'We can do this,' repeats Nathan excitedly. 'It's all there for the taking.'

'I need some time to get my head around it,' I say. 'Give me twenty-four hours to think.'

'This opportunity might not be there in twenty-four hours,' he pleads. 'We need to strike whilst the iron's hot.'

'I'm not going to make a rash decision now, Nathan.' My voice surprises me – its tone tinged with calmness, belying the chaos that is raging through my head. 'AT Designs was set up using Tom's money. Almost every penny of his inheritance went into founding this company and I'm not about to blow all our hard work on a whimsical fancy thousands of miles away.'

'When you say, "our" hard work, are you referring to mine and yours? Or yours and Tom's?' Nathan's blue eyes are unflinching as he looks at me.

'Both,' I say.

'I've given my all to this company,' he says, 'and yet ten years after Tom's death, he still takes top billing.'

'Oh, for God's sake, you're being ridiculous,' I snap, closing the door in a futile attempt to stop the whole company listening in on our domestic.

'But I'm right, aren't I? No matter what I do or how much I achieve, I will never be able to escape Tom's shadow.'

'You've worked here for less than three years,' I say. 'Let's not get ahead of ourselves.'

I see him smart and wish that I could suck the words back in.

'You need to understand how much AT Designs means to me,' I say, careful to keep my voice gentle and my features soft. 'We've worked so hard to get it where it is – you, me, Tom, all of us.'

'Who are you doing it all for, Alice?' he asks, turning away from me. 'Because if it's Tom, he's not coming back.'

I swallow hard at his true words. No one is more aware of that than I am. 'I'm doing it for *us*,' I say. 'You, me, the girls. It's what keeps me sane.' I attempt to smile but I know it's not reaching my eyes.

'Will you at least think about it?' he says. 'For us.'

I nod, but I've already made my decision. How can I risk the business when I'm not even convinced our marriage is going to survive? Despite his protestations on Saturday night, I'd allowed the poison of paranoia to worm its way through my system as soon as he'd gone to bed. At 11 p.m., I'd believed him and felt nothing but relief. By two o'clock the next morning, I was wallowing in self-pity and overcome with an incandescent fury that I'd allowed him to trick me. If I'd known where his 'mistress' lived, I would have gone round there and dragged her out by her hair.

Thankfully, when I woke up yesterday, my emotions were a little calmer despite the banging in my head, and we'd managed to have the kind of Sunday I wouldn't have thought possible just a few hours before. We smiled at all the right times and asked the girls all the right questions over a roast dinner, but there was still a palpable feeling that something was off. The elephant in the room wasn't so big that the girls would notice it, but it was there nevertheless. And the shadow of it still remains today, so how can I possibly plough everything I've worked for into something I know so little about?

And yes, Nathan's right; Tom *is* still at the forefront of my mind all these years later. Whether it be trying to second-guess what he'd do when Sophia plays up, to how he'd advise me to handle this very situation. I hear his voice so clearly, see his face so vividly, that it sometimes takes my breath away. He wouldn't want me to risk throwing everything away. I know he wouldn't. I just need to convince Nathan that's what *I* think and not what I know Tom would have thought.

12

'Are you coming up?' Nathan asks that night, wrapping his arms around me as I iron Olivia's school uniform.

I can't help but stiffen at his touch and try to convince myself that I'm still reeling from David Phillips over-stepping the mark. It's easier that way, as it hurts too much to acknowledge that it's actually Nathan I'm recoiling from.

'No, you go on,' I say, 'I'll be up in a bit.' I reach over the ironing board for my wine glass on the table.

'Don't you think you've had enough?' he asks, and I immediately feel my hackles rise.

'No,' I state firmly.

'Don't make this about you and me,' he says, wearily.

'What are you talking about?'

'That,' he exclaims, pointing to the wine glass and the bottle standing beside it. 'You're drinking more than I've ever known you to.'

I don't want to admit that it's a problem – that it's become a crutch I need to lean on.

'You've got to keep things in perspective,' says Nathan, 'and drinking isn't going to help. Don't confuse whatever's going on with it being about us – because we're good.'

'Are we?' I ask, unable to keep the bitterness out of my voice.

'Yes!' he exclaims, as he comes towards me, pulling me in. 'You've got a lot going on at the moment and you need to tackle everything one step at a time, otherwise it'll feel too overwhelming.'

I wish I had his ability to compartmentalize everything, instead of having to live in the constant roar of noise as my brain battles to sort the wheat from the chaff.

'Come on,' he says, knowing me too well. 'What's causing the most grief inside that head of yours?'

I'm still struggling to prioritize it myself, and even if I could, I'm not sure I'd be able to express it.

'Are you thinking about Japan?' he asks.

I don't want to say that it's the least of my problems, so I nod instead.

'Okay, well you know my views on it. I can only say it as I see it and I think it's a once-in-a-lifetime opportunity that we'd be crazy to miss. But, it's ultimately your decision and I'll stand by you whatever you decide.'

'Will you?' I ask, looking directly at him.

'Yes, of course,' he says. 'Look, I can see why you've jumped to conclusions, but if I was having an affair, do you honestly think I would be so careless as to leave hotel bills and jewellery lying around?'

He attempts to laugh and I manage half a smile. He's right. He's an intelligent man who would have the art of subterfuge nailed if he wanted to. He wouldn't allow an errant bouquet to turn up at the home of his wife instead of his mistress. Any indiscretions would be micro-managed, to within an inch of their lives.

'I called the hotel in Tokyo and they confirmed that they'd given me the wrong bill. I only paid three hundred and twenty something dollars. You can check it against the company credit card if you like.'

I shake my head, but know I probably will.

'And I have no idea where the earring came from. I can only assume it's one of Sophia's friends', so no doubt we'll get to the bottom of that in time. And the bouquet, well, I guess it just got sent to the wrong address.'

'I called them,' I say, watching him. 'They confirmed that it'd been sent to the correct place and that the sender was Nathan Davies.'

'What?! Are you serious? That's what they said?'

I nod. 'They confirmed that you sent them, and that Rachel was indeed the lucky recipient, supposedly.'

'They actually said "Nathan Davies"?'

Did they? Or had I given them his name? I can't remember.

'This is crazy,' he says, rubbing a hand through his hair. 'If I had something to hide, believe me, I'd hide it.'

And he would. That's the shred of hope I hang on to.

'I guess all this is the reason that you're nervous about the Japan deal?'

'Well, it doesn't exactly help,' I say. 'You're asking me

to take out a huge debt, for a project that I'm not even convinced you'll be around to see the end of.'

'I would never, ever, cheat on you,' he says, taking hold of my hands.

I so want to believe him. His eyes look like they're telling the truth. I *could* believe him if I could just allow myself to.

'Why don't you leave that?' he says, his fingers trailing lightly down my back. 'Come upstairs.'

'I'll come up when I've finished,' I say, pulling away from him.

'Okay, but don't make me wait too long,' he says, nuzzling my neck with feather-light kisses that threaten to make my knees buckle.

I *could* go up. I *want* to go up, but I'm afraid of making a fool of myself. If I give in, then I'm saying that I believe what he's telling me. And what if I'm wrong? Will he wallow in his ingenuity? Lose respect for his wife? Laugh about it with his mistress? The incessant rattling in my brain grows louder and I pour myself another glass of wine in a bid to quieten it down.

My laptop is open on the dining room table and I wake up the screen with a swipe of my finger. Pixels of colour instantly burst into life as a photo of us all at Disneyland two years ago comes to the fore. From the outside, we look happy, like a normal family, enjoying everything that life has to offer. But if you look really closely and give it more than a cursory glance, you can see a pain in mine and Sophia's eyes. It's as though there's a glaze; a transparent barrier that holds the world back at arm's length. Too fearful of letting anything get too close, knowing that it can be snatched away the moment you let your guard down.

Against my better judgement, I open up Facebook and start trawling through the exaggerated lives of my 'suggested friends'. Gina Fellowes, a friend of a friend I once knew, is currently at Manchester airport and looking forward to a 'sick, no-holds barred' hen weekend in Ibiza. Michelle Truman, the wife of my second cousin's son, is 'feeling blessed' at her best friend's granddaughter's christening. I already feel worse than I did a few minutes ago.

I become fascinated by the power of algorithms as name after loosely connected name is offered up as a potential 'friend'. I vaguely remember Jack Stokes from my first job in London and Lindsay Brindley as one of the mothers from Sophia's Year One class. The tenuous connections make me feel uneasy, as if someone is trawling through my head, ravaging the cobwebbed corners that store information that is no longer needed. When I see the face I want to see, more than anyone else in the world, I almost gloss over it as being too familiar to concern myself with. But as I continue to scroll down, the image starts burning itself into my brain.

Tom Evans, *my Tom*, is on Facebook.

I race back up the screen, not knowing whether I

want to be seeing things or not. In my haste I miss him and force myself to slow down as I go through the images again.

My heart feels as if it's stopped when I see his face peering out at me; like a hand is in my chest and squeezing the life out of it. His eyes bore into mine, from the same photo that Sophia keeps in a frame on her bedside. My fingers trace the outline of his lips, and if I try really hard I can almost feel them pulsing.

How have I not seen this before? Why hasn't he been flagged up to me, his wife, as a contact? I didn't even know he was on Facebook. Surely his account would have been closed down by now. I feel sick as I click on his photo, frightened to see the friends he made and the conversations he had before he died.

There's a photo of him on his news feed, the last one I took, on the day he left for Switzerland. He's wearing the navy shirt I bought him for his birthday. His eyes, so much like Sophia's, glisten in anticipation of his trip, excited for what lay ahead.

I look around the dining table, to the chair he had been sitting in the morning he went. He and Sophia had been side by side, smiling at me as I came down from the shower with a towel still wrapped around my head.

*

'What are you two up to?' I'd asked, their faces full of mischief.

Sophia giggled. 'Can I show her, Daddy? Can I show her?'

'Show me what?' I'd said suspiciously.

'You're so rubbish at keeping secrets, Sophia,' he laughed, nudging her with his elbow. They'd looked at each other conspiratorially, as they so often did, the pair of them as thick as thieves.

'We've got something for you,' she said.

'O-kay,' I said, looking between them, panicking that I'd not marked our temporary separation with anything in return.

Sophia reached down onto the floor. 'Ta-dah,' she said, bringing up a homemade card and placing it in my hand. Jewels and gems had been stuck haphazardly onto the front, the white glue still visible and tacky – the glitter sprinkles not yet having had a chance to stick. I tried to hide the fact that there was more falling on the carpet than there was on the card.

'Ooh, what's this then?' I asked.

'Open it, open it,' she'd said, bouncing up and down on her chair. I glanced across at Tom, his eyes ablaze with love, for her, for me. He'd give us the world if we asked for it.

Inside was a photo of us at our wedding, looking at each other at the altar. The words underneath read:

It hurts to be apart,
but believe me when I say
I'll love you all the more,
until my dying day.

'That's the nicest thing you've ever said to me,' I said, reaching across the table to kiss him. 'Is this your guilty conscience kicking in?'

'Oh, that's charming,' he'd laughed. 'We've gone to all this trouble and you think it's some kind of conspiracy.'

'So, there aren't three other wives and mothers down the road getting the very same treatment this morning then?' I said, knowing that Chris, Ryan and Leo would no doubt be offering the same sentiment to smooth the way towards their departure, on what had become something of an annual jolly.

'Absolutely not,' he'd said in mock protest. 'Jules's card has got green jewels on it. Yours has got blue.'

'Go on, get out of here,' I had said.

He'd kissed me. 'I'll see you in five days. You sure you're okay to hold down the fort until then?'

I thought of the meetings lined up for the week and felt the usual rush of excitement. I couldn't remember ever being as happy or fulfilled.

'I suppose I'll have to be,' I'd said teasingly as his lips grazed mine. 'I'm the talent after all. Remind me why the company needs you again?'

'You'll miss me when I'm gone,' he'd laughed. And then, all of a sudden, he was.

When Jules's husband Leo had called me the following night, to say that Tom was missing, I thought he was joking.

'He's probably still in the bar at the top of the mountain where you left him,' I'd said, unconcerned.

'No, I'm serious Al,' he'd replied. 'Tom went out on his own after lunch and he's not come back.'

A chill had run through me, though I still wasn't unduly worried. He was a good skier and it wasn't unusual for him to go off and explore. I looked at my watch and at the darkening skies outside the living room window, choosing not to acknowledge that Switzerland was an hour ahead.

'Okay, so it's gone six there?' I'd asked, my logical brain trying to overrule the feeling of panic that was building within me. 'He's very likely to be sitting in the warm somewhere, trying to remember the time you were supposed to be meeting tonight.'

A heavy breath crept down the line. 'We were supposed to be meeting two hours ago,' said Leo quietly.

'Have you called anyone?' I asked. 'Have you checked his room, the hotel, the restaurant?' I'd tried so desperately to keep my voice steady. 'Is there a gym or a sauna he might be in?'

'He hasn't checked his skis back in,' Leo had said,

and my whole world had begun to close in around me.

'Well, you need to find him,' I said, a slight hysterical lilt to my voice. 'Leo, you *have* to find him.'

'We've been everywhere we can think of,' he'd said. 'We'll give it another hour and then we'll report him missing.'

'No, you can't wait another hour,' I wailed. 'Anything could happen in that time. He might be lying somewhere, unable to get up. He could have fallen down a crevasse and if it snows . . . Leo, another hour could be the difference between life and death.'

'I'll talk to reception now,' he'd said sombrely. 'But if he calls you in the meantime, tell him to stop pissing about.'

If Tom is trying to scare them, I'd thought, I'll kill him myself.

I had sat by my phone, willing it to ring, for the next hour. Watching every sweep of the ticking second hand as it rotated through the minutes on the clock above the fireplace. 'Come on, Tom,' I said out loud. 'Where are you?'

When Jules's number flashed up on the screen, I could only imagine it being bad news. She would have been delegated by the boys, in an attempt to break it to me gently.

'What's going on, Jules?' I'd said, barely able to breathe.

There was an excruciating silence at the end of the line. 'Jules?' I shouted.

'Still nothing,' she'd said gently. 'The rescue team have been called in and they're trying to ascertain where Tom was last seen and his likely route. Leo will call as soon as he hears anything more. Do you want me to come over?'

I'd wanted to say 'yes' but felt that doing so would elevate what might still be a stupid prank into a full-on crisis. It was as if acknowledging the severity of Tom's situation would somehow make it worse.

'No, I'm fine,' I'd said. 'I'm sure we'll all be laughing about it by the morning.'

I couldn't even begin to think about going to bed, but sleep must have found me for a few snatched minutes as when I woke up there had been a text from Tom, simply saying, Send help.

'He's texted me, Leo,' I screamed down the phone moments later. 'He needs help.'

'I know,' he'd said. 'I got one too, but the weather's closed in on us. It's too dangerous to go up the mountain in the dark.'

'Please do *something*,' I'd cried. 'What about the rescue team? Are they there?'

'Yes,' he said. 'Everybody is doing everything they can.'

'Well it's not enough!' I'd raged. 'He's called for help. Send a helicopter, we've got to get to him.'

'We don't know when he actually sent the text,' he said. 'There's barely any signal up here, so between his phone and my phone, there could be a considerable time lapse.'

'I don't care,' I'd cried, hugging my knees to my chest. 'Just find him before it's too late. Please.'

The days that followed had been a blur of visitors and flowers. The long-stemmed white lilies that I'd once loved became a beacon of lost hope. Their sweet aroma now the pungent odour of gut-wrenching grief and loneliness. People came to the door with sorrow and lasagne – I didn't hear anything other than, 'Just pop it in the oven at 180.'

Every ring of the phone had the potential to bring the best or the worst news. Every knock at the door could have been Tom or the Grim Reaper, personally confirming his death. It was numbing and excruciating all at once.

I couldn't sleep for fear that I'd miss him when he called and spent night after night staring at the phone, willing it to ring. Even when all hope was lost; when there wasn't a chance he'd be found alive, I initially refused to hold a memorial for him. How can you commemorate someone's life, if you can't be sure that they're dead? But it seemed that people needed an outlet, some form of closure so they could accept he wasn't coming back.

The church was ablaze with colour, with me refusing entry to anyone who wore black. It was to be a celebration of his life, not confirmation of his death. Yet whilst my soul still prayed that he'd walk through the door, my lucid self felt I'd let him down by accepting his fate.

Over the weeks that followed, Sophia became a limpet on my already depleted resources. 'Why isn't Daddy coming back?' 'Where is he now?' 'If he isn't dead, why isn't he here?' 'When will I see him again?'

Every other minute was spent answering her questions as best I could. The minutes in between were spent holding her close to me, the pair of us too frightened to let the other go in case they never came back.

A guttural sob takes me by surprise and my memories throw me back out with a jolt. I can't stop crying as I read the only message on Tom's Facebook noticeboard.

Had the best lunch in Verbier today. 'Potence' (flame-grilled meat) and a cheese fondue. Going to make this part of my staple diet when I get back home!

There's a photo of a medieval-looking device, alight with flaming chunks of meat hanging from it. Underneath, Tom had written the caption:

Life is good!

'Life *was* good,' I correct him.

How could he possibly have known that within a few hours *his* would be over? I brush away tears as I look at when it was posted. The night before he died would have been 25 February 2009.

My blood runs cold as I read the date. 22 June 2018. Today.

13

'I'm sorry I'm late,' I say as I rush into the gym cafe the following morning.

'You okay?' asks Beth, with a concerned expression.

I thought I'd done a pretty good job of concealing the bags weighing my eyes down, and hoped that lashings of mascara would have disguised their red rims. I'd eventually fallen asleep on the couch and have vague recollections of Nathan helping me into bed in the small hours. He'd held me as I silently cried.

'The last twenty-four hours have been . . . well . . .' I can't even finish the sentence because I don't know what to say. Should I start with us not getting the Japan job and Nathan wanting to buy it and do it ourselves? Or should I skip straight to the part where the ghost of my former husband is seemingly posting on Facebook?

'What's happened?' asks Beth.

'I've had a problem with the car this morning,' is all I feel confident enough to say without breaking down. It's not a lie.

'Oh,' is all she says.

I force a smile. 'Yeah, I woke up to two flat tyres, so I had to call Range Rover out and they ended up putting it on a truck and taking it away. Not a great start to my morning.'

'And I bet new tyres don't come cheap.'

'Exactly.'

'From the look of you, I thought you were going to say something had happened with Nathan. How did that go? Is everything okay?'

'Mmm,' I mumble, for fear that if I say any real words, my thin veneer will crack.

'So, was he able to justify his actions?' she presses. 'Did you hit him with everything you had?'

I nod. 'He says he's not having an affair.'

'Well, I could have told you that much,' she says, her features pinched. 'When will these men take ownership of their actions? When will the women who sleep with married men hold their hands up for the part they play? They all think they can do what they like, regardless of who it hurts, but there has to be consequences. They have to be ready for that.'

Her eyes drift off and I imagine her picturing her ex with his new girlfriend, wondering if they're even aware of the pain they've caused.

'It's a good job I believe in karma,' she says. 'What goes around, comes around. Somehow or other they'll pay.'

I force a smile, wondering what purpose that serves if the damage has already been done.

'You *want* to believe him, don't you?' she asks, looking at me.

'Of course,' I say. *I don't know what to believe anymore*, is what I mean.

I want to tell her about Tom being on Facebook. I can't stop thinking about it, imagining him out there, living a life without us. The thought is totally incomprehensible, yet I'd rather it be true than the Facebook Support Team being right when they said it must just be a technical glitch.

'I'm afraid there are one thousand and forty-five Tom Evans*es* on the site,' their operative had said last night.

But only one of them is presumably dead, I'd wanted to say.

'Is there nothing you can do?' I'd pleaded instead. 'Can you at least tell me where this Tom Evans, *my* Tom Evans, is posting from?'

'For reasons of confidentiality, we're unable to do that,' he'd said. 'Have you tried contacting him directly?'

I couldn't say no. That would just make me look insane. Why would I have contacted them to ask where he was, before asking *him*? But that's what I'd done – because I was too scared to go the other route, too terrified that I might get a reply.

'Did you hear back on Japan?' Beth asks now, and I'm grateful to her for changing the subject.

'We didn't get it. The developer pulled out of buying the site.'

'I'm sorry – you really wanted that, didn't you?'

I nod. 'So much so that Nathan almost convinced me that we should buy it and build it ourselves.'

'Wow,' she says, looking at me in awe. 'Are you going to?'

I shake my head. 'No, AT Designs means too much to me. It was created by Tom and me, and if anything happened to it because of a bad decision I made, I'd feel I'd let him down in the worst possible way.'

I think back to how hard we'd both worked to get the company off the ground, even when Tom was still holding down a full-time job as a civil engineer.

It had long been a dream of mine to start my own interiors company and just after we found out I was pregnant with Sophia, Tom convinced me that it was time to turn it into a reality. I put my card in shop windows, dropped leaflets, designed a website; anything to get my name out there.

A couple of nearby residents commissioned me to redesign a room or two, and a local playschool asked me to create a new library space for the children. There was no real money in it though, as by the time I finished hand-painting a life-size farmyard mural on the wall, I was out of pocket, but the look on their faces was reward enough for me in the beginning.

Once Sophia arrived, I spent every minute that she slept tiptoeing my way through the designs and ideas that were strewn on the floor of the back room of our flat. But there still wasn't enough time to get everything done before she woke up again and I'd often find myself awake at two in the morning, playing catch up. One night when the hormones and tiredness had got the better of me, Tom had held me in his arms and promised to be around more than he already was.

'But you can't,' I'd cried. 'You're busy enough with your own work. I can't expect you to do any more than you're already doing.'

'I'll quit,' he'd said. 'I don't want to be a civil engineer for the rest of my life.'

'Quit?' I'd said, panicking. 'But we need your money coming in. AT is barely making anything.'

'So, we'll use my inheritance,' he'd said. 'It's what Mum and Dad would have wanted.'

'All of it?' I'd asked.

He'd grimaced. 'I'll put a little bit by, just in case Daniel ever manages to turn his life around.'

'But if your parents had wanted to leave some for your brother they would've.'

'Yes, but they based their decision on the life he's leading now,' he'd said. 'If he comes out of prison at some point and sorts himself out, then I know they'd want me to help him.'

'Do you think that's likely to happen?' I'd asked, careful to tread lightly, knowing that his brother's life choices had brought shame and embarrassment on the family.

'It might,' he had said. 'You'd have to know Daniel to see the potential. He's just somehow got caught up in doing bad things.'

Tom was a good man and our achievements had been a source of great pride to him. I still feel an enormous sense of responsibility to him, and to his parents, to ensure that it always remains so.

I look at Beth. 'Maybe if there wasn't all this other stuff going on, I might have been convinced. But right now, I just can't see the wood for the trees. *Everything* feels so complicated.'

'With Nathan, you mean?'

'It just all feels a bit too much to deal with.'

Beth opens her mouth to speak but appears to think better of it.

'So, how's things with you?' I ask. 'Did you think anything more about Millie's dad?'

'Mmm, she brought it up again at the weekend,' she says. 'I've had a chat with her, just to see how she feels about it all and whether she really wants to know more about him.'

'And she does?'

'That certainly seems to be the way it's looking,' she says. 'And I suppose I want to know where he is and what he's doing too.'

I hear my phone ringing in my bag and immediately feel my pulse quicken, wondering if it's Nathan, the office or Olivia's school. Since when did I want to avoid so many people?

It's an unknown number and I force myself to answer it. 'Hello,' I say gingerly, alert to the potential bad news it could be bringing to my door.

'Mrs Davies?' asks a male voice.

I hesitate before answering. Only cold callers would refer to me so formally. 'Yes,' I say, through a resigned sigh.

'It's Mark Edwards at Range Rover. Just to let you know that your car's all ready for you. I'm afraid we've had to replace all four tyres.'

I resist the temptation to say, I bet if it had been *Mr* Davies you'd been dealing with, it would only have been two.

'Why? What was the problem?' I ask instead.

'Well, the two front tyres were already flat, as you could see, but by the time the car reached us, both rear tyres were on their way as well.'

'That's ridiculously unlucky,' I say, a tad sarcastically.

'Indeed,' he says. 'You might want to rethink where you park it in future.'

'Why's that?'

'Because it appears that all four tyres were slashed with a knife.'

A chill runs through me as I imagine someone systematically working their way around the car, thrusting a blade into the rubber.

'You've gone white,' says Beth, as I numbly end the call. 'What is it?'

I force a smile. 'That's probably because they told me how much the car was going to cost.'

'That'll teach you for buying one for the same money that you could buy a house,' she says, laughing.

'Indeed,' I say, ashamed at the comparison.

I know she's only joking, but the comment makes the divide between our lifestyles painfully obvious. Perhaps everything that's been happening lately is my payback; a warning not to take anything for granted.

'So, what's the next step?' I ask, in an attempt to bat my paranoia away. 'How are you going to go about finding Millie's father?'

'Well, I'm not sure the official channels are going to be much help. I applied for child maintenance a few years ago and they opened a file, but they never managed to track him down. I don't know if they keep looking – I don't suppose they have the time.'

'And if someone doesn't want to be found . . .'

'True enough,' she says. 'But I did have a look on the internet, with the little information that I have.'

I reach into my bag for a pen and pad, relishing the idea of having someone else's problem to focus on instead of my own.

'So, what have you got so far?' I ask, turning to a fresh page and writing Beth before underlining it.

She smiles wryly. 'So, he had his own business.'

'And?' I ask.

'Surprise, surprise, it no longer exists.'

'Okay, what about his parents?' I ask.

There's a flash of something in her eyes, but as quick as it came, it's gone again. 'I didn't meet either of them, so no leads there.'

I wrinkle my nose. 'Did he have any hobbies? Any places he used to go?'

'He worked really hard and was away a lot. He was hugely ambitious, and he wanted the best for us.' She laughs hollowly. 'Or so I thought.'

She stops and looks lost in her thoughts, as if it's only just dawning on her that when he said he was working, he was actually with the other woman.

'Did you own a place together?' I ask, in an attempt to bring her back.

'We didn't get that far,' she says. 'He was just about to move in with me.'

'So, there's no paper trail at all?' I say.

She shakes her head ruefully. 'It's embarrassing. How can I know so little about my child's father?'

'Come on,' I say. 'Don't beat yourself up. It's just one of those things, though I do hope you know his name.'

She looks at me witheringly, but there's humour in her eyes. 'Yes,' she says. '*And* his date of birth, actually.'

'See,' I jest. 'What else do you need to know?'

She rolls her eyes, but I can see that she appreciates me adopting a more light-hearted approach.

'So, come on,' I say, my pen poised. 'What's his name?'

'Thomas Evans,' she states boldly.

I can see her lips moving and hear a muffled sound, but I can't even begin to compute what she's saying. My head fills up with a hotness that feels like it's trapped, with no way out. I need air to breathe, but I panic that I can't take it in quickly enough.

I want to throw myself across the table and hold a hand to her mouth, so that she can't say anything more. But because I don't, she continues, blissfully unaware.

'Date of birth, 21 May 1976.'

Her head tilts to the side, a look of concern on her face, and I try to stand up, but feel so dizzy that I immediately fall back down again. I can't breathe, my lungs won't let me, and my body burns.

'But . . . but it can't be,' I falter. 'That's not possible.'

The last thing I remember is Beth mouthing, 'Are you okay?', seemingly in slow motion. Then everything goes black.

PART 2

Nine Years Earlier – Beth

14

It had been a long day – I was off the back of parents'
evening and knew I was staring down the gun at thirty
English tests. Jacob's attempt to rearrange '*is pen pig
the in my*' into a sentence was on top of the pile; '*My
penis in the pig*' was beautifully written, but not quite
what I was looking for. I didn't know whether to laugh
or cry.

'Just come for one drink,' Maria had pleaded, and
for a moment I had been sorely tempted to go for three.
Would a class of seven-year-olds really worry if I didn't
correct their grammar and just gave them a big red tick
and gold star instead? But then I remembered Mrs
Pullman, who had expressed concern that little Bertie's
answer to *What could you do better at?* had gone
unchecked. How was I to know he'd write *spillings*?

'No, I'd better get off,' I'd said. 'I'm definitely up for
Friday though. My treat, so name your poison.'

'I'll hold you to that,' Maria had laughed as she pulled
her coat on, and I smiled ruefully. I was still thinking I
should have gone when I was in my car driving down the
A23, my hands twitching on the steering wheel, waiting
to see if the good fairy or bad fairy would win out.

Just one, said the dark, forbidding figure on my left shoulder.

Go home and do your marking, piped up the pure, angelic voice on my right shoulder, just that little bit louder.

I was pleased I'd listened to her, because as soon as I was indoors, and changed my tartan skirt and polo neck for a dressing gown and slippers, I was happy to be there, safe in the knowledge that I wouldn't have to leave my snug haven until the next morning.

I didn't promise I wasn't going to have a drink though, and poured myself a generous glass of red wine as I psyched myself up to tackle Jacob's vocabulary conundrum. One final look at my phone and then I'd hide it under a cushion and pretend that I was controlling *it*, rather than *it* controlling me.

As soon as I saw the notification from Better Together, a dating website I'd signed up to, I was intrigued. Enough to make me want to read the message in its entirety, enough to put me off marking for just another few minutes.

Hi – just read your profile and you sound like you're up for some fun.

Was I? Is that how Maria had presented me to the online dating population? A girl who was looking for some fun?

She'd been in hysterics as she set me up on the site, as had I, but we were two bottles of wine in by then, and *everything* had seemed funny. She'd agreed to change the wording from 'sex-maniac' to 'liberated woman who knows what she wants' to 'looking for a good time, life's too short to be serious'. I couldn't even remember if that was the final profile we'd settled on, but I guessed it might have been if this guy thought I might be up for 'some fun'. I didn't know whether I should be proud or horrified. I supposed that all the time I was behind a screen, I could be anything I wanted to be.

What did you have in mind? I typed, though as soon as I sent it, I held a cushion up to my face and squirmed. If I allowed myself to imagine I was in a bar having this conversation, I saw myself sitting there, my body giving off all the right language, yet my mind in turmoil at what my mother would think. You can never stray too far from a Roman Catholic upbringing.

I'm not looking for anything serious either. Fancy meeting up? he replied.

I wasn't sure he'd understood the sentiment in my words. When I said life was too short to be serious, I didn't mean I didn't want a serious relationship. I was just trying to get across the devil-may-care attitude I pretended to have. I was twenty-eight, with ovaries fit to burst, and a mother who had attended church every Sunday for the past ten years, so that Father Michael would see his way to marrying her only child when the time came. Of course I wanted a serious relationship, if only to appease those who demanded it!

I'd convinced myself that maybe Mr 'Up for some fun' was best avoided, but that was until I saw his photo.

'Blimey,' I said, out loud, making Tyson jump. He looked at me with his chocolate-drop eyes, staring out between his daft floppy ears, waiting for his equally sappy owner to elaborate. 'Well, I wouldn't kick *him* out of bed on a cold night,' I said, as Tyson cocked his head inquisitively to one side.

Here was a man who knew what he was about. His confident stance, sense of style, those 'take me to bed' eyes and that smile. 'Oh, that smile,' I said to Tyson as he laid his head down on my feet. 'Does it *really* matter if he's not looking for anything serious?'

When? I replied, brazenly.

Tonight?

I almost choked on my wine. If we met up on the strength of this conversation it'd beat even Marcus, the blind date that Mel, another teacher at school, had set me up with. At least we'd enjoyed a twenty-four-hour virtual courtship before meeting in the flesh. At this rate, I could see myself waking up in this dreamboat's bed tomorrow morning.

I looked down at my dressing gown and the stain that Tyson had caused when he'd jumped up at me a week ago, making me spill the cup of tea I was holding. And my slippers, one of them chewed through at the toes by my ever-faithful, if sometimes infuriating, furry friend. I didn't look in the least bit glamourous, but it wouldn't take long to get myself back round the right way. Then I remembered I had winter legs – and *no* smile, not even George Clooney's, would have warranted me shaving them.

Tomorrow? I replied, pleased with myself for playing hard to get.

Sure. Westbury Hotel in town, just off Bond Street? Polo Bar 7.30 p.m.?

I was momentarily stumped by his authoritativeness, unused to being told what to do, but there was a little part of me that quite liked it.

See you there, I said, already working out what the hell I was going to wear. He'd made it sound posh without even trying.

'So, you're just going to turn up there and . . . what?' said Maria the next morning, open-mouthed. She gives off the impression that if she was single she'd be out on the prowl every night, but she's only that brave because she's happily married and living the single life vicariously through me. The reality of dating sends her into a head spin, as if I needed another over-protective mother figure.

'Yes,' I said simply, because there was nothing more to add, though I knew she'd have a dozen more questions.

'But what if . . . I mean, what happens when . . . ?' None of her sentences were finished.

'This was *your* idea,' I said, laughing. 'You're the one who forced me onto a dating site.'

'But I wanted you to meet a lovely man to marry, not to have sex with a stranger in some anonymous hotel.' Her expression was pinched and disapproving.

'Er, excuse me,' I said in mock outrage. 'Less of the anonymous hotel. I'll have you know that the Westbury is a very well-respected establishment.'

She laughed and threw a packet of crisps across the staff room at me. 'You know what I'm saying,' she said. 'Just be careful.'

I jest, but despite shaving my legs, I really wasn't intending to sleep with him that night. Not until I saw him. Not until I saw that smile, and then all bets were off.

15

'Do you usually go to bed with men on the first date?' asked the man, who I now knew as Thomas, as we lay on the most expensive-feeling sheets and pillows I'd ever laid on.

'Do you usually *expect* it?' I replied, because he seemed to me to be a man who usually got what he wanted.

He propped himself up on one arm and traced my cheek with his finger. 'This is not what I usually do, but I'm afraid I couldn't help myself with you.'

I rolled my eyes and started to get up, assuming that we'd both got what we'd come for. There was really no need for the post-coital sweet talk.

'Where are you going?' he asked, catching hold of my wrist.

'Home,' I said, suddenly uncomfortable. Funny how allowing myself to be tied up and rendered helpless by this stranger in the name of love-making somehow seemed safer than this unexpected invasion of my space.

'I'd like to see you again,' he said, releasing his grip.

I smiled. 'That's very gentlemanly of you, but you and I both know that's unlikely to happen. There's honestly no need for pretence here.'

He looked hurt. 'I think we've got something special.'

I laughed as I stepped into my dress. He would have perhaps seen it as me making light of the incredible time I'd just had, but I knew it was my defence barrier going up, ever-ready to take the knock that I was sure was coming. That's why I always made sure to get in there first.

'Look, I had an amazing time,' I said. 'A *really* amazing time, but you made it quite clear that you're just looking for some fun, and I'm happy with that. Really, I am. Let's not make this any more awkward than it needs to be.'

'I'm away a lot,' he said. 'That's why I can't commit to anything serious.'

That's one I'd not heard before.

'But if I was around more, I'd definitely want to see where this went.'

'Of course,' I said, as if placating an upset pupil in my class. 'And if I was around more, I'd like to see where this went too, but alas . . .' I childishly refused to let him have the upper hand, to make him think that I was in any way disappointed.

I sat back down on the bed and ran my hand across his bare chest, onto his toned shoulder and down his tattooed arm. If he carried on smiling like that I'd have to get undressed and do it all over again.

'You want to, don't you?' he asked, as if reading my mind.

I smiled. Of course I did, but there was no harm in leaving him wanting more.

'When you're next in town, give me a call and let's see if we can hook up.' I sounded like I'd swallowed a 'How To Play It Cool' manual. He pulled me down on top of him, his tongue searching my mouth. It took all of my willpower to pull myself off.

'I'll surprise you,' he said as I reached the door.

'You do that.' I smiled, wishing he would, but knowing he wouldn't.

So to say I was gobsmacked when he texted a week later is an understatement. I was already talking about him in the past tense to Maria the morning after I'd met him at the hotel, as if he was just a dream I'd had.

'I swear to God, he was the sexiest man I've ever seen,' I'd mused, as I'd allowed my tea to over brew. Maria had listened enviously, no doubt imagining it was her. 'But he wasn't as sexy as your Jimmy,' I'd added.

'Who are you kidding?' she'd said, swiping me around the arm with a tea towel that had been in the staff room for years. I had a recollection that it might have been on my rota to take it home and wash it every once in a while. I couldn't remember ever doing so. '*Every* man's sexier than my Jimmy,' went on Maria, 'but I love him all the same. Will you be seeing him again?'

'Oh shit,' I'd said, as I'd caught sight of the manila-envelope coloured tea and pulled the bag out, burning my fingers. 'Of course not. It was a one-night only perform-ance and I'll happily live off it for the rest of my life.'

Surprise! his text said, almost making me drop the phone.

Make him wait, I said to myself. *No need to be over-keen.* If I'd been in class, it would have been okay, but I was planning lessons in the library, and every second that passed felt like a day. I was quietly impressed that I lasted over four minutes.

Who's this? I texted, knowing damn well it could only be him.

It's Thomas . . .

Sorry ??? Sometimes I'm my own worst enemy.

From the other night . . . we met at the Westbury. I tied you up and then I . . .

Well, that served me right. I looked around the library, imagining that the conversation was being played out over a tannoy, and blushed furiously.

I typed and deleted Hey, what's up? five times, before hitting send.

I'm in town tonight and want to see you.

Was he asking me or telling me? Either way, it turned me on and I knew I was going to go, no matter what prior engagement stood in my way.

I'm not sure I'm free, I replied, knowing that my diary was clear.

No problem, he wrote, calling my bluff. Another time perhaps?

Fuck.

Let me check, I texted back, far too quickly.

I waited for what felt like an inordinate amount of time, but in reality, it was probably only two or three minutes. *Treat 'em mean, keep 'em keen – that's me!*

I'm supposed to be having dinner, I typed. But I might be able to move it. What was wrong with me? Why didn't I just say, *Yes, I'm free and I'd love to see you?*

Great, I'll come to you. There's a nice hotel over your way called the Clarendon. I'll meet you there at 7.30 p.m.?

For dinner? I asked presumptuously.

He ignored my question, instead asking, What do you do?

Wasn't that information we should be sharing over a meal? I cringed as I recalled falling into bed with him without knowing anything about him. He knew even less about me. But that was when I honestly believed it was going to be a glorious one-night stand, something I'd embarrassingly become accustomed to over the previous three years.

In my defence, whilst my friends were living their late teens and early twenties in a hedonistic whirl, I had been playing the faithful wife to Joel. Well, we weren't married, but we may as well have been, as we lived the life I'd expected to be living fifty years later. We stayed in when everyone was going out. We drank tea whilst they were necking jäger bombs. And we had Tyson whilst they were responsibility-free and able to jump on a Ryanair flight to Ibiza at the drop of a hat. How I had yearned for that life. So much so that after six years, I stuck Tyson under my arm and walked out.

'Keep everything,' I'd said, with a flourish of abandonment.

'But you *can't* leave,' said Joel. 'You can't go, just like that.'

'We both deserve better,' I'd said honestly. 'We both deserve *more*.'

'Well, leave Tyson here then,' was all he'd said, and I knew I'd made the right decision. We still bumped into each other every once in a while, but he could barely bring himself to say hello. Not because I'd left, but because I'd taken Tyson with me.

The idea of embarking on a new relationship with Thomas made me tingle. Now *that* would be worth staying in for.

I'm a teacher, I said finally, in answer to his question.

I'd better be good then, otherwise you'll have to keep me behind after school.

I smiled. Maybe that's exactly what I'd do. I could be the strict teacher, happy to dish out discipline. I'd delight in punishing him for his low mark in a test and would gladly put him in detention for starting a fight.

I resisted the temptation to search for 'sexy professor' images on Google, but I couldn't concentrate for the rest of the afternoon as I mentally scanned my wardrobe, whilst listening to the children take it in turns to read *Horrid Henry*.

Thomas wasn't there when I arrived, at least not in the places I looked. He didn't specify whether he would be in the lobby, the bar, the restaurant or a room. My stomach flipped at the thought of him in the latter, but if we went straight to that, there was every chance that I'd leave knowing nothing more about him than I already did.

I'd only just ordered a vodka and orange when I felt a silent presence behind me, the heat of breath on my neck. I could smell expensive aftershave, emanating from freshly washed skin.

'I'm sorry I'm late,' he whispered, before leaning around to kiss my cheek. 'I was just finishing my homework.'

I looked down, through the horrendously magnified glasses that Maria had lent me, at my pencil skirt and pale pink twinset, pleased that my efforts hadn't gone unnoticed.

'Can I get a large gin and tonic?' he said to the barman, all the while stroking my leg through the crepe material. His hand stopped moving as his fingers reached the clasp of my suspenders and he turned to look at me with a wide grin.

'I've made a dinner reservation, but I think we might have to take a rain check on that,' he said, raising his eyebrows in question.

I nodded – it took all of my willpower not to unbutton him right there and then.

I followed him to the lift and moved aside as an elderly couple got out. We stood there, a foot apart, unspeaking as the doors closed. If I imagined this scenario in my head, I would have put money on me to burst out laughing; the role-playing and me being mute would have tickled the immature side of my character. But the atmosphere was so sexually charged that I didn't feel anything other than an overwhelming desire to get our clothes off as quickly as possible.

'So how did I do, Miss Russo?' he said afterwards, with a naughty glint in his eye.

I rolled over onto my side and propped my head up on a bent arm.

'I would say that you are a very willing pupil with an eagerness to learn. Your ability to focus on the job in hand is exemplary, needing only the most basic of tuition to reach a more than satisfactory conclusion. Overall, an outstanding performance and I look forward to welcoming you into my class again soon.'

He smiled, his full lips parting ever so slightly to reveal a row of perfect white teeth.

'Dinner?' I asked, having worked up an appetite.

His eyes bored into mine with an intensity that pulled at my groin. 'Or shall we just skip straight to dessert?'

Butterflies fluttered in my tummy as he touched me. It didn't matter what was on the menu, no dish was worth missing this for.

16

'You didn't tell me you had a dog,' said Thomas when he came around to my flat for the first time a few weeks later. Seeing as we'd only met four times and had gone straight to bed on all of those occasions, it was hardly surprising that we'd not yet had the opportunity for small talk.

'This is Tyson,' I said proudly, as if I was introducing him to my child.

Thomas couldn't help but laugh as he went to pet him. 'But he's the cutest dog I've ever seen.'

'Don't be fooled,' I said. 'He lives up to his name – cockapoos can be ruthless.'

'He's not one of those territorial dogs, is he?' asked Thomas, in between planting kisses on my lips. 'The type who won't let you go into the bedroom with a man – no matter how hot he is.'

'He *can* be, but he should be all right with you.'

Thomas smiled as his hands wandered onto my behind, pinching it.

'Ow,' I laughed, swiping him round the shoulder.

'So, shall we test your theory?' he asked, as he began to unbutton my jeans.

'No,' I said, playfully pushing him away. 'We're going to eat first.'

'Aw, seriously,' he whined, sounding like a disgruntled little boy. 'Can't we just . . . ?'

'No, absolutely not. If I keep choosing sex over food, my mother will wonder what's happened to me.'

'You'd tell your mother something like *that*?' he asked incredulously.

I couldn't help but laugh at the horrified look on his face. 'No, I meant she'll notice that I've lost weight.'

'Oh, right.' He dipped his finger into the béchamel sauce in the pan.

'Honestly, you're worse than the kids in my class,' I remonstrated, swatting his hand away. 'Will you just behave yourself for a minute and get the wine out of the fridge.'

'I've got something to ask you,' he said later, as he tucked into my homemade lasagne.

'Mmm,' I replied, though I wasn't really listening – too busy concentrating on whether the pasta sheets were cooked enough.

'I'm in the middle of setting up a deal with a really important client.'

'O-kay,' I said, hesitantly, wondering how that could possibly have anything to do with me.

'He's coming over to London next month and it's important that I create the right image. I need to present myself correctly, you know?'

I wrinkled my forehead as he pressed on. 'It would just help my cause if he could see that I have a girlfriend and that I'm a serious guy.' My expression went from one of confusion to one of surprise, but although I thought I knew where this was going, I still wanted to hear it from him. 'I just wondered if you were free to, you know, come with me.'

'Are you asking me to be your trophy girlfriend?' I said, having to stop myself from giggling, though I don't know whether it was from embarrassment or excitement.

'It's okay, if . . . you know, you don't want to. I understand.' He looked at me with doe eyes, like Puss in Boots from *Shrek*.

'Don't pull that one,' I laughed. 'I'd love to come. What do I have to wear? Do I need to be a slutty girl-friend or a posh bit of totty? Oh, can I be like Vivian Ward in *Pretty Woman*! All the gear, no idea.'

He looked at me as if I was completely mad. 'You can just be you,' he said, before smiling and adding, 'You won't be needing to coax any slippery suckers out of their shells.'

He knew the lines from my favourite film! I think that might have been the moment I began to fall in love with him.

As the weeks passed, I began to feel more comfortable around Thomas and dared to be confident that we had something special going on. Walking hand in hand into the restaurant to meet his business associate seemed like the next big step, and I felt dizzy with excitement, conscious of other diners watching us as we followed the maître d' to our table. A good-looking man with olive skin and dark smouldering eyes stood up as we approached.

'Mr Rodriguez, good to see you. This is Miss Russo.'

Mr Rodriguez took my hand and brought it up to his lips. 'Very pleased to meet with you.'

'Likewise,' I said, looking furtively around for his 'better' half.

'Alas, my wife has been called away,' he said. 'So, I'm afraid it's just me this evening.'

I didn't know whether to be disappointed or not. There was a shred of relief that I didn't have to make superficial small talk, but that then meant I would have to listen to their business dealings.

Thomas looked at me, as if to say sorry, and ordered a bottle of Laurent Perrier Rosé.

As it turned out, the conversation was actually very enlightening, and if nothing else, I felt my social standing had been elevated somewhat just because I now knew the difference between a Meursault and a Petit Mouton.

'Who knew wine could sound even better than it tastes?' I said, as we just made it onto the 23.50 from Waterloo. It was the last train from London to Guildford, so everyone was packed in like sardines, with Thomas and I pressed up against each other.

'Yeah, sorry about that,' he said, his face belying the fact that his hands were surreptitiously travelling up under my lace top, and into my bra. 'I hope you weren't too bored.'

I closed my eyes and a breath caught in my throat as his fingers deftly teased my nipples. If it wasn't illegal I would have gladly let him take me there and then, regardless of who was watching.

'N-no, I mean it,' I managed. 'I found it really interesting.'

He raised his eyebrows suggestively. 'Which part? Was it the juicing of the luscious, ripe grapes, or the fact that you can make thousands of pounds from buying and selling wine? What turns you on the most?'

'All of it,' I said as his hand slid down into my trousers. His fingers just reached the lace top of my knickers before I grabbed his wrist and looked at him wide-eyed.

'What?' he said, all too innocently.

'Patience is a virtue,' I said, in between kissing him. 'In one hour, *all* of your dreams will come true.'

Except they didn't. Instead, we spent the first two hours after we got to my place searching for Tyson, who had, it seemed, let himself out of the back door.

'But there's no way I would have left it open,' I said, verging on hysteria when we still hadn't found him. 'I'm sure I would have checked that it was locked before we went out. Don't you remember seeing me do it?'

He ran a hand through his hair. 'I can't say that I did, but I wasn't really paying attention.'

'It's the last thing I normally do before I go out,' I cried. 'How can I have been so stupid?'

'Hey, don't beat yourself up about it,' he said gently. 'We'll find him – he won't have gone far.'

As soon as the sun was up the next morning, we both headed out in different directions, our breaths billowing in the cold air as we shouted his name. 'Tyson, Tyson! Come on, boy.' I choked on the words, furious with myself for the stupid mistake I'd made and terrified of what might have happened to him. 'Please Tyson,' I begged. 'Please come home.'

Thomas and I met again an hour later at the park where I usually took Tyson for his walks.

'No sign?' I stupidly asked, willing my dog to be at Thomas's feet.

He looked at the ground, shaking his head glumly.

'I need to go to work,' I said. 'We should go.'

'I'll stay, if it's all right with you,' he said. 'I've got a meeting I can push back, so I'd like to carry on looking.'

'Oh, yes, well, of course that would be amazing, if you really don't mind.'

I'd not seen him looking quite so sombre. 'I feel responsible too. If I'd not distracted you, perhaps this wouldn't have happened.'

I thought back to the night before, when I'd asked Thomas to do my necklace up.

'This is beautiful,' he'd said as he admired the delicate diamond hanging from a silver chain.

My hand had instantly gone to it, my fingers feeling its weight.

'Thank you. It was a gift from my dad.'

'Well, he obviously has very good taste.'

I didn't tell him that he'd *had* very good taste. Instead, I batted away the tears that threatened to fall every time my dad was mentioned and closed my eyes as Thomas kissed my neck. The fifteen minutes we'd then spent having sex instead of getting ready meant that I'd been in a mad panic to get out of the door to catch our train. Perhaps I'd not had time to check that the back door hadn't been left ajar. I *could* blame Thomas, but what was the point? It was a distraction that I had readily encouraged.

'Thanks,' I said, kissing him at the park gate, his lips cold.

'I'll call you with any news,' he said. 'If I find him, is there a cafe or something around here that I can wait in until you come back?'

Was there? I'd lived in the area for five years, but suddenly I couldn't even recall the shop where I usually got a coffee on the way to work.

'It's okay,' he said, sensing my difficulty. 'I'll find somewhere.'

'No, no . . . of course, sorry, I'm not thinking straight. Here, take my key.' I struggled to get my house key off the ring that carried a worn photo of me and Dad. I was prepared to give Thomas the key to everything I held dear, but not that.

'Are you sure?' he asked. 'Is there an alarm or anything I need to worry about?'

'No,' I said quietly, paranoid that anyone might overhear how lax my security arrangements were.

'Keep me posted, won't you?' I said as I reluctantly left him.

All morning my mind alternated between Tyson and a man I was fast falling for, and when I'd heard nothing by lunchtime, I could feel myself welling up.

'I can cover for you if you want to go home,' said Maria as she rubbed my back.

I shook my head. 'I'm better off here. There's nothing I can do at home, apart from wait.'

'Honestly, I can do your classes this afternoon; you're no use to the children when you're like this.'

'Are you sure?'

'Yes, go on, go,' she said. 'I'll tell the head.'

As I walked from the station to my flat, my mood was lifted a little at the sight of 'LOST' posters on every other lamp post along the route. Anyone with information was being urged to call an unfamiliar phone number.

'Do I assume I have you to thank for the posters?' I asked Thomas when I got home. I didn't dare call the number on my phone as I risked 'Hot Guy', the childish pseudonym I'd saved him under, appearing. I made a mental note to change it, even though it *was* still accurate.

'Yes,' he said sheepishly. 'You don't mind, do you?'

'Of course not,' I exclaimed. 'That's really sweet of you.'

'No one's called yet, but I'm hopeful. I didn't know what else to do.'

'Thank you,' I said, kissing him.

'Are you okay if I go to this meeting? I was able to put it off for a few hours, but I could really do with getting it done today, if you don't mind.'

I was astonished he even felt the need to ask. 'Of course, you should go.'

'But I'll be back tonight, if that's all right, and I'll leave you my phone, just in case anyone calls about Tyson.'

'Don't be silly,' I said, shaking my head. 'Take your phone with you.'

'No,' he said adamantly. 'I won't be able to answer the call if it comes in. We can't take the risk of missing it.'

'But—'

'Take it,' he said as he put his jacket on and handed me the phone. 'I'll be a couple of hours. Feel free to answer any call that comes in.'

It felt very odd to have someone else's phone in my possession, especially one that belonged to a man I was seeing so casually, yet knew so intimately.

I held the phone in front of me as I walked around the park, calling for Tyson, and showing anybody I encountered a photo of him. I could almost feel my eyeballs burning the screen every time I looked at it, willing it to light up. When it did, just as I reached the gate, where another poster had been attached, I couldn't answer it quickly enough.

'Hello,' I said gingerly.

'Oh, hi,' said a male voice. 'I'm calling about the dog.'

My heart soared, making me feel as if it might lift me off the ground. Yet the very real possibility of being told that something had happened to him quickly followed. 'Yes?' I said, urging the man on, my chest a mangle of emotions.

'Is there a reward?' he asked, stopping me in my tracks.

'Er, I . . . I don't know,' I stuttered.

'Well, is there or not?'

'Does it matter?' I said, suddenly indignant. 'Have you any information or not?'

'Well, it all depends on how much the reward is.'

I took the phone away from my ear and stared at it aghast, horrified that the safe return of my beloved dog was reliant on how much I paid. Wasn't this akin to kidnapping and demanding a ransom?

My head wrestled in vain to win the tug of war with my heart. It was a poorly fought battle.

'A thousand pounds,' I said, suddenly aware of how

much I wanted Tyson back. The ache was so profound that I would pay five times more. I wonder if he heard it in my voice.

'Whoa,' the voice said. 'You really like this dog, huh?' I stayed silent whilst he conducted a muffled conversation at his end. 'We'll think about it and let you know tomorrow.'

The call abruptly ended as I cried, 'I'll give you five thousand!' into the dead air.

17

My sleep was interspersed with vivid sightings of Tyson. He was around every corner, running through every meadow. I could hear myself laughing as he bounded towards me, my arms outstretched ready to embrace him, but as he leapt up into them, a car came from nowhere and mowed him down. My own screaming woke me up.

'Ssh, it's okay, it's just a bad dream,' whispered Thomas as he wrapped his strong arms around me. My heart was racing, and my breathing came in short sharp pants as I struggled to get myself back around the right way.

'It's okay,' he repeated over and over, and for a few moments I believed him, but then came the sudden rush of reality as the harsh facts presented themselves.

'But it's not,' I cried. 'It's not okay.'

'I'll deal with it tomorrow,' he said. 'If that man's got Tyson, I promise we'll get him back.'

'And if he hasn't?'

'I'll get him back,' is the last thing I remember him saying, before I dozed off again.

He was gone by the time I woke up, my hand instinctively reaching down to the floor beside the bed, giving

Tyson the sign that it was okay to jump up. I waited momentarily for my face to be licked or the unmistakable swish of an excitable tail going from side to side. It felt like I'd been punched when I remembered he wasn't there. My body ached with yearning and I thought, as I so often do, about the passage of time. How so much can happen in twenty-four hours – in one hour – one minute. That's all it takes for your whole world to turn on its axis. In just a moment, everything can change, and your life will never be the same again.

That's how it had felt when my dad died suddenly. He'd uncharacteristically taken the day before off work, and we'd gone out on the boat – just the two of us. It was the most perfect day; the sun scorched in a bright blue sky and the light breeze worked in our favour as we sailed my namesake out onto the Solent. We had anchored off the coast of the Isle of Wight and called a tender to take us to one of Dad's restaurants.

'How are you, my friend?' asked the head chef, Antonio, as he kissed Dad on both cheeks.

'Very good,' Dad had replied, his accent so much more Italian whenever he spoke to a fellow countryman. 'I couldn't be better.'

'And my, how you've grown,' Antonio said to me. 'I remember you when you were down here.' I'd smiled as he'd held a hand out a few inches from the floor. 'What are you now? Fifteen, Sixteen?'

'Thirteen,' I'd giggled, secretly pleased that he thought I looked older.

'Bellisima!' he said. 'And Mrs Russo? Is she not with you?'

'No, it's just me and this one today,' Dad had said, ruffling my head as if I was three. I flattened my hair self-consciously. 'Father and daughter time.'

If I had been cross with him for treating me like a child, it didn't last long, as he poured the tiniest amount of white wine into one of the glasses set on the table.

'Don't tell your mother,' he'd said, winking.

I remember the sun shining and Dad offering to swap seats because he had sunglasses and I didn't. I remember the starched white tablecloths and the smell of olive oil and garlic as bowls of seafood spaghetti wafted past us on their way to other diners. If it hadn't been the last meal we shared, I doubt I'd be able to recall what we had, but because it was, I can see all too clearly my carbonara and Dad's arrabbiata being set down before us.

'This is the life,' he'd said, as we tucked in. And it was. I couldn't imagine having a better time.

'One day this will all be yours,' he'd continued, sweeping his arm over the packed veranda we were sat on. You couldn't squeeze another table in if you tried. All of his restaurants, the one on the Isle of Wight and the four others on the mainland, were always fully booked, more often than not for months in advance.

'But I can't cook,' I'd said, worrying that I wouldn't be up to the job.

Dad laughed heartily. 'When did you last see *me* in a kitchen?'

'You're always in it at home,' I'd replied, confused.

'But I don't go to work and cook, do I?'

I'd shrugged my shoulders.

'You just need to run the operation,' he'd said. 'As long as the chefs can follow Grandma's recipes, you'll be fine.'

As always, Antonio had joined us for a drink after our meal and, as always, I'd spent their mostly Italian conversation fixated on watching the smoke rings he created.

I was fluent in Italian, but it was still an effort to keep up, and anyway, they were just talking shop, so I zoned out. Now, of course, I wished I'd concentrated on every word Dad spoke, no matter how boring I thought it was, because ever since, his is the only voice I yearn to hear.

The next morning, back home, he had woken up, made Mum a cup of tea and collapsed on the kitchen floor with the teaspoon still in his hand. She'd tried to revive him, and the ambulance was quick to come, but it was already too late. He'd had a brain haemorrhage at just forty-nine.

The house had been full of people, even before I'd woken up, and I'd walked out onto the landing to cries and panic from the floor below. I knew something had happened, but it didn't occur to me that it had anything to do with Dad. How could it? We'd just spent the best day together. He'd been perfectly normal, and he'd let me have some wine. It was our little secret. How could he no longer be there to share it?

My hand was still dangling down the side of the bed, ever hopeful of feeling Tyson, when my phone rang, making me jump. *Hot Guy* lit up the screen. I really had to change that.

'Hi,' he said tightly.

'What's up?' I asked, immediately aware of his clipped tone.

'That man's called again,' he said grimly. 'I've got a good mind to call the police . . .'

'And say what? People offer rewards for their pets' safe return all the time. It's not a crime to take it.'

'But we didn't offer a reward,' he said.

'No, but I would have done, if I'd thought about it. This guy's obviously chancing his arm, but if he's got Tyson, then I'll happily pay whatever it takes to get him back.'

'He says he's got him and wants two thousand pounds,' said Thomas.

'Do you believe him?' I asked.

'I think we should take him seriously, in the absence of anything else. I've got his address.'

'So, what should I do?' I asked, my voice wobbling. 'What's the next step? Should I get hold of the cash?'

'God no. I don't want you turning up at some strange guy's house with that kind of money on you.'

I gulped. '*Me?* You want *me* to go?'

'Well, no . . .' he faltered. 'Not if you don't feel comfortable.'

'Look, I know I'm asking a lot of you,' I said, 'especially after everything you've done already, but would *you* mind going? You know Tyson – you'll know if it's him. I'll give you the money and as soon as you're happy, you can hand it over.'

It dawned on me how ridiculous it all sounded. 'God, listen to us,' I went on. 'It sounds like something out of a film!'

I still felt uneasy when we met outside the bank and I surreptitiously handed Thomas a brown envelope stuffed with a hundred twenty pound notes. 'I feel like I'm in the middle of a drugs bust,' I said, laughing nervously. But Thomas was rubbing at his chin, deep in thought.

'You sure you're okay to do this?' I asked.

'Nothing will give me greater pleasure,' he said.

I saw a flicker of something cross his features, a tightening of his jawline, a blackness momentarily descend over his eyes. I'd not seen that look on him before.

'You won't do anything silly, will you?' I said, feeling unsettled.

'Of course not,' he replied, a little too quickly.

Unconvinced, I waited by the phone, eager for news. I didn't know what I was more nervous about; it not being Tyson, or Thomas discovering that it was all a ruse and decking the guy.

When it rang, I said a quick Hail Mary on both fronts.

'I've got him,' said Thomas.

My hand flew to my mouth in relief and my chest seemed to cave in as it rid itself of the stress and anxiety I'd been holding within it.

'Oh thank God,' I cried. 'Was it okay? Any problems?'

There was a long enough pause to make me think that all was not well and panic gripped me once again.

'By the time I got there, the bloke said he wouldn't hand him over for a penny less than three grand.'

'Oh,' I said, more concerned about where Thomas had got the extra thousand from than having to pay more to get Tyson back. No amount of money would have been too high a price.

'So suffice to say, the idiot lost out. He should have stuck to his original price, because his audacity pissed me off so much that he only ended up with a thousand.'

'Is that *all* he ended up with?' I asked cautiously.

'I'll drop him back shortly,' he said, ignoring the question.

The knock at the door came just after seven, and I raced towards it, narrowly avoiding the chewed-up ball that Tyson loved to play with. To see him there with

Thomas on the doorstep, his tail wagging, made my heart feel as if it was about to burst.

I beamed as Tyson leapt up to greet me. 'Where have you been?'

I fell to the floor as he whirled about like a dervish, not knowing whether to jump onto me, nuzzle my hair or lick my face.

'Thank you,' I said, looking up at Thomas. 'Thank you so much.'

'I'm sorry that it cost you so much to get him back,' he said.

'I would have paid much more,' I said, laughing, as I ruffled Tyson behind the ears. 'You coming in?'

'No, I need to go and see my mum.' He looked down at the ground and I felt as if I should say something. He'd not divulged any information about his background or his family – mind you, neither had I.

'I'll call you tomorrow,' he said, slipping the envelope, with what looked like the surplus cash, onto the hall table before leaning in to pull me up.

'I can't thank you enough,' I whispered, our faces almost touching.

'I'm just so happy that I was able to get him back for you.'

His lips brushed mine and I so desperately wanted him to stay. If it hadn't been his mother he was going to see, I would have done everything in my power to convince him to. I was that close to letting him know

177

how I felt, regardless of the consequences. If he ran in the opposite direction then so be it, but I needed to get across the effect he was having on me because it was unlike anything I'd ever felt before.

When he didn't call the next day, and the weekend had been spent staring at the phone, willing it to ring, I convinced myself I'd done something terribly wrong. What had I said? Nothing, *yet*. But the power of the unspoken word should never be underestimated. Had he known what I was about to say? Was he scared that I wanted to take our relationship one step further? I didn't know what that was yet, but I couldn't let him go. Though perhaps, in *not* saying something, I already had.

'Are you sure he's not married?' asked Maria in the pub after work.

'I have absolutely no idea,' I said, having wondered the very same thing the night before.

'Would you carry on seeing him if you found out he was?'

'Absolutely not,' I said, taking umbrage that she even needed to ask. 'I would never cross that line and besides, that isn't the type of relationship I'm looking for.'

'What type of relationship *are* you looking for?' she asked. 'Because, honestly, right now, it seems that this one is based on sex.'

'But it's *really* good sex, M,' I sighed.

Maria rolled her eyes, but she couldn't suppress a

grin. 'You can't allow that to cloud your judgement,' she said. 'There's more to a relationship than mind-blowing orgasms.'

I raised my eyebrows as if questioning the validity of her statement. 'Is there?'

'A relationship cannot survive on sex alone; it has to have something more. You need to be compatible in *life*, not just in bed.'

'We're harmonious in many ways,' I said. 'We talk . . .'

'A few post-coital words do not constitute a conversation,' she said, laughing.

'We've got something deeper than that. Well, at least I thought we had.'

'Does he know that?'

I pulled an apologetic face.

'Oh great,' she said, lifting her hands in frustration. 'So you're now pining like a love-sick puppy for a man who doesn't even know that you've fallen for him. Have you gone this long without speaking before?'

I nodded.

'So, nothing's changed apart from how you feel. And just because you've now decided you want more, he's supposed to jump to?'

I nodded meekly.

'Jeez, the poor man's not telepathic, Beth!'

'I know, I know,' I said. 'I *will* talk to him, if I ever get the chance.'

She took hold of my hand. 'Listen, this may not be

what you want to hear at the moment, but I'm being serious when I say there has to be more to a relationship than—'

'I understand your concern,' I said, patting her hand like my grandmother used to do to me.

'Stop taking the piss,' she laughed, pulling it away.

'You'd be surprised how intellectually stimulating we find each other as well.'

'I'll bet,' she said, rolling her eyes.

'I mean it!' I exclaimed. 'We've spoken at length about the value of wine, its investment potential and the upsides to repack sales.'

She looked at me blankly. 'I don't even know what you're talking about.'

'Aha! See? We're connecting on a far more cerebral level than you give us credit for.'

I thought it wise not to mention that straight after said conversation, he'd almost made me climax on a packed train.

My phone rang, and smiling, I showed Maria that 'Hot Guy' was ringing. 'Looks like it's time for my bootie call,' I said, as she choked on her wine.

'Well, if you're remotely serious about this guy, I suggest you change that to his actual name.'

'Hey, it's me,' he said, as I stuck out my tongue at Maria.

'Me?' I queried, letting him believe that he could be one of a hundred.

'Do you have many men's faces buried between your legs?' he asked.

Touché.

Still, I stayed silent for a few seconds, as if waiting for the penny to drop. 'Oh, hi,' I said, eventually. 'How are you?'

I thought I heard him snigger. 'I'm good, how are you? How's Tyson doing after his little adventure?'

'He's all good,' I said. 'Thanks to you, he doesn't seem any the worse for it, as far as I can see. What's going on with you?'

'I was just sitting here thinking about you and I wondered if you were around tonight to hook up?'

'Tonight?' I repeated, for Maria's benefit, though I immediately regretted it as the voice of reason was shaking her head and wagging her finger at me. 'Er, I can't really do anything tonight. I'm in the pub with my friend Maria.'

'How late will you be?' he said. 'I could meet you afterwards.'

There was a very real flip in my stomach at the idea of 'hooking up'. It must have been written all over my face as Maria rolled her eyes theatrically and threw her arms into the air in exasperation.

'Why don't you come here?' I said, throwing a curve-ball, not thinking for a second that he'd knock it out the park. Maria's eyes widened and she looked down at herself before shaking her head.

SANDIE JONES

'Sure, where are you?'

Oh. My. God, I mouthed to Maria, as I ran a background check of myself in my head. What underwear did I have on? When did I last shave my legs? Was the flat tidy?

'We're in the Tiger's Head in Woking,' I said, my voice belying the panic I felt. 'The one overlooking the green.'

'Okay, I'll be there in around forty minutes,' he said.

'Cool, see you then.'

'Well, you played hard to get,' said Maria after I'd hung up. 'And now you've thrown me under the bus as well. Look at the state of me.'

'You look gorgeous,' I said, fluffing up her dark curls. 'Anyway, I thought you weren't about all that superficial bollocks. It's not about looks and physical attraction, Maria. God, you're *so* shallow.'

She swiped me across the arm, probably all too aware that I was only taking the mickey out of her to stop myself from spontaneously combusting with excitement.

'Oh, so he's here then,' she said a little while later. I briefly marvelled at how she knew when she had her back to the door, but I realized my wide grin must have given the game away.

'Hi,' I said, way too over-enthusiastically. I lent up to kiss his cheek, but he turned and gave me a kiss on the lips. 'This is Maria.'

'Pleased to meet you,' he said, offering his hand. She

looked a little miffed that she wasn't getting a kiss and I had to suppress a giggle.

'You too,' she said, in her clipped telephone voice.

Two bottles of wine later and Maria's ancestral Scottish lilt was beginning to make itself heard. My accent, on the other hand, had apparently become more Italian, as Maria had laughingly observed.

'So, you're in the wine business, eh?' she asked Thomas. 'How much would this . . .' She took a look at the label. 'So, how much would this Merlot be?'

He smiled as she pronounced the T. 'Well, this bottle wouldn't be worth more than you paid for it, other than you'd expect to pay twenty pounds more in a restaurant and five pounds less in a supermarket.'

'So, where's the big money angle? Cos me and my Jimmy would be up for some of that.'

I looked at her and rolled my eyes. She and Jimmy barely made it through the month, but maybe that was all the more reason to invest.

'Well, it's all about the fine wines,' he said. 'Their values increase and decrease, and you just have to know when's the right time to buy and sell, much like stocks and shares I suppose. But this is much more of a dead cert than the London Exchange could ever be.'

'So, we'd be buying wine?' asked Maria.

'Yes, but not to drink.' He laughed. 'You'd keep it in a safe place, in optimum temperatures, until you wanted to sell it. All of my clients make over a two hundred per cent return, minimum.'

'But who would we sell to?' she asks, her expression confused.

'Well, you'd normally sell it to the highest bidder, and because I've always got clients who are looking to invest large sums of money, I'm normally able to outbid anyone else because I've got people lined up who want it.'

She gave me a nudge in the ribs. 'So, we wouldn't really need to do *anything*, your "hot guy" would do it all for us.'

'O-kay, it's time to go,' I said, not wanting Maria's loose tongue to reveal any more secrets.

She wound her window down as she got in her taxi. 'You two lucky ducks go and have a fun time,' she said, blowing us kisses. 'Go give each other multiple orgasms.'

I turned to Thomas, wide-eyed and laughing. 'I am *so* sorry. She has an alcohol threshold that should never be crossed.'

'Don't worry,' he laughed, pulling me towards him. He took my breath away as he kissed me, his hands entwined in my hair. He almost knew to support me as my knees threatened to buckle. 'So, what about it?' he whispered into my ear.

'What about what?' I asked, breathlessly, not wanting him to stop.

'Let's go give each other multiple orgasms.'

18

I was too busy being kissed as I fished for the keys in my bag to notice that the front door to the flat was ajar. It wasn't until I went to put the key in the lock that my blood ran cold.

'Come on, what's taking you so long?' said Thomas as he nuzzled my neck, seemingly oblivious to Tyson's frantic barking.

'Look,' I blurted out, not even thinking that I might alert whoever was in there. 'It's open.'

Thomas looked up and instinctively walked around me, so he was between me and the door. 'Call the police,' he said authoritatively, holding an arm out to stop me moving forward.

'Don't,' I said, my breath catching in my throat as he pushed the door slowly open. 'Someone might be in there.'

In a split-second panic, I ran through the items that a burglar might take that could never be replaced; the necklace from my dad, his wedding ring, framed photographs of us on the mantlepiece. I could see them all so clearly, being carelessly shoved into a holdall, their value so paltry to anyone but me. The very thought was enough to cause a ripple of pain through my chest and my bottom lip to wobble.

'Just call the police,' Thomas repeated, and I nodded, adrenaline rushing through me, making my hands shake. I could barely hold the phone in my hand, let alone make a call.

'Please be careful,' I begged as he stepped into the darkness, whilst I waited on the front step, holding back tears.

The seconds turned into minutes as I watched lights going on one by one. When Tyson's barking and whining eventually subsided, I knew Thomas must have reached him. I allowed myself to believe that if *they* were okay, *it* was okay. That maybe I'd just left the door open. Again.

I realized I'd been holding my breath when Thomas came back with a worrying grimace on his face.

'I'm really sorry,' he said, as my heart sank. 'You've been burgled and it's a bit of a mess. Tyson's okay, a bit shaken up. Looks like he was shut in the kitchen – he's nearly scratched the door to ribbons.'

Sobriety hit me like a sledgehammer.

He pulled me into him and kissed the top of my head. 'I'm so sorry.'

'I haven't called the police yet,' I said. 'I was hoping it might be a false alarm.'

'I'm afraid not,' he said. 'Tyson's barking might have scared them off eventually. But I doubt they'd make such a mess and not take anything.'

'Is it definitely safe?'

He nodded. 'It looks like they came and went through the front door.' He ran a finger down the door frame and I could see that it was splintered a little.

'Bastards,' I spat, before cautiously following him inside.

Nothing can prepare you for how it feels to have your home violated. To see all your personal possessions, things you've worked hard for, strewn across the floor. Every drawer was pulled out and upturned and every cupboard emptied in an attempt to find . . . what? It was a normal two-bedroom ground-floor flat, pretty basic, nothing special. But it was mine, and to know that someone had been in there, rifling through my letters, trawling through my underwear drawer and helping themselves to whatever took their fancy, made me feel sick to the pit of my stomach.

I fell to my knees on the floor where my jewellery box had been upended, too frightened to turn it over, in case I couldn't see what I so desperately wanted to see. I forced myself to take a deep breath.

'I've popped Tyson back in the kitchen until the rest of the flat is straightened out a bit,' Thomas said as he entered the bedroom. 'Are you okay?'

I nodded and counted to three in my head, psyching myself up. *Please don't do this to me*, I prayed silently to whichever God was listening. *If you'll just make this okay, I promise I'll come to church more.*

'Can you see if anything's been taken?' he asked gently as I turned over the box.

'Yes,' I sobbed, my heart breaking. 'The necklace my dad gave me, his wedding ring, some earrings.' I ran a hand over the carpet, willing my fingertips to feel the sentimental items I treasured. 'The other stuff doesn't matter, but my dad's . . .' I couldn't hold back anymore.

'Ssh, it's okay,' said Thomas as he knelt down on the floor and rocked me in his arms. 'We'll call the police, they might be able to get it back.'

'No, no they won't – they never do.'

'They'll try. Is there anything else?'

I stood up and rubbed at my head, trying to work the fury and frustration out. I couldn't even remember what used to be there just a few hours before. Did I still have that fancy camera I treated myself to a couple of years ago? Or had I lent it to Maria? Was my laptop at home or at school? I couldn't think straight.

The living room was even more of a mess; every piece of paper had seemingly been pulled out of the dresser, where I had developed my own haphazard filing system, and thrown onto the floor.

I looked around the sea of invoices, bills and payslips that lay at my feet. My mother's will, which she had given me on the strict understanding I wasn't to open it until she passed away, lay next to its ripped envelope. After twenty years of it being in my safekeeping, I'd allowed a stranger to come along and destroy that trust.

Even seeing the cards that the children from my class had made for me, lying forlornly on the floor, made me cry. Their bright colours and kind words so at odds with the sickening scenario they were now a part of.

'It's difficult to tell,' I sniffed.

Thomas nodded and punched digits into his phone. 'Hello, I'd like to report a burglary,' he said, before giving my address. 'They could be here in five minutes or five days,' he said as he hung up. 'There's not much manpower left in the burglary squad these days.'

'Can you stay?' I asked.

'Of course.'

It wasn't until I really looked at the chaos surrounding me that I realized how many secrets my home held. I considered myself to be a private person, only letting those closest to me in, yet in just a few minutes, a criminal had found out so much about me. He knew that I was a primary school teacher at St Mary's in Guildford and how much I earned. He now had all my bank account details and my current balance. Even the seemingly innocuous details about me, such as my eclectic fashion sense, my love of yellow, the book I was reading, and my fondness for the Brontë sisters were all laid bare, making me feel overtly vulnerable. It was only as my eyes caught sight of the solicitor's headed paper, which my mother's will was attached to, that I realized that the son of a bitch also knew things that I didn't even know myself.

I worked my way through the wreckage fastidiously, refusing to allow my emotions to overwhelm the job in hand. But no matter how hard I tried, everything felt contaminated, sullied by a stranger's touch.

'Do you want to carry on doing this now?' Thomas asked as he was putting all my books back in the bookcase. 'We can do the rest in the morning.'

I looked at him and wanted to cry again.

'Do you want a cup of tea?' he asked.

'Thank you.'

'What for?'

'For just being so kind.'

He looked away, as if embarrassed.

I went into the kitchen and opened the fridge, lifting a bottle of white wine out of the door. 'I'd rather this.'

'Yep, great,' he said, following me in, watching as my shaking hands fumbled with the seal covering the cork.

'Here, let me,' he said, and I watched as his strong tattooed arm took the weight of the bottle away from me. I couldn't remember the last time I felt so safe, which was ironic seeing as I was stood in the middle of a crime scene.

19

'Tell me about your family,' he said, as we lay in bed later that night.

It seemed momentous, not only because we were talking properly, but because it was the first time that we were in bed without having ripped each other's clothes off to get there.

'There's not much to tell,' I said. 'My dad died when I was thirteen and it's just been me and Mum ever since.' Just talking about him brought a lump to my throat. The thought of the only part I had left of him – his ring and the necklace he bought me – being in someone else's careless hands turned my stomach.

'So, no brothers or sisters?' he asked.

'Nope, a spoilt only child,' I said, forcing a laugh.

'Me too. Though I bet I wasn't as spoilt as you,' he joked.

I smiled, knowing he was probably right. There weren't many girls who got a pony for their seventh birthday, and a boat named after them. I can still remember the gasps of schoolfriends as they arrived at my house for birthday parties. If it wasn't the long drive that stumped them, it was the swimming pool and extensive gardens.

Every year, the celebrations were more outlandishly themed, from animals to Disney and circus acts, to my personal favourite, the actual Chitty Chitty Bang Bang taking us all for a ride.

Mum would look on, quietly embarrassed, whilst Dad, the Italian showman, took centre stage, making all his daughter's dreams come true. The very next day though, it became tradition for him to take me around all his restaurants and into the kitchens, where the hard work really happened.

'No matter how lucky we are, we must never lose sight of what it took to get here and where we came from,' he used to say to me.

His wise words had stuck, as I'd barely missed a day's work since. Even when I was genuinely ill, I'd think of the children who were expecting me and would drag myself into school.

'I wasn't *that* spoilt,' I said, defending myself.

'What? With the dad you had?' he said, laughing. 'I find that very difficult to believe.'

I pulled myself up and turned on the light. 'I wasn't aware I'd spoken about my dad,' I said, my voice clipped.

'What?' he said, still laughing.

'When did I talk to you about my dad?' I had no reason to be suspicious, but I couldn't help feeling uncomfortable.

'After we'd had dinner with Diego Rodriguez,' he said.

'I don't remember that.'

'You were a little tipsy,' he replied, smiling, as his finger traced my lips. 'It must have been somewhere between the train station and home because, if you remember, we were pretty busy at all other times.' He raised his eyebrows suggestively.

I felt myself blush at the flashback of being pressed together on the train and the overwhelming urgency to get back to the flat. All the details in between were sketchy.

'We were talking about the wine business and you told me that your dad was a successful restaurateur and that in another life, me and him would no doubt be in business together.'

That *did* sound like something I would say, forever holding a candle to my father's entrepreneurial spirit.

I smiled. 'He'd either be buying wine from you, or selling you his collection. He had a nose for a fine wine.'

'Did your mum ever remarry?' he asked.

'God no. Dad was the love of her life. No other man stood a chance.'

It's funny. I'd desperately wanted to share exactly this kind of information with him, had thought that we weren't really a proper couple until we did, but now that we were, it didn't feel right, and my protective barrier was going up again.

'What about your parents?' I asked, deflecting the conversation back onto him.

'My mum has dementia and is in a home, and my dad lives in Sydney with his new wife.'

'I'm sorry to hear that. Do you see her very often?'

'As much as I can,' he said sadly. 'I try to go in a few times a week.'

'That must be really difficult. Does she know who you are? Is she able to recognize people?'

'It's a bit hit and miss,' he said. 'She has good days and bad days, but unfortunately she's at a stage where it's really starting to take hold.' His voice caught in his throat. 'Is your mum in good health?'

'She is, yes,' I said, whistling and touching the wooden surround of the headboard. 'She's made of stern stuff and puts me to shame.'

'In what way?' he asked.

'In *every* way. She's on the go 24/7; doing a yoga class, walking a neighbour's dog, helping out at church, volunteering down at the soup kitchen. If I have half the energy and a quarter of the conscience that she has when I'm her age, I'll be very happy with my lot. She's a force to be reckoned with.'

'So, she doesn't work as such?' he asked.

'No, not in the sense that she earns money, though she probably works the same hours as a full-time job. But that's not why she does it. She's just a selfless person who gets a great deal of satisfaction from helping others. Making someone's day easier is reward enough for her.'

'So, she doesn't have to worry, financially?'

I laughed. 'Good grief no. The only financial pressure she's under is to spend more. She's still in the house we all lived in as a family, but it needs some money spent on it. She's essentially only living in the downstairs rooms, and yet she still won't put the heating on or change the rickety old windows that are letting a cold draught through. The pool hasn't been used for years and the stables are derelict. I'd love to see it restored to its former glory, but she reckons she's happy with it the way it is.'

'So, what's she spending all her money on then?' he asked incredulously.

'No doubt she's giving some of it to worthwhile causes and I'm sure there's a reason why Father Michael has a little twinkle in his eye every time he sees her.'

Thomas raised his eyebrows playfully.

'Oh no, I didn't mean . . .'

'So, you don't think it's because she plays his organ every Sunday?' he said.

'That's outrageous,' I shrieked, hitting him with a pillow. 'You know what I mean.'

'She must be getting a return somewhere. It wouldn't make sense to leave it lying dormant.'

I shook my head. 'It's all in a building society, earning a pittance in interest. It could be put to work, so that she makes money without losing any of her capital, but she's a tough nut to crack.'

'She should invest in the wine business,' he said, laughing.

'What, and give all her money to a shady character like you? No chance.'

'I'll try not to take that personally,' he said, through a smile. 'I'd do it as a favour.'

'And what would *you* get out of it?'

He smiled. 'Well, normally I work on commission, but for you . . .' He moved himself down the bed, his lips setting my skin alight as he went. 'For you, I could do a special deal.'

'What kind of special deal?' I asked, my back arching involuntarily.

'Well, if you keep letting me do this to you . . .' A breath caught in my throat as I felt his tongue. 'Then I'd be *very* happy to take payment in kind.'

20

'Mum, you've got more of a social life than me!' I was looking at her calendar hanging in the kitchen, the bottom of it moving ever so slightly in the draught coming through the windows.

'What, dear?' she asked absently as she disappeared into the larder. Tyson waited patiently outside, knowing that a treat was likely to come his way.

'How are there possibly enough hours in the day to get all this done?' I asked, as I surveyed the colour-coded event listings. 'What does this all even mean?'

'Well, it's quite simple really,' she said, pretending to sound put-out. 'Blue is for the church, orange is for friends, and pink is for me.'

'How does that help?' I asked, unable to understand her system.

'It just means I can prioritize at a glance,' she said. 'So, if a blue event comes in and there's already a pink event scheduled at the same time, I know that I can move it to accommodate the blue event.'

She really is that selfless, but I still felt the need to double-check. 'So, if there was a blue event and a really important pink event came in, what would you do?'

'I can't think of an important enough pink event that would take precedent,' she said, leaving me in no doubt.

I shivered and pulled my coat around me as I felt the draught again, and was unable to stop myself picking at the flaking paint on the wall.

'Mum,' I said carefully, 'I think the house is in need of some work.'

She stopped stock-still, her hand in mid-air, holding a teaspoon of sugar. 'Why do you say that?'

I didn't think I'd need to explain the obvious but attempted it anyway. 'It's too cold in here. Look – the curtains are moving. And we ought to get those damp areas looked at – they can't be good for your chest.'

'There's nothing wrong with my chest,' she said indignantly.

'No, but there will be if that wall stays like it is.'

'It'll cost too much,' she said.

'But it will be worth it,' I said, putting an arm on her shoulder. 'It's not as if you're doing anything else with the money. It's just sitting there.'

'Well, that's where I like it,' she said, bristling, and I couldn't help but laugh.

'What are you saving your money for?' I asked, suddenly serious.

'For a rainy day,' she said, moving away from me to put a pan of sweet-smelling berries on the Aga. 'And for whatever you may need in the future, when I'm no longer here.'

'But I don't want you to provide for me, I want you to spend your money on you. On making sure you're fit and healthy, safe and warm . . . I want you to enjoy living here.'

'I do enjoy living here,' she said, her voice wobbling ever so slightly. 'Of course, it's not the same house that it once was, when you and your father were here, but . . .'

'Do you want to stay here?' I asked, knowing that if I looked up, she'd be staring at me, horrified that I even needed to ask.

'Of course,' she exclaimed.

'But what about buying something smaller, something more manageable?' I asked.

'Oh no,' she said, shaking her head. 'The only way I'll be leaving this place is in a wooden box.'

'Okay, so if that's the case, then perhaps we could get some work done, not only to make it more comfortable for you, but to make it look really lovely again,' I said, over-enthusiastically. 'We could get all the walls watertight and paint them in bright colours. Maybe even take one or two of them out. Imagine this as a great big space with an island and a new oven.'

'Oh, I'll not be getting rid of my Aga,' she said, defensively. 'And you can't take that wall out, because of the wine cellar behind.'

I peered around the door to the windowless store room at the end of the corridor, its bare brick walls housing indistinguishable bottles.

'What have you got in there?' I asked, walking towards it. Mum followed me, both of us ducking our heads to clear the low joist.

'That stuff hasn't been touched since your dad . . . I don't know why I keep it really, it must be well past its best.' She attempted to laugh, but I could feel her pain.

'Oh my goodness, Mum, I can't even read what these are, there's so much dust on them.' A cough caught in my throat and I battled to stop my eyes from watering as I picked up a bottle at random.

'Well, this one is a cognac,' she said, taking it from me and wiping it with the tea towel in her hand. 'Your dad used to love his cognac. We'd have all his suppliers over for a dinner party, and they'd all know to bring a bottle of this or a fine whisky. You would have been too young to remember, but they were very glamorous affairs.'

I vividly recalled sitting at the top of the grand staircase, peering through the banisters at the women in their furs arriving with well-turned-out men who seemed far older than them. Even then I could see the divide in their relationships; the bonhomie between the men, who would disappear into the drawing room, and the wives who seemed happy to be left to make small talk in the entrance hall. Only my mum would look wistfully after her husband, wishing she was with him instead.

'We might be able to do something with these,' I said, pulling out another bottle that had a 1966 seal.

'What do you mean?' she asked.

'They could be worth something,' I said. 'I know someone who might be able to sell them. Only if you'd want to, of course.'

'Who would want this old stuff?' she asked.

'You'd be surprised.'

'Well, if you think it'd be worth doing . . .' she said. 'More importantly, who's this friend?' She looked at me with a naughty glint in her eyes and I felt my cheeks flush. 'Oh goodness, I've not seen you go like that in a long time.'

I bowed my head. 'It's nothing,' I said, fooling no one, especially my mother. 'He's just a friend.'

'Well, feel free to invite him round,' she said. 'See if anything takes his fancy.'

I smiled and followed her back into the kitchen.

'Do you want a piece?' she asked, as she took a lemon drizzle cake out of the oven and set it down on a cooling rack.

'I'll take a slice with me if that's okay. I don't want to ruin my appetite before Maria's barbecue.'

I didn't tell her that Thomas was coming with me to said barbecue and that I felt sick to the pit of my stomach at the thought of him meeting my friends. And indeed them meeting him. I really wanted it to go well.

I knew something was wrong the minute I opened the door. Whilst *I* was dressed up as if I was going to the

Queen's garden party at Buckingham Palace, Thomas was wearing a pair of jeans and a worried expression.

'You okay?' I asked, concerned.

'I'm really sorry, but I'm going to have to bail out of the barbecue.'

'What? Why?' I said, fighting the disappointment that was slowly working its way around my body.

He looked at his feet. 'It's mum.'

'Oh God, is she okay?' I asked, ushering him into the hall and closing the door.

'She didn't have a very good night, and is very disorientated and confused today.' He looked at me with sad eyes. 'I'm sorry, I just feel I need to be there.'

'Of course,' I said, rubbing his back, though what good that ever does I don't know. 'Of course. You should go.'

'I'm really sorry to let you down,' he said. 'I was looking forward to meeting your friends.'

'It doesn't matter – we can do it another time.'

'Will you still go?'

I was taken aback by the question. It hadn't occurred to me not to. Should it have?

'Well, yes,' I said.

'Ah, okay, it's just that I was wondering if you wanted to come with me.' He looked down at his feet, shuffling from one to the other.

'Go *with* you?' I said, in surprise. 'What, now?'

'This is going to sound really weird, but I don't know

how long she's got left, and as different as she is to the person I knew as my mum, I'd still really like you to meet her, before . . . well, you know . . .'

I felt like I'd had the wind taken out of my sails as the magnitude of what he was saying sunk in. In the space of just a few minutes, I'd gone through a whole plethora of emotions from excitement to selfish disappointment, and concern to utter surprise. I had no idea which of those my mouth would choose to convey.

'I . . . I . . . Well, of course, I'd love to,' I faltered. 'If you think it'll be okay.'

His eyes seemed to light up as he nodded.

'I wouldn't want to cause her any more anxiety though.'

'It'll be fine,' he said, through the tiniest of smiles. 'You'll brighten up her day.'

21

'It's best to keep conversation simple,' Thomas said as we pulled up in the car park of the care home. 'And it's always wise to agree with her, no matter how absurd it sounds.' He attempted to laugh but it didn't sound real.

'We'll go through the normal routine. She won't know who I am, I'll remind her, she'll acknowledge it and then immediately forget.' He cleared his throat before continuing. 'Though if last night is anything to go by, she may be even more confused than usual.'

He bowed his head and I put a hand over his. If I had the right words, I'd offer them, but I didn't want him to think me patronizing.

'Hello Elise,' he said cheerily as we walked into the brightly lit reception. 'You're looking good.'

The girl, younger than me, giggled coquettishly and immediately touched her hair. I'd not yet seen him converse with another woman and his effect was obvious. She was yet to register my presence and I waited for him to introduce me.

'Where is she today?' he said instead.

'She's in the common room,' Elise replied, her eyes still alight.

He led the way down the carpeted corridor, the smell reminding me of my grandparents' house. Whatever that smell is, it's not good or bad; just old, much the same as when you walk into an antiques shop or a second-hand book store.

I immediately regretted not bringing some flowers as we walked into a large room with windows for walls and individually coloured and styled upright armchairs. There were vases on the little tables between them, each holding a sorry-looking bunch of flowers, carelessly arranged. I hoped it wasn't an indication of how the vulnerable residents were treated.

I followed him over to the corner, where a dot of a woman sat peering longingly out of the window at the gardens beyond. Just looking at her broke my heart and I selfishly hoped she wasn't who we were here to see.

'Mum?' called Thomas, warily. She immediately looked up at him, her eyes searching for some kind of recognition. 'It's me.'

She smiled and nodded.

'This is my friend, Beth.'

I stepped forward and offered my hand, but she wasn't forthcoming. I looked at him, fearful that I'd done something wrong. He winked at me and shook his head.

'Come and sit down,' she said to me, patting the chair beside her. 'You get a beautiful view of the garden from here – it's my favourite place to sit.'

'It's gorgeous,' I said.

'Don't tell anyone,' she said, leaning in conspiratorially. 'But I often come down here when everyone is still asleep, even the nurses. You see so many wonderful things at that time in the morning; the squirrels come out to find their nuts, the blackbirds have a squabble in a puddle. Sometimes I can even see a rhododendron as it opens up throughout the day. Slowly, slowly, its petals stretch out towards the sun . . .'

'So, what have you been doing since I last saw you Mum?'

'Well, Frank's been in to see me,' she said quietly. 'That was nice.'

'What, Dad?' Thomas asked, shooting a glance at me and raising his eyebrows. 'What did he have to say?'

'Oh, you know. We were talking about the days when we went dancing. He'd take me to the Rivoli Ballroom and we'd be the first on the floor and the last off.' She gave a little laugh, her eyes lighting up. 'I said to him about the time that The Beatles were there, but he doesn't remember it. I mean, how can you forget seeing The Beatles?'

She reached across to me, placing a hand on my lap. 'You remember The Beatles, don't you Sarah?'

I went to correct her, but thought better of it. 'Of course, they were the best.'

'Exactly, see, there you go Frank,' she said. 'Helen

206

remembers it. My parents wouldn't let me go, would they Frank?'

She giggled like a naughty schoolgirl and I wanted to pick her up and pop her in my pocket. Get her away from this sterile environment, where no matter how hard they tried to make it look any different, it still resembled God's waiting room.

'So, he'd come over and skulk about in the back lane, waiting for me to get changed out of my nightie and into my itsy bitsy miniskirt.' She laughed to herself. 'My father was incensed when he saw me in it the first time: "You're not going out dressed like that." So, I'd storm off upstairs and come back down in something that covered me from my neck to my ankles. "That's more like it," he'd say. He never found out that I'd just shove my teenie weenie skirt into a carrier bag, along with a bottle of wine that I stole from their drinks cabinet.'

She laughed again, and I couldn't help but join in her merriment. I could happily listen to her all day and was already working out a way to come and see her more often.

'Your Aunty Sheila came to see me,' she said, looking at Thomas. He threw me a sideways glance, careful to keep his smile painted on. 'She's very unhappy at that place she's staying,' she went on. 'Says that they'd treat a dog better than they treat her.'

Thomas sat there, sadly nodding his head.

'I didn't like to boast and tell her how wonderful my

son is,' she went on, giving me a nudge with her elbow. 'I wouldn't be here if it wasn't for him. Anyone else wouldn't bother; they'd just put me in one of those terrible places that she's in and leave me to rot. But not my boy; he looks after his mum.'

I felt my heart lift as I looked at him. 'He's a good man,' I said.

She patted my hand.

'Now, you see next to the purple rhododendron bush, there's a delphinium, well that was one I planted in the springtime and look at it now. The gardener said to me, "Joyce, you shouldn't put that there, it'll get over-shadowed by the hornbeam."'

'Mum loves her plants,' Thomas said, smiling.

'But I stood my ground,' she went on. 'And look how beautiful it is.'

She certainly seemed to know her stuff, as the window perfectly framed the wild English flowerbed she'd helped create.

'That's why I always like to sit here. This is my special place.' She looked out wistfully, seemingly lost in thought.

'What did you have for dinner last night, Mum?' asked Thomas.

She smiled. 'We had a tea dance yesterday afternoon, so we had sandwiches and scones and a band came in to play. Oh Frank, you would have loved it; they sang all our favourite songs. Do you remember that song we had at our wedding? 'Raindrops Keep Fallin' On My Head'. Well, I danced to that with Eileen, because you weren't here, but I imagined it was you.'

'I remember,' said Thomas, throwing me a rueful glance.

I looked at him, suddenly aware of how painfully difficult this must be. Who could possibly imagine that the woman who had rocked you in her arms, snuggled down beside you in bed to read you a story, been the only person who could comfort you when you fell and hurt yourself, would ever mistake you for someone else? Or at times, stare straight through you as if she's never seen you before. The cruelty of the disease rocked me to the core and I felt a new sense of love and respect for Thomas as he pretended to be the husband his mother had separated from over twenty years ago.

'And what was that song we used to sing to our boy?' Joyce went on. 'You know the one . . . *dom, dom, where it began . . .*' Thomas shrugged his shoulders and looked away, embarrassed, as she sung louder. '*You can't begin to know it . . .*'

'"Sweet Caroline",' called out her nearest neighbour, whose head I couldn't even see over the top of the chair.

'That's it Maude, join in.'

Joyce picked up my hand and we swayed our arms above our heads, as the impromptu singalong gained momentum. Clearly Maude was of the loudest voice, despite her feet not being able to touch the ground.

Even one of the nurses, who was administering tablets in little plastic cups, was singing her heart out. I couldn't help but smile as I joined in the chorus, the scene reminiscent of something out of *One Flew Over the Cuckoo's Nest*.

'Why don't you join in with *your* song?' I teased Thomas, as he looked increasingly uncomfortable.

'Now would be a good time to go,' he said, smiling and rolling his eyes. 'We're going to head off now, Mum,' he said over the din.

Suddenly her eyes narrowed as she looked at him. 'Who are you?' she said, abruptly. 'What do you want?'

'Mum, it's me,' he said as he knelt down in front of her, taking her hand in his.

'Get away from me,' she shouted, physically pushing herself back in her chair. 'Nurse, nurse, help. Somebody help me.'

Her panic was increasing with every syllable and I moved out of the way as two uniformed nurses rushed towards her.

'It's okay, Joyce,' one of them said as they restrained her. 'You're safe.'

'But he's here, he's here.' She was screaming, her hands shaking as her arms flailed.

'You should go,' one of them said, turning to us.

I couldn't stop tears springing to my eyes, my confusion seemingly akin to Joyce's own.

'We need to calm her down,' the nurse said. 'It would be better if you went.'

She was still screaming, 'He's here, he's here,' as we quickly walked away down the corridor.

22

'I'm sorry about that,' Thomas said as we drove away from the care home. His jaw was twitching involuntarily, making him look like he was struggling to contain his true feelings.

'Are you okay?' I asked.

He bit down on his lip and turned away. 'It's so difficult to see her like that,' he said. 'She was such a different woman when . . .' His voice cracked. 'When she was my mum.'

I put my hand over his, resting on the automatic gearbox. There was nothing I could say, even if I could get past the lump that was lodged in my throat.

'She was incredible,' he choked. 'She was the woman who remembered everybody's birthday and had a card and the perfect present wrapped and ready the day before. She was the wife who turned heads whenever she walked into a room, on the arm of her proud husband. She was the mother who stayed up all night to make me a Gremlin costume, only to get to school the next morning to find that it wasn't fancy dress until the following week!'

I sensed an uplift in his tone. 'I trust she took you home to change?'

He shook his head and smiled. 'No, she figured it would do me good – make me more aware. It was the hardest lesson I've ever had to learn – imagine sitting there, amongst my uniformed friends, wrapped in fur with huge cardboard bat wings for ears. I've never got my days muddled up again.'

'I was speaking to *my* mum this morning,' I said. 'I don't know if it's of any interest, but she's got some cognac, whisky and a few bottles of wine that she said you could take a look at – you know, if you're free sometime . . .'

'Seriously?' he asked, his eyes widening.

'Yes, maybe we can pop over there, when you next come down.'

'Why don't we go *now*?' he asked, excitedly. 'She doesn't live too far away, does she? Will she be home?'

'Well . . . yes, probably, but I don't think . . .' I started, as I struggled to comprehend how we'd gone from the disappointment of him not meeting my friends, to now, me meeting his mother and the possibility of *him* meeting *mine*. Things were moving at a whippet's pace and it thrilled and terrified me in equal measure.

'Why don't we pop into Maria and Jimmy's instead?' I said, playing for time. 'They might still have some sausages sizzling.'

'Would you mind if we didn't?' he asked, his eyes on the road ahead. 'I'm not really in the mood for a party. I can drop you off there though, if that's what you'd prefer.'

I didn't want to be anywhere without Thomas. 'No, let's go to my mum's then,' I said hesitantly. 'I need to pick Tyson up anyway.'

He looked across at me. 'We can leave it – if you think it's too soon . . .'

How could it be, when I'd just met *his* mother?

I texted Mum to let her know we were popping over and she texted back: I'd better put the icing on that cake then!

'Crikey,' mused Thomas, as we turned into the gates of my childhood home. He whistled through his teeth as we drove along the drive, the house not yet in view.

I squirmed, embarrassed by our perceived wealth.

Mum was at the door when we pulled up and I hurried in, expecting Thomas to follow. Instead he was looking around, agog at his surroundings.

'Mum, this is Thomas,' I said, in an effort to shake him out of it.

'Mrs Russo,' he said, almost jumping to attention. 'So very pleased to meet you.'

I watched as Mum gave him the once over and could tell from her expression that she was quietly impressed. I let out the breath I'd been holding in.

After the niceties were exchanged, I said, 'Thomas can look at that wine whilst he's here.' I picked up the last remaining crumbs of lemon drizzle and popped them in my mouth. It was sacrilege to leave even the tiniest morsel. 'If you want him to?'

'Well, only if you've got time,' she said, already up out of her chair and walking towards the cellar.

I rolled my eyes and tilted my head at him to follow, whilst I helped myself to another slice of cake.

'So . . . ?' I whispered as she scuttled back in a few minutes later, clearly as eager as I was to convey her thoughts.

'Ooh, he's lovely, Beth,' she enthused. 'A real gentleman.'

I smiled and felt warm inside. That's how much Mum's opinion mattered.

'Is it serious?' she asked.

I nodded. 'I think so . . . I hope so. I really like him.'

'And he *really* likes you,' she said, knowingly. 'I can tell by the way he looks at you.'

I giggled like a schoolgirl, only pulling myself together when Thomas reappeared in the room. It was so obvious that we'd been talking about him and I felt myself flush as he raised his eyebrows questioningly.

'So, do you want the good news?' he said into the awkward silence.

Mum and I both nodded.

'You've got a really good collection there, Mrs Russo.'

'Please call me Mary,' she said, her voice akin to the put-on telephone voice I used to tease her about when I was younger.

'Some of them are worthless,' went on Thomas, 'but you've got a few there that I'd love to sell for you.'

We looked at him expectantly.

'I would hazard a guess, at a conservative estimate, of five thousand pounds.'

'Five thousand pounds?' Mum and I shrieked in unison.

'There's some vintage cognacs in there and one or two whiskies that someone will pay handsomely for. It might even go higher.'

'Wow,' I said, looking between him and her. 'You've been sitting on a treasure trove.'

'Goodness, I can't even begin to get my head around it,' she said. 'So, would you be able to sell them for me? They're no use to me here.'

'If that's what you want, then I'd be very happy to sell them for you.'

I looked at Mum and we both nodded.

'Okay, so let me go and catalogue them all properly and let's see what we can get.'

'Are you okay for him to do this?' asked Mum, under her breath. 'They say you should never mix business with pleasure. I don't want him to feel awkward if they don't fetch as much as he thinks they will.'

'It'll be fine,' I said. 'He's very professional. I've seen him deal with clients and he knows what he's doing. If it doesn't reach that figure, it's no loss, is it? They've been sitting there gathering dust for over twenty years, so anything we get is going to be a bonus.'

Mum nodded thoughtfully.

'Okay, so I've got everything I need,' Thomas said

when he walked back in the room. 'I'll see who's in the market and get you the best price I can.'

'So, this is what you do for a living?' Mum asked.

'Yes,' he said, smiling.

'That must be interesting. I had no idea such a thing even existed.'

'It's a growing industry,' he said. 'Back in the eighties, it was something you did to be flash and pretentious, when everybody thought they were Gordon Gekko.' We all laughed, remembering Michael Douglas's character making unethical get-rich-quick deals.

'But it's got a bit more serious in recent years,' Thomas went on. 'Now, it's actually about the wine and the genuine connoisseurs, who know what they're buying. It's *real* money now, being used to make *real* investments, by people who are passionate about what they're doing.'

'So, they're making a living out of it?' asked Mum, slightly awestruck.

He nodded. '*They* are. *I* am. For some people it's just a game they like to play, alongside their proper jobs. But for me, it's a very real business.'

We both watched as he walked slowly towards the French doors that overlooked the garden. I couldn't help but feel embarrassed by the cracked panes and peeling woodwork, remembering how they used to be the feature of this once-impressive drawing room.

'So, this is *all* yours?' he said as he looked out. It was more of a statement than a question. 'Where does it end?'

217

Mum got up to join him. 'Well, it's as much as the eye can see really. It disappears into a valley beyond the horizon and then runs straight down to the river at Godalming.'

He whistled through his teeth.

'Of course, it's not what it once was,' she said. 'We used to have a livery over on the right, so there were always horses in the field, and the swimming pool was the centre of many a party, adults and children alike.'

'I bet you had some good times,' he said.

She nodded. 'It was a very social house, always full of people, even though we were only a family of three. There would always be somebody here; family, friends, colleagues. We even put up friends of the church in the pool house one year. Do you remember that?' she asked, looking at me.

'Vaguely,' I mused. 'Weren't they refugees that Father Michael brought over?'

'Yes,' said Mum, with a laugh. 'Your father thought I was completely mad, but I couldn't turn them away. It's not in my nature.'

'Wouldn't you like to get the place back to how it was?' Thomas asked Mum, as I waited with interest for the answer.

'Of course, but it would take an awful lot of money to do that,' she said.

'But we could at least make the house more

comfortable for you,' I said. 'You've got the money – it's sitting there doing nothing.'

'Yes,' agreed Mum. 'But once you start something like this, it tends to run out of control very quickly. The more work you do, the more problems it uncovers, especially with a house of this size and age. We've got the money to start it, but we haven't got the bottomless pit that I know we'd need to finish it. And plus, I need to live, God willing, for as long as I can.'

'Would you mind me asking a personal question?' said Thomas.

Mum and I looked at him, neither of us objecting.

'Do you have a mortgage on this place?'

'Goodness me, no,' said Mum, shaking her head vehemently, as if he'd asked if she was having an affair with the Pope.

'Mum doesn't believe in having credit of any kind,' I offered, by way of explanation.

'My husband never borrowed a penny from anyone,' she said, proudly. 'His family built up the business through sheer hard work and determination, first in Italy and then over here. Folk used to think they were the mafia.' Her shoulders shook as she laughed at the memory. 'They must have thought he was extorting money! But he was just an honest, hard-working man who didn't owe anybody anything. He used to say, *If you haven't got it, don't spend it*, and he would turn in his grave if I went against that now.'

'So, why don't we invest the money you *do* have,' I said, not knowing where the idea had even come from. It sounded absurd before I'd even finished the sentence, but still I went on. 'If we can double that money, we can get the work done *and* you'll have enough to live on.'

I looked to Thomas for confirmation. 'There are lots of investment opportunities out there,' he said. 'I, for one, have never had a client walk away with less than a hundred per cent return. Even from the very first deal.'

Mum looked at me with wide eyes. 'Are you suggesting I put *everything* into wine?'

'You think it's foolproof, don't you?' I said, turning to Thomas.

'Well . . . yes,' he said, 'but . . .'

'Tell Mum about Rodriguez,' I said. 'Tell her how much he started off with and how much you helped turn it into.'

'He's probably not the best example,' he said.

'Why?' I asked, wondering which part I'd misunderstood.

'Because I have clients who have done even better than him.'

'Oh,' I said, standing corrected. 'Well, why don't you tell Mum about them then?'

'Rodriguez is a new client and is just dipping his toe in the water at the moment, but he's already turned thirty thousand into a hundred thousand in just a few months. Beth met him the other night, and he's very happy with what I'm doing for him, isn't he?'

I nodded enthusiastically.

'But my biggest client, Seamus Harrison, started off with a budget of twenty thousand two years ago, and it currently stands at just over a million. He's been able to give up his job in the city and go back to Ireland, where he spends his time training racehorses. He'd never have been able to do that without shrewd investments.'

'And I suppose you make your money from their windfalls?' asked Mum.

'I work on commission, yes,' he said. 'I love what I do; the biggest kick being the ridiculous amounts of money that I can raise for my clients.'

Mum nodded thoughtfully and as I caught her eye, she raised her eyebrows as if silently posing the question I could hear loud and clear. *Are you absolutely sure you know what you're doing?*

'Shall we see how we get on with the wines we've got to sell first?' I said, in answer. 'If that's successful, we can talk about further investments.'

'Sounds like a sensible plan,' said Thomas. 'Let's start from there.'

23

'Well, that was relatively painless,' I said, as we waved goodbye from the car.

'She's lovely,' Thomas said, offering her a wide smile and sticking his hand out the window as we pulled away, crunching gravel as we went.

'She liked you, too,' I said, unable to stop smiling.

The two most important people in my life liked each other, and as I leant back on the headrest, it felt as if everything in my world was aligned. Great tentacles of happiness spread their way through my body, working their way to the very tips of my fingers, making them tingle. I wanted to hold onto this feeling for as long as I could, knowing that within seconds something could happen to snatch it away.

'I'm not going into work until later tomorrow,' I said, dreamily.

'Oh, why's that?' he asked.

'I'm supposed to be planning the outdoor pursuits trip that we're going on the week after next.'

'Ah, yes, is this the five days of hell in Snowdonia?' He grimaced. 'With thirty snotty-nosed kids, who are going to be up all night, and murder all day.'

I laughed. 'You can come if you want.'

'I'd rather stick pins in my eyes,' he said, shuddering.

'Don't you want children?' I asked, taking myself by surprise.

The pause that followed, whilst he considered his answer, was enough to pop the precarious happy bubble that I'd put myself in. *I've overstepped the line. He thinks I'm too pushy. Why have I ruined everything?*

'Eventually,' he said. 'But only at the right time, when I know I'm with the woman I want to be with for the rest of my life.'

I could sense him turning to look at me, but I stayed focused on the road ahead, too scared to see the look in his eyes, in case they said it wasn't me.

'So anyways,' I said, far too casually, 'I wondered if we could go back to your place tonight. I'd love to see where you live – have somewhere to picture you in when we're not together.'

'Ah, that would have been awesome, but I'm up at the crack of dawn tomorrow.'

I could feel my bubble deflate even more, as if it were a very real, tangible thing. But instead of wallowing in my own paranoia, I took a different tack.

'That's okay, I'll get up with you and go home.'

'That's not going to work,' he said. 'It's Sod's Law. Any other day would be fine, but I need to be at the airport by five thirty in the morning.'

I turned in my chair. 'The airport? You didn't tell me

you were going anywhere.' I could hear the accusatory tone in my voice and flinched. He didn't owe me anything.

'What . . . ? Yes, I did. I told you I was going to Spain for a couple of days.'

Suddenly, it wasn't about him *going*, but him not *telling* me he was going.

'When?' I asked, knowing full well he'd not said a word.

'The other night, after the burglary. I told you I was going to Spain to meet an investor who had some vintage rioja to sell.'

If he'd have said any other time, I would have believed him. But after the burglary I was feeling particularly vulnerable, and if he'd told me he was going away, I'm sure I would have remembered – nervous at the thought.

'You didn't,' I said. 'This is the first I've heard of it.'

He laughed. 'I definitely told you. You said that it was a shame that we weren't away at the same time. Anyway, what's the biggie?'

'There is no "biggie",' I said, putting the word in speech marks. 'You just didn't tell me, that's all.'

'Well, I'm sorry if you don't remember, but I'm telling you again now. I'm going to Spain tomorrow and am back on Wednesday.'

'Don't talk to me like I'm a child,' I said, my voice rising. 'I don't care that you're going away. You can *do* whatever you want, *go* wherever you want, with *whoever* you want to go with, but don't tell me I already knew something when I didn't.'

'Jeez, why are you getting so stressed out about it? Is it because you haven't been to my place yet?'

'It's got nothing to do with that,' I said, though I had to admit, it didn't help. He'd come to my flat over a dozen times, we'd been to London probably the same again, yet his place, which was allegedly just west of town, had somehow managed to elude us.

'Listen, when I get back from Spain, I'll do dinner at mine,' he said, sounding conciliatory. 'Would *that* make you happy?'

'Don't you dare patronize me,' I screeched, incensed. 'Making out as if you're doing me a favour.'

'You're being ridiculous,' he said, pulling up outside my flat and turning the engine off.

'Don't bother getting out,' I yelled as I retrieved Tyson from the boot. 'You'd better get off home for your beauty sleep.'

'Are you being serious?' he asked incredulously, through the open window. 'You're honestly going to leave it like this?'

'Have a nice trip,' I said, without looking back.

24

When 'Hot Guy' flashed up continually throughout my lunch hour the next day, I had to turn my phone over.

'Problem?' asked Maria through a mouthful of ham sandwich.

'Not really,' I said tartly, unable to keep the vitriol I felt from spilling out.

'I can't believe you've still got him stored as "Hot Guy" on your phone,' she laughed, in an attempt to defuse the atmosphere. 'Does he know?'

I shrugged and felt tension creeping up from the base of my neck. 'I'm seriously thinking of renaming him Dickhead.'

'Uh-oh,' she sang. 'Trouble in paradise. Is this your first lovers' tiff? What did he do?'

'We rowed about going to his place,' I said. 'He made something so simple so complicated.'

'About *going* to his place, or *not* going?' she asked.

'I wanted to go, but he said it wasn't convenient.' Even as I was saying it, it sounded immature. 'So when we got back to mine, I forbade him to come in.'

Maria choked on her sandwich. 'That's a bit extreme, isn't it?'

'He was an *extreme* arsehole, so the punishment befitted the crime.'

'So, this is him, trying to crawl back into your good books,' said Maria, giving a nod to my phone, still vibrating its way along the staff room coffee table.

'He flew to Spain this morning, so I'm assuming he's ringing me to say that he got there safely. But he can call all he likes, because I really don't care.'

Maria rolled her eyes and picked up my phone, which was in danger of buzzing itself off the table.

'Jesus, he's called twenty-three times,' she said. 'I think he's done his penance, don't you?' It started ringing again, and she accepted the call before throwing the phone at me.

'Yep,' I barked down the phone, with all the sassiness I could muster.

'It's me,' he said.

'No shit, Sherlock. What do you want?'

'I've had an accident,' he said. 'I'm in hospital.'

My blood ran cold and I momentarily lost the ability to focus. 'What? Where?' was all I could manage.

Maria instinctively came towards me, her presence a welcome anchor in the stormy sea I'd suddenly been immersed in.

'I'm in Spain,' he said, his voice slow. 'I've been hit by a car.'

'Oh my God,' I said, bringing my hand up to my

mouth. 'Are you going to be okay? Where are you? I'll come over.'

'No, it's fine,' he said. '*I'm* fine, just bruised and sore. They're going to take an X-ray. They suspect I've got a broken arm and they're keeping me in overnight, just as a precaution.'

'What about the car?' I asked, though I don't know why.

'Well, that's got a me-shaped dent in it,' he said, attempting to laugh before saying, 'Ouch, that hurts.' I wondered how people in pain actually had the where-withal to say 'Ouch'.

'I can come out there,' I said, as Maria nodded in agreement, intimating that she'd cover for me. 'I can be there later tonight, if I can get a flight. Honestly, I—'

'No,' he said with surprising force, though it was probably the best course of action as I was beginning to babble and struggling not to cry.

'Will you be okay? Have they said when you might be able to fly home?'

'Not yet, but it doesn't look like I'll be out of here any time soon. I'm just worried that I'll not be able to get back to see you before you go off on your trip.'

I fell back onto the staff room sofa. 'Listen, about last night—' I started.

'I'm sorry,' he said, cutting across me. 'It was a silly argument and I'm sorry that it got out of hand.'

'I'm sorry too,' I said. 'I got a bee in my bonnet and was completely unreasonable.'

'You weren't,' he said. 'You're right about my place. Once we're both home, why don't we spend the weekend together? Stay at mine and I'll show you the delights of Maida Vale.'

Now that he was offering it, it didn't seem nearly so important. It didn't matter where we stayed, just as long as we were together. Him having an accident seemed to hammer the point home even more.

'Are you sure you don't want me to come over?' I said.

'No, honestly, I want you to stay where you are. But before you go, I've got some good news.'

'Oh?'

'I managed to sell your mum's wine collection, just before the accident. In fact, it's why I was on my phone and probably not paying attention when I crossed the road.'

If I didn't already feel guilty, I certainly did now.

'Guess how much I got?' he went on.

'No, go on,' I said, wondering if it even mattered anymore.

'Seven thousand,' he said, as excitedly as one can sound when they're probably in traction and being held together with metal pins. I reminded myself of my tendency to over-dramatize.

'Wow,' I said, listlessly. 'That's amazing.'

'It means she'll be able to get cracking with the work,' he said. 'It'll at least tide her over until the big one comes in. That's if she decides to do it, of course.'

'Let's talk when you get back,' I said. 'Are you sure you don't want me to come over?'

'Honestly, I'm fine,' he said. 'I just wanted to let you know and to say I'm sorry. I'll call you later, once I have more news.'

'Okay.'

There was a pause before he said, 'I love you.'

In that split second I almost knew he was going to say it, yet I still wasn't ready for it and didn't know how to respond. Would he think I was weak if I said it back? Would he hate me for not? I wanted to, because it's how I felt, but my brain was waging a war against itself, weighing up the pros and cons of being honest.

'You too,' was what I eventually came up with, and immediately regretted it. It wasn't enough – he deserved more.

'See you, then,' he said despondently, and I put the phone down, furious that I'd caused his insecurity all because I wanted to what? Save face? I couldn't stop a tear from springing onto my cheek.

'Hey, hey . . .' said Maria, as she carefully lifted a bourbon biscuit out of her tea and ate it whole before coming to sit down next to me. 'What's going on?'

'He said, "I love you",' I blurted out.

She snorted. 'And *that's* why you're so upset?'

I nodded. 'I didn't say it back,' I sobbed, and immediately realized how ridiculous I sounded.

To be fair to Maria, she didn't do what I would have done if I'd been in her shoes. She refrained from slapping me around the cheek and telling me to pull myself together.

'*And* he's been in a car accident,' I cried, as if it was secondary to me not telling him how I felt.

'Okay, so *now* I want to slap you,' she said, making me laugh.

'I'd do it to myself if I could,' I said, sniffing.

'There's nothing to stop you,' she smiled. 'I assume he's okay, if you're able to stress about other inconsequential bollocks?'

I nodded, embarrassed.

'So, he's gone from being a complete dickhead two minutes ago to someone you love so much you can't tell him?'

'Something like that,' I said, smiling.

25

I couldn't wait to see Thomas when he eventually got home four days later. Despite his promise to go to his flat, he asked if I could just be patient for a little while longer as it was in a bit of a state, and all the time his arm was in a sling, he wasn't able to get it ready for me.

'You deserve more,' he said on the phone. But I didn't care where we met by then, I just needed to see him.

I jumped up onto him as I opened the door, wrapping my legs tightly around him, breathing him in, not wanting to ever let go.

'Steady on,' he laughed. 'Watch the arm.'

'I love you,' I whispered, in between kisses. His mouth broke into a wide grin, and all the pent-up emotions I'd unknowingly held within were released. Like a flock of birds taking flight.

I'd prepared dinner, but knew that our sexual appetite would probably need to be sated before our desire to eat kicked in. Without breaking our kiss, and somewhere between his T-shirt coming off and my jeans being unbuttoned, I guided him into the kitchen and deftly turned down the temperature on the oven.

'You are incredible,' he said afterwards, as we lay spent on the bed.

Still out of breath, he lifted himself off the pillow and leant in to give me the softest of kisses. 'I love you and don't ever want to be away from you again,' he whispered.

I felt a knot in my stomach as I realized I'd have to remind him that I was about to go away for five days. I wondered if there was any way I could get out of the school trip. For the first time in my life, I seriously considered throwing a sickie. My yearning to be with Thomas clearly overrode my normally resolute conscience.

'You haven't forgotten I'm going away on Monday, have you?' I said quietly, not really wanting him to hear me. Because if he didn't hear me, I still had time to think of a reason not to go.

He pulled away from me. 'Shit!'

It was hard enough as it was, I didn't need him to make it even more so.

'But it's only for five days.'

'Shit, I'd forgotten all about that.' He leant back heavily on the headboard and ran a hand through his hair.

Don't say it. Please don't say it.

'Do you *have* to go?'

He said it.

'I can't let the kids down, can I?' I didn't know who I was trying to convince.

'But there are other teachers going?'

233

'Yes, of course, but there's a very strict adult to child ratio and I'm supposedly the team leader, so it's not easy to pull out, especially when I haven't got a valid reason.'

His brow furrowed. 'Aren't I a valid enough reason?'

I couldn't tell whether he was being serious or not and swung my legs off the bed in a bid to change the atmosphere.

'It killed me being away from you this week,' he said. 'I don't want to do it again.'

I knelt on the bed and kissed him. 'It's only five days,' I said, half laughing. 'You'll manage.'

He sat himself up even straighter. 'Listen, I've been thinking.'

This sounded ominous. I sat back down next to him.

'I want us to live together,' he said. 'Because when I'm away from you, all I can think about is how quickly I can get back.'

My heart felt like it was about to jump out of my chest. 'Seriously?' I squeaked. 'What, here or at yours?'

'I can work from anywhere,' he said, 'and Mum's not too far from here – it's manageable. But you've got your *whole* life here and if you came to live with me in Maida Vale, you'd have to change jobs and be further away from your friends and your mum. It makes sense for me to live here. I'll contribute towards your mortgage – assuming you have one?'

I nodded. 'Yes, unfortunately I don't share my mother's

school of thought on debt. Well, I would if I had the choice, but . . .'

'Okay, so I'll pay the mortgage and we can halve the bills and food – what do you think?' He sounded excited, but unsure – as if he didn't want to show too much emotion in case he'd called it wrong. I couldn't wait a second longer to put him out of his misery.

'Yes, yes, yes,' I screamed, straddling him and kissing him deeply. If I'd ever been as happy, I couldn't remember when. 'When shall we do it? As soon as I get back? What about next weekend?'

He laughed and rolled me over, his weight pinning me down on my back. 'I'll move some bits in whilst you're away if you don't mind. And when you come home on Friday I'll run you a bath, make love to you and cook you the best meal you've ever had.'

I squealed. 'In that order?'

'Absolutely! You'll have spent a week in a hostel with no running water by then!'

I swiped his tattooed arm and he fell on me, nuzzling my neck and tickling my sides until I could barely breath.

'Did you tell your mum the good news?' he asked, when I eventually begged for mercy.

'Oh God,' I said, pulling myself up and pushing my hair out of my face. 'In everything that was going on with you this week, I totally forgot.'

* * *

I wish I'd lied and told him that she was thrilled, because the very next morning we were sat round at hers instead of being in bed, so excited was Thomas to tell her.

'Oh, my goodness, that's wonderful news,' Mum said, clapping her hands together. 'Who'd have thought that a few dusty old bottles languishing in a cellar could be so valuable?'

'It's gone a bit crazy,' said Thomas. 'I was in Spain this week and was offered some really exciting cases; there was a crate of Moncerbal and a dozen Les Manyes which will be gold dust to investors. I already know that I'll be able to sell them for five times as much as I buy them for.'

'So I assume you're going to buy them?' asked Mum. 'If you know you're on to a sure thing.'

'Absolutely,' he said, smiling. 'It's too good an opportunity to turn down. I'm already being chased by a few people who have heard the word through the grapevine.'

If he hadn't looked at me expectantly as he delivered the punchline, I would have missed it altogether.

'That was awful,' I groaned.

'The old ones are always the best,' he laughed.

'So you'll not be holding on to them for very long?' asked Mum.

Thomas shook his head. 'Unfortunately, I doubt I'll have them in my possession at all. I'll sell them on, probably the same day that I buy them.'

'How much will you be buying them for?' asked Mum, suddenly forthright.

'One hundred and fifty thousand secures the deal,' said Thomas. 'And I've already been offered four hundred and fifty thousand by a client in Russia. But I'm going to hang out for more.'

'So an investor is going to buy them through you and you're then going to sell them on to someone who is honestly going to pay that kind of money?' I found myself asking.

'Pretty much. I'll take my ten per cent commission on each transaction and everybody's happy.'

I looked to Mum, trying to read her mind.

'Why can't *we* buy the wine?' I don't know if I meant my thoughts to be aired publicly.

'What?' exclaimed Thomas, though I noted Mum stayed silent. 'Where are you going to find that kind of money?'

I glanced at Mum again and she gave me a nod.

'We can do that,' I said. 'It will pretty much wipe us out, but if it's only for twenty-four hours, and comes back fivefold, it would have been a very good day's work.'

'It would certainly mean I could get all the work done and not have to worry anymore,' chipped in Mum.

Thomas looked from Mum to me and back again. 'This isn't the right deal for you, Mary. It needs to happen faster than you would be able to manage and, I don't know, it just feels . . .'

'I can make the transfer first thing Monday morning,' she said, sitting up straighter in her chair, as if she really meant business.

'I think you should start smaller,' he said. 'There will be plenty of other opportunities. I'll know the right one when I see it.'

Her whole body seemed to shrink, as if somebody had released her air valve.

'We want to do *this* one,' I said adamantly. 'If you're absolutely sure that we can double our money . . .'

'At the very least,' he said.

'Then I want to do it,' I said. '*We* want to do it. Mum?'

'If you're happy, then I'm happy,' she said.

Thomas smiled and shook his head. 'You two have enough chutzpah to serve an army.'

Mum and I looked at each other, taking it as a compliment.

'But if that's what you want . . .'

'Absolutely,' I said, before turning to Mum and laughing. 'And if it all goes wrong, I'll sell the flat and reimburse you.'

'I might hold you to that,' she said, smiling.

26

The alarm went off, waking me from a dream I was having about Prince Harry. We were holding up a bank, demanding money, with sawn-off shotguns. His bala-clava fell off and he quickly put on a mask instead, but it was *his* picture on the mask. What was *that* all about?

'Wakey, wakey,' said a sleepy voice beside me.

I groaned. It couldn't be time to get up – I was sure I'd only just gone to sleep.

'I don't want you to go,' Thomas said in my ear as he spooned me from behind.

His words jolted me, reminding me that in a few hours' time I'd be on a coach, trying to convince thirty children not to eat too many sweets, and holding a sick bag for those who didn't listen.

'Can't you tell them you're really ill?'

'No!' I exclaimed as I pushed myself up. This was hard enough without him putting pressure on me. 'That's not who I am.'

He reached over to stroke my bare back, sending tingles down my spine. 'But it's a big day today. Once the deal's gone through, we need to go out and celebrate.'

I'd momentarily forgotten about what else was happening today. Maybe that's what my dream was about. Was it a warning?

'We can do that on Friday night,' I said, leaning in to kiss him. 'We'll have lots to celebrate then because we'll officially be living together as well.'

'Mmm, don't forget to leave me a key. I'll take the next few days to move my gear across.'

After dropping Tyson at my mum's, we'd spent yesterday clearing out the spare bedroom to create some space for Thomas's stuff, though he assured me he didn't have much. Still, I wanted him to feel as if this was his home as much as mine, so gently encouraged him to bring whatever he wanted.

'Will you let me know as soon as Mum's money hits your account?' I said, as he kissed me at the door. I don't know what I felt stranger about; leaving him at my place, or having him in possession of my family's life savings. Good job I trusted him.

'I'll keep you posted every step of the way,' he said. 'In an ideal world, both ends of the deal will happen today, but if your mum's money doesn't clear then we might be looking at tomorrow.'

'And then we'll *really* have something to celebrate,' I said, smiling. 'I love you.'

He kissed me deeply. 'Love you too. I'll see you on Friday.'

'Hey Mum,' I said into the phone, once I'd gone around the corner and lost sight of Thomas.

'Hello darling, you okay?'

'Yes, I'm just on my way into school.'

'Looking forward to the trip?'

'Yes and no,' I said, honestly. 'If it was a normal week, I would, but Thomas is moving a few of his things into the flat and—'

'Is he now?' she teased. 'So, this is getting serious.'

'I should hope so,' I laughed. 'You're just about to give him a hundred and fifty thousand pounds!'

'Are we definitely going ahead with that?' she asked, a little quieter. 'I was going to ring you just before I went to the bank to, you know . . . well, just to double check that you're still happy.'

Despite being *more* than certain that we were doing the right thing, I still felt almost sick with nerves.

'Absolutely,' I said, ignoring it. 'This is going to allow us to do everything we need to do to the house.'

'Well, I went out and bought some magazines yesterday,' she said, sounding like an excited little girl. 'And honestly, Beth, there are some truly beautiful houses out there.'

I laughed. '*Yours* is truly beautiful – it just needs a little bit of TLC.'

'Well, I think I've found the kitchen I want. It's a country shaker style with basket handles and a white granite worktop. I was thinking I might get a microwave as well – all the houses in the magazines seem to have one. I probably won't use it, but it all fits into the kitchen design now, doesn't it? You should see what can be done these days Beth, and don't get me started on the bathrooms . . . they have walk-in rain showers now, none of this mouldy old curtain around a bath business. My hips will thank me for that, I can tell you!'

She may have been making a joke of it, but I hadn't really appreciated, until now, how she'd been living. Having the work done would make a big difference.

'Let me know once you've transferred the money,' I said. 'Maybe we can go out at the weekend to have a look around and get some more ideas.'

'This is so exciting,' she said breathlessly. 'I'll call you as soon as I've been to the bank. Have a good time, won't you?'

And I had. Until the second day, when I hadn't heard anything from anybody.

'Have you had any problems with your phone?' I asked Maria over breakfast.

The children were nearby, eating their porridge, albeit begrudgingly. When the 'chef' overheard one of them complain that it tasted like cardboard, he said he'd do the teachers something 'a bit more grown-up'. I didn't know whether to laugh or cry when he served up the same porridge, with a jar of strawberry jam slammed down on the table between us.

'Service here is murder,' said Maria, and for a moment I didn't know whether she was talking about the phone network or the meal we'd just been given. 'Jimmy sent me an email to say that he'd been trying to call and text, but nothing got through. I don't think I've received anything from anybody since we got here.'

'That explains it then,' I said, feeling relieved, though I still couldn't shake off the queasiness in the pit of my stomach. I pushed the bowl of what looked like cement mix away from me. 'I expected to hear from Mum and Thomas, but I've not heard a peep.'

'Give them a ring on the landline at reception,' she said.

'Good idea.'

I called Thomas first, but it went straight to answer-phone. He normally had a personal voicemail greeting, so I put the phone down and redialled when I heard an automated message.

A robotic-sounding woman answered. ' . . . *Leave a message after the beep.*'

'Oh hi,' I said, still unsure I'd called the right number. 'It's me, Beth. Just wanted to let you know that no messages or calls are getting through to me here. I hope everything's okay and the deal went through. If you could call the hostel and leave a message for me, just so I know that all is well, that would be great. If I don't hear from you, I'll assume you've trashed my flat and run off with the money.' I forced a laugh before putting the phone down.

When I called Mum, she picked up straight away.

'Oh, thank goodness,' she said, her voice a little panicky. 'I've been calling you and texting you. I got a little worried when I didn't hear back.'

I didn't know whether that was because she thought I'd fallen down a mountain, or something had gone wrong with the deal.

'No, everything's fine,' I assured her. 'My mobile's not working up here, so I'm calling you off a landline.'

'As long as all is well,' she said, before adding, 'Has Thomas received the money?'

'Yes,' was my immediate response.

'So, did it all go okay? What did we get in the end? I've been dying to hear.'

'It went fine,' I said, not knowing why I was lying. 'I've not managed to speak to Thomas this morning yet, but he'll have the final numbers for me when I do.'

I heard her exhale down the line. 'Well, that's a relief. I barely slept a wink last night for worrying.'

'There's nothing to worry about, Mum. As soon as I speak to him I'll give you a call back.'

'Okay darling, I feel better for having talked to you.'

Nausea continued to swirl around, slowly snaking its way up towards my throat.

'Excuse me,' I managed to blurt out to Maria as we passed each other at the door to the ladies. A second later and she'd have been wearing the contents of my stomach.

'Are you okay?' she asked gingerly through the flimsy door.

'Er, no,' I managed, stating the obvious. 'I don't feel so good.'

'Oh God, you don't think it was that porridge, do you? We'll all be in here in a minute.'

'I don't think I'm going to manage canoeing this morning,' I said, just before the thought of it brought along another wave of nausea.

'No worries, do you want me to stay here with you?' she said.

'No, I'm fine,' I said, opening the cubicle door.

'Jesus, you look like shit,' she exclaimed. 'What do you think's going on?'

'I don't know,' I said honestly, doubting that the growing feeling of trepidation about the deal could cause me to be physically sick. 'If you could cover for me I'd be really grateful.'

'Of course,' she said, rubbing my back. 'Did you manage to get hold of Thomas?'

It was all I could do to shake my head. 'Not yet, I'll try him again later.'

'Why don't you go back to your room and get some rest? I'll check in with you at lunchtime to see how you're feeling.'

I managed to send the children off with a smile on my face, trying to ignore my nagging conscience when little Theo said, 'But Miss Russo, it won't be as much fun without you.'

'Of course it will,' I said, ruffling his hair. 'We've got abseiling this afternoon and I wouldn't miss that for the world.'

Except the world, it seems, is a precarious place. One tiny tilt of the axis and we're all at sea.

'Have you definitely not got any messages for me?' I asked at the hostel lobby, just before lunch. 'Might someone else have taken a call?'

The man shook his head unhelpfully.

'I'm really sorry, but I don't think I'm going to be able to stay the course,' I said when Maria came to visit me in my room. It wasn't strictly true – I *could* have seen it through – but I didn't feel well enough to be scaling down mountains and building a raft in the middle of a lake. At best, I was going to have to base myself at the hostel, which was unwelcoming at the best of times, least of all when you're ill and want your own bed. I didn't let on that I felt compelled to get home as quickly as I could, just to check that everything was okay with Thomas. Once I was satisfied, I would come back, free of the apprehension that was slowly poisoning my body.

I held my phone on my lap for the taxi journey to the station, impatiently waiting for the service bars to light up. We were a good four miles from the base of Snowdonia when my phone sprang into action. Ping after ping resounded as the driver tutted, no doubt used to townies who were restless and testy, eager to get back to civilization.

Is everything okay?

Did it happen?

Can you call me when you can please?

I've seen a wonderful kitchen

Just let me know when it's done

I'm worried – please call me

Message after message illuminated the screen. Every single one of them from Mum.

27

By the time I pulled into London Euston I'd called Thomas ten times and was verging on hysteria. If he wasn't dead, he'd better have a bloody good excuse.

When I turned the corner of my road and saw his car parked up outside the flat, I felt all the air rush out of me. It didn't rule him out of having had an accident, or worse. But it *did* mean that he was there, we were still together, and he hadn't done the dirty on us with Mum's money, because rightly or wrongly that's all I could think about.

Shame flooded through me as I recalled the already hazy journey. I was unable to believe that the thoughts I'd allowed to infiltrate my mind were truly mine. Seeing him come out the front door, with his overnight holdall slung casually over his shoulder, I went to call out. But I stopped, to give myself just another few seconds to pull myself together. To wipe the guilt, that I was sure would be obvious, from my face.

His face broke into a wide grin as he reached his car and I wondered if he'd already seen me, but was pretending not to, so as not to spoil the surprise. I tried to walk faster, thwarted by my case's wheels having to negotiate the uneven pavement.

I stopped dead still in my tracks as Thomas leant into the passenger window of the car. I wanted to see him talking to a male colleague or perhaps even my mum, who he'd thoughtfully taken out to lunch to celebrate the deal. I wanted to see *anyone* apart from the attractive blonde woman he was kissing.

Feeling as if I'd been punched in the stomach, I instinctively crouched down behind a hedge on someone's path. I don't know if it was because my legs collapsed beneath me or that I was scared of being seen. How would anything, ever be all right again, if I acknowledged what I'd witnessed? If Thomas knew I'd caught him out.

I needed to think before I acted, but I didn't have much time. I heard the car start up and gathered my thoughts. *Think. Think. Think.*

I stood up, just in time to see the car go past, the smiling woman looking out the passenger window at me as she went by. There was no recognition from her. No appreciation that the man she had just kissed was my boyfriend. All she would have seen in me was a young woman who was returning from a trip, perhaps glad to be home and looking forward to seeing her lover. All I saw in her was the bitch who had just taken him away.

Already breathless from shock and grief, I scurried across the road as quickly as my lead legs would carry me. I had a momentary thought, as I put my key in the door, that he might have changed the locks, but why would he do that? He was cheating. He wasn't trying to take my life away from me, although I feared it was one and the same thing.

I rushed through to the spare bedroom, expecting to see his treasured possessions filling the familiar space, but nothing had changed since I was last there. My wardrobe, where his clothes had hung happily with mine, was devoid of his shirts and trousers. Only the faintest scent of him remained, to prove he ever existed.

My ravaged brain couldn't compute what was going on. Had he gone away for a couple of days with his mistress? Was he going to come back on Friday, pretending that all was well and assuming that I'd be none the wiser? Or had I just witnessed him walking out of my life?

I ferreted for my phone in my bag, but I was all fingers and thumbs as my heart beat against my chest. Tears clouded my eyes *and* my judgement.

'I don't care about her,' I said out loud. 'We can get through this, just please come back home.'

I called him again, and the by-now-familiar woman's voice read out the banal announcement.

'You need to call me, *right now*,' I hissed, barely able to breathe. 'If I don't hear from you in the next hour, I'm going to call the police.'

I slid down the wall onto my bedroom floor, the room which just a few days ago had been where we'd made love, where he'd said he wanted us to live together, where he begged me not to leave him. Had it *all* been a lie?

No, it couldn't have been. He couldn't have pretended to love me that well. He couldn't have faked what we had. It was impossible.

But then I remembered his parting shot. Had it *always* been about the money?

I pictured my mum's smiling face, excited about restoring her beloved house to its former glory. I could see her in the warm glow of her kitchen, the room where Dad used to whirl her around, and could hear her saying that she'd never leave. That all the time she had him, me and the beat in her heart, she would never let anything happen to the house we all loved.

My throat contracted and I raced to the bathroom, where my stomach was quick to dispel the sandwich I'd managed on the train. With my head still hanging over the toilet, I noticed that where there'd been two tooth-brushes neck to neck in the cup on the basin, only one now remained.

As soon as I felt able to, I called Mum, not knowing what I was going to say.

'Has the money definitely left your account?' I blurted out before she'd even finished reciting her phone number.

'Oh, hello darling,' she said, sounding perplexed. 'Yes, why?'

'But have you *actually* checked?' The panic in my voice made me sound more cutting than I meant to be.

'Yes, why?' she asked hesitantly, feeding off my own distress. 'Has Thomas not received it? I thought you said he'd received it.'

I was stumped to know what to say for the best. Should I tell her I lied? Was there any chance that it had somehow gone to someone else's account by mistake? Could Thomas be exonerated of any wrong-doing, apart from kissing a woman who wasn't his girlfriend? Should I tell her that I think we've been scammed? Did she need to know that every penny she had is probably on its way to Rio de Janeiro?

If you're about to break the heart of the person you love most in the world, how's best to do that?

I knew I couldn't do it over the phone – she deserved more than that, so I jumped in my car and spent the time driving there going over and over what was happening. Trying to think of a single logical reason why Thomas would have done what he'd done. My own pain paled into insignificance when I measured it against my mum's. Her lost pride. Her broken promise to my dad. The future that she thought she had, snatched away from her . . .

And it was *all* my fault.

28

I don't even remember driving towards Treetops, Thomas's mum's care home. But I found myself sitting at the junction, just half a mile away, being beeped and honked at.

You've got one more chance, I said to myself, as I hit *call* on Thomas's mobile number.

The tone ran long and constant, as if flatlining. Even the robotic woman had given up on him.

'Fuck!' I said, slamming the steering wheel.

I didn't know what to do. I sat at the junction, debating which way to go. Turn right, and I go to my mother's and tell her what I've done – what *he's* done. Turn left, and I go towards the only link that I have to Thomas. The car behind blared its horn with impatience – I looked in my rear-view mirror and saw an agitated man waving his hands at me, forcing a decision.

There was a different girl on reception as I approached the desk, feeling sick with trepidation. If she told me I couldn't see Joyce, I feared I might burst out crying. I took a deep breath – I needed to stay calm and in control.

'Oh hi,' I said, trying to sound casual – as if I came here all the time. 'Is Elise not around?'

The girl looked covertly from side to side. 'She's been dismissed,' she whispered.

'Oh,' I replied, shocked. 'Why?'

She leant in. 'Apparently she wasn't checking credentials. She let just about anyone in – didn't even take their name.'

'That's not good, is it?' I said. 'You have to be so careful.'

'Exactly,' she said. 'So we're asking all visitors to sign in with their name and who they're here to see.'

I picked up the pen hesitantly, allowing my overactive imagination to wonder if they'd already been put on alert. Had Thomas warned them that I might come looking?

Just in case, I wrote a false name and moved slowly away from the desk, as if waiting for someone to pounce. *But I've not done anything wrong*, I countered in my head. *If they're going to ambush anyone, it should be him.*

'Is Joyce in her usual place?' I asked nonchalantly.

'Ah,' she said, and I froze, waiting for my heart to start beating again. 'Her son's already here. I think they're in the lounge.'

Of all the scenarios I'd allowed for, Thomas being here wasn't one of them. *Shit.*

I briefly thought about running away. But I'd come here to find him, and shockingly, despite being together for almost six months, this care home and his mobile phone number were my only hope of tracking him down.

I saw Joyce, in her chair over by the window, talking animatedly to a man with his back to me.

I wanted to run over to him, throw my arms around his neck and beg him to tell me I'd got this all wrong. That something had happened to his phone. That he wasn't having an affair. That he'd invested my mother's money wisely. That he was still the man I'd fallen in love with.

My pace quickened as I got closer. My ragged breath came in short, sharp pants as the enormity of the next few seconds dawned on me. They would dictate the rest of my life.

'Thomas?' My voice didn't sound like my own.

He turned around to face me.

It wasn't him.

In that split second, I tried everything to turn this man into the person I wanted to see. *Expected* to see. If he just had blue eyes, instead of brown, a straighter nose, a stronger jawline, it *could* have been him. But it wasn't.

'Can I help you?' the man asked.

I looked to Joyce for help, but she was looking at me as if she'd never seen me before.

'I'm sorry, who are you?' I asked.

He looked taken aback, his features clouding over. 'I'm Ben Forrester. Who are you?'

'There must be some mistake,' I said, ignoring his question. 'The lady at reception said you were Joyce's son.'

'I am,' was all he offered, warily.

'So, you have a brother?' I asked, clutching at straws.

'No, I do not, just a sister. Can I ask what this is all about?'

I felt my insides crumble, as if a tiny pickaxe was chipping away at my core beliefs, my morality, my self-preservation, slowly destroying everything I held true.

'Joyce,' I said, breathlessly, leaning down beside her chair. 'Do you remember me? I was here a few days ago with your son Thomas.'

'Now, just wait a minute,' said the man, starting to stand up as Joyce shook her head fearfully.

I racked my brain trying to remember what she'd called me. My real name wouldn't mean anything to her. 'I'm . . . Helen,' I said, remembering. 'I was here with Thomas. We spoke about Frank and The Beatles. You told me how you'd sneak out of the house so that your dad didn't see you in your miniskirt.'

'Okay, that's enough,' said the man, grabbing my arm tightly and hauling me up.

'Joyce, I was here with *him*,' I screamed as he pulled me away. 'You called for help. You said it was him. You kept saying, "He's here."'

I felt the grip on my arm tighten. 'Please Joyce. Try to remember.'

'*Who* were you here with?' asked Ben Forrester, his nostrils flared.

'I don't know,' I said, sobbing as the truth of the words sunk in. 'I honestly don't know.'

29

Mum took one look at me and ushered me into the hallway.

'What on earth has happened?' she asked, putting her arm around my back.

'I can't . . . I just can't . . .'

'Calm down,' she soothed as she walked me into the kitchen. 'Here, sit down.' She moved a pile of interior magazines to the side of the table, each neatly marked-up with Post-it notes.

I felt my heart break.

'It's Thomas . . .' I sobbed.

She pulled me to her and held my head against her stomach, rocking me gently. 'Darling, what is it? What's happened?' I briefly wondered how she couldn't guess, but if she'd had that kind of cynical mind, then she would never have agreed to this crazy plan in the first place. Or had I agreed to it on her behalf? It certainly felt like it.

'He's gone,' I choked. 'He's gone with all the money.'

The rocking stopped abruptly and she held me away from her, staring at me, her eyes unblinking. I could only imagine the vice-like grip that was squeezing her insides, making her feel as if she couldn't breathe.

'What . . . what do you mean?' she faltered. 'What are you saying?'

'He's a conman, Mum. He duped me, then you, into believing that he was doing it for *us* . . . that he had *our* best interests at heart.'

'Where is he?' she asked matter-of-factly.

'I don't know.'

'Well, where does he live? That might be a good place to start.' There was an acerbic tone to her voice. An accusatory edge. 'Had you thought of that? He can't just disappear into thin air, can he?'

My head fell into my hands. 'I don't know where he lives.'

'What do you *mean*, you don't know where he lives?' she asked coldly. 'You've been seeing him for months.'

'I've never been to his place,' I admitted.

She threw her arms up in the air before taking herself off and circling around the kitchen, deep in thought.

I knew the question was coming, even before she asked it.

'So, where does he work then?' she said eventually.

'He didn't have an office. He could work from anywhere – as long as he had his mobile phone.'

'And you thought that *all* this made him seem like a good bet?' she asked, her voice rising. 'I honestly can't believe what I'm hearing.'

Her disappointment in me was palpable, which hurt so much more than my broken heart, or the stolen money.

I remembered the last time I'd disappointed her. I was fourteen and she'd found a cigarette in the pocket of my school blazer. I'd wanted her to ground me. I'd wanted her to scream at me. But all she said was, *You've let me down.* It was the worst possible punishment and I vowed I'd never disappoint her again. And I hadn't, not until today.

'I *will* fix this,' I said, a sudden fury bursting out of me. How dare he come into my life like a wrecking ball, destroying everything I hold dear?

Mum fell down dejectedly onto a chair. 'And how do you intend to do that?'

Despite everything, I foolishly believed that *she* would find the solution. Like she always had. In my mind, she was the adult and I was the child, so I naively hadn't expected the question and the onus to fall to me.

'I will not let him get away with this,' I said. 'I will track him down and make him pay for what he's done.'

Mum sat there, sadly shaking her head. 'It could have been worse,' she said, in barely more than a whisper. 'There could have been children involved.'

I pictured myself doubled up over the toilet, and suddenly wondered why I'd not realized that I was five days late. I instinctively touched my tummy, desperately trying to drown out the voice that said, *Maybe there are.*

PART 3

Present Day – Alice and Beth

30

Alice feels a churning in her stomach as she prepares to get out of the car. Her mum had done the school run for the past five days, as Alice had taken to her bed with a supposed virus. Nobody need know that she was in the midst of despair, devastated by the revelation that her beloved Tom had been having an affair. That he'd fathered a child with her best friend.

She checks her reflection in the rear-view mirror, barely able to recognize her sallow skin and sunken cheekbones.

'Okay Olivia, let's go,' she enthuses as much as she can.

The pair of them walk quickly, Alice with her head down and Olivia skipping to keep up.

'You're giving me a stitch,' she moans.

Alice catches sight of Beth's car parked up ahead and thinks about turning back. *I can't do this*, she says to herself. *But Livvy needs to go to school*, she counters in her own mind as she forces herself to keep walking.

'We need to talk,' a voice says, as Alice draws level with Beth's old Volkswagen.

Alice tugs on Olivia's hand and breaks into a half run.

'Alice, please,' calls Beth, a little louder. 'We can't pretend this isn't happening.'

'That's exactly what we're going to do,' says Alice, under her breath.

It's the only way she can bear to get up in the morning, because if she acknowledges the facts – that her dead husband and best friend betrayed her in the worst possible way – she is terrified of the damage it will do.

It didn't matter that Beth might not have known Tom was married. It didn't matter that she and Beth didn't even know each other then. The sense of deceitfulness still punctured her lungs, making her feel as if she can't breathe.

'This isn't going to go away,' says Beth as she catches up with Alice and Olivia.

The little girl looks up at her mum, puzzled as to why she's not listening to Beth.

'You're being very rude,' she says. 'Millie's mummy wants to talk to you.'

It's only then that Alice stops, dead in her tracks, and turns to face the woman who has taken away everything she knew to be true. She knows that Millie is standing beside Beth, but she cannot allow herself to look at her for fear that she will suddenly see Tom so clearly in her features that she will cry out. A very real pain is piercing her heart.

'Thank you,' says Beth calmly. The seconds stretch out like hours as the two women look at each other for the first time since Beth's admission. As soon as Alice had come round from her blackout, she'd insisted on getting up and driving home, despite the first aider at the gym telling her to stay where she was. For a moment, she thought she'd had the weirdest dream, but Beth's face peering into her bubble, like an ugly caricature, jolted her back into the real world. Alice had had to get as far away as possible, as quickly as possible, as panic descended on her. She couldn't remember how she'd got home or what anyone had said to her over the ensuing days. She had just laid in bed, with her head under the duvet, unhearing and unseeing as she grappled with the scale of the deception that had befallen her.

'I've been calling and calling you,' says Beth quietly.

'There's nothing to say,' says Alice, her voice nothing more than a squeak. She clears her throat, determined not to show her true pain.

'I had no idea my Thomas was your Tom,' says Beth. 'How could I have?'

'You should have made it your business,' chokes Alice, as tears immediately spring to her eyes. 'You must have known that the man you were . . . the man you were seeing, was married. How could you not have known that?'

'Because he was very good at hiding it,' says Beth. 'Don't forget, I've been wronged too in all of this. I thought the father of my—' She stops and looks down at Millie. Alice still refuses to follow her gaze.

SANDIE JONES

'Why don't you two go play?' Beth says to the girls. 'The bell will go in a minute.'

They both reach up to give their mum a kiss and run off. 'As naive as I now know myself to be,' Beth goes on, 'it didn't occur to me for a second that he was married.'

'But you said that you'd seen him with someone,' says Alice. 'That must have been me. Unless you're going to tell me there were others.'

It's the first time the thought occurs to Alice and she clutches at her chest.

Beth looks down to the ground. 'I don't know if the woman I saw was you. It all happened so quickly, I can't remember. She was blonde and beautiful, but I thought he was cheating on *me*. That *I* was the victim. If I'd known there was another woman, another family . . .'

'I'm not just *another* woman,' hisses Alice, all too aware of the other mothers around them. 'And we're not just *another* family. Tom was my husband and father to our much-loved daughter.'

'I'm sorry,' says Beth. 'But he was also Millie's father.'

Alice snorts in derision. 'He didn't even see Millie, for Christ's sake, so don't go making out he was Father of the Year.'

'But now I know why he left us so suddenly,' cries Beth.

'Did he even know you were pregnant?' Alice asks, her eyes narrowing as she looks at the nemesis she used to call her best friend. 'Did he know before he died?'

266

Beth shakes her head solemnly. 'I never got the chance to tell him. All this time I thought he'd been living the Life of Riley, with no thought to what he'd done to me, but deep down I knew he wouldn't have left me like that.' She looks at Alice before going on. 'We were too in love for him to just get up and go. Now I know it wasn't his choice and it makes me feel better.'

Alice feels the exact opposite. She hadn't thought she could feel any worse about Tom's death. She was sure she'd reached the bottom and had scratched her way back up again, leaving marks on the wall as she came. They served as a reminder of where she'd been and how she'd do anything to stop herself from ever going back there. But she could feel herself sliding back down into the pit of despair again, the pain just as great as when he died.

'How long did it go on for?' asks Alice, her voice cold.

'We met six months before I got pregnant and then he just disappeared.'

Alice racks her already exhausted brain, trying to work out the logistics. At first, she'd ruled it out as being a complete impossibility – a notion that could only be a million-to-one coincidence. But as the dates and the facts burrowed themselves under her skin, the probability of Beth's *Thomas* and her *Tom* being the same person had become too hard to ignore.

'I'm not going to do this here,' says Alice, turning and walking off.

'You can't just ignore it,' says Beth. 'We need to talk it through.'

Alice stops and turns around, her features hardened, her voice sounding unlike her own. 'We don't need to talk through anything. I was his wife. Sophia is his daughter. That will never change and that's all we need to discuss.'

She rushes off towards her car, leaving Beth standing stock still on the kerb.

'I'm back,' Alice calls out, as cheerily as she can manage as she opens the front door.

'Hey,' shouts Nathan. 'I'm upstairs.'

She slowly makes her way up the stairs, taking every step to fix her smile onto her face. She doesn't know whether she's doing it for Nathan or Sophia's benefit.

'You okay?' she asks, poking her head around Sophia's bedroom door.

'Mmm,' she answers, without looking up from her mobile phone.

Alice waits, hoping for a more eloquent response from her intelligent, well-educated daughter. But she's left staring at the top of her head. Again.

'I really think we need to talk about this whole phone business . . .' starts Alice, but Sophia is already rolling her eyes. 'I would also appreciate a little respect.'

'Yes Mum,' she says, placing it on her lap and sitting up straighter. Alice is sure she can see her hand itching to pick it up again.

'I don't mind you using it for normal communication between your friends, your *real* friends, but not for the seven hundred you've got on Facebook or whatever it is.'

Sophia stifles a smirk. 'Nobody's on Facebook anymore. It's Snapchat.'

'Okay, well whatever it is, I'd prefer you to spend your time on real life and not the made-up one on social media.'

'I don't make up anything,' she protests.

'I hope you don't, but everybody else on there probably does.'

She tuts, and Alice shoots her a look.

'These people's lives are fake,' says Alice, picking up the offending item. Sophia looks at it as if it's a baby that her mother is about to throw into a road. 'They're not lives that you can aspire to because they're not real, and I think it's putting you kids under an awful lot of pressure to *be* a certain way and *look* a certain way.'

'I don't take any notice of that sh—' Alice raises her eyebrows to stop her daughter finishing her sentence. She looks away sheepishly. 'There's some useful stuff on here too, it's not all rubbish and fake.'

'Give me one example,' Alice urges.

Sophia holds out her hand and Alice reluctantly gives her phone back to her. She taps and swipes away. 'So, for example, I can see where all my friends are.'

'How is that useful?' Alice blurts out, a little louder

than intended. Though she can't help but wonder whether, if there'd been such a tool when she was married to Tom, it might have alerted her to him having an affair with Beth. But then she thinks that if such a thing *had* existed, they might have been able to find Tom on the mountain, and he would have come home to her with only a few bruises to show for his misadventure. *Would he have left me anyway?* she asks herself. *Would he have gone to Beth as soon as he found out she was pregnant and left the family that he already had, to be with her?*

She banishes the thought, because it is no longer important. What she'd believed to be true for the last ten years is a lie and she hates herself for living half the life she could have been living. She could have been anyone, could have gone anywhere; instead she has been paralysed, forever fearful that something would happen to a loved one, or take her away from those who needed her.

Well, no more. She is going to be the person she lost all those years ago; live with abandonment, shake off the paranoia that has plagued her for so long. She's going to love the husband she's got, not the one she lost. She's going to be the wife Nathan should have had all this time, not the hollowed-out version she's mostly been.

'Look,' says Sophia patiently as she shows her phone to Alice. 'This is how I can check out where all my friends are.' Alice screws her eyes up to see miniature cartoon characters dotted across a map. 'There's Hannah. She's in a car going along Upwood Road.'

Alice looks a little closer and is astonished to see a blonde-haired avatar sitting in something resembling a toy car.

'That's insane!' exclaims Alice. 'You can actually see what everyone is doing?'

'Sometimes, yeah. So, there's Jack and he's listening to music.'

A boy wearing headphones is grinning back at her.

'And there's me!'

Sophia closes in on a girl with bunches, smiling out of the very house they're sitting in.

Alice can barely find the words. 'That is so wrong, on every level. I don't want you on there.'

'Mum, everyone's on it.'

'I don't care. I don't want your whereabouts being advertised to whoever's watching.'

'You can turn it on and off.'

'Well then turn yours off. Wait, who's that next to you?'

'That's Nathan!' Sophia laughs.

'What's *he* doing on there?' asks Alice, her voice high and taut. 'Why does he need to be on there?'

'I put him on,' says Sophia, her eyes alight with mischief.

Alice looks at her daughter, wide-eyed. 'Well, you'd better turn his location off, or whatever it is you need to do. I don't want either of you sharing it with the world.'

'I can't take Nathan off – I have to do that from his phone.'

Alice is about to call him but thinks better of it, as she acknowledges that knowing his location might come in useful one day. Though as soon as the thought enters her head she forces herself to dismiss it. 'Okay, well, do whatever you have to do.'

Sophia nods conciliatorily and Alice walks towards the door, but her head immediately fills with negative thoughts. She's better when she's talking – she knows that much now – it gives her something to concentrate on. It's the gaps in between that allow panic to set in. She fights against every fibre in her body that is telling her not to do what she's about to do.

'We'll be going to the airport in fifteen minutes,' she says, clearing her throat. 'You sure you're going to be all right?' She resists the overwhelming urge to throw herself onto Sophia's bed and cling to her.

If she could only pretend that this is just another ordinary day, when her former husband was who she thought he was, and she wasn't about to get on a plane and fly thousands of miles away, she'd be fine. *What if it crashes? What if I die? What if the children need me?* The irrational thoughts reverberate around her head as she turns to look at her daughter, wondering if it's the last time she's going to see her beautiful face. *No*, she chastises herself. *I am not that woman anymore.*

'Grandma will be here in time to make you tea,' she says in a bid to drown out the negative thoughts.

Sophia rolls her eyes. 'I don't understand why she has to be here. I'm nearly sixteen – I can look after myself.'

'That may be so, but there's Livvy to think of,' says Alice, hanging on to the door for support. 'It's not fair for you to have the responsibility.'

'Well, why doesn't she go to Grandma's and I stay here?'

Alice sighs heavily. 'We've been through this enough times. Will you please just do as you're told? You know the plan, and that's the end of it.'

'When are you going to start treating me like a grown-up?' Sophia huffs as Alice walks out.

'When you start acting like one,' says Alice, under her breath, acutely aware that she sounds like her own mother twenty years ago.

She goes into her bedroom, where Nathan is packing, and can't help but notice the difference between their organization skills. Whilst her case is lying open with its contents hastily chosen and messily arranged, Nathan has laid out his outfits on the bed, each with the corresponding pair of shoes and colour-coordinated accessories.

'Hi darling,' he says, pulling her towards him. 'All okay?'

She smiles tightly.

'You sure you want to do this?' he asks as he kisses her.

'Absolutely,' she says.

'What time's your mum coming?'

Alice looks at her watch. 'She's going to pick Livvy up from school and then do the girls' tea here.'

'And you're okay with it all?' He hesitates before going on, as if fearful of opening a can of worms. 'About leaving the girls?'

'Yes,' she says, ignoring the weight that is sitting on her chest. 'No problem.'

'And we're going to have fun, as well as see to business?' he says.

'Of course,' says Alice, and she means it, because she can't remember the last time she let her hair down. She might need to up her medication in order to get herself there, but she'll get there – she's determined to.

'I can't believe the turnaround in you,' he says, kissing her on the nose. 'One minute you're adamant that AT Designs should save money by holding back on our expansion plans, and the next you're offering a million pounds for a site in Japan that you've not even seen. What changed?'

She could tell him. She could say that the man she's been doing it all for, to keep his memory alive, not wishing to let him down, was nothing but a cheating bastard. But she doesn't want to give Tom the credit. She wants Nathan to think that what she's about to do is what *she* wants to do, rather than having been dictated to from beyond the grave.

'I think you're right,' she says. 'It's about time we put ourselves on the map, and if we have to come out of our comfort zone to do it, then I'm prepared to take that chance.'

'I love you, Mrs Davies,' he says.

'And I love you, Mr Davies,' she replies, without wishing for a second that she was still Mrs Evans.

31

'It doesn't look big enough, does it?' says Alice in astonishment at the sliver of barren land she's standing in front of.

'You'd be amazed what they can fit on this,' says Nathan, 'especially here in Tokyo. They're used to building tall and thin, because space is always at such a premium. They just go upwards.'

'So, it's going to be five floors?' she asks.

'Yes,' says Nathan. 'It'll be the same height as the athletes' village over there. We can't go higher than that.'

Alice shields her eyes from the midday sun as she looks across the river to the vast, brand-new white block standing proudly amongst the cranes and metal-framed structures that will create the Olympic site.

'This is a prime piece of real estate,' says Alice, excitedly. 'Look how close it is.'

Nathan smiles. 'I know. It may look like a dusty car park, but this is going to be in such huge demand. I can't actually believe that we're getting it for such a good price.'

Alice looks over to the towering blocks beyond, where columns of mirror-like windows appear seemingly endless against a blue sky. She feels a knot forming in her stomach. Can they really take on the big boys in a country so far away? In a culture so far removed from their own?

'We can do this,' says Nathan, as if reading her mind. He looks at his watch and tugs gently on her hand, beckoning her back to the waiting car. 'We're going to be late if we don't get a move on.'

The chill of the air conditioning hits her as she gets in and the suited chauffeur offers her a cold towel. She accepts gratefully and lays it gently on her face, careful not to disturb the make-up she's so meticulously applied. She'd caught sight of the platinum ring on her right hand as she put her mascara on earlier, its diamonds no longer an indelible link to Tom, but a nod to his affair with Beth. After all, who's to say it hadn't been meant as a present for *her*?

As Alice had acknowledged that she would never know, she'd ripped it off and thrown it carelessly into her handbag. She had somehow felt different without it, as if something had changed within her. How could it not have? The realization that she'd lived a lie for most of her adult life – the ten years spent with Tom and the ten years spent without him – hit home. A life based on deception and deceit. But now she was finally stepping out of the shadows, a complete woman, no longer peppered with holes that the bullets of the past had left.

She checks her reflection in her compact mirror and wipes the merest hint of under-eye smudging away. Her bright-red lipstick, that matches her blouse, still stands the test of time.

'You look gorgeous,' says Nathan, taking hold of her hand and giving it a squeeze.

By the time they reach the lawyer's office, on the twenty-fourth floor of one of the skyscrapers Alice had seen from the Olympic site, her carefully applied mask of confidence is on the wane.

'Don't desert me now,' says Nathan, noticing. 'We can do this.'

She runs her tongue around the top of her teeth, the dryness in her mouth threatening to stick her lips to her gums.

'Mr Nathan,' says a petite Japanese woman through a face mask. 'A pleasure to meet with you. Mr Yahamoto is here. Please come this way.'

They're ushered into a corner room where its occupant is pacing the floor with his phone at his ear. He offers the merest of smiles before signalling for them to sit down at the glass boardroom table.

Feeling like a child playing in an adult's world, Alice forces herself to inhale, long and slow. She shifts her stance, sitting taller and pushing her shoulders back, hoping that the gesture will give her more of a presence.

'Hai. Hai,' says the man in front of them, in a clipped tone, before abruptly ending the call.

'Ah, Mr Nathan,' he says whilst bowing, 'a pleasure to meet with you finally. And this must be Miss Alice.'

Alice smiles and offers as much of a bow as she can from a sitting position.

'How are you enjoying Tokyo?' he says, handing them both handleless cups. 'Please – some green tea.' Nathan eyes the murky liquid dubiously, whilst Alice accepts gratefully.

'So, is everything good to go?' asks Nathan. 'Are we ready to exchange?'

'Yes, I have notification that we are almost there,' says the lawyer.

Nathan taps his hand against the side of his chair impatiently – Alice can hear his wedding ring knocking the metal arm.

His obvious agitation is making Alice even more nervous than she is already. She tries to bat away the uncomfortable sensation rising within her, the creeping tentacles that are snaking up from her stomach and into her chest. *Can we just get this over and done with before I change my mind?* she says silently.

'Ah-ha,' says Mr Yahamoto in answer, making her jump. 'The email is in. We're ready to go.'

The printer in the corner of the room spews into action and he goes to it, retrieving the document he was waiting on.

'So, here we have the papers for you to sign,' he says, carefully lining them up in order as he presents them to Alice.

'As I understand it, you are the sole owner of AT Designs?'

'Yes,' she says croakily, before clearing her throat. 'Yes.'

'And Mr Nathan has explained everything to you regarding the covenant?'

Alice looks to her husband beside her, who nods and puts his hand on hers.

'Excellent. So, I need you to sign here, here and here,' says Mr Yahamoto, demonstrating with a pen, before he offers it to her. She declines and reaches into her bag on the floor for her 'lucky pen', the one Tom had given her to celebrate signing the contracts on their first house. It was the one she'd used for anything important since, superstitiously believing that it would bring her joy and luck. Her fingers clasp around its embossed silver case, feeling the weight as she lifts it out.

'Could I borrow your pen after all?' she says to Mr Yahamoto, apologetically. She places her pen on the table, watching it wobble as it finds its place.

'Of course,' he says, handing her his bog-standard biro.

She scrawls her signature wherever a pencilled cross is marked.

'So, this signifies that you have now exchanged, and ten per cent will be transferred to the vendor.'

Alice smiles tightly, still toying with the cheap biro in her hand. *How significant*, she thinks, *that the most monumental of decisions for Alice and Tom Designs has been signed off with a pen other than the one Tom gave me.*

'Completion will take place next week, but we have all the papers we need to do that, so I do not anticipate there being any problems.'

'It's been a pleasure,' says Alice, standing up from the table and offering an outstretched hand.

'The pleasure is all mine.' The lawyer bows, then holds the door open for them. 'Ah, Miss Alice,' he calls out, just as she steps into the lift. 'Your pen. You forgot your pen.'

'Keep it,' she says as the doors close.

32

The champagne has gone to Alice's head. She didn't feel it before, but now that she's sitting on the toilet, its seat heated, she's finding it difficult to focus. She's trying to concentrate on the back of the door, but it's moving, as if she's on board a storm-tossed boat. She reaches out for the toilet paper, but it's not quite where she thought it was – her hand a few centimetres short.

'Shit,' she says out loud, wondering how many drinks she's had and wishing she'd had just one less. She likes the way alcohol numbs her nerve endings, which normally happens sometime between glasses three and four. But she feels like she's had a bottle, and some.

Then she remembers the tablets she took to calm her nerves on the plane, not thinking for a second that the double dosage would do anything other than send her to sleep, which they had. But now she can't help but wonder if it was a good idea to drink with them in her system.

The operating instructions for the toilet seem to be swaying in front of her eyes and she snorts with laughter every time she pushes a button and it does everything apart from flush.

'You have had *far* too much to drink,' laughs Nathan as she weaves her way back to the table.

'I thought we were celebrating,' she slurs, sitting down heavily on the chair being pulled out for her.

He reaches across the table, taking hold of one of her hands. 'Shall we go to the room?'

'Ooh, is that an invitation, Mr Darcy?' she asks loudly, starting to get up again. The heel of her shoe buckles beneath her ankle and Nathan moves in to steady her.

She knows she's lost the ability to moderate her volume level. 'When I get you upstairs, I'm going to—'

'Ssh,' laughs Nathan. 'I'm not sure everyone in the restaurant needs to know.'

When they get out of the lift she shrugs off his attempt to steer her down the corridor towards their room and leans against the wall as he struggles with the key card.

'I'm going to keep you up all night,' she says, moving towards him and grabbing hold of the lapel on his jacket. She wants this, *needs* this. It had been weeks since they'd had sex.

'I want you to make love to me like you've never done before,' she says as she kisses him, her tongue teasing his, her teeth biting down softly on his lips.

'What's brought this on?' asks Nathan, arching an eyebrow.

She can't tell him that for almost ten years, it's been Tom who's been at the forefront of her mind. Wondering if he can see her, refusing to really let herself go, for fear that it will hurt him to see her give herself to another man.

She hates herself for only half loving Nathan all this time, because that's what she's done. Whilst she has been pining for a man who slept with another woman, fathered another child, she'd missed out on giving herself, in all entirety, to the man who deserved it most.

'I've been such a fool,' she says, as tears well up in her eyes. 'Will you ever forgive me?'

'For what?' Nathan asks warily. 'What have you done?'

'Nothing, that's the problem,' she says. 'I've not done enough.'

He looks at her quizzically as she pushes him against the back of the door, her hands reaching down to the zip of his trousers. It's hardly surprising that he's ready for her and his tongue responds, his own need for release evidently as urgent as hers.

'What was *that* all about?' he says afterwards, as they lie on the plush carpet.

'That's how it should have been all this time,' says Alice, her own body still shuddering with the after-effects.

Nathan rolls onto his side to face her. 'What's changed?'

'Everything,' she says, honestly. 'Everything feels different.'

His brow furrows. 'Because of the deal? Or because you've been brave enough to come away?'

She almost expects him to say, *I told you that the*

world wouldn't end, and silently thanks him when he doesn't.

'I just think that this is the start of a new phase in my life,' she says, relieved that the drunken fog is beginning to clear.

'Well, this is a new approach I could grow to love,' he says, smiling. 'If it means sex like that . . .'

Alice laughs. 'I mean it, things are going to change. I'm not always the wife you deserve, the mother my children need or the businesswoman I know I can be.'

'I think you do a pretty good job,' he says, 'considering.'

'Considering what, though?' she asks. 'That I had a breakdown when my first husband died?'

'I didn't mean—'

'I know what you mean,' she says, 'and I agree with you. I don't want what happened to define me. I'm sick and tired of being that person. Even when I pretend that I'm not, I know that deep down I still am.'

He nods.

'So, I just want to say that I'm sorry, and from now on I'll give myself to you wholeheartedly.' She leans in to kiss him. 'I love you,' she says, before inviting him to take more.

'I could get used to this new wife I've got,' he says, as he lifts himself up off the floor. 'But just let me go to the toilet first.'

Alice sighs and watches his naked body as he walks

into the bathroom as if seeing him for who he truly is, for the first time. She's lying, sated and content, when Nathan's phone pings from the inside pocket of the jacket he'd thrown to the floor in his urgency to get his clothes off. She wouldn't normally look, but it might be the girls trying to get hold of them. Forcing herself to stay calm, curbing any irrational thoughts that something must have happened to them, she reaches across to retrieve it.

She looks at the message, then looks again, her eyes blurring the words beyond recognition. She thinks she knows what it says, but closes her eyes, to give them a chance to unsee it.

I need you. Now xx

The blood that so recently felt warm as it coursed its way around her body turns icy cold. She scrolls up and down, looking for any evidence of who she's fighting against in the battle for her husband's affections. But there's nothing, other than the anonymous phone number it's been sent from.

She hears the toilet flush and needs to think quickly, but her heart is racing so fast that it's making her hands shake. She fumbles to take a screenshot and sends it to herself, before deleting the message she had read and the one she sent. Nathan comes out of the bathroom just as she manages to put the phone back into his jacket.

'Are you still on the floor?' he asks, laughing. He

holds a hand out to pull her up and it takes all her strength not to recoil. How could he profess his undying love? How could he swear that he's not having an affair, when all along he's been sneaking around, living two truths? How could he let her sign the deal today, knowing that he'd lied to make it happen? The thought makes her feel nauseous.

'So how about we do that all over again?' he breathes into her ear as he stands behind her, guiding her towards the bed. She can feel him, but her desire of just a few moments ago has been replaced by a rage so incandescent, so ferocious, that she fears she might do something rash if the wrong instrument should fall into her hands. She clenches her fists in an effort to stop herself tearing him limb from limb.

'I'm tired,' she manages, through gritted teeth.

'Well, the new you didn't last very long,' laughs Nathan, as he gently lowers her onto the bed. 'I'm pretty wired, would you mind if I went to the bar?'

She's sure she's stopped breathing. Was he honestly seeking her permission to cheat? Because that was surely what he was about to do. She had no idea who the woman was, but it seemed as if she could be here, in Japan. She tried to put aside how warped that made Nathan. What had he gained from dragging her all the way over here apart from getting her to sign the contracts, which she could have done in London? Had he brought his wife *and* his mistress to satisfy his sick ego?

She shivers involuntarily as she recalls how she'd waxed lyrical to Nathan about everything she'd done wrong, how she wanted to change and give him what he deserved. He must have been laughing at her the whole time. What a fool she's been.

As soon as Nathan's out the door, Alice gets up and frantically goes to the minibar, breaking the miniature Bombay Sapphire cap in her impatience. She doesn't even think twice about drinking it directly from the bottle. It burns her throat as she pours it into her mouth neat, grimacing at the taste.

She knows it won't bring answers, but it makes things just a little bit easier to bear until she makes her next move.

Her phone is sitting on the bedside table, its new content making her feel as if it's somehow complicit in Nathan's chicanery. She picks it up, staring unmoving at the screensaver picture of Sophia and Olivia poking their tongues out. Negative thoughts crowd her head-space, each battling for supremacy. It feels as if her whole world is balancing on a precipice. She needs to talk to someone. She needs to talk to Beth.

Her thumb hovers over the number, stored under *Your Best Friend* in her contacts. Alice can't help but smile at the memory of Beth changing it, unbeknownst to her, when she went to the ladies in the pub. The next morning, on her way to school, *Your Best Friend* had lit up the phone screen. Alice hadn't been able to get out of the car for laughing. What she wouldn't give to be laughing with Beth now. Couldn't they just go back to how they were? Pretend it never happened?

Alice dials, before immediately stopping the call, choosing instead to log on to Facebook in the hope that Beth has posted a cryptic message that will somehow make everything all right again. All she needs to say is that she got it wrong, that of course it's not the same Tom, how could it be? But there's nothing other than an advert for the school fete this coming Saturday. Alice remembers she'd promised to man the face-painting stall, but that wouldn't be happening now.

With a shaking hand, she types in Tom Evans and waits as it collates all the one thousand and forty-five Tom Evanses listed. She hopes and expects that since her phone call to Facebook to inform them of the error, there will now be one less. But his face is still there, staring out at her as if everything is how she believed it to be, and all she wants to do is reach into her phone and gouge his eyes out.

She clicks on his profile and a new photo fills the screen. It feels as if she's been kicked in the chest – the air rushes out of her as she looks at it through a blurry haze. An attractive woman, whom she's never seen before, has her arms wrapped protectively around a toddler. The pair, both with fur-lined hoods and red-tipped noses, pose against the backdrop of a snow-covered mountain. Below, Tom has written, My Girls – My World.

33

'He can't be alive,' says Alice out loud, still poleaxed on the bed. 'He just *can't* be.'

But then she remembers that this time last week, she'd also thought it was impossible for him to have loved another woman and fathered another child.

She shakes herself down. She can't deal with this right now. She needs to find Nathan.

She moves around the room, picking up the clothes that had been carelessly discarded as their lovemaking had built in momentum. The lace knickers that had lent themselves perfectly to being peeled off by Nathan's teeth now look sordid, the expensive black dress that he'd sexily unzipped, teasing her back with his fingertips as he did so, now makes her feel cheap as she slips it back on.

She squeezes her feet back into her three-inch heels in a desperate bid to get out of the confines of the room, where the air feels like it's being sucked out. She doesn't know whether she wants to find Nathan or kill Tom a second time as she walks unsteadily down the corridor, forcing a smile at the hotel employee in the lift.

If she knew where she was going, and what she was

going to do when she got there, it would help, but right now, all she knows is that her paranoid fears about her husband having an affair have finally been proven, and she needs to decide what she's going to do about it.

The bar is just as busy as when she'd sat there enjoying a bottle of champagne with Nathan before dinner. She'd felt excited then, finally buoyed by optimism for the future. Now, she has a lump in her chest and a sickening sensation swirling in her stomach.

Despite her trepidation, she strides in with her head held high, trying desperately hard not to look how she feels; panic-stricken. She surreptitiously takes in everyone there, not sure if she wants to see Nathan or not. If he's here, she will need to go to him and ask what the hell is going on. If he's not, she's got an even bigger problem on her hands. Where is he? And who's he with?

She thinks back to the earring and bouquet, and the bill from this very same hotel. She'd let Nathan convince her that the charges for cocktails, room service and a couples massage had been a mistake. He'd promised her that he'd never seen the earring before and that the florist delivering the bouquet was a million-to-one co-incidence. How had she allowed herself to be played? Maybe because knowing the truth about Tom had made her look at Nathan in a whole new light. One in which she refused to believe that he was like her cheating first husband.

The realization that one man she loved would do that

to her is hard enough to take. Now that she's faced with the prospect that *both* of them have makes her question what *she's* doing wrong. All she's ever done is love them the best way she knows how. How could that not be enough?

She holds her breath as she looks around the bar, willing Nathan to be there, because right now, that is the lesser of the two evils. If he isn't, she doesn't want to go where her mind will undoubtedly take her. She doesn't want to acknowledge that whoever just sent him that text might be in Japan.

Does she live here? Is this where he met her? Has she got something to do with the site? Is that why he's so keen to do it, so that he can spend more time here, be with her, knowing that Alice wouldn't be keen to travel? She wonders if her announcement that she was going to come had surprised him. He wouldn't have been expecting it, that was for sure. Had she scuppered his plans? His chance to be with *her*? Perhaps not, because as she fruitlessly scours the faces in the bar, she's hit by the realization that he's gone to her anyway.

She orders a Baileys with ice – the first drink she can think of when the bartender asks. The man playing Sinatra on the piano looks over and gives a cheery nod. She smiles weakly and sips her liqueur, resisting the urge to knock it all back.

Despite being in a strange city, on the other side of the world, where Alice's imagination could so easily concoct a horror story about what could have happened to Nathan, there's no part of her that's worried about his safety. Perhaps because deep down, she'd hazard a guess that it's not his safety that's being compromised – it's his morals.

'May I?' asks a gentleman, indicating the stool next to Alice.

'Of course,' she says, smiling, her subconscious having already registered in that split second that he's attractive.

'Can I buy you a drink?' he asks in an American accent.

Her first instinct is to say no, but then she wonders, why not? Why shouldn't she accept a drink from this handsome man? Why shouldn't she enjoy his company and flirt with him a little? She might go even further if the opportunity arises. Panic rises within her as she contemplates the idea of going to bed with the man in front of her. As exciting as the prospect may be, she cannot even begin to understand how people who are married, who are supposed to love their partners, can cheat. Her heart palpitates at the mere thought of it.

'I'll have a G and T please,' she says. 'A double.'

The barman smiles and sets about slicing a cucumber into a crystal bowl, its cool, fresh fragrance finding its way across the bar.

'Are you staying here or just visiting?' asks the man, tilting his head towards the opening into the lobby.

'We— I'm staying here,' Alice says, her interest piqued

enough to change her story, if only to see how far this game can go.

'I see,' he says, his piercing blue eyes never leaving hers. She wonders if he can see straight through her.

'What about you?' she asks, crossing her legs and flicking her blonde hair over her shoulder. 'Are you staying here?'

'Yep, just for tonight. I've been trying to sleep for four hours, but I'm battling horrific jet lag and the harder I try, the more it eludes me.'

'Where have you flown in from?'

'I've worked a double shift, flying from New York to Shanghai and Shanghai to here.'

She can't even compute the geography involved. 'So, you're cabin crew?'

He nods modestly. 'Pilot.'

She smiles. *Does he think I was born yesterday?*

Beth unexpectedly springs into her mind and Alice feels a pang in her chest. She remembers Beth telling her that she'd always fancied the idea of dating a pilot. 'Imagine that uniform,' she'd breathed, as they had adopted the downward dog pose in their yoga class. 'Imagine him walking in with the cap under his arm and picking me up to the sound of "Up Where We Belong" . . .'

As Alice had tried to picture the scene, which she'd been able to conjure up all too easily, she'd lost concentration and collapsed into a fit of giggles. 'But they're never what you think they're going to be, are they?'

'Are you speaking from experience?' Beth had squealed in astonishment.

'No,' Alice had replied in mock horror. 'I mean, whenever you hear them on the tannoy on the plane, they always sound so gorgeously smooth and authoritative, and then when you get off, there's a puny little fella who looks far too young to be flying a metal tube thirty-six thousand feet up in the sky. They're not all Richard Gere, is all I'm saying.'

But looking at the man in front of her now, Alice notes that he isn't that far off. His dark hair curls ever so slightly at the collar and his steely eyes follow the barman's every move.

'Can I get a Scotch and soda?' he asks.

Alice raises her glass to him and he gives a smiling nod.

'Will the Scotch do the trick?' she asks. 'Get you to sleep?'

'I'd like to think so, but right now all I want it to do is stop my eyeballs from burning.'

He smiles, and she laughs a little louder than she'd intended. She pulls herself up, then wonders why she should.

'I don't know what's worse – the inability to sleep, or the need to sleep far longer than you're permitted to. You'd think I'd be used to it by now.'

'How long have you been a pilot?' Alice asks, showing herself to be a willing player in his game.

'Fifteen years,' he says, with a glint in his eye. 'So, what brings you here?'

'Business, actually.' As soon as she says it, she's overcome with panic as she remembers that she's signed contracts for a site worth a million pounds. With a faithful husband and business partner by her side, it had felt manageable; nerve-wracking, but manageable. Now, adrift in the ocean, without Nathan's anchor, the thought leaves her nauseous.

'What kind of business?' he asks.

'I'm in property,' says Alice, clearing her throat and sitting up straight in an attempt to shrug off the impostor syndrome that always seems to linger whenever she achieves something she doesn't feel she deserves. 'Interiors and development,' she adds, taking ownership of the words this time.

'Interesting,' he says. 'Are you buying or selling?'

'I've just bought a site today,' she says. 'I'm building twenty-eight apartments on it.'

He looks like he's been given an electric shock. 'Wow, really?'

'You seem shocked,' she says lightly. 'Did you not realize that women are able to do that in this day and age?' She didn't dare let on that without Nathan, she would never have entertained the idea. She brushes off the insecurities that snake through her and tries to silence the voice that says, *And without Nathan, you'll never complete.*

'Not at all,' he says carefully. 'I'm just genuinely impressed. Does that make me a male chauvinist?'

Alice shakes her head.

'So, you're doing this all on your own?' he asks, stepping into dangerous territory again.

'Without a man, you mean? Well, it's my company, my talent, my money.' She didn't feel the need to share that most of the funds had been raised by a loan from the bank.

'Well, hats off to you,' he said, holding up his tumbler. 'And I'd say that to a woman, man or child. It takes a brave person to do what you're doing, especially in a market as competitive as here. I'm in awe.'

And so you should be, she says silently, before asking herself why she's even contemplating not being able to go ahead without Nathan being on board.

'So, I'm guessing you're from England?'

Alice nods as she takes a sip of her drink. 'London.'

'I love British women,' he says. 'The accent drives me wild. There's just something so damn sexy about it.'

'We can talk real dirty as well,' she says.

'Oh yeah . . . ?' he says, encouraging her to go further.

Alice raises her eyebrows suggestively before leaning in to whisper, 'Mud, Dirt, Soil . . .'

The man throws his head back and laughs. 'You Brits have also got a wicked sense of humour.'

Alice smiles, her eyes boring into his. She'd forgotten what it felt like to flirt; to feel attractive and desired.

The power it gave her was an aphrodisiac in itself. Maybe she was now beginning to understand how unfaithful partners were able to let their guard down. Was it really this easy?

'Look, I don't normally do this,' he says. 'But –' she smiles sweetly, pretending that she believes him – 'would you like to join me for a drink in my room?'

'For just a drink?'

He smiles, and her insides flip over.

If her husband wasn't cheating and lying to her, then she wouldn't be in this position, but he is, so . . .

The thought of what Nathan might be doing right now breaks her heart, and as she looks at the handsome man in front of her, she wonders why she shouldn't allow this stranger to glue a little of it back together. *Would going to bed with him make me feel better?* she thinks. *Would I feel that I'd somehow got one over on Nathan? That we'd be on a level par?*

The pilot leans in close. 'Is that a yes or a no?'

She locks eyes with him. 'What's your room number?'

'1106,' he replies.

'I'll meet you there in five minutes.'

He takes his glass and Alice watches him as he walks out of the bar. Every fibre in her body is on high alert, even the tips of her fingers are tingling. She forces herself to stay where she is, to calmly finish her drink, all the time counting loudly in her head to silence the nerves that are circling in her stomach.

'Can I get the bill please?' she asks the barman.

'Mr Anthony has already signed for it, madam.'

Slick. He's obviously done this before.

She lowers herself off the stool, careful not to make eye contact with anyone in case she sees their disapproving expression. She smooths down her dress as she walks through the lobby, pretending that what she's about to do is perfectly normal. It must be, because her husband does it with no trouble whatsoever. In fact, both her husbands seemed to share a similar lack of conscience.

As she waits for the lift, she can't determine whether her body is shaking with nerves or fear. She looks at herself in the highly polished gold doors and is taken aback by the reflection. There's a smudge of mascara around her eyes, and she wets a finger to rub it away. She pinches at her cheeks and watches as the blood instantly rushes to colour her pallid skin. She ruffles her feathered fringe and tucks one side of her hair behind her ear.

Forcing herself to take deep breaths, she walks slowly along the low-lit hallway, her heels sinking into the plush carpet. Just as she draws level with the door, it swings open and he's standing there, his eyes wide.

'There you are!' exclaims Nathan. 'I was just about to send out a search party.'

'I got a second wind,' she says, brusquely. 'I couldn't sleep.'

'Now you know how *I* felt,' he says.

'Where have you been?' Alice asks, as she steps out of her shoes. She can't bring herself to look at him for fear she'll see the truth.

'In the bar,' he says, without missing a beat. 'But if I'd known you were awake I would have stayed here and carried on where we left off.'

He comes up behind her as she stands at the dressing table taking her earrings out.

'You were incredible,' he whispers into her ear.

Alice closes her eyes as he kisses her neck, imagining that it's the man in the bar. When she opens them to see Nathan, she can't help but feel duped.

34

By the next morning, Alice has made a decision. In order for her to go into battle, she needs to know who she's fighting against. Nathan, Alice has decided overnight, isn't going anywhere. Why would he, when his whole life is with her? He'd lose his home, his kids, his job, the lifestyle to which he's become accustomed, for what? A sleazy bit of rough on the side? It's easier for Alice to think this way, believing she's in control, and can dictate the outcome. Because if she allows any other scenario to play out in her mind, she simply wouldn't be able to function.

So she needs to find out who the threat to her family is, and once she does, she'll know what to do about it. But in the meantime, she's going to try her damnedest to be the wife and mother she needs to be to stop her world from going off-kilter. Though that doesn't mean she's going to give her all to her philandering husband; she slips out of bed just as he moves towards her with an outstretched arm.

She takes a quick shower and puts her hair up into a messy top-knot – there's no point in doing anything else when the humidity outside turns even the sleekest style into a ball of frizz. She knows she's trying to keep her mind occupied – to stop it from alternating between Tom and Nathan, asking the questions she so desperately wants to know the answers to.

But what will she do with the answers once she has them, if they're not the ones she wants? Is Tom still alive, living happily with his new family? Had he set the whole thing up? But then why would he be so audacious as to continue using his real name? Who is Nathan having an affair with? Will it make a difference if it's someone she knows? Will she stay if he promises it didn't mean anything? Will it crucify her if he says he's fallen in love? She can't possibly say how she'll react without knowing what she's dealing with.

It pains Alice to admit it, but Beth had been right all along. She'd had a sixth sense that Nathan was cheating, probably because she'd had it happen to her and knew the signs to look for. But then Alice pulls herself up at the stark realization that, in fact, Beth's partner *hadn't* been unfaithful to her. Tom was already married. It was Alice he was unfaithful to, not Beth. The intense fury that she'd tried so hard to contain was in danger of boiling over.

She remembers listening to Beth over and over as she'd relived their intense love affair, revealing their most intimate moments against the backdrop of its sudden demise.

'How could he do it to me?' Beth had cried as Alice

held her. 'I thought we were everything to each other. He told me he loved me and never wanted to be without me.'

Alice could even recall asking Beth if he might have been married.

'There's no way,' she'd said abruptly, seemingly offended by the suggestion. 'He used to stay over. How could he do that if he had a wife and, God forbid, kids at home?'

Alice stops buttoning up her shirt. He'd stayed over? So it *couldn't* have been Tom. But as fast as her brain wants to grab onto the tiniest semblance of hope, it removes itself from her grasp just as quickly, as she acknowledges that Tom had often been away with work. She laughs wryly at the memory of him going backwards and forwards to Dublin, in a supposed attempt to win new business. Had the client even existed? Had the whole set-up been an elaborate ruse to be with Beth?

She pictures Tom kissing her and Sophia goodbye at the front door, with his overnight holdall in his hand.

'I wish I didn't have to do this,' he'd say.

'So do I, but it'll be good for business,' Alice would reply. 'So go make it worth our while.'

He'd look back at them forlornly, like a lamb going to slaughter, and Alice used to feel a little piece of her heart break each time. Now, she wonders, how long it had taken him to get his game face on and get round to Beth's. She imagines it was only a matter of minutes.

SANDIE JONES

Alice does all that she can not to blanch when Nathan takes her hand as they walk down to breakfast. He sits down and orders a coffee whilst Alice heads to the buffet that is laid out along one wall of the huge room. She's debating between fruit or cereal when a male voice behind her says, 'I missed you last night.'

Taking her time to turn around, assuming that whoever it is must be talking to someone else, her mouth drops open and a thousand words crowd the space in her brain as she's faced with a uniformed pilot. He looks like the man from a dream she thinks she's had.

'I'm sorry . . .' she starts, without really knowing where she's going with it.

'Don't be,' he says, smiling. 'It happens all the time. I get stood up by beautiful women every night of the week.'

Somehow, she doubts that. 'I'm not here on my own,' she says, feeling like a schoolgirl caught playing truant.

'I know,' he says, his eyes avoiding hers as he picks up what looks like granola in a glass pot. 'I saw you walking in with your husband.'

Alice's cheeks flush and her pulse quickens as she scans the room, desperately trying to remember where they'd been seated.

'Anyway, it was very nice to meet you,' says the pilot. 'And good luck with that venture of yours.' He continues along the buffet without missing a beat.

Her heart's done exactly the opposite as she sees Nathan heading towards her.

'What are you having, sweetheart?' he asks, as he literally rubs shoulders with the man Alice could have had sex with last night.

She *could* have done, perhaps *should* have done, but she hadn't. Nathan, on the other hand, most probably had, as he certainly wasn't in the bar where he claimed to have been. Yet, he was only gone for an hour or so. Would that have given him enough time? If the woman who proclaimed to 'need him, *now*' was waiting in a room down the corridor, then it gave him plenty.

Alice can't help but scan the room as she walks back to the table, picking out any lonesome woman and assessing whether she might have had sex with her husband last night. There are disappointingly few possibilities, but it doesn't stop Alice fawning over Nathan, just in case they're being watched.

She puts her hand on his as they talk, careful to give him her full attention. He, in turn, seems to give her his, which confuses her. Why would he do that if he knows his mistress is there, watching?

'Looking forward to going home?' he asks, as she leans in for a kiss. He doesn't flinch.

'It will be good to see the girls,' she says.

'Has it been as hard as you thought it would be? Coming away? Leaving them at home?'

'Actually, no,' she says, honestly. She imagines that's probably because she's had other things to think about.

'It would be nice if we could do this again,' he says.

'Perhaps a little more often. If last night was anything to go by, I'd like to do it a *lot* more often.'

She remembers their love-making before she'd seen his phone; the warm tingle of alcohol making her lose her inhibitions, the sense of abandonment as she finally cast off the shackles of the past, content to give her all to the husband who deserved it. The words of the text flash in her mind and it hits her again, hard, that he doesn't.

'It's funny,' she says, watching his reaction carefully, 'but this time yesterday, I was so excited about this project.'

His brow furrows. 'And now?'

'Now, I don't feel like I want to do it.'

'But what's changed in that time?'

Everything, she wants to say. 'Nothing,' she says instead. 'I just don't want to do it.'

Nathan sits back in his chair and laughs. 'Well, it's a bit late to change your mind.'

'Is it?' she asks, tilting her head to one side. 'What if I wanted to pull out?'

He runs a hand through his hair. 'Well, you can't . . . we've exchanged. We'd lose the hundred grand deposit.'

'But losing one hundred thousand would surely be better than losing a million?' she says.

He picks up her hand and holds it to his lips. Any notion of his mistress being in the room evaporates. 'I understand why you're nervous, it's only natural, but it will be okay.'

'I just don't know if it's the right thing to do,' says Alice. 'I don't know if I'm prepared to risk AT's money . . . Tom's money.' She thought she'd throw that one in there, just to remind Nathan whose money they were playing with. She doesn't care if it makes him flinch a little. And ironically, she no longer cares what Tom may or may not think about what she's doing. He'd lost that right.

'We can't back out now,' says Nathan. 'We're too far in.'

Alice reclaims her hand. 'But there's not really a "we" in it, is there? This is all on *my* shoulders. It's *my* money, *my* reputation and *my* responsibility if it all goes wrong.'

'But it won't,' says Nathan. 'This is going to be the best thing that's ever happened to us and I'm going to be with you every step of the way.'

She smiles sweetly, but she doesn't believe a word he says anymore.

35

'Is Nathan not with you?' asks Alice's mum, Linda, as she greets her at her own front door with a hug.

'No, he took the train straight to the office from the airport,' says Alice. Not because that's where she believes he is, but because that's where he told her he was going. 'How have the girls been?'

'Livvy has been a dream.'

'And Sophia?'

Linda rolls her eyes. 'Like you were twenty years ago,' she says.

Alice smiles, but she can't help but think that actually, she and Sophia are nothing alike. Whilst Alice went through her teens as a troublesome bundle of hormones, not yet privy to knowing she'd grow out of it, Sophia is in a whole other world of hurt. In a place where sometimes Alice can't reach her.

But who can blame her? She's endured the horror of having her father walk out one morning and never come back, and for someone so young, it's no surprise that those feelings of abandonment and paranoia are still so near to the surface. Scratch at Alice just a few weeks ago, and you would have found the same emotions, but she's not sure they'd be there now.

'I'd rather six Olivias than one surly teenager,' says Linda. 'But Sophia has been through a lot. She's a good girl – she just needs a bit of time to find her place in the world.'

'I know,' says Alice, but she can't help but wonder if there was any more she *could* have, *should* have done.

'Just be honest,' her mother had said, when they were told it was no longer viable for Tom to be found alive. 'It's all that you can do.'

Alice hadn't had a minute to process her own grief, yet she was expected to impart the worst possible news to her seven-year-old daughter.

'Would you like me to do it?' her mother had asked gently, as the three of them huddled on the sofa together.

Alice had shaken her head, but a pool of nausea swirled in her stomach.

'Sophia, I've got something to tell you,' she'd said, her trembling hands holding her daughter's.

'Is Daddy coming home today?' Sophia had squealed in delight, as she sat bouncing up and down excitedly.

Alice shook her head as her eyes filled with tears.

'Shall we make some cookies?' Sophia had asked, oblivious. 'To give to him, when he gets here.'

Alice had pulled her close and breathed her in, squeezing her eyes shut and wishing with all her might that they could rewind a week, to a time when their worlds were normal. Now nothing would ever be normal again.

'Daddy's had an accident,' Alice had said, slowly and deliberately. She didn't want to get it wrong because Sophia would remember this moment for the rest of her life.

'Is he okay?' she'd asked.

'He was skiing, and he got lost on the mountain.'

'So when will he be coming home?'

'They've been looking for him for the past three days and nights, but they can't find him. They think he might have fallen down somewhere.'

Sophia had pulled a face. 'Ouch. Is he hurt?'

Alice had felt she wasn't doing a very good job and hated herself for delaying the truth, but she just wanted her daughter to have a few more moments of innocence. She'd felt her mum's hand on her back, the presence and reassurance of one mother to another. Her lips had quivered, and her voice wobbled.

'He's dead,' she'd managed.

She'll never forget the look on Sophia's face as the realization dawned.

'So . . . so Daddy's not coming back?' she'd stuttered. 'Ever?'

Alice had shaken her head. 'No, but he will always be here with us – he will always be with you wherever you are. Looking down on you, watching over you.

Whenever you're sad, he'll be by your side, holding your hand.'

A big tear had dropped from Sophia's cheek. 'Will I feel him?' she'd asked, looking up at her mum pitifully. 'Will I feel his hand in mine?'

'Y-yes, of course,' Alice had choked. 'You'll know he's there.'

Sophia's mind, no doubt, had flashed through a million memories – of her and Daddy in the park, looking for conkers; of him tickling her until she could hardly breathe; of watching *You've Been Framed* on TV together and laughing mercilessly at other people's misfortunes.

'We'll be okay,' Alice had lied.

She'd lain awake that night, holding Sophia close to her, her little body taking up not even half the space in their bed that Tom's had just a few nights before. How could he be gone? How could someone so loved, so needed, wake up one morning, walk out the front door and never come back? How was that even possible?

'Perhaps we don't give her the credit she deserves,' says Linda, snapping Alice back into the present. 'For getting to where she is today, knowing what she's been through – what you've *both* been through.'

Alice nods numbly and fights the clenching in her throat that tells her that tears are imminent.

'Oh darling, what's wrong?' asks Linda as she pulls Alice towards her and kisses the top of her head.

Should she tell her mother what's been going on? She so desperately wants to offload everything in her head, hear her mother say that she's got it all wrong about Tom. Linda loved him like her own son and wouldn't have a bad word said about him. But as much as Alice wants to share her newfound knowledge, she knows that it would be a selfish act. It might make *her* feel better for a moment, but it would crush her mother, and then she'd question whether Sophia should be told. No, there is nothing to be gained from saying anything.

'Nothing, I'm fine,' she lies. 'I just missed the girls.'

'Well, you should do it more often,' Linda says. 'It does you good to get away from it all every now and again.'

Alice doesn't have the heart to tell her that she'd taken half the problem away with her.

'So, anyway, come on, tell me, how was Japan?' asks Linda, as she fills the kettle and clicks it on.

'It's a beautiful place, so much culture, and the people are just lovely.'

'And the project? Is that all going ahead?'

Alice smiles, hoping that it reaches her eyes, as her mother will be the first to notice if it doesn't.

'Yes, it's an amazing opportunity,' she says, sounding like she's reading from a textbook. 'Really exciting.'

'I'm so proud of you, Alice,' says Linda. 'Of everything you've achieved.'

Alice smiles. 'I think I might have bitten off more than I can chew with this one.'

'Nonsense,' says Linda. 'You will rise to the challenge, as you always do.'

'Thanks Mum. It means a lot.'

'And I assume Nathan is fully supportive?' she asks without looking at Alice, as if she's been waiting for the right time to broach the subject.

Alice marvels at her mother's knack of always hitting the nail on the head. 'It's all his idea,' she says. 'He's fully behind it.'

'But is he fully behind *you*?' her mother asks.

Alice smiles tightly in answer and Linda looks away pensively.

Her mother has never voiced her opinion, but Alice can tell from her expressions and the look in her eye sometimes that she has reservations about Nathan. She had gently urged Alice to slow down when it had all seemed to be going too fast.

'Just give yourself some time,' she'd said when Alice came home aglow after their fourth date. 'You don't need to rush into anything. If this man is right for you, he'll wait until you're ready.'

But somewhere between the jigs and the reels, her sound advice had gone unheeded, because three months later Alice discovered she was pregnant.

'How can this be?' she'd cried hysterically into Nathan's arms. 'This wasn't supposed to happen.'

'I know you're frightened, but I promise you, I'm not going anywhere.'

'I can't put another child through that,' she'd said through her tears. 'I can't put Sophia through that again.'

'Not everyone dies at thirty-two,' he'd said, gently.

'It's not just about dying. It's about a child losing one of their parents for *any* reason: death, divorce . . . I just can't put another child through that.'

He'd kissed the top of her head and rocked her gently. 'You won't be on your own. I'll always be here for you – for *all* of you.'

'Don't you dare make a promise you can't keep,' Alice had sobbed. 'That's not fair.'

'I swear to you, I'll not let you down. Would it make you feel better if I moved in with you? Will that prove to you that I'm not about to go anywhere?'

Alice had nodded gratefully.

'But Tom's not yet been gone a year,' her mother had said when she heard the news. 'You're still grieving. Take your time – there's no need to rush into anything. You hardly know this man.'

Now, for the first time, Alice wonders if her mother had seen something she hadn't.

36

As soon as Alice sees Olivia running across the play-ground, with her arms outstretched, she feels equal measures of happiness and guilt.

'You're back,' she squeals as Alice picks her up and swings her around. 'Is Daddy home too?'

Alice imagines her answer if she decides that Nathan's cheating is not something she's prepared to put up with. *No darling, he's moved out. You can see him every other weekend.* Her chest tightens.

'Yes, he'll be home in time for tea,' she says.

'Yay,' Olivia shrieks excitedly.

Alice turns around and smiles when she sees Sophia coming towards her. 'Hey, what are *you* doing here?'

Her elder daughter's arms hang limply by her side, but as Alice pulls her closer, she feels them slowly come up and wrap around her.

'I had to return some books to the English department,' she says. 'And then I saw this little monkey doing PE on the field, so I thought I'd hang around and walk down.'

'Ah, that's so nice,' says Alice, kissing Sophia's forehead and pushing her hair away from her face. 'Everything okay?'

'Yeah.' Sophia shrugs.

'What's been going on since I last saw you?'

'You've only been gone three days,' she exclaims.

'So, nothing new to report?'

'Gossip, you mean?'

Alice smiles. 'That obvious, eh?'

Sophia rolls her eyes. 'You're worse than my mates.'

Despite her attempt to look and sound normal, Alice is anything but, as she constantly scans the playground, looking for Beth from behind her sunglasses. She can't shake the heaviness that's sitting on her chest – the foreboding feeling of waiting for Beth to turn up, not knowing whether she's about to throw a grenade in her already fragile world. Hoping for the best, Alice puts her head down and hurriedly leads the way out of school.

'Hello Alice,' says Beth from her left, blindsiding her.

Heat rushes to her skin, making her feel light-headed. The girls are just a few feet behind her and she has no idea what Beth is going to say or do.

'We still need to talk,' she says quietly.

Alice looks directly at her, all too aware of little Millie standing at her mother's side. *Will I see Tom in her, now that my eyes have new knowledge?* she asks herself, too frightened to look.

'Can Olivia come to play?' asks Millie.

Beth raises her eyebrows questioningly at Alice.

'Not today,' says Alice emphatically, her eyes flashing a warning look to Beth.

'Perhaps another time,' says Beth to her daughter.

'Aww, that's so unfair. Why can't I go to Olivia's then?'

'Because you have to wait to be invited,' says Beth patiently. 'I assume we're still invited to Olivia's party on Sunday?' She's looking at Alice, who for a split second has no idea what she's talking about.

'What?'

'Olivia's party? Is Millie still allowed to come?'

The penny drops as Alice remembers the twenty invitations Olivia had excitedly taken into school two weeks ago. 'Um, I don't know . . .' she stutters. 'I'm not sure there'll be . . .' She pulls herself up. Of course Olivia's birthday celebrations will go ahead. Just because her father is having an affair doesn't mean that their lives have to be put on hold. But still Alice's heart beats double-time at the thought of a house full of nine-year-olds, their pushy parents and her unfaithful husband. She almost groans out loud at the added complication of Beth and Millie being thrown into the mix.

'Please say I can still come,' says Millie tearfully, whilst tugging on Alice's skirt.

'Come on, let's go . . .' starts Beth, pulling the child away.

'Of course,' says Alice, forcing herself to look at Millie. The little girl's eyes are filled to the brim and just as she sticks her bottom lip out, a big fat tear runs down her cheek. The jolt that Alice had expected to feel when she looked at her doesn't come and she crouches down to Millie's height.

Is that you in there, Tom? She looks into Millie's eyes, searching for a sign, anything to prove that her beloved husband, the man she thought would never betray her, would do what Beth's suggesting.

'Of course you can come,' Alice says to Millie. 'Olivia wouldn't have it any other way.'

The little girl's dismay instantly turns into a grin and she instinctively throws her arms around Alice and kisses her cheek. 'Thank you,' she squeals.

Alice avoids eye contact with Beth as she returns to full height.

'When are you free to . . . you know . . . ?' asks Beth quietly.

'Mum, can I go and sit in the car?' asks Sophia, obviously assuming that the two mums are going to have a long chat, like they usually do.

'Yep, sure,' says Alice, fishing for the keys in her bag.

'Hi Millie-Moo,' says Sophia, as she affectionately ruffles Millie's hair. The little girl laughs and Alice feels like she's stopped breathing.

It's only then that the full implications of what Tom has done hit her. She's spent the past week wallowing in self-pity at the realization that her first marriage was a sham. She'd swung from wanting Beth dead to being glad that Tom was no longer alive in her efforts to process what had happened, but at no point did she remember appreciating that she and Sophia might be half-sisters.

'We need to sort this out,' says Beth, as if reading her mind. 'We can't carry on, in this state of limbo.'

Alice feels like she might crumple to the floor, but steels herself, refusing to give in.

'I'm not going to do it here and I'm not going to do it at Livvy's, I mean Olivia's, birthday party.' She sees Beth baulk at the self-correction, as if noting that she's no longer in the inner circle who know Olivia well enough to call her Livvy. Alice presses on, keen to convey that *she'll* be the one calling the shots. 'We'll arrange something for next week, once we've both had a chance to work out what this all means and the consequences that come with you having had an affair with my husband.'

Alice couldn't help herself.

'Mrs Davies, Mrs Davies,' calls out Miss Watts, making her way towards Alice.

Alice fixes on a smile. 'Hi.'

'Could I have a word please?' She looks to Beth. 'Perhaps in my office would be best.'

'Yes, yes of course,' says Alice as she begins to follow her inside, not knowing what to do with Olivia.

'I'll keep an eye on her,' says Beth, sensing her predicament. 'The girls can have a play.'

It was all that was needed to force Alice's decision. She caught hold of Olivia's hand and marched her inside.

'I'm sorry,' says Miss Watts quietly once they're in

her classroom, so Olivia can't hear from the corridor outside. 'I just wanted to have a word with you to see if we might be able to find out what's going on with Olivia at the moment.'

'Is there a problem?' asks Alice, careful to temper her impatience. She doesn't need this on top of everything else.

'Well, yes, I'm afraid there is,' she says, wringing her hands together. 'Another parent has called to make a complaint.'

'A complaint?' says Alice, not sure that she heard right. 'About what?'

'They are suggesting that Olivia is bullying their child.'

Alice almost laughs. 'My Olivia?'

'Erm, yes, I'm afraid so,' she says. 'We've had said child in for a chat and she won't say very much. I think it's because she may be frightened.'

'Are you sure you've got this right?' asks Alice, unable to believe that her daughter could possibly be guilty of what she's being accused of.

'We've also spoken to Olivia,' says Miss Watts. 'But she says that she's not been horrible to anyone. But, in these situations, I find there is rarely smoke without fire.'

Alice shakes her head. 'I understand that you have to investigate this, but are you absolutely sure you've got this the right way round? Just last week I was called in to pick Livvy up from the nurse, after Phoebe had pushed her in the playground. Could it be that it's actually Phoebe who's bullying Olivia?'

Miss Watts pulls that therapist face again and Alice feels an overwhelming desire to punch her.

'Phoebe isn't actually the child in question,' she says.

'She isn't?' queries Alice. 'Well, if it isn't Phoebe, who is it?'

'I'm afraid I'm not able to divulge that information.'

'So, let me get this straight,' says Alice, feeling like a pressure cooker. 'Are you honestly expecting me to ask my eight-year-old child who she's supposedly bullying, because you're not prepared to tell me?'

'Well, as we've spoken to both girls, I'm hoping that it will rectify itself, but I just wanted to make you aware of the situation as the girl's mother has threatened to take things further if it's not resolved.'

'Are you kidding me?' asks Alice incredulously. 'They're eight years old for Christ's sake.'

Miss Watts looks down at the floor, as if she suddenly wishes she was anywhere but here.

'Who's the child?' asks Alice again.

'I'm afraid I really can't say.'

If she knew it wouldn't reflect badly on Olivia, she'd drag Miss Watts across the classroom by her cheap lapels until she told her.

'Well, then I guess I'll just have to find out for myself,' Alice snaps as she storms off.

37

'Shit, shit, shit!' says Alice as she slams the steering wheel.

'Why are you saying the s word Mummy?' asks Olivia, wide-eyed.

'Because Mummy is pissed off,' says Alice. 'If one more person thinks I'm going to take their shit, then they've got another think coming.' She looks in her rear-view mirror to see Sophia turning to her little sister and putting a finger to her lips, in an effort to stop her from saying anything more. Alice smiles, but it's a painful facade. If only the world consisted of just the three of them – then she'd be happy.

She's halfway home when she decides to call Nathan.

'Shit,' she says again when there's no answer. She does a U-turn in the middle of the road. 'I'm just going to pop to the office.'

Sophia groans, whilst Olivia whoops. 'I hope Lottie's there. She always plays with me.'

As Alice pulls into the small car park behind the office building, she calls Nathan again. When he doesn't pick up, she can only assume he's somewhere he shouldn't be. From now on, he'll *always* be somewhere he shouldn't be, at least in her head.

'Sophia, are you coming up?' asks Alice.

'No, I'll wait here. Try not to be too long.'

I'll be as long as it takes, thinks Alice as she takes the stairs two at a time, with Olivia trailing behind her.

'Hey, you're back,' says Lottie excitedly, sounding much like Olivia when she saw Alice. 'How's it going Livs?' she asks, holding a hand out for Olivia to high five.

'Hi Lottie,' says Alice, as cheerily as she can manage. She looks her up and down, taking in her lean, long legs, encased in tight black trousers. Her hair is pinned up with what looks like a pencil securing it, blonde strands fall down, framing her elfin face.

'Can you just do me a favour and keep Livvy occupied whilst I have five minutes in my office?' asks Alice.

'Sure. Do you want to come and help me do some colouring in?' she asks Olivia.

For the first time since seeing the text to Nathan, Alice is able to sit down and work out who it might be from. Her stomach knots as she recalls it from the camera roll on her phone. As ludicrous as it sounds, she wonders if it's changed since she took the screenshot. Might there be *more* words, to give her more of a clue as to who it's from? She hopes there are less; that the incriminating sentence, so short, yet so hurtful, has been magicked away into cyberspace.

Disappointingly, what she finds is what she remembers.

I need you. Now xx

She types the number it was sent from into her phone and holds her breath whilst she waits the split second to see if it matches any of her contacts. If it does she doesn't know how she'd ever recover from the deceit. But if it doesn't, she's no further forward to finding out who it is. She counters that the latter is the best option – just.

When nothing shows up, Alice sets about methodically working through her contact list to see if it might jog a memory or a feeling. Though it quickly becomes apparent that ninety per cent of the people she knows are ruled out on the grounds of gender, age or sexual preference. The only real possibility is Lottie. The number definitely isn't hers, or at least not the one Alice has. She could have a second phone, but as Alice looks out through the glass wall at her and Olivia, their heads together as they pick colours from the marker box, she knows it *can't* be her. She's attractive, but childlike. Assured, but awkward. And besides, what would *she* find appealing about going to bed with a man old enough to be her father? And her boss, to boot.

Nevertheless, she calls Lottie's number, just to be sure she has the right one stored, and watches, waiting for her to pick it up. Alice can see the phone sitting on the desk, but Lottie shows no signs of going to it.

'Lottie,' she calls out, 'have you got a minute?'

Lottie drops what she's doing and scurries into Alice's office.

'I had trouble calling you whilst I was in Japan,' Alice says to her. 'Your mobile just kept ringing and ringing.'

'Ah, yes, sorry,' says Lottie. 'Mine got stolen, so I had to get a new one.'

Alice bats away the heat that's creeping up from her toes. 'Oh,' she manages, momentarily stuck for anything better.

'I did let Nathan know though,' says Lottie. 'I sent him my new number, just in case either of you needed to get hold of me.'

'*Did* you?' says Alice numbly, as all the reasons she'd had for ruling *against* Lottie being Nathan's mistress, suddenly become arguments *for*.

'I'll send it to you now,' says Lottie, unaware that Alice can't begin to function until she gets it.

Alice's phone pings and the numbers blur, but she can already tell that it's not a match. She lets out the breath she didn't realize she'd been holding in.

'So, how did it go in Japan?' asks Lottie, oblivious to Alice's need for privacy.

Alice smiles tightly and nods. 'It was good – we complete next week.'

Lottie dances up and down on the spot, clapping her hands together.

'Oh my God, how exciting,' she says.

Alice wonders if they really will complete next week when there's such a huge obstacle in between now and then. But then the pilot's surprise, her mother's words, and Lottie's excitement ring loudly in her ears. And she wonders why the hell she shouldn't. With or without Nathan.

'Have you seen him today?' asks Alice, as if Lottie is privy to the innermost workings of her mind.

'Who?' she asks.

'Oh, sorry, Nathan. Have you seen Nathan?'

'No. To be honest, I wasn't expecting to see either of you after a ten-hour flight. I thought you'd both go straight home.'

'Has he called in?' asks Alice.

'Hold on,' Lottie says, poking her head around the door. 'Has anyone spoken to Nathan this afternoon?' she calls out across the open-plan office. It's an innocent enough question, and one which just a week ago would have been quite normal. But now it feels accusatory, as if she's tracking him. Lottie's question is met with shaking heads and nonplussed expressions.

Alice tries to call Nathan one more time, but it goes straight to his answerphone. Her fingers tap thoughtfully on her phone case. *Where are you, Nathan?* she says to herself. She looks out the window, to the car park below, and can just about make out Sophia's fast-moving digits operating the phone in her lap as she sits in Alice's car, waiting.

'I'll be back in one minute,' she says to no one in particular. She runs down the stairs, back to her car, and knocks on Sophia's window, making her daughter jump.

'Roll the window down,' mouths Alice impatiently, as she watches her daughter roll her eyes.

'What?' says Sophia gruffly.

Alice doesn't have time to deal with her daughter's bad mood, caused, no doubt, by something she's seen on social media.

'Can you get that Chatsnap thing of yours up?' she asks her.

'Yeah, why?' asks Sophia, her tone loaded with suspicion.

'Because I could really do with finding Nathan,' says Alice, stopping herself short from saying anything more. Sometimes the more words you use, the more mistrust you create.

Sophia looks at her through narrowed eyes. 'What for?'

'Can you do it or not?' asks Alice impatiently.

'Jeez, chill your beans,' says Sophia as she swipes her thumb and moves her fingers at lightning speed.

'Watch who you're talking to,' warns Alice. 'I'm not one of your mates.'

'It looks like he's somewhere on Park Lane in London,' she says hesitantly. 'The Hilton.'

Alice wants to ask if he's in bed with someone. After all, this app seems to be able to show a myriad of other activities. 'Thank you,' is all she says. 'I'll see if I can reach him there.'

'Mum, is everything okay?' Sophia asks, with more than a hint of worry in her tone.

Alice forces a smile. 'Of course, why wouldn't it be?'

'Do you promise?' asks Sophia, her sassy attitude suddenly replaced by the vulnerability of someone half her age.

It takes all of Alice's resolve not to pull her daughter to her and hold her tight. Instead she crosses her fingers behind her back and hopes her smile reaches her eyes.

'Yes darling, I promise.'

38

'Just tell me the truth,' Alice demands loudly after dinner has been cleared away, her patience spent.

'I promise, Mummy, I haven't done anything,' cries Olivia.

'So why are another little girl and her parents saying that you did? You cannot go around hurting people Olivia, with words *or* actions. I will not stand for it.'

'But I'm not, Mummy! Phoebe is mean to *me*.'

'We're not talking about Phoebe,' says Alice. 'We're talking about another girl who thinks you're being mean to *her*. Honestly, Olivia, I will not be called in by the school to be told that you're a bully.'

'I'm not a bully,' she screams, before running up the stairs and slamming her bedroom door.

'Right, that's it young lady. You stay in there until the morning and by then you'd better be ready to tell me the truth.'

Alice feels riddled with guilt as she takes Olivia a glass of water half an hour later, only to find her daughter fast asleep yet still fully dressed. Tiny whimpers emanate from her chest as Alice changes her into her pyjamas.

This is not the kind of mother I am, Alice tells herself

as she sits on the edge of her bed with her head in her hands. She'd do anything to crawl under the duvet and shut everything out – wait for the storm that she knows is brewing to pass. But she has to be stronger than that. She will not be defined by her weaknesses again.

Her phone pierces the uncharacteristic quiet in the house and she wearily reaches across the bed for her handbag. Maybe she *will* lie down, for just a few minutes.

'Hi darling, it's me,' says Nathan when she picks up. She can already tell from those four words that he's had a drink. 'You're not going to believe it, but I've bumped into Josh, an old pal of mine,' he slurs. 'You remember him, don't you? I introduced you to him once.'

Alice couldn't ever recall meeting Josh. She'd remember if she had because the people Nathan had introduced her to over the years were few and far between. He'd said that losing his parents when he was young had made it difficult for him to form friendships. Certainly the ones he had now were all part of their wider circle of couples, even his golf buddies were husbands of friends Alice had acquainted him with.

There had been many a time when she'd wished Nathan had more of a backstory. That he'd brought an extended family into her life, as Lord knows her own was small enough. It would have been nice to feel part of a bigger picture; to have family to call on and spend time with. But he'd pretty much turned up, seemingly out of nowhere, and it's only now that she wonders if her perceived saviour was actually a wolf in sheep's clothing. Had she been so damaged that she had been prepared to overlook issues that would otherwise have been glaringly obvious? Had she been so insecure that she'd ignored any niggling doubts?

'Isn't he your old school friend?' she asks now, helping Nathan out, because she doesn't have the energy to listen to him embellish his lie.

'Yeah, that's the one,' he says, falling straight into her trap. 'God, you've got a good memory. Anyway, I had a bit of an impromptu meeting at the bank and then I bumped into Joe and one thing has led to another.'

'Josh . . .' Alice corrects him. 'I thought you said his name was Josh.'

'What . . . ? Yes, Josh – that's what I said.'

He's too drunk to get his first story straight, and Alice is too tired to care. It's not as if she needs any more proof that he's up to no good – she's got all that she needs. Now, she only has to decide what she's going to do about it.

She wants to wait up for Nathan to come home, if for no other reason than she'll be able to smell the cheap perfume on him, or see if his mouth is stained with someone else's lipstick. It's almost as if she needs to hurt as much as she possibly can in order to force herself to make the right decision. But try as she might, the argument with Olivia has left her exhausted and her eyes are battling to stay open as the bongs ring out for the ten o'clock news.

She can't even remember taking her tablets, but she must have done, as the next time she opens her eyes it's morning and she's none the wiser as to whether Nathan came home at ten thirty or three thirty. It occurs to her as she reaches an arm across the empty bed that he still might not be home. She squints at the green digits reading 06.20 on the illuminated clock on the bedside table and lifts her head off the pillow. She can hear the shower running and is furious with herself for not knowing whether it's Nathan coming in or going out.

She wants to go back to sleep so she can turn off the noise in her head that the new day brings. But try as she might, her senses are already alert to the problems that lie before her. Defeated, Alice throws the duvet off in frustration. There's too much to think about now – her brain a whir of activity. There's no point in lying in bed any longer.

The steam billows out of the bathroom as she opens the door. Nathan, naked and wet from the shower, turns towards the draught.

'Morning darling,' he says as he rubs a towel two-handed across his back.

'How was your evening?' she asks tightly as she stands in front of the mirror, putting her hair up.

'Long and boring,' he says, with a laugh. 'It seemed like fun at the time, but now, in the cold light of day, when I'm tired and hungover, my memories are quite different.'

I bet they are, Alice thinks to herself.

'How was yours?' he asks as he comes up behind her, his hands reaching around to untie the belt on her robe. She pulls it tighter around her.

'Come on,' he pleads. 'We've got time for a quick one.'

There's no part of her that wants to have a 'quick one', especially when she doesn't know where he's been. And until she does, there won't be any *quick* ones, *slow* ones or any *other* ones.

'I need to get ready,' she says, shutting him down. 'I've got a busy day.'

'We've both got a busy day,' he says sulkily, as if it's a competition. 'I might need you to sign some papers for Japan.'

She manages a nod as he kisses her.

'I'll see you in the office,' he says as he walks out.

She takes her time in the shower as a showreel of where Nathan might have been last night plays out in her head. The images are vivid – in high-definition and with surround sound. She sees his lips on somebody else's, his hands tenderly holding her face as he professes his love. The unidentified woman calls his name out as his hands move lower, but Alice blocks out that image, preferring to focus on forming the woman's face, as if doing so will provide irrefutable evidence of the encounter.

The tips of her fingers are beginning to wrinkle and her hair is squeaking as she plans the day ahead, skipping over the parts that she doesn't want to acknowledge. *I'll blow-dry my hair; it'll make me feel better. I'll drive*

Olivia to school and try to find out who my daughter is bullying. I'll work on the drawing room of Belmont House; I'm thinking the maroon crushed velvet with a gold accent. I'll find out who my husband is sleeping with. I'll make a nice paella for dinner tonight; I wonder if there are any king prawns in the freezer.

She works her way through the first items methodically, her day in the office going exactly according to plan until her self-imposed drawn-out lunch can't be protracted any further. She knows the next item on her list requires attention and purposefully looks at the over-eaten core of her apple to see if just another second can be gleaned from nibbling at the remains.

She peers over the top of her computer screen, through the glass into the space beyond. She can just make out the top of Nathan's head, sat at the desk in his office on the other side.

With her eyes flicking from him to the screen between them, she enters his personal email address on the log-in screen before confidently typing his password.

INCORRECT PASSWORD ENTERED

Her brow furrows. *I must have hit a wrong key*, she tells herself, already knowing she hasn't. She types it in again, more slowly, more precisely.

Incorrect again. Alice feels as if she's trying to hack Google.

She tries their other favoured keywords; insecure variations on birthdays and the girls' names they'd made up together for online shopping accounts, when neither of them could imagine the other needing to spy on them. Nothing will open sesame.

Nathan is up out of his chair and heading in her direction, but she's too busy trying to crack the password to notice.

'Hey,' he says, as he swings open the glass door.

Her ears instantly go hot, and his words are momentarily muffled. She tries to change screens as quickly, yet as casually, as she can manage.

'Hi,' she says, finding her voice.

'I'm just popping to the bank to make sure everything's finalized, ready for Monday.'

She looks at him. 'Oh, I thought you did that yesterday?' It's a question she expects him to answer.

'Er, yeah, I did.'

'So, what do you need to go again for?'

'Erm . . . they need your passport,' he says, though Alice may be imagining the hesitation.

She unlocks her desk drawer and blindly sifts through the mess of paperwork, make-up and stationery that's in there.

'There it is,' tuts Nathan, leaning in to retrieve it from underneath a chequebook and some fabric samples.

'Wait!' says Alice, grabbing hold of his wrist. 'I'll come with you.'

'There's no need. I literally just need to drop it in so they can take a quick copy.'

'All the same, I should come,' she says. 'Just in case they need anything else.'

'It's honestly a waste of your time. It'll be a two-minute job.'

Alice starts picking up her phone and keys from the desk. 'No problem – I could do with getting out of here for a bit.'

'This is ridiculous.' Nathan lets out a huff as she ushers him out of her office. 'It doesn't take two of us to go to the bank.'

'Come on, we can chat on the way,' says Alice.

He stops at the bottom of the stairs and turns around to face her. 'Look, stop!' he says, his brow vexed.

Alice stops in her tracks.

'I didn't go to the bank yesterday,' he says abruptly, his eyes avoiding hers.

It takes a moment for Alice to process the admission. 'But you said—'

'I know what I said, but I didn't go.'

So now it's beginning to come out. He's got himself into a hole and knows that I'm about to discover that he wasn't where he said he was.

'So, where *were* you?' she asks, her heart in her mouth. It seems to take forever for him to answer.

'I was trying to get something for Livvy.'

That's the last thing she was expecting. 'Sorry, what?'

'For her *birthday* . . .'

He's speaking to her as if she's stupid, as if she should understand what he's saying; but she can't, for the life of her, work out what Olivia's birthday has to do with him not going to the bank.

'I wanted it to be a surprise,' he goes on.

'I'm sorry,' she says, shaking her head. 'What are you talking about?'

'I told you I'd gone to the bank yesterday afternoon, but I went to see someone about a present for Livvy.'

Alice raises her eyebrows, waiting for more.

'I went to look at a dog.'

'A *dog*?' she repeats incredulously. 'Since when have we wanted a dog?'

'It's just something that Livvy mentioned a little while back and I thought it might be a good idea. I wanted it to be a surprise for all of you.'

'Isn't that something that you and I should discuss first?' asks Alice. 'I'm not sure that I would want one just now. It's a huge commitment.'

'Yeah, I know, but I think it would be fun.'

'Where did you go then?' asks Alice. 'To see this dog.'

'It was over Kent way.'

'And?' she asks, trying hard not to let her doubt in his story show in her voice.

'And what?'

'Did you like it?'

'Er, no, it wasn't right for us.'

'What was it?'

'Mmm, it was one of those crossbreeds, like a labra-doodle or something.'

'Ah cute,' says Alice. 'What colour?'

'Chocolate brown,' he says, quicker now, warming to the theme.

Alice looks in his eyes, trying to see any hint of deceit. 'So why are you telling me this now?'

'Because you've put me in a corner,' he says, as if he's aggrieved. 'It's going to be obvious, when we get to the bank, that I didn't go yesterday. But if you hadn't insisted on coming . . .'

Alice refuses to take the bait and opens the door to the car park. She walks briskly around the corner, leaving Nathan to catch up.

'And what about Josh?' she asks, as they fall in line with each other on the high street, narrowly missing a collision with a twin buggy. 'Or was it Joe?'

'They should ban those things,' says Nathan in an effort to change the subject.

'So, Josh?' presses Alice, not letting him off. 'Where did you meet *him*? Or is that a lie as well?'

'I'm not *lying* Alice,' he says. 'Jesus, I just wanted it to be a surprise.'

'The dog part or the Josh part?'

'You're being ridiculous,' he says wearily. 'I got the train down to see the dog and bumped into Josh at Waterloo, on my way back. He was just heading home after work and one beer turned into three . . . you know how it is.'

'So, what time did you get in?' she asks as he holds the door to the bank open for her.

He attempts to laugh. 'I wish I knew. Around one. Maybe two.' He sounds more unsure with every number.

'So you weren't with *her*?' asks Alice, surprising even herself. Of all the times and places she'd imagined having this conversation, it wasn't now, in a bank queue. She wishes she could suck it back in, but the best she can hope for is that he didn't hear her.

'*Her*?' he repeats, as if he's hoping he's misheard.

Alice turns to look at him, jutting her chin out in an act of defiance. She doesn't say anything because she doesn't trust her voice.

'Are we honestly going to go there again?' he asks incredulously, under his breath.

'I haven't even started,' hisses Alice.

He throws his arms up in the air. 'What are you going to accuse me of this time?'

'I saw the text,' is all she says.

Nathan looks around, checking who's in listening distance. A mum with a noisy toddler is in front of them and an elderly gentleman is a few feet behind them. Neither will be able to hear very much.

'What text?' he says.

'The text from *her*.' She almost spits it out. 'The one where she begs for you.'

Nathan shakes his head and looks at her as if to say, *Poor Alice, you need help*. She remembers a nurse doing the very same thing when she was in the unit, and how she used to fantasize that when she got out, she'd break into her house and just sit there in the corner of her front room. She wouldn't speak, just slowly shake her head and pull her mouth into a pitying smirk.

Alice opens the photos on her phone and hands him the screenshot of the text he'd received in Japan. She watches as the colour drains from his cheeks.

'Did you go to her Nathan? Did you give her what she needed?'

She's never seen him speechless before. He always has just the right words for every situation. But not for this one, it seems.

'I didn't want to tell you,' he starts, and Alice can already feel the tightening at the back of her throat that signals tears are imminent.

'I can't do this here,' she says, turning and striding out of the bank.

Nathan catches up with her outside and forcibly pushes her into an alley, out of sight of shoppers.

'Listen to me,' he says, authoritatively. 'I don't know who she is.'

Alice laughs and cries simultaneously. 'Are you serious? You're honestly expecting me to believe that?'

'I didn't want to tell you because I didn't want to worry you. I've had three or four similar texts, all from the same number, but I don't know who it is.'

Alice wipes her nose with the back of her hand. 'I can't believe this is the tack you're going to take. I expected more from you, Nathan. You're an intelligent man – I thought you'd have your excuses all ready to go, but I'm truly disappointed that that's all you've got to offer.'

He takes hold of her shoulders, his face just a few centimetres away from her. 'You need to believe me because it's true. I've tried calling the number again and again, but it just rings. I've texted it but had no response.'

'And yet there's nothing on your phone to prove your story,' says Alice. 'In fact, there's no trace of anything apart from the one message that I saw. No attempt by you to find out who it is. No attempt to block the number. Nothing, apart from a dirty text.'

He gets his phone out, scrolls through his recent calls and turns the screen to face Alice. 'Look, there,' he says, jabbing a finger at a number. 'I've called it fifteen times today alone.'

'God, you must be crazy about her,' snorts Alice derisively.

'For fuck's sake, I don't know who it is,' he says as he rakes a hand manically through his hair. 'Here, take it, try it yourself. If we're having some mad passionate affair, you'd assume she'd pick up as soon as she sees it's me.'

Alice nods numbly.

'Well, go on then. Call it. See what happens.'

Just as Nathan had predicted, the line rings out.

'What more do I have to do?' he asks, his frustration evident. 'I do everything I can to be the man you want, the man you need, but I still get it thrown back in my face. The only thing you make me feel I'm doing right is being a father. Nothing else is ever good enough for you.'

Alice wipes away the tears from her cheeks. Is she asking for too much? Expecting a fairy tale that doesn't exist?

'Look, I understand how it must look right now,' Nathan goes on, 'and if I'd known you'd seen the text then I would have explained sooner. I don't know what's going on or who's messing with me, but I promise you I'm not having an affair. You and the girls are my world.'

Alice allows Nathan to pull her into him because, despite everything, she needs to be held.

'You need to find out who's doing this,' she says into his chest.

'Don't worry, I will,' he says. 'Now let's go back into the bank and do what we came here to do.'

39

'Okay, okay, no running,' Alice calls out from the kitchen, as ten overexcited nine-year-olds race in from the garden and up the stairs. 'Livvy, not upstairs please. There's more people at the door.'

If she wasn't out of breath from blowing up the balloons, and didn't have twenty party bags still to fill, she'd go to the door herself. But as per usual, she'd thought she still had plenty of time, only realizing there was less than half an hour to go when Olivia danced into her bedroom in her Elsa dress.

'Shit,' she says out loud. 'Nathan, can you get the lemonade in from the garage and find somewhere to hang the piñata?'

'I'm on it.'

'Grandma's here!' squeals Olivia from the hall.

Alice instantly feels calmer now that backup has arrived. 'In the kitchen, Mum,' she calls out.

Screaming kids whizz back past her, followed by Linda, who raises her eyebrows as if to say, *Are you mad?*

'I know, I know,' Alice says. 'It just seemed like a good idea at the time.'

'Right, where do you want me to start?' asks Linda, in her typical no-nonsense way.

'Mummy, can we do the piñata?' Olivia calls out from the conservatory.

'No, not just yet Livvy, you've still got one or two friends who aren't here. Mum, can you just put the sausage rolls in the oven?' Alice asks Linda, feeling her fringe sticking to her forehead. 'And a few bowls of crisps out on the table? It'll give them something to nibble on.'

'Hi Linda,' says Nathan as he comes in from the adjoining room, leaning in to kiss her on the cheek. 'You okay?'

Alice watches her mum smile and make all the right noises, but it seems forced. As if she's dealing with a bothersome cold caller who she'd like to tell to sod off, but feels obliged to continue listening to, at least until they'd got to the end of their script. *Does she feel 'obliged' when speaking to Nathan?* Alice wonders. *Has it always been that way?*

'I'm good,' she says. 'What's going on with you?' But she's already turned her back on him to put a baking tray into the oven.

'We're completing on Japan tomorrow,' he says, going up behind Alice and wrapping his arms around her. 'You should be very proud of your daughter. She's going to be an international property tycoon.'

Linda laughs, but Alice is sure there's a bitterness to

it. 'I'm always proud of my daughter, Nathan. So it's all going ahead then?' She directs the question at Alice.

'Mmm, four o'clock tomorrow. I can't decide if I feel sick with fear or excitement.'

'It's a big commitment,' says Linda. 'It's a lot on your shoulders.'

'I'll be right there beside her,' says Nathan.

Alice shrugs him off and a tense silence hangs in the air, only broken when Olivia bursts in from the conservatory, crying.

'Look what Phoebe did to me,' she wails, holding her arm out.

Alice throws Nathan a look that says, *If that bitch of a girl has made my daughter cry at her own birthday party, I'm going to kill her.*

He glares back at her, silently saying, *Okay, calm down. I've got this.*

'Look, there. She scratched me. Ow,' cries Olivia, though no real tears are yet to materialize. Alice gives her arm a rub and a magic kiss.

'Okay girls, can we please be kind to each other,' says Nathan, going through to the conservatory and ushering the sea of blue polyester floating and spinning in front of him out into the garden. 'If you carry on twirling, Phoebe, you're going to make yourself sick.'

Alice hopes she might, though not on the polished wood floor.

'Is that the little girl you think's bullying Olivia?' asks

Linda, as the two girls link pinkies and vow to be friends again.

Alice rolls her eyes. 'I honestly don't know *what's* going on. One minute they're at each other's throats and the next they're making up again. I didn't realize I'd told you.'

'You didn't,' says Linda. 'I was talking to Beth when you were away.'

Alice's stomach lurches at the sound of her name, knowing that she's going to be here any minute.

'Well, believe it or not, it's now being suggested that it's actually Livvy that's being mean,' says Alice.

Linda folds her arms and takes a territorial stance, like a mother hen ruffling her feathers, ready for battle. Alice can't help but laugh. 'She might not be the angel you think she is.'

'Absolute rubbish,' says Linda. 'And I'll take on anyone who says otherwise.'

The doorbell rings and Alice immediately feels breathless. 'Mum, would you mind?' she says, tilting her head towards the front door.

Despite Beth insisting that she has to get off, Alice can hear her mum insisting, even louder, that she must come in. Her heart drops and she knocks back the biggest mouthful of wine that she can manage when she hears Millie coming down the hall saying, 'Just come in for a bit, Mummy, and then you can go.'

'Hi,' says Beth, looking as if she's quite literally on the back foot.

'Hello,' says Alice tightly.

With the people that matter to her all in one place, the magnitude of the secret they share weighs heavy on her shoulders. She's not ready for it to be revealed, here and now, and shoots Beth a warning look, which if her old friend knows her at all, she'll take notice of.

'Welcome to the mayhem and mess,' says Linda warmly, totally oblivious to the palpable tension between the other two women. 'What can I get you to drink? And Millie darling, what would you like?'

Alice looks to her mum, her breath catching in her throat. What would she say if she knew the little girl she was offering the crisp bowl to was Sophia's half-sister? And would Nathan be secretly pleased if he knew Tom had toppled from his place on the pedestal in such spectacular fashion?

But you might not be so squeaky clean yourself, she says to him silently, still unsure whether to believe his story about the unknown number. She wants to, but knows that if she does, she's in danger of being as gullible as Beth was in trusting Tom. The admission that gullibility might be *all* that Beth is guilty of jolts her.

Alice can't help but look at her, as if seeing her properly for the first time since her revelation. There's a very real vulnerability in her eyes. A pain not unlike her own. The result of them both having had the lives they thought they had ripped out from beneath them.

It isn't Beth's fault that Tom did what he did. How

was she to know that he was married, with a child? Alice hadn't seen that lying, duplicitous side to Tom either, or maybe she had, but she just didn't realize it at the time. Even now that she's had time to digest it, she still can't believe that he was cheating on her, on *both* of them, playing them for fools. They were both victims, who could do worse than support each other through this unimaginable ordeal.

'Go on Millie, go and join in. I'll stay here with the grown-ups,' Beth encourages.

And it's not her fault either, thinks Alice, as she steps forward and offers Millie her hand.

'Shall we go and see what all the noise is about?' she says to the little girl dressed as Disney's Anna. Millie nods enthusiastically and waves a quick goodbye to her mum.

Alice leads Millie out to the garden, where Nathan is struggling to blindfold a boy who is dressed as a mini Jack Sparrow. She refrains from saying that it might be easier if he just pulls his bandana down over his eyes. Before they've even counted to three, the boy is hacking at the colourful donkey suspended from a tree as if he's making his way through a dense jungle with a machete.

'Whoa, steady on Captain,' says Nathan. 'Hey Millie. You want a go in a minute? If you're as good at this as you are at *Minecraft* the donkey doesn't stand a chance.'

Alice looks on, marvelling at how at ease he is with the kids. Not just his own, but everyone else's as well.

Despite everything, she would never be able to show enough gratitude for the way he took Sophia on, without question. For adopting a child that was never his until he made her feel as if she was.

Alice heads back into the kitchen and tops up her wine, taking a grateful sip before turning to Beth.

'Could I have a word?' she says, whilst nodding her head in the direction of the front room, away from the noise.

Beth forces a smile and follows Alice. The two women walk into the living room and Alice shuts the door softly behind them, playing for time, not knowing where to start.

'Listen,' she says, wringing her hands together. 'I'm finding this all really difficult to deal with. It's come at me like a rocket and I can't deny that I'm having trouble processing it all and what it means.'

Beth nods, her lips pressed tightly together, as if they're the only thing stopping her from shouting out.

'I'm devastated by Tom's deceit,' says Alice, holding herself back from revealing what's on Facebook. She needs to deal with that on her own, before involving anyone else, as it will only serve to complicate matters. 'But I will come to terms with it in my own time,' she goes on, 'and in my own way, as I'm sure you will.'

Beth nods.

'And as much as this newfound knowledge pains me,

it is the realization that I've lost our friendship that pains me even more.'

'You don't have to—' starts Beth.

'No, please,' says Alice, holding a hand up. 'Let me finish. All I've thought about is how it affects me and Sophia, not thinking for a second about you and Millie. I'm sorry for that – it was selfish and wrong. I can't even begin to imagine how this news has affected you, and for any part I've played in making that even harder, I'm truly sorry.'

Beth's eyes widen at Alice's admission.

'I hadn't realized quite how much your friendship meant to me until you weren't there,' Alice goes on. 'We've only known each other for what, two years?'

Beth nods. 'Almost three.'

'But yet it feels like a lifetime,' says Alice. 'I've not always found it easy to make friends and, as you know, I'm not the most social mum in the playground.'

'I've never seen you move so fast as when you drop Livvy off,' Beth says with a little smile.

'Exactly!' says Alice. 'So friends don't come easy to me, but you . . .' She feels tears spring to her eyes. 'You and I feel like kindred spirits, and if we allow our friendship to suffer because of someone else's duplicitous character, then there are no winners in this sorry state of affairs. I lost Tom once, and now I feel like I've lost him all over again. I don't think I can cope with losing you too.'

'I'm so sorry,' says Beth, her face crumpling. 'If I'd known I was about to throw a bomb into your world . . .'

The two women approach each other awkwardly until Alice opens her arms and pulls Beth into her. 'What do they say?' Alice laughs snottily. 'You should never allow a man to come between friends.'

'Something like that,' sniffs Beth. 'So, we're all good?'

'We're all good,' says Alice, acknowledging how different it feels to have Beth back on side. 'We can work out a plan, going forward, together.'

'Is everything okay with Nathan now?' Beth asks as they walk back to the kitchen.

'It will be,' says Alice, suddenly confident.

40

'I thought that donkey would be able to withstand more of a beating,' jokes Nathan as he comes back into the kitchen, his arms so full of piñata debris he can't see where he's going. He staggers blindly towards the bin. 'I was hoping for at least half an hour of entertainment from that. What's next, Mum?' He lets out an exaggerated sigh as he picks up a glass from the worktop and takes a mouthful of red wine. 'God, this kids' entertainer malarkey is hard work – no sooner are they on one thing than they want to know what's coming next—'

'Nate,' Alice interjects, feeling infinitely stronger. 'This is Beth.'

'Ah, the infamous Beth,' he says, looking down to wipe his hands on a tea towel. 'I was beginning to think you were a figment of Alice's imagination, or a hunky rugby player she's been seeing on the side.'

He looks up, ready with one of his wide grins that would beguile even the most unwelcome of guests. 'Pleased to finally meet—' The rest of his sentence is cut off as his glass flies from his hand and smashes onto the island, splintering into a thousand tiny pieces.

'Argh!' shouts Alice, jumping back from the missile.

'Oh goodness,' calls out Linda. There's a splash of red liquid on her white skirt, but her eyes are on Olivia's birthday cake, sat on the worktop with nine candles, soaked in red wine and pockmarked with shards of glass.

It's only Beth and Nathan who don't make a sound, seemingly frozen in time, like someone has pressed the pause button on them.

'Okay, stay away kids,' says Alice, throwing an arm out across the conservatory door, where several pairs of eyes are craning to see what's happened.

'But look at my cake,' shrieks Olivia. 'Olaf's all red.'

The colour has drained from Nathan's face – his expression suspended in disbelief whilst all around him chaos reigns.

'B-but how?' he manages in barely more than a whisper.

A crippling heat descends upon Alice as she looks to Nathan, to Beth and back again. 'How *what*? What the hell's wrong, Nathan?'

'I . . . erm, I just . . .' he stutters.

'Are you okay?' Alice asks her husband, as Linda reels off kitchen roll and starts soaking up the pooling liquid.

Nathan looks to Beth, his eyes blinking rapidly. 'What? Erm, yeah . . . yeah I'm fine.'

'What's going on?' Alice can't help but notice the change in the atmosphere. As if somebody had come in and wired five hundred amps into a socket. That somebody appeared to be Beth.

Alice looks to her, but she just shrugs her shoulders and smiles.

'Nathan?'

'God, I don't know what happened there,' he says, running a hand through his hair and attempting to laugh. 'You look just like somebody I used to know and for a moment I thought you'd come back from the dead. I got the fright of my life.'

Beth smiles sweetly. 'Oh, I can assure you I've not died. Unless, of course, I'm in some parallel universe, living another life, and I've come back to haunt you.'

Nathan laughs awkwardly. 'Yes . . . yes, maybe.'

Whilst Alice and Linda clear up the mess, Nathan and Beth stand rooted to the spot.

Alice's sense of unease refuses to budge. The look on Nathan's face was unlike anything she'd ever seen before, as if he really *had* seen a ghost. Yet Beth is the epitome of calm, as if she has everything under control.

Alice knows the thought she's trying so desperately hard to stop infiltrating her mind. It can't be. It isn't possible. She'll settle for any other explanation than *that*, because if she gives *that* room to breathe, it will suck all the breath from her.

'I'll just go and change,' says Nathan. 'I'd better go

and see if I can get Livvy a new cake as well.' He leaps over the pool on the floor, where Linda is on her hands and knees, cleaning it up.

'What's got *him* all of a fluster?' she asks.

Alice looks to Beth, hoping for an answer, but she just smiles and says, 'Here, Linda, let me help.'

'Excuse me for just one second,' says Alice as she follows Nathan up the stairs.

'Jesus!' he says as he looks down at his splattered chinos in their bedroom mirror. 'I don't suppose *that's* going to come out.'

'Are you going to tell me what that was all about?' asks Alice, trying to stay calm, whilst under water her legs are kicking furiously to keep her afloat.

He turns on a kilowatt smile. 'Honestly, nothing. That woman, your friend . . .'

'Her name's Beth,' hisses Alice. 'Why do you find that so hard to say?'

'Beth,' he says, slowly and deliberately, 'looks just like a girl I used to know.'

'An ex-girlfriend?' presses Alice.

Nathan's head drops. 'Yes, actually she was. Back when I was in my early twenties.'

'So what happened?'

'We were together for a few months, had a great time, but then . . .' His voice trails off.

Alice waits. She's not going to help him out.

'Then we split up, and about a year or so later, I

heard she'd died in a car crash.' He looks up at Alice imploringly, but she feels nothing.

'Funny, you've not mentioned that before.'

'It's not something that's ever come up,' he says. 'The woman downstairs just looks so much like her – that's all.'

'Beth,' Alice says, her voice strained.

'Yes, Beth,' he repeats. 'It gave me quite a fright.'

'So much so that it made you drop the glass you were holding?'

'Well, yes.'

Alice watches as he takes his trousers off and finds another pair in his immaculately organized wardrobe.

'So, you and Beth don't know each other?' Alice can't believe that she's pursuing this line of questioning. That she could honestly think that her second husband is also having an affair with her best friend. Because that's what she's thinking, if she'll just allow herself to admit it.

'What? No, of course not.'

'You've never seen her before in your life?'

'Well, I don't know, maybe. If she's perhaps been at school when I've been there . . . I don't know.'

'You'd better go and get your daughter a new birthday cake,' Alice says, her eyes narrowed.

'Yes,' he says, raising his eyebrows and attempting to laugh. 'Honestly, you couldn't make it up, could you?'

No, Nathan, you couldn't, thinks Alice.

41

'Okay, so are we all here?' asks Alice, commanding the attention of the team as they gather in her office the following morning.

They nod their heads in unison.

'As you know, we're completing on Japan this afternoon, so it's going to get pretty hectic around here over the next few weeks, and I just want to double-check you're all on board and ready.'

Mumblings of agreement reverberate around the office and Lottie lets out a squeaky whoop of excitement and then covers her mouth, as if it was entirely involuntary. Alice smiles, thankful for the humour it injects into the otherwise tense proceedings.

'You may well get excited, Lottie, because you and I are going out to Japan at the end of next week to see the site.'

Alice watches with glee as Lottie's mouth drops open.

'When . . . when was that decided?' stutters Nathan.

About the same time that I decided to take back control of my life, Alice thinks. Which, if she hazarded a guess, happened somewhere between six and seven o'clock last night. Right around the time that Beth had given her a kiss on the cheek and whispered. 'Let's never allow a man to get between us again.'

After Nathan had gone to bed early with a migraine, apparently brought on by the party, Alice had poured herself a large glass of red wine and sat at the dining table, with the lights dimmed. She'd imagined herself sitting there for hours, as her brain frantically tried to work out what was going on. But as she waited for the normal irrational thoughts to start mocking her, her mind became perfectly calm. Suddenly, the muddied puddles were replaced with crystal clear pools that she could see her reflection in, looking like the person she wanted to be. Happy and content, without the artificial support props of alcohol and antidepressants.

She used to be that person once, back when life was simpler, before she allowed men to cloud her judgement and dictate her path. Well, no more. She was not going to allow the men she loved, who she thought loved her back, define who she was, and what she could be. This was *her* life and she was going to take it by the horns and own it.

She'd picked up her full glass and poured it into the sink, mesmerized by the swirls of dark burgundy as the water carried what had become her cornerstone away. Surprised by the power that surged through her as she did so, she systematically opened the remaining six bottles, some she'd only bought earlier that day, and drained them.

When she went up to bed, her tablets, which made

her sleep just that little bit easier and smoothed out the rough edges of her paranoia, called out to her from where she hid them behind the bubble bath she never used in her medicine cabinet. She allowed them to goad her for a little while as she alternated between looking at them, thinking she needed them, to looking at herself in the mirror and knowing she didn't.

She credits both those decisions with how in control she feels this morning, and the team seem buoyed by this new sense of confidence and authority. Everybody, it seems, apart from Nathan, who is still sitting there in a haze of confusion.

'I'm also going to organize some meetings with fabric houses and furniture makers,' Alice goes on. 'See if we can make some new contacts, build new relationships. We're going to need people onside once we get started.'

'Oh my God, I am *so* up for this,' says Lottie, beaming from ear to ear.

Alice returns her smile. 'Okay, let's get to work.'

The team gather their things and head back to their desks. Only Nathan remains, which Alice isn't remotely surprised about.

'Since when are you making executive decisions like that without consulting with me?'

Alice doesn't look up from her computer screen. 'Since I remembered that *I* own this company.'

'And what's that supposed to mean?' he asks, standing in front of her with his hands burrowed deep into his trouser pockets. 'Are we going to harp on about Tom again? The prodigal son who so thanklessly put his inheritance into setting up AT Designs?'

Alice looks at him with a smile, immune to the barbed snipe. He can say what he likes about Tom now – she doesn't care. But she will not let it be implied that without him she wouldn't be where she is today. For the first time, she allows herself to wonder if she might've even gone further without the men in her life, both seemingly intent on holding her back.

'Tom may have put the start-up money in,' says Alice calmly, 'but I have worked my arse off to get this company to where it is today. We wouldn't have the house, the cars – even the expensive shoes you're standing in – if it wasn't for me. Nobody has put more into AT Designs than I have. And if that threatens you Nathan, then I suggest you start thinking about what else you might like to do.'

Alice thinks she sees a flash of vitriol darken his features, but his expression quickly changes to one of bemusement, which riles her even more.

'I'm going to get a sandwich,' he says.

'You do that,' says Alice.

As soon as his back is turned, she lets out the air that she'd held in to bolster herself up. Those swallowed breaths that give you extra confidence and stop your nerves from jangling, at least not loud enough for anyone else to hear.

She watches as he disappears from view, picks up her

phone and scrolls through until she finds the number for Liz, her old solicitor. The one who dealt with Tom's estate, and the one who advised her to get a pre-nup before marrying Nathan.

'Alice, how are you?' Liz asks warmly. Her voice immediately takes Alice to those dark days after Tom died. If it had been this time last month, she would've allowed herself to be transported back there, to wallow in the mire, but not today.

'I'm well,' she says. 'How are you?'

'Busy, but when are we not?' She gives a little laugh. 'What's going on with you? It's been a while. What is it? Six years?'

'About that, yes.'

'And how is Sophia and little Olivia?' Alice feels touched that she remembers the names of her children. 'Not so little any more, I bet?'

'Livvy's nine going on twenty-four, and Sophia is everything you'd expect a fifteen-year-old girl to be,' says Alice. She can't for the life of her remember Liz's children's names and is instantly disappointed in herself. 'I'm sorry to bother you, but I'm after some advice, if you don't mind.'

'Of course.'

'You may remember I was getting married to Nathan around the time we last spoke. I was looking for some advice about a pre-nup.'

Alice is sure she can hear the disapproval in Liz's 'Mmm.'

'We're going through a bit of a rocky patch,' Alice goes on. 'It's just a tentative enquiry at the moment, but I'd like to get an idea on where I'd stand financially, should we separate and divorce.'

Alice can hear Liz rustling some papers on her desk and imagines her sitting on a maroon leather chair in a mahogany-adorned chamber. 'I'm sorry to hear that,' she says, sympathetically, and it takes all of Alice's resolve not to cry. Maybe she's not as tough as she's pretending to be. 'Well if I remember correctly, you decided not to go ahead with the pre-nup.'

'No, that's right,' says Alice, and she can almost hear Liz silently saying, *Silly girl.* 'It wasn't something either of us wanted to do,' she goes on, trying to justify every bad decision she made back then.

'So, what assets do you have?' asks Liz. 'Just a rough idea.'

Alice tots everything up as quickly as she can. 'Well, I don't have specific figures, but the house is in my name and is worth about two million. AT Designs is profitable and has cash in the bank, but I've just recently taken a loan out for a million pounds to buy some land in Japan. We're building twenty-eight apartments near to the Olympic site.'

'Wow, that sounds interesting,' says Liz, but Alice is sure she can hear disbelief in her voice. 'And the business is solely in your name?'

'Yes.'

'So, can you remind me what Nathan brought to the marital table.'

Alice goes quiet, trying to find something worthwhile to say, but sensing the unfavourable answer, Liz puts her out of her misery.

'Okay, so despite Nathan turning up with nothing but the shirt on his back, he can still make a claim on your wealth if you separate.'

Alice winces at the lawyer's brutal choice of words. 'So that's not looking too good for me, then?'

'It would have been wise to secure your future a little,' says Liz, 'whilst you still had the chance. But you were in love and sometimes love is blind.'

Alice can't help but notice her use of the word 'were'. *Does that mean we aren't any more?* she wonders. *I guess that's why I'm calling her.*

'But I can draw something up to give you more detail if it should get to that stage,' Liz goes on. Right now, Alice can't see any chance that it won't.

'Thanks,' she says. 'But just before you go . . . About Japan – Nathan has largely been dealing with the business end of the transaction up until now. We've – I've – already paid a hundred thousand on exchange, and I'm about to complete this afternoon. I know I'm asking a lot, Liz, but is there any way you could take a quick look at the contract, just so, you know . . .'

'I assume a conveyancing solicitor has read through it before now?' asks Liz.

'Well, yes,' says Alice. 'My lawyer is based in Japan and he seems happy enough, but as I say, Nathan's been dealing with that side of things. I would just appreciate you checking it through, especially if I'm going to be on my own, going forward.'

'You're not leaving yourself an awful lot of time,' comments Liz. 'And I can't claim to be an expert on international property law, but if you send it over now, I'll take a quick look at it.'

'Thanks Liz, just let me know how much I owe you.'

'If it's all straightforward it shouldn't take me too long. You're lucky you've caught me in the office. Any other day this week and I would have been in court.'

'Thanks Liz, I really appreciate it.'

Alice puts the phone down just as Lottie is passing her office.

'Lottie, would you mind asking Matt for a copy of the Japan contract?' she says, as nonchalantly as she can manage.

'Yep sure,' she says breezily.

A few minutes later, Matt pops his head around Alice's door. 'I hear you're after the Japan contract?' he says. 'I believe Nathan's put it in the safe, under lock and key.'

'Good job I've got a key then.' Alice smiles as she reaches into her desk drawer and throws Matt a small bunch of keys. 'Would you mind?'

When he brings the contract in, he closes the door behind him.

'Can I have a word?'

'Sure,' says Alice, knowing it's unlike him to ask. 'What's up?'

'The company credit card has taken some pretty hefty hits recently.'

The news is no surprise to Alice.

'That's okay,' she says. 'I've been hitting it hard with fabrics and furniture for Belmont House. There was some stuff we needed to pay for up front.'

'Well, that's the thing,' he says. 'I know where we are with Belmont, but it already feels as if the Japan project is running away from me.'

Alice looks at him, her brows knitted. 'What do you mean?'

'Large sums are already being spent, mostly with one company, and I understand that we need to be a little organic on this, but I could do with a bit of a heads-up so that I can prepare for whatever's coming at us over the hill.'

'There must be some mistake,' says Alice. 'I've not spent money on anything over there yet. Perhaps a couple of hotel bills and the odd lawyer's bill, but that's it.'

Matt scratches at his head. 'That's not going to have busted through our twenty-grand limit.'

'Twenty grand?' exclaims Alice. 'We couldn't possibly have spent that kind of money.'

'We have, and most of it has gone to a company called Visions. Do you know who they are?'

Alice shakes her head. 'Have you spoken to Nathan?'

Matt nods. 'I mentioned it when the balance reached ten thousand and a couple of times since, but he said everything was fine and that the payments were all accounted for. But now we're at our limit, there's nowhere for us to go.'

'Might our credit card have been cloned or something like that? It definitely sounds as if there's been a breach somewhere. Can you check it out?'

'Sure. I'll find out what's going on and report back.' He offers a tight smile and turns to leave Alice's office.

She flicks through the contract that he leaves with her, but without speaking lawyer language, it's double-Dutch. She can't see any anomalies, but scans a copy straight over to Liz for her to check.

I'm popping to the bank reads a text from Nathan and Alice instinctively walks over to the window.

So *why do you need your car?* she wonders, as she watches him hurry towards it, peering around furtively before sliding behind the steering wheel.

42

Alice watches through the windscreen as Nathan types something into his phone. There's an uncomfortable sensation rising up from her toes, and as much as she tries to shrug it off, she just can't shake it.

As he reverses out of the parking space, Alice grabs her keys and bolts down the stairs. She wants to know, once and for all, what the hell he's up to.

She keeps her distance as his car manoeuvres its way through the mid-morning traffic, heading out of town.

He's only gone a couple of miles when he slows down and indicates left, into the Holiday Inn car park. Despite herself, Alice still wants there to be a perfectly reasonable explanation for why he's taken time out of his working day to go to a hotel. But the evidence against him is mounting.

Alice pulls into a space a few rows behind Nathan and hopes that the rain will obscure his vision in the same way it's dulling hers. She keeps the windscreen wipers on full power, yet they still struggle to offer her a clear view through the glass.

Ten minutes slowly pass, with Nathan still in his car. Alice switches off her wipers to try and retain some level of inconspicuousness, which makes it all the harder to stake out the women she sees; squinting through her rain-splattered windscreen as they make their way to or from their cars, waiting for one of them to head towards Nathan.

A dark car reverses into the space beside Nathan's, but Alice can't see the make or model. It doesn't seem to matter, as five minutes passes without movement. Alice is on the verge of leaving when she sees the car's door open and a woman get out. There's a flash of long dark hair, but it all happens too fast as the woman quickly gets into the passenger seat of Nathan's car.

Alice is rooted to the spot in shock and anger, fighting off the overpowering temptation to run over there and pull her out by her hair. Her hand is on the door handle, her pride pushing her out. She wants to kill him, and then her, but just as she's about to listen to her heart, her head steps in and attempts to take charge. *Breathe*, it tells her. *Stop and breathe.*

The two vital organs vie for control, pushing and pulling, like an internal tug of war. She slams her hands on the steering wheel and cries out, 'You lying bastard.' It wasn't as if she hadn't given him the chance to confess, to get it all out in the open – yet he'd *still* prevaricated.

But she's seen it with her own eyes now. She's not been the paranoid, needy wife Nathan has made her out to be. She's been right all along, and the overriding emotion is one of relief. Relief that she doesn't have to keep trying to catch him out. Relief that when he lies to her, she'll know the truth. And relief that she's been cast adrift in the ocean, with just her two girls by her side.

Just a few days ago, the thought would have killed her. But she feels differently now that she's no longer beholden to anyone else. Now, all she has to do is dodge the obstacles that tie her to a marriage that isn't what she thought it was. The house, the business and Japan suddenly seem superficial compared to the only real hurdle she's heading towards at a hundred miles per hour: the children. She has to do *everything* in her power to push through the complications, animosity and bitterness that will no doubt spill over from this ultimate deceit. She has to stay strong and true to her girls in her efforts to protect them from the fallout.

There's nothing more to see here. It doesn't even matter who it is anymore – it won't make Alice stay with a man who would rather be with someone else.

Just as she puts the car into gear, the woman gets out of Nathan's car, screams something that Alice doesn't quite catch and slams the door. A couple of people in the vicinity automatically look in their direction, but, fearful of getting involved, put their heads back down and hurry by. Alice winds her window down to get a clearer look through the rain, just as Nathan's car screeches forward, no doubt leaving rubber on the tarmac. The woman shouts something again and gesticulates with her arms, but

Nathan's car keeps on moving, at speed, out of the car park.

Alice wishes she'd driven away a few seconds ago, before she had seen the woman who has wrecked her marriage. Before she knew who she was.

With her heart hammering through her chest, she gets out of the car and runs across the car park, lifting her jacket over her head to protect her from the lashing rain. She has no idea what she's going to say, as she wets her lips, desperate for some moisture in her dry mouth.

The woman's still standing there, with her back to Alice, staring after Nathan's car. Alice feels sick as she is faced with the gut-wrenching deceit.

'Beth!' she croaks, hating her voice for letting her down.

Beth turns around, her wet hair stuck to her face. Alice can't tell if the drops on her cheek are tears or rainwater. She sees Alice and is instantaneously paralysed. It takes a few seconds for the shock to subside, but it feels like minutes for Alice, her eyes not leaving Beth's.

'Al-Alice,' Beth stutters, seemingly incapable of forming a full sentence. She looks in the direction that Nathan's car went, as if it will somehow magically tell her whether Alice had seen him or not. 'Wh-what are you doing here?'

'I'm not sure I'm the one who needs to answer that question,' hisses Alice, her stare unmoving.

'It's . . . it's not what you think,' stutters Beth.

'I can't even begin to get my head around this,' cries Alice. 'How could you? How could you do this to me, *again*?'

'I'm not having an affair with him, Alice,' says Beth, pulling herself up, suddenly seeming more in control. 'You've got this all wrong.'

'Have I?' snaps Alice. 'What other possible explanation can there be?'

The two women stare at each other through the pouring rain.

'Get in the car,' says Beth eventually. 'We need to talk.'

'I knew it!' cries Alice, chastising herself as she gets into the passenger seat of Beth's car. 'I knew something wasn't right yesterday – as soon as Nathan saw you. It was so obvious, but I didn't want to believe it – *refused* to believe it. Anyone but you, Beth. Why? Why would you do this to me? First Tom and now Nathan.'

Beth turns to look at Alice. 'I'm *not* sleeping with Nathan.'

Alice takes her phone and pulls up the number of the mystery text sent to her husband. Beth's face freezes as a ringtone emanates from her handbag on the back seat. Alice shakes her head and reaches for the door handle.

'Wait!' Beth calls out as she stretches across to pull the door to.

'I've heard all I need to hear,' says Alice.

'You haven't heard the half of it,' hisses Beth.

Alice, sensing a shift in atmosphere, falls resignedly back onto the seat. 'Are you in love with him?' she asks.

'I was once, yes,' admits Beth. 'But that was a long time ago.'

Alice turns, her eyes wide. 'How long has this been going on?' she asks incredulously.

'Years,' says Beth. 'Long before I met *you*.'

Alice feels like her brain might explode, unable to compute what she's being told. She can't even form the words if she wanted to.

'You look surprised,' says Beth coldly.

'This . . . this has been going on all this time and you knew Nathan was my husband all along?'

'Yes,' says Beth. 'But in my defence, this started way before you two got together. I met Nathan before you did.'

'What?' gasps Alice. 'How is that even possible?'

'Because he's not *your* Nathan,' says Beth calmly. 'He's *my* Thomas.'

43

'What the hell are you talking about?' Alice shouts, her indignation spilling out.

'Well it turns out that things aren't quite what they seem,' says Beth, her tone acerbic. 'I met and fell in love with a man I knew as Thomas Evans some ten years ago.'

Despite having thought she'd built a barrier, to immunize herself against the hurt that knowledge caused, Alice still feels a pain slice across her chest. She wants to close her ears off to what Beth is saying, but yet she wants to know – *has* to know.

'We were really happy,' Beth goes on. 'I was completely in love with him and thought we'd be together forever. But then I saw him with you . . .'

'You *saw* us together?' says Alice, in barely more than a whisper. 'So you knew who I was. You've known all this time that I was Tom's *wife*.'

'Well, you see, that's where it starts to get interesting.'

Alice numbly shakes her head, no longer listening to what Beth's saying. 'You've known *all* this time that I was Tom's wife. You've sat and let me talk about him, held me when I've cried about him, all the while knowing that you had an affair with him. Had a *child* with him.' Her shoulders convulse as a sob catches in her throat. 'Why would you *do* that?'

'It wasn't like that,' says Beth, her voice softer. 'The man I knew as Thomas Evans left me for you.'

Alice looks at her with a confused expression. 'But that's not possible. I was his wife – how can that be?'

'Because the man I thought was Thomas was actually Nathan.'

'I . . . I don't understand – you're not making any sense.'

'It didn't make any sense to me either – not at first. But do you remember Nathan taking you to Albany Avenue in Guildford?'

'When?' asks Alice, unable to remember ever going to Guildford, let alone the road name.

'Around ten years ago. You waited in his car – he had a silver Audi at the time – outside a flat – *my* flat.'

Slowly the memory begins to form, but it's vague at best. 'Didn't he move from there to Battersea?' muses Alice, her voice sounding as hazy as the recollection. 'I think he grabbed the last few things whilst I waited outside.'

'That was my flat,' says Beth.

'No,' says Alice, more confidently. 'He was sharing the place with a guy who was a lift engineer or something – I remember it now – Ben or Blake his name was – it definitely began with a B.'

'You're right – Beth. That was my place, and that was the day Nathan left me for you.'

Alice shakes her head vehemently.

'Come on Alice, you *saw* me, I know you did. You looked straight at me as you went past in the car. You must have known what you were doing, or at the very least, known what *he* was doing. Did he tell you about me? Did you hatch the plan together? It turned out pretty nicely for you, didn't it?'

'I honestly don't know what you're talking about. I'd never seen you before you pitched up at school with Millie.'

Beth lets out a disbelieving snort. 'When Nathan and I met, he told me he was a wine dealer. He also told me that his mother was in a care home with dementia, made me believe that I'd been burgled and even abducted my dog, before "rescuing" him back for me.'

'Why would he do that?' asks Alice.

Beth shrugs her shoulders. 'For the money, in the short term – he stole some jewellery and personal possessions that might have fetched a few hundred pounds, although their sentimental value was a lot higher. And I paid a ransom, for want of a better word, to get my dog back, which would have gone straight into his pocket.'

Alice looks at her, bewildered.

'But Nathan likes to play the long-game, so in creating those distressing situations, not only did he earn financially from them, but he earned my trust – made me think he was my saviour.'

SANDIE JONES

Alice remembers Nathan making her feel exactly the same way. *A wolf in sheep's clothing*.

'And when the time was right, he pounced,' says Beth with tears in her eyes. 'When he knew he had my trust – when he knew I felt secure – he stole one hundred and fifty thousand pounds of my family's money.'

Alice's eyes widen, unblinking as she stares at Beth.

'But why would Nathan need your money? He had more than enough of his own when I met him.'

'He didn't have a pot to piss in,' says Beth scathingly. 'Everything he came to you with was ours – he took every penny that my mother had, and didn't the pair of you have a grand old time spending it. I bet you couldn't quite believe your luck, could you? But whilst you were living the high life, my mother was slowly dying of embarrassment and shame.'

Alice's blood runs cold.

'It broke her heart and took her soul. It was everything she and my dad had worked for, and without it, she couldn't carry on living in the house that she cherished, the house that she had shared with my father.' Beth's face crumples as the tears come. 'And I allowed him to do it.'

A part of Alice wants to reach out to her old friend, but she stops herself – the trust that they'd once shared shattered.

'So she sold the house, and less than two weeks later died in her sleep, her pride unable to survive the move.' Beth blows her nose on a tissue.

'I'm sorry, but—' begins Alice, wondering how any of this has anything to do with her, but Beth cuts her off.

'She didn't speak to me again after what happened. And above all else, I'll never forgive him for that.' She looks at Alice. 'So, what did you do with all our money? Did he pay off the house? Did he plough it all into AT Designs? Or did the pair of you just have a fine time spending it? Either way, you've not done too badly out of my family's life's work, have you?'

'I think you've got the wrong man,' says Alice. 'And you've certainly got the wrong woman. I was more than capable of standing on my own two feet when I met Nathan, financially, if not emotionally. Tom received a significant inheritance after the death of his parents and it was largely put into the company, which in turn paid off the mortgage. I was totally self-sufficient by the time I met Nathan. I didn't take anything from him, nor did he offer. The house is mine, the company is mine, the site in Japan will be mine.'

'So, you're telling me that he brought nothing to this marriage, nothing of any financial value?'

Alice shakes her head. 'Not a penny, and yet now I'm told he's entitled to half of everything I own.'

'You've spoken to a solicitor?' asks Beth in surprise.

'Yes, earlier today,' admits Alice. 'I've asked for some advice on where I stand if we separate. Something's not been right for a while, but seeing his reaction to you at

Olivia's party yesterday, I knew for definite. I guess you must have really surprised him.'

Beth smiles wryly. 'He wouldn't have been expecting me, that's for sure.'

'Now I know why you went out of your way to avoid him,' says Alice. 'I'd not thought about it before, but last night, I remembered all the times you could have bumped into each other, yet every time you'd somehow manipulated yourself out of it. You must have both felt like you were sitting on a timebomb, working out ways to avoid each other whenever I was around. But yesterday you made a conscious decision to do what you did. Why now, Beth?'

'You don't get it, do you?' says Beth. 'That day, when I saw you both outside my flat in Guildford, was also the last time I saw *him* – until yesterday.'

Alice feels winded. 'What?'

'He disappeared off the face of the earth and it was only a good few years later that I saw a picture in the paper, of you receiving a design award. I didn't think I'd ever be able to recognize the woman in the car that day, but I knew it was you the minute I saw it. So I used you to track him down.'

That admission, more than anything else, cuts Alice the deepest.

'Now I'm here to claim back what's mine.'

'You want *money*?' asks Alice, her voice tight. '*That's* what this is all about?'

'I want what's rightfully mine. What he stole from my family.'

'And you've waited this long to get it?'

'I needed to take my time, work out the best way to do it, pounce at the most opportune moment, just like he did with me. I had to be sure he had the money to give.'

'So how are you going to go about getting it back?'

Beth looks down into her lap and wipes away the tear that is threatening to fall. 'By blackmailing him.'

Alice lets out a derisory laugh. 'With what?'

'I had hoped that making him look like he was having an affair would do the trick. That by the time he found out it was me, he'd be so close to losing you that he'd do anything to make me stop.'

'So, the texts . . . ?' starts Alice.

Beth nods. 'And all the other things . . . the hotel bill, the earring, the flowers, the tyres . . . '

'That was all *you*?' asks Alice, disbelievingly. 'But why? Why would you do that to us? To me?'

'Because I hated you for having the life that I was supposed to be having. You had it *all* . . . the perfect job, the perfect children, supposedly the perfect husband . . . I just wanted you to hurt as much as I had been hurt. But I went too far. Olivia didn't deserve to be brought into this.'

Alice cocks her head to one side as a new fire sparks

within her. She'll take whatever Beth throws at her, but not if she's going to bring her children into it. They're off limits.

'Olivia?' she questions.

Beth looks anywhere but at Alice. 'I made a formal complaint to the school about her,' she says quietly.

'Oh my God!' Alice exclaims.

'I'm sorry,' says Beth, barely audible.

Alice goes to get out of the car before Beth leans across and grapples with the door.

'Please – wait,' she says.

Alice leans her head back resignedly onto the headrest and closes her eyes.

'So what is Nathan going to do now?' she asks. 'Now that he knows it's you.'

'He's told me he'll have the money ready by tomorrow.'

Alice laughs sarcastically. 'We'll have less money then than we've got now. Japan completes this afternoon.'

'Are you still going ahead with that? After everything I've told you?'

'Doing the Japan deal isn't dependent on Nathan,' says Alice, matter-of-factly. 'It depends on me – whether *I* want to do it or not – and right now, I don't see any reason why I shouldn't. In fact, what you've said only makes me want to do it more.'

'Is Nathan doing it with you?' asks Beth.

'Financially, you mean?'

Beth nods.

'No, this is all on me – I've taken a loan out for it.'

'Good,' says Beth. 'Don't let him anywhere near it.'

'And what are *you* going to do?' asks Alice. 'Now that I know everything. Now that you can no longer blackmail him.'

Beth turns to look at her imploringly. 'Don't tell him, Alice.'

'What?' she says, exasperated. 'After everything you've done, you honestly expect me to do you a favour?'

'Please,' begs Beth.

'What if everything you've told me is a lie?' says Alice, looking directly at Beth for the first time. 'What if you've made this all up? And even if you haven't, why should I do anything you say? Look at what you've done to me, to my family. Right now, Nathan doesn't look like he's actually done anything wrong, at least not by me. So why would I show you loyalty over him?'

'Because he pretended to be *your* dead husband,' blurts out Beth, stopping Alice in her tracks. 'Please – if for no other reason – do it for that.'

Alice feels a jolt. *Tom.*

'So, Nathan told you that his name was Thomas Evans?'

Beth nods. 'Born on twenty-first of May, 1976.'

'So regardless, you've known for ages that your Thomas and my Tom were two entirely different people. Yet you still implied that he was one and the same person.'

'Yes,' whispers Beth.

'So . . . so you never actually knew *my* Tom?' Alice asks tentatively. '*Your* Thomas Evans was Nathan.'

Beth nods.

A rush of relief floods through Alice, reigniting every tiny flame that she'd bequeathed to Tom over the past ten years. 'So Tom *was* the man I thought he was?' she asks, with tears streaming down her cheeks. 'He was never the man you made me think he was.'

'No.'

Alice lambasts herself for ever believing otherwise. She knew her Tom hadn't been capable of what Beth was accusing him of. She steels herself before asking the next question, unsure of the answer she wants to hear, unsure of what her best friend is truly capable of.

'He's on Facebook . . .' she starts. 'My Tom is on Facebook living a new life . . .' She can't bear to look at Beth, knowing that her expression will tell her all she needs to know.

'I'm so sorry,' Beth chokes. 'I wanted you to think that he might still be out there. That he'd left you because he *wanted* to. Just like Nathan had left me.'

Alice closes her eyes tightly, willing her heart not to break all over again. 'But the photos?'

'Surprisingly easy,' says Beth quietly. 'They're all on your phone, and how often have you left it on a pub table whilst you went to the bar, or given it to me to hold whilst you were in the toilet? The picture of the other woman and child was a random photo from the internet.'

'God, you must *really* hate me,' cries Alice.

'I thought you were part of it,' says Beth after a long pause. 'I saw the house and the cars, and just assumed that it was my mother's money that was paying for it all.'

Alice feels numb and wearily pulls on the door handle.

'What are you going to do?' asks Beth as Alice goes to step out. 'Are you going to tell Nathan you know everything?'

She doesn't even have the energy to reply.

44

Alice feels like there's a tennis ball lodged in her throat, blocking her airways, as she makes her way up the stairs to the office.

'Whoa, I didn't think you were going to make it back in time,' says Nathan, moving in to kiss her. 'Where were you?'

She stares at him, not knowing what she's looking for, but there's nothing to suggest he's the man who's defrauded her best friend and her mother. Nothing to explain why he'd used Tom's name before he'd even met Alice. And nothing to suggest he knows he's about to be rumbled. His calmness almost floors her. She moves past him without a word.

'We've got fifteen minutes until we complete,' says Nathan as he follows her into her office.

'Great,' she murmurs.

'You okay?' he asks. 'You look tense.'

'Nervous,' she manages.

'That's not a bad thing,' he says. 'You wouldn't be human if you weren't.'

She smiles tightly.

'Get the champagne on ice, Lottie,' is the last thing

she hears Nathan say as she closes her door behind him.

Her phone rings, displaying Liz's number. She'd forgotten all about her.

'Liz, hi.'

'Hello Alice – have you got a minute? I just wanted to come back to you on this contract.'

'Yep, sure. Anything I need to be worried about?'

'Well, only that there's a clause that I've just had checked out. I thought it might just have been a discrepancy caused by translating the contract from Japanese to English, but I checked with a colleague and it's a pretty important one – I hope it's not too late.'

'No, but we're close,' says Alice. 'Completion's scheduled for about fifteen minutes' time.'

'Well, it looks to me as if there's a covenant on the land.'

'Yes, my lawyer in Japan mentioned something about that,' says Alice. 'He'd flagged it up to Nathan, who assured me that all was well.'

'But it means that nothing more than a temporary structure can be built on the land you're buying. A shed, car port, something along those lines, perhaps, but certainly not a permanent apartment complex.'

'Well, that doesn't make sense,' says Alice tightly. 'We've got planning for twenty-eight apartments.'

'I can't see how that can be the case,' says Liz. 'Because as I say, the land you're buying is within the urbanization control area, and as such, no brick buildings are permitted.'

Alice feels as if the blood flowing around her body has reached a dead end. 'But surely Nathan would have flagged that up to me,' she says, rubbing at her forehead with the palm of her hand. 'Why would he have let me go ahead with the purchase, if nothing can be built on it?'

'I don't know,' says Liz tentatively.

Or maybe Nathan already knows there's a problem, thinks Alice. 'But why would he advise me to go ahead with it?' she says aloud. 'It'll risk the business, our salaries, our home, all of it. It doesn't make any sense.'

'I'm only reporting what we've found,' says Liz.

'Who's the vendor?' asks Alice abruptly.

She hears Liz turning over papers at her end.

'A company called Excelsior. I really think you need to get to the bottom of this before you agree to completion. It would be ill-advised to go ahead on what I'm seeing here.'

The name means nothing to Alice. 'Okay, thanks for your help,' she says, and puts the phone down. She starts typing an email to Mr Yahamoto, heading it up 'Private & Confidential'.

Dear Mr Yahamoto,
It has come to my attention that there are one or two discrepancies in the contract for the purchase

of Embassy Docks, Tokyo, that I would like you to comment on, ahead of completion.

Therefore, I would like to postpone completion until such time that I am confident that all is as it should be.

Please inform the vendor's solicitors of this decision immediately and let them know that we will revert to them in due course.

I would like to remind you to exercise discretion in this matter, and remain aware that I am the sole purchaser and so should therefore be your only point of contact.

Yours sincerely,
Alice Davies

Alice grabs her handbag from her desk and heads out through the open-plan office. 'I'll be back in five minutes,' she calls out, to no one in particular.

'Hey, where are you going?' says Nathan, frantically. 'Alice!'

She races up the high street, and is out of breath by the time she arrives at the bank. On seeing her, the manager grabs a cup of water from the cooler and offers it to her.

'Mrs Davies, are you okay?'

'I need to stop the transaction,' she says, breathlessly. 'We're not completing.'

Five minutes later she's waiting in the manager's office

as he prints off confirmation that the transfer has been halted. If her fears are unfounded, then she may have just lost out on the deal of the century. *A no-brainer*, as Nathan would say. But if her instinct is right . . .

Beth's words ring loudly in her ears. *Don't let him anywhere near it.*

Her chest falls and rises heavily, every fibre in her body fighting against the growing possibility of Nathan being more corrupt and cruel than she could even begin to imagine.

Her phone rings and, seeing it's Nathan, she hesitates, as if it's going to stop him from saying what she thinks he's going to say. Knowing that if he does, it means that everything Beth has said is true.

'Jesus, Alice,' barks Nathan down the line. 'What the hell are you playing at?'

'What's up?' she says, as calmly as she can, though even *she* can hear the quiver in her voice.

Don't say it. Please don't say it.

'Why have you stalled completion?' he says, and with those five words, Alice's world comes crashing down around her.

She hangs up and with shaking hands calls Beth. 'You won't be getting any money back from Nathan,' Alice says.

45

The deceit is crippling, like an unknown force rippling through her body, slowly shutting down her vital organs, one by one.

Beth drives the car in silence, the pair of them contemplating their next move whilst Alice's phone rings off the hook.

'How can you be so sure that Nathan's the vendor?' asks Beth eventually.

'Because the vendor is the only other person who would have been told that completion's delayed,' she says.

'And you were buying it for a million pounds?' asks Beth incredulously. 'How much do you think Nathan bought it for?'

'It's worthless!' says Alice, as she bangs the dashboard with a closed fist. 'He'd have got it for a song because nothing can be built on it. It's no man's land.'

'Shit,' says Beth. 'He was going to do it all over again.'

Alice leans back on the headrest as a text from Matt pings through on her phone.

Good news! Looks like the payments to Visions are all kosher as they're a subsidiary of Excelsior – the vendors on Japan! Will talk you through when you're back in the office.

'What do you want to do?' asks Beth.

Alice counts to ten in her head, concentrating on taking slow deep breaths in and out. 'I want to kill him, is what I want to do.'

'Who was that disgusting man?' asks Beth, sounding as if a lightbulb has gone on in her head that no one else can see. Alice waits for her to offer more.

'That creep who owned Temple Homes. The one who assaulted you.'

Alice shakes her head, not knowing what he's got to do with anything. 'David,' she says. 'David Phillips.'

'Where's that site? The one he wanted you to work on.'

'Bradbury Avenue,' says Alice, a slight irritation to her. How was this solving the very big problem of Nathan?

Beth snatches a look at her watch. 'Will it still be open?'

'What, the site?'

Beth nods.

'I don't know. Why?'

'Call David and find out if you can meet him there.'

Alice turns in her seat. 'Why would I do that?'

'Just ask him to meet you there now.'

'Absolutely not,' snaps Alice. 'I never want to speak to him again.'

'Just do it,' says Beth, her eyes not leaving the road in front of her. 'I've got an idea.'

'And what do I do if he says yes?'

'We'll revert to Plan B.'

Alice begrudgingly looks up his number, unsure of whether she deleted it from her phone after their encounter. She almost hopes that she has.

When she sees it, she fights the urge to lie to Beth. 'I don't want him to think that what he did was okay,' she says quietly, remembering his hands on her behind, his rough fingers kneading her breast.

'Believe you me, he won't get away with it,' says Beth, 'if you please just do as I say.'

'Are you honestly asking me to *trust* you?' says Alice, her voice high-pitched and laden with irony.

'Yes,' says Beth firmly, and for some reason Alice believes her.

'David!' she enthuses, superficially. 'It's Alice. How are you?'

'Oh, Alice,' he replies. 'Well, this is a surprise. I thought after—'

'It was a misunderstanding,' she says. 'And not something that should interfere with business.'

'Well, I'm pleased you feel that way. I have to say, I was somewhat surprised by your overreaction.'

Alice bites her lip, desperately trying to stay calm.

'Listen, I was wondering if I could take a look at the site after all? Just to get a clearer picture of your vision for the interior. That is, if you'd still like me to . . .'

'Of course,' he booms. 'It's still very much a building

site, so we have to be careful, but I'll gladly show you around. When are you free?'

'I was thinking in maybe half an hour or so, around six, if that works for you?'

'I'm afraid the site is closed for the day now,' he says.

Alice looks to Beth who spins her finger, intimating for her to wrap the conversation up.

'Ah, that's a shame as I'm literally coming past it. Never mind, perhaps another time.'

'Well, if you're passing, I suppose you could pop in. It's all supposedly locked up – health and safety and all that.' He laughs throatily. 'But if you go around the back, there's a loose hoarding that you can slide across. Don't tell anyone I told you though, or they'll come down on me like a ton of bricks. I've already been paid a visit because kids treat it like a playground, and if anything happens to one of them, apparently it'll be on my head. How ridiculous is that?'

'Crazy,' says Alice, desperate to get off the phone as Beth gives her the thumbs-up.

'Perhaps we could meet for dinner to discuss the way forward. I'd hate for you to miss out on this opportunity, just because—'

Alice cuts him off, unable to listen to this odious little man any longer.

'Fine, I'll give you a call tomorrow,' she says before putting the phone down and turning to Beth. 'Now what?'

'Just ask Nathan to meet you there,' says Beth authoritatively.

'But what for?'

Beth turns to look at her and they share a momentary understanding. An unspoken agreement that everything will be all right.

'Where the hell are you?' barks Nathan through the loudspeaker. 'What's going on? We've *got* to complete on Japan.'

Alice feels bizarrely detached – as if she's landed in a movie of someone else's life.

'Did you hear me?' he goes on. 'Time's running out.'

'Who for, Nathan?'

'What do you mean, who for? Us. You. AT Designs . . .' He sounds slightly hysterical. 'If we don't do it now, we're going to miss this opportunity. I've worked so hard for this, Alice.'

'You have,' she agrees, though on the opposing side to her, it seems. 'Meet me at the Temple Homes development on Bradbury Avenue.'

'What? Why?'

'We got the go-ahead on the job I pitched for.'

'This isn't the right time Alice – we need to get Japan done first.'

Alice looks at Beth, her eyes wide, her thoughts frantic.

'Just get him there,' hisses Beth, under her breath.

'The only chance of getting "this done" is if you meet me at Bradbury Avenue.'

393

'Jesus, I'm on my way,' he says gruffly.

'Wait here,' says Beth, as they park up in one of the adjacent roads to the Temple Homes site.

'What? No!' says Alice as she wrestles to undo her seatbelt. 'I'm coming with you.'

'Just give me five minutes with him,' says Beth, leaning back into the car. 'He needs to know what he stands to lose if he doesn't give me the money back.'

Alice leans her head back onto the headrest and laughs falsely.

'Do you honestly believe that he's going to pay you back?' she asks.

'If he knows he's about to lose everything . . . you, the girls . . .'

'Do you think he cares enough?' says Alice impatiently. 'What part of his behaviour in the last hour has made you think that he has mine and the children's best interests at heart? He thinks he's about to defraud me of a million pounds. He'll be intending to leave immediately – he'd have to, before I found out that he'd sold me a worthless piece of shit. Do you honestly think that on his way to wherever he's going to go and hide, he'll suddenly develop a conscience and think, *Oh, hang on – I'd better pay Beth back her mother's life savings from ten years ago?*

'If what you've told me is true, we need to work together to make sure he never does this to anyone else, ever again. It's the best we can hope for.' She softens her tone. '*I've* done what you've asked me to do. Now let me go and speak to him.'

Beth considers this for a moment, as if sizing up the options. 'I'll give you five minutes, then I'm coming in.'

Alice walks around the back of the boarded-up site until she comes to a loose panel that she can just about squeeze through. She looks up at the four-storey building, its slab floors and ceilings being held in place by metal stilts. A dormant crane stands against the open-sided structure.

She climbs the concrete staircases up to the top floor and looks down to where Beth's car is parked. Nathan's BMW speeds down another adjacent street before coming to an abrupt stop as he bumps it up onto the pavement. Everything about him looks chaotic, whilst Alice feels strangely calm.

He finds the same loose panel as she did and jumps over the pipework laid out along the muddy trenches.

'Alice!' he calls out.

'I'm up here,' she replies, the whipping wind carrying her voice.

'What the hell is going on?' he says when he reaches her, a little out of breath. 'Why have you dragged me out here? We haven't got time for this, you need to authorize the bank and Yahamoto and get Japan done.'

'I'm not completing on Japan,' she says, her voice wobbling.

He starts to come towards her. 'You have to, darling. We'll lose a hundred thousand pounds if we don't.'

'Is that not enough for you, Nathan? Wouldn't you have been wise just to take the deposit money and run?'

'Wh-what?' he says, as his eyes slide from side to side. 'What do you mean?'

'But you wanted to hold out for the big one, didn't you?' Alice goes on. 'You got greedy. What were you going to do with the money, Nathan? Do you have another life all lined up, ready to walk into? Were you going to use the money to charm your next victim? Like you did me.'

'Darling, you're not well,' he says, opening his arms out to her. 'I know you're back on the tablets, you're drinking too much, you're allowing things to get to you and mess with your head. You need help.'

Without even thinking, she steps forward and slaps him hard across the face. He holds his burning cheek with his hand and looks at her in shock.

The mask finally slips. 'You're going to go through with Japan,' he hisses. 'Get on the phone now and authorize completion.'

She stands there, jaw set, but her heart is beating so fast she's sure she can feel it banging against her ribcage. 'I'm not doing it, Nathan.'

He lunges at her and pins her against a concrete pillar. 'You don't have a choice,' he says, his breathing heavy. 'Just get on the phone and do it.'

396

'No,' she croaks, shaking her head as much as she's able to.

He hits the wall above her head with his fist. 'Fucking do it. Now!'

Alice recoils as his knuckles pass within millimetres of her face. She feels unable to breathe, her lungs burning, as she struggles to keep calm. Nathan grabs her roughly by her cheeks and she's sure she's stopped breathing altogether.

'Nathan!' calls out Beth from the top of the stairs.

His head spins around. 'You?' he questions, as if unable to believe what he's seeing. He looks from Beth to Alice and back again. 'What the fuck . . . ?'

'Is it true, Nathan?' asks Alice, his grip on her face weakening. 'Did you steal Beth's money?'

His eyes are wide, his pupils dilated.

'You owe me,' hisses Beth.

'For what?' laughs Nathan hollowly. 'It was your *own* greed that brought you down.'

'You killed my mother,' she says.

'That's a little over-dramatic, isn't it? Did I force either of you to give me money? Or did you give it to me willingly?'

Alice wants to close her ears, so that she can't hear what her husband was capable of in a different life.

In this life, she says to herself.

'You were going to do it again, weren't you?' says Alice, trying desperately hard not to cry as the reality hits her. 'You were prepared to walk away from our marriage and children, for money.'

'I've done my time,' he spits. 'There isn't another man on this earth who would have put up with what I've had to. Constantly having to reassure you, convince you that nothing was going to happen to me, that I wasn't going to leave you like your beloved Tom did. You sucked me dry, Alice.'

'Don't you dare put yourself in the same sentence as him,' she screams, hitting Nathan's chest with all the strength that she can muster. 'You will *never* be the man he was. He was cut from a different cloth. You don't even come close.'

He grabs hold of her wrists and leans in so that his face is just millimetres from hers. 'Cut from a different cloth, you say? I very much doubt that. I think we're a lot more similar than you think.'

'Leave her alone,' says Beth, stepping forward.

'Or what?' he snarls.

Beth raises her arm to hit him, but Nathan catches it and twists it up and around her back. His face is distorted and beads of sweat are dotted on his forehead as he moves towards the edge of the building, taking Beth with him.

'Get on the phone,' he says to Alice. 'Authorize the deal.'

'Why are you doing this?' she asks. 'When did you become this person I don't recognize?'

'*You* made me like this,' he spits. '*You, her, him* . . .'

'*Him?*' Alice questions.

'Darling Tom,' he says, snidely. 'The golden child who could do no wrong.'

Alice shakes her head in confusion, whilst Beth winces as he tightens his grip on her.

'You're not making any sense,' says Alice. 'What has Tom got to do with any of this?'

'He took what was mine,' says Nathan. 'You both did.'

Alice looks to Beth, her expression as puzzled as her own.

'You think that AT Designs is all yours?' he shouts at Alice. 'Well, it isn't. Whatever Tom put in, half of it was mine. So all this time you've been bleating about it being Tom's company, how *his* interests have got to be protected, how you've got to do right by *him* . . .'

'Nathan, you're . . . you're not making any sense,' stutters Alice, feeling as if she's being suffocated by his words. 'What do you mean? What are you saying?'

'A million pounds for Japan is what I'm due. It's rightfully mine. It's what I should have had all along.'

'Why?' asks Alice.

'Because Tom and I *are* cut from the same cloth.'

Alice shakes her head. 'You couldn't be further from the man he was if you tried. You're nothing alike.'

Nathan throws his head back and laughs. 'And yet so similar, don't you think?' He waits for Alice to take the bait, but she looks at him, dumbfounded.

'Come on,' he exclaims. 'Didn't it ever occur to you how similar we are? How our profiles match in certain lights? How our mannerisms mirror each other?'

Alice can't separate her lucid thoughts from the living nightmare she finds herself in. She thinks back to seeing Nathan walk into the garden of the psychiatric unit; feels his warm eyes taking in his surroundings before they settle on her. They'd seemed gentle, familiar. Had she been drawn to him because there was a comforting resemblance to the man she'd just lost?

Had the way he sometimes ran his hand through his hair reminded her of someone else? Had his slightly lopsided grin subconsciously infiltrated her brain, masquerading as someone else's? Had she fallen for him because he seemed so much like Tom?

'Wh-what are you saying?' falters Alice.

'I'm Tom's brother,' says Nathan bluntly.

46

The floor feels like it's falling away as Alice's legs buckle beneath her. She lands heavily and tries to focus but everything around her is spinning.

'Alice!' she hears a woman cry, but it sounds muffled and a long way away. She turns towards the direction she thinks it came from, though she can only see the blurred outline of two bodies close together.

'Y-you . . . you can't be,' she croaks, her mouth feeling like it's filled with cotton wool. 'That's impossible.'

'Well, you're looking at the impossible,' he says.

'You're *Daniel*?' she asks, unable to process the question, let alone the answer.

'Oh, so he *did* talk about me,' says Nathan acerbically.

Alice can barely speak, the words that are circling in her head are banging against the sides of her skull.

'When did you know?' she asks. 'Why didn't you tell me who you were when you found out who I was?'

'Oh darling, I've always known who you were,' he says patronizingly. 'As soon as Tom died, I came looking for you.'

'No, no,' says Alice, shaking her head, refusing to believe what he's saying. She thinks back to that day in the unit. He was there to see someone else. He was there by chance. 'No, you're lying. You came to see someone else.'

'I came there to see *you*,' he says. 'I knew you'd be desperate by then, and you were. You would have clung to anyone who showed you sympathy.'

Alice is still shaking her head vehemently.

'That was the easy bit,' Nathan goes on. 'If I'd known I'd have to wait all this time to get the money, well . . .'

'But . . . but why?' Alice manages.

Nathan's face clouds over. 'Did you honestly think it was fair that the inheritance from my parents, *our* parents, should all go to Tom?'

The Evans family had split into two uneven factions before Alice and Tom had even met. It seemed they'd done all they could to help their volatile and capricious son and brother. And by the time Alice was welcomed into the family fold, there was little to show for Daniel's existence aside from a few childhood photos on the mantelpiece.

Alice remembers them being the ironic backdrop as her and Tom, along with his heartbroken parents, sat in their dining room, stunned by the news that their youngest son had been convicted of fraud and sentenced to four years in prison. His mother's face was crumpled with grief, as if she'd lost the only child she'd ever had, and his father's stiff upper lip was close to collapsing.

'I don't want that boy's name mentioned ever again,' he'd said. 'He's been trouble ever since he was sixteen and there's no part of me that's surprised to find him in the position he is now. It's as if this was always going to be his path. Well, long may he walk it, but he'll be doing it on his own.' He'd put his arm around his wife and she fell into him, her agony unlike anything Alice had ever seen.

'You can't just freeze him out,' Tom had said softly. 'He'll always be your son.'

'He's no son of mine,' his dad had said.

'They disowned you,' Alice says to the man she no longer knows. Her eyes regain their focus as she stares at him. There is no part of him that she recognizes as her husband. 'They wanted nothing more to do with you.'

'But Tom would have put them up to that. I know he would.'

'No, you're wrong,' says Alice. 'He tried to do the exact opposite, but your parents wouldn't hear of it.'

'I only have your word to take for that.'

'So when you came out of prison, you assumed Tom's name and date of birth?' Even as she's saying it, it sounds too absurd to be true.

'Well, I couldn't exactly use my real name,' he says, half-laughing. 'As a convicted fraudster I was going to find it hard going. Tom, or Thomas as my parents used to call him, was, apparently, a good upstanding citizen, and as I knew more about him than anyone else, he seemed the obvious choice.'

Beth looks at Alice, wide-eyed, as his admission takes hold.

'So, you planned all this from the outset,' says Beth, her voice shaking. 'You were always looking to defraud me. It wasn't just an opportunistic one-off.'

Nathan laughs heartily. 'What? You think I fell in love with you first, and robbed you second?'

'But, I—' starts Beth.

'I also knew who *you* were before I met you. Those dating sites are an invaluable source of vulnerable, needy women, looking for a knight in shining armour. I didn't need to read too hard between the lines of your profile to find out who you were. By the time we met, I knew your full name, what you did for a living, who your father was and where your mother lived. All I had to do then was wait for you to get greedy – and boy, did you get greedy.'

Beth turns and raises her free hand, striking him on the face. He pulls her hair, yanking her head back, and she screams.

'Beth!' Alice calls out as she struggles to get up.

Beth is writhing, frantically trying to get a grip on him as he stands behind her with his hand furled in her hair, pulling on her scalp.

Alice runs unsteadily to where they're standing, perilously close to the edge. 'Get away from her,' she screams, raising her arms. But just before she gets there, Beth kicks up with her foot, her heeled boot landing square in Nathan's crotch. He momentarily lets go of her as he doubles over in pain and in that instant she pushes him with all her might.

He stumbles backwards as if in slow motion, and Alice tries to grab him, but instead of taking her hand, he reaches for Beth's. Beth squeezes her eyes shut as she's pulled towards the sheer drop, and in that split second Alice has to decide who she's going to save. She lunges at Beth with everything she's got, tackling her side-on. The force sends both Beth and Nathan upwards, seemingly flying through the air, their arms flailing. Alice reaches out and feels a hand grip onto hers. She closes her fingers around it as tightly as she can and pulls back with every shred of strength she can muster.

It's only then, as the body falls heavily on top of her, that Alice is aware of the choice she's made.

It was the right one.

EPILOGUE

I clamped my eyes shut as the floor fell away beneath my feet. The air whipped through my hair and I steeled myself for the cold, hard ground that was coming up to meet me.

I forgot to breathe – it seems that when you think it's going to be the last breath you take, you want to hold onto it for just that little bit longer.

Alice could only save one of us, and after everything I've put her through, it didn't deserve to be me. But it seems that a true friend will always be there, to catch you when you fall.

ACKNOWLEDGEMENTS

To my amazing agent, Tanera Simons, at Darley Anderson for her unwavering support and encouragement. Nothing prepares you for the leap into the unknown of the publishing world and she has been at my side when I've been too scared to open my eyes.

To everyone at the DA Agency who work tirelessly to get their authors books into the hands of as many readers as possible. They really are the best in the business. Special thanks go to Mary Darby and Kristina Egan in the Rights Department for translating my words into twelve languages. And Sheila David for her work on the secret project!

To Editors Extraordinaire, Catherine Richards at Minotaur Books in the US, and Vicki Mellor at Pan Macmillan in the UK. This novel has had many lives, and I'm so grateful that they helped me give it the best life possible.

From marketing and promotions, to audio and sales, the work that goes into publishing a book should never be underestimated. I am so incredibly lucky to have publishers who go the extra mile in ensuring that my books get out there. Heartfelt thanks to Andy, Kelley,

Joe, Sarah, Nettie and Sam in the US, as well as Matt and Becky in the UK.

Thank you to my very special friends, Jo, Karen, Lynn, Nicky and Sam for their support and understanding when I've been lost to writing, edits and deadlines. Unreturned phone calls, cancelled get-togethers and postponed trips have not made me the best of friends.

To my mum, who will tell anyone who stops for long enough that her daughter is an author, and to my Aunty Carol; if I can do it, so can you! Dust that typewriter off!

The biggest love and thanks go to my husband and children for putting up with my alter-egos Alice and Beth – who weren't always the easiest people to live with. They certainly weren't very good at cooking, housework and keeping on top of the laundry! You'll be pleased to hear that normal service will now resume (at least until I'm possessed by another character!)